Devid Khandelwal desperately wants to experience the supernatural. After years of studying everything from crystals to tarot to spellcasting, nothing has happened that would tell him the Shadow Realm is real. And that kills Dev. As a last-ditch resort, he purchases a summoning board, an occult tool that will grant him his ultimate desires.

Cameron Habersham is Dev's best friend. Cam loves Dev like a brother and will do anything for him, as long as he looks good doing it. So when Dev asks him to perform the summoning board's ritual, he reluctantly agrees, but he knows nothing will come of it. Nothing ever does.

However, within a day, Dev and Cam's lives are turned upside down as wishes begin to come true. They discover the existence of a supernatural world beyond their imagination, but peace between the species is tenuous at best.

Dev finally gets to see the Shadow Realm, meets the man of his dreams, and is inducted into the local male coven. But for all the desires that were summoned into existence, Dev soon realizes the magical community dances the line between good and evil, and Cam ends up on the wrong side of everything.

The old adage is true: Be careful what you wish for.

# SUMMONED

Magus Malefica, Book One

*J.P. Jackson*

A NineStar Press Publication

www.ninestarpress.com

# Summoned

Printed in the USA

ISBN: 978-1-64890-257-4

First Edition, April, 2021

Also available in eBook, ISBN: 978-1-64890-256-7

CONTENT WARNING:

This book contains sexually explicit content, which may only be suitable for mature readers. Depictions of death of secondary characters, gore, abuse, graphic violence, kidnapping, imprisonment, and torture.

# Chapter One

"IT'S HOW MUCH?" Cam scoffed, glaring at Damien behind the counter.

"$299.99, plus tax." Damien's tongue piercing got in the way of the 's', and the word came out more like 'pluth'.

"Ignore him, Damien. New piercing? I like it." Dev tried to ameliorate his best friend's rude comment, then turned to scowl at Cam. "Honestly, why did I ask you to come?"

"Because you love me." Cam tapped a finger on the box Dev clutched in his hands. "Dev, your parents are going to kill you if you spend that much money." Cam cocked an eyebrow at Dev. "And seriously, man, how are you going to pay for...whatever that thing is?"

"With this." Dev pulled out his wallet and flipped the black leather cover open to extract a brand new, slick, and shiny, never-been-used MasterCard.

"And where the hell did you get that?"

"Special offer for impending university graduates." Dev sneered. If all went well, he'd be graduating in the next couple of weeks. Cam, however, had dropped out the previous year to figure himself out as a rebellion against his parents' divorce. His mother had fiercely argued against the idea for two months until she gave up and agreed to Cam taking the year off.

"Oh dude. Just say no." Cam had never been supportive of Dev's interest in the occult, but this was going to be the last purchase.

Unless this purchase worked. And Dev *knew* it would.

It had to.

Dev placed all his hopes and dreams on the fact that this was going to work.

DEV COULDN'T WAIT to open up his latest acquisition.

When he and Cam had arrived at Dev's house, all he wanted to do was rush up the stairs to hide out in his bedroom, tucked away from any distractions or family drama, intent on inspecting his newest possession. Well, any distraction other than Cam, who had accompanied him home.

Instead, as Dev started up the stairs, looking back over his shoulder to ensure Cam was following, he careened into his sister Amna.

"Ugh, you oaf!" Amna shoved him backward, pushing him into Cam. "Oh! Whatchya got in the bag? It looks like it's from that witchy store you like!" Amna slid a finger into the bag to pull it towards her to inspect. Dev pulled his prized possession towards him.

"Cam, come on, let's go." Dev snarled at Amna.

Cam, however, wasn't keeping up. He'd wandered into the kitchen. Cam was playing nice.

"Hi, Mrs. Khandelwal." Dev's mom loved to cook and proudly fed her family traditional meals. Tonight's fare, from the smell of things, was Rogan Josh. Dev hated curry with a passion. He wasn't fond of lamb either and the two together were wretched. He decided going out for fast food was a better alternative.

"Cam," Dev ground up his face with displeasure, "let's go."

Cam shot daggers back at Dev. He shook his head, rolling his eyes as he returned his attention to Dev's mom. "Nice sari!" Cam smiled. "Later, Mrs. Khandelwal."

Upon entering Dev's room, Cam flopped onto the bed and began examining his too-long fingernails, preening them while lying on his back. Cam's shoulder-length sandy-brown hair, which had a slight wave to it and a multitude of natural blonde and auburn highlights, splayed out behind his head, making his pose look model-esque. His three-days' worth of stubble added to that. Dev would never have used the description of "male model" in front of his lifelong pal. The last thing Dev wanted was to feed Cam's ego. Cam's head filled most spaces he inhabited.

"Get your damn boots off my bed." Dev slapped Cam's feet.

"Oh my god. Yes, Mom." Cam toed off the designer rainbow-snakeskin boots. The *thud, thud* ricocheted in the tiny bedroom.

"What are those things made of? Lead?" Dev quipped in response to their noisy removal.

"That's the sound of a quality product, bitch." Cam gave Dev the side-eye. Dev caught the glance. They glared at each other for all of a second, then burst into laughter.

He continued to stare at Cam, who returned to plucking away at some unseen dirt beneath a thumbnail. He had to admit, Cam was too handsome for his own good. They had known each other since grade school and had been, for the most part, inseparable. Dev had stood by idly as Cam used his good looks to get what he wanted. Not that Dev would describe himself as ugly. Far from it. But between the two, Cam always got the good-looking guys first, and that encouraged Cam to parade around, flaunting his beauty.

Dev had invited Cam to tag along on his afternoon shopping excursion. The out-of-the-way pagan store, Magix & Mystix, held all sorts of goodies, most of which Dev couldn't afford, hence the credit card, but he'd had his eye on this particular object for the last couple of months and had squirrelled money away like a miser in order to afford it. All that saving, though, still hadn't amounted to the amount of cash required.

But his luck had changed when a kiosk from a local bank had opened in the Student's Lounge at the University. The handsome, bicep-bulging booth occupant, wearing a shirt obviously a size too small, promised an enticing introductory percentage rate on the credit card, stating the bank offered the cheapest one in the city. And with this purchase from Magix & Mystix in mind and the desperation to get his hands on it, Dev signed the credit card contract in a heartbeat.

All the way downtown, and during their short walk to the store, Cam had proclaimed he was being led through the seediest parts of Edmonton's dark alleyways on their way to make the purchase and complained often about how they were going to be robbed, stabbed, or murdered in some grisly fashion.

None of that had happened.

But Dev had finally got his paws on the summoning board, and as he pulled the rectangular box out of the store's signature black paper bag, his stomach tensed with excitement. The coveted item had a silver pentacle stamped in the center with one word superimposed over top.

## *Desires*

There had been a whole series of summoning boards: *Spirits, Wealth, Justice,* the board Dev had been after, *Desires,* and the last in the series, locked away behind glass, *Demons.* Dev understood enough to know summoning demons wasn't something even his expert level of knowledge should attempt. He was happy enough to leave that particular object where it was. Locked away.

After sliding off the box lid, the sought-after summoning board was professionally wrapped in layers of black tissue paper. Dev peeled each thin layer away, his enthusiasm growing with each sheet.

"Honestly, I don't get what you see in all this stuff." Cam waved his hand through the air, a flippant gesture meant to dismiss Dev's impressive occult collection.

Of course, Cam was referring to the contents of Dev's room, crammed full of books, candles, incense burners, and trinkets on every flat space. The occult was Dev's jam. Crystals, runes, tarot decks—you name it, Dev had it. The occult. He had read, studied, and practiced everything from card readings to spirit summoning. But despite his keen interest, admirable level of knowledge, and dedicated study, Dev hadn't had a single otherworldly encounter or brush with psychic phenomenon.

That *killed* Dev.

"Shush. You be nice. Otherwise my demons will get you." Dev chuckled, knowing full well Cam's interest level focused more on his latest pair of shoes. Dev made a mental note to check for holes in the floorboards.

Dev, on the other hand, would have done anything to be a witch, sorcerer, or seer of the hidden. A pastime his Indian-born mother did not appreciate.

*"Devid, why? This is all bad. You need to find a nice girl, get married, have children. I want to be a grandmother."* Dev pictured his mother's face as her lips mouthed words. He would sit in a state of catatonia while she spouted off such sentiments. Like this morning, at breakfast.

He had come out years ago. But Dev would close his eyes and sigh as his mother continued to say things to him, clinging to a misguided hope perhaps his penchant for men was a passing phase. So far, that had not proven true, and even though Dev had stabs of guilt about his attraction to muscled, hairy-chested bearded guys, those wretched guilt pains didn't stop him from fantasizing about burly men and on rare occasions, pursuing them, however shyly. And Dev's mom had little good to say about Cam. Cam was also gay. Scruffy too, and even more of a furball than Dev, although both sported a hirsute body. Cam, by his own admission, was a bit of a quandary. Walking down the street no one would suspect Cam's sexual preferences. Cam's tankish stride, wide square shoulders, set closer to the pavement than the sky, plowed through most crowds like a stocky football player. His unruly hair made him look manlier, like Jason Momoa. But when Cam opened his mouth, and these were his words, not Dev's, "Unicorns and rainbows just fly out, and honestly, if you can't figure out I'm gay, then how dense are you, really?" That was an exact quote. Flamboyant from sun up to sun down, which Dev loved. He wished in some small way he could be as brave and carefree about his sexuality as Cam. That wasn't the case, especially growing up in a first-generation-born Canadian household that still held true and fast to many an Indian custom, like the kalava he wore around his wrist. The red string bracelet was there to appease his mother and signify Dev's adherence to Hinduism, but nothing could have been further from the truth.

Cam snapped Dev out of his mental wanderings. "Dev, the moment you actually manage to harness a demon and have it do your bidding, I'll concede to wearing discount clothing." Cam cocked an eyebrow and pursed his lips at Dev, who met his gaze. They both smirked. In no world, anywhere, would Cam ever resort to wearing anything so common.

This was the nature of their relationship. Cam was eternally bitchy, and Dev was perpetually spooky. The dynamic was weird, but the friendship worked for them.

"Come on," Dev said, pulling Cam's attention to the task at hand. "Do this with me."

"What? Bitch, no."

"Why not? What the hell have you got to lose?"

"Just, you know, for some crazy-ass reason you manage to pull off some kind of beast wrangling, I don't want to be dragged into the depths of the pit by some shrieking harpy demon. Especially in this outfit. I'm not ready to go to hell looking like this."

"That's not a thing, Cam." Dev shook his head at Cam with a *'god, you don't know anything!'* kind of look.

"How the hell would you know?"

"I know. Now get down here."

"Ugh, all right fine. It's not like any of this has ever worked before." Cam slid off the bed and sat opposite Dev on the floor, cross-legged. The comment bit at Dev. It hurt, but Cam's flippancy wasn't trying to put him and his interests down. Cam pointed to the newest acquisition, "What exactly is this thing?"

"A summoning board."

"Yeah, you've said that. What *is* it, though? Like, what's it supposed to do?" Cam asked, "And what are all those squiggly things?" Cam pointed toward the script patterning the outside of the board, his finger getting far too close to the board for Dev's comfort.

"Shh. It's nothing." Dev slapped his hand away. "It's only there to make the board look all gothic and shit."

"Mmmhmm. K. So...what am I supposed to do? Run around the thing three times and chant 'Bloody Mary'?" Cam asked.

"Oh my god, you're such an idiot. No, you moron. It's for summoning your greatest desires," Dev instructed.

"Really? So, like, a big monster boyfriend?" Cam winked, cupped his own crotch, gave the bulge a couple of squeezes, and tossed Dev an over-dramatic come-hither look.

"I just...I can't with you right now. Is that all you think about?"

"Nope. Bastard better be good-looking too. And rich. It takes money to keep me looking this good." Cam ran his hands over his designer-clad torso and overpriced jeans.

"I swear to god, I don't know why I bother with you."

"Because you love me."

"Sadly, yes. I do. Why? I have no idea." Dev got up and rummaged around his room.

"Okay, so what the hell are you doing now?"

"We need things."

"This is getting complicated."

"Shush."

Dev rushed around his room, gathering the trinkets they needed to do their first summons. And as fast as a desperate person would sell their soul to the devil, he returned to where Cam sat, mimicking his crossed-leg sitting position with the board between them. He handed Cam a marker and three post-it notes.

"And...?"

"Write down three wishes."

"Damn, are we summoning a genie?"

"It's called a Djinn, and no, we are not...at least, I don't think. Why do you make everything a challenge? Write something down." Dev prodded Cam with the end of his marker.

"Good lord, all right. Fine."

Cam got busy scratching stuff down. He had his first wish written in a flat second, the other two he had to think on.

Dev on the other hand had already planned *exactly* what he was going to wish for. He'd come up with this plan the first time he spied the board in Magix & Mystix. He had dreamed of these particular desires for years. All his hopes lay on this last purchase.

This was it.

The last straw.

The last time any of this hocus pocus would be attempted.

Dev had promised himself if this didn't work, he would give all of it up, for good. He was worn out from Cam's remarks. The steady stream of one-liners and quick-witted comments were berating and made him feel hollow and silly. It was playful teasing on Cam's part, but the jabs still hurt. His best friend thought his deepest held beliefs were nothing but nonsense and phooey.

Dev *believed* in magic. He would have staked his soul on a bargain with the devil.

Not having had any experiences with the supernatural had shattered Dev. The desperation every time he watched a movie or TV show where paranormal beings existed left a tennis-ball-sized lump in his throat. Why hadn't he seen any? The sense of abandonment weighed heavily as if a hole of emptiness filled his chest cavity.

*Yeah, okay, so TV wasn't real.* Still.

Dev spent many a sleepless night searching for some hint within the myriad of books he owned. Some trivial sign the Shadow Realm was waiting for him. There were so many others who had already travelled through the veil! All you had to do was go online. There were endless chat rooms and blogs of those who had seen ghosts, been visited by the fae, and seen horrifying encounters of those possessed by demons.

Dev believed. Wholeheartedly.

He believed in magic to the marrow of his bones.

So, this was it. And with all the heart-wrenching, utter loneliness and consuming desire for the Shadow Realm to be real, he wrote down his three wishes:

*I want to have a supernatural power.*

*I want to see the Shadow Realm and be part of it.*

*I want my friends and family to respect me for my knowledge of the occult.*

Dev folded the tiny notes in half. He didn't want Cam to see them because then they wouldn't come true. He tossed them into the copper cauldron he had placed in the center of the board. The instructions on the back of the box were specific. All wishes were to be written on paper, personalized with blood, and placed into the inner ring. Finally, the paper had to be burnt in order to release the energy created while making the desire tangible.

Cam gave Dev his pieces of paper.

"No! Not like that, geez." Dev tossed them back at Cam.

Cam threw his hands up in the air. "What the hell?"

"Fold them in half like I did and put them in the copper bowl."

"Fine." Cam did as instructed. "There, happy?"

"Not quite. Give me your hand."

"Why?"

"For the love of..." Dev grabbed Cam's hand and deftly managed to stab a finger with a thumbtack.

"What the ever-loving fuck, dude?" Cam ripped his hand away and grabbed his finger. A small pinprick of blood welled up to the skin's surface. He brought the finger up to his mouth.

"Don't you dare!" Dev pointed at Cam.

Cam stopped and glared at Dev with a '*well what?*' kind of look.

"Squeeze your finger so the blood drips onto your papers, but get it in the bowl, don't get blood on my floor." Dev pricked his own finger and held his digit over the bowl.

Three drops of blood fell into the copper cauldron. Followed thereafter by three of Cam's.

Dev lit a match and pitched the flaming splinter into the bowl, pushing the post-it notes around so they caught fire.

"Go open the window," Dev instructed Cam.

"Your mother will kill you if you burn the house down." Cam got up, went over to the window, and slid the pane open. A gust of air blew into the room, ruffling loose papers on Dev's desk.

"Okay, now come read this with me." Dev gestured for Cam to sit beside him.

"I swear if anything happens…" Cam warned while he rearranged himself next to Dev, inspecting his finger and sucking at the miniscule wound.

"It will. I know it will."

"You always say that." Cam rolled his eyes and sighed with exasperation.

"Come on, read this."

"Ugh, fine."

And together, they read the incantation off of the instruction sheet that came with the board.

*"With passion of heart, I seek to find, those Desires I want. Wishes to be mine."*

"That's it?" Cam's head tilted to one side in disbelief.

"That's it." Dev shrugged.

They waited for a few heartbeats. Loud ones that thudded against the inside of Dev's chest.

"Okay, I'm bored now. And my finger hurts. You owe me a macchiato." Cam grabbed his designer boots and slid them on. "You coming?"

Dev gazed into the cauldron as the last of the papers charred and blackened and tiny wisps of smoke curled up toward him and dissipated.

Nothing had happened.

His heart ached. His shoulders slumped, and he hung his head.

"Come on," Dev flinched as Cam threw an arm around his shoulder and squeezed him in a one armed bro hug. "I'll buy."

"Yeah, all right."

But, Dev couldn't give up hope. Maybe you had to sleep on it. Maybe the moon cycle had to change over in order to power up the wishes.

*Something* had to happen.

As the two left the room, Dev eased the door closed using both hands on the doorknob while silently praying to any god or being who happened to be listening.

*"Please hear me,"* he whispered.

INSIDE THE EMPTY room, behind the closed door, the summoning board's squiggly writing around the outside edges that was 'only there to make the board look all gothic and shit' shifted. As if the doodles and lines were dancing or marching.

The entire border rotated, widdershins, and the inner ring of the board spun in the opposite directions, changing the symbols.

The wind blew in through the open window and the curtain fluttered in the breeze.

# Chapter Two

DEV WOKE TO the racket of his younger fraternal twin sisters' screaming. He groaned, turned over in bed, and pulled the pillow over his head. He had studied late into the night after coming home from coffee and dinner with Cam. Finals were only a few weeks away.

"No! You cannot wear my sweater, Bhanu. I don't care what Mom said," Amna screeched.

"Seriously? Peach looks wretched on you and besides, it doesn't fit you." Bhanu's tone dripped with acid. Dev swore the sizzle of the burn was audible. This was going to get ugly, and fast.

"Ugh." Dev flipped the covers back and crawled out of bed, standing up and flexing his shoulders backward. His spine cracked and popped. Wearing only his boxers, he pulled open his bedroom door to find his younger sisters still screeching at each other in the hall.

"Will the two of you please shut up?" Dev added to the level of noise in the hallway while rubbing sleep out of his eyes.

"Oh my god, Dev, put some clothes on!" Amna covered her eyes with both hands, mocking some sense of propriety. If neighborhood rumors were true, Amna had a reputation for being in the "fast and loose" camp and not the "good girl." Bhanu defined the good girl category, if not the prissy and bitchy role as well. Amna though, really liked the boys, which made Dev giggle because judging from the collection of posters of the men adorning the walls of her room, Amna and Dev drooled over a similar taste in men. But if gossips were to be believed, Amna got all the action whereas Dev had been left high and dry. At least that's what Bhanu had told him.

"You know, you should consider shaving," Bhanu flicked a finger up and down, "You're never going to get a date with all that..." Bhanu's face scrunched up as she took an exaggerated gasp and spat out, "hair." She stuck out her tongue in a gag.

"Ha! Shows what you know. The bears can't keep their hands off all this." Dev ran his fingers through the fur covering his chest and tummy.

The girls threw their hands up in unison, in protest and disgust, turned and exited, taking their argument downstairs to the kitchen.

Dev retreated into his room. He wished the bears were after him. Truth was, he hadn't had a date in months. But between fourth-year courses at the "U," working part-time in the family's dry cleaning shop, and spending every other precious moment reading about and practicing runes and tarot cards, he hadn't put himself out there.

And if he didn't go out once in a while, he'd never get a date. Or laid. That would be...

Goosebumps erupted on Dev's flesh thinking about the possibilities. He hadn't done the deed yet. Sure, he'd kissed and even given a blowjob once, but that had been the extent of his sexual forays. He had pictured his first time in his head and fantasized regularly. He wanted that magical experience to be with the man of his dreams. Bigger than him, more muscular than him, and at least with as much body hair. A 'Ginge' would be the creamy icing on top of the sex cake. He had a hard on for redheads.

Dev let out a sigh and adjusted his crotch which had begun to respond to his private musings of big, muscled redheads. No time to think about such things now, and certainly no privacy to do anything about it. Even with a promise of a locked door, Dev's sisters would barge in or batter the door down. Nothing was sacred.

Glancing around his room, Dev took stock of all his baubles. Everything sorted tidy and organized in numerous bookshelves lining every wall around his room. Crystals were stored next to the window where the sunlight and moonglow would charge them. Books were kept by his bedside for late night reading, sorted by subject matter. Tarot decks with varying themes and bags full of runes occupied another unit. Hidden behind a box set of tarot cards on the center bookshelf lay a bag of divination bones Dev had spent a boatload of money on. And the bones were real. Not some fake plastic resin crap. They were the real deal. Dev swore an actual human phalanx had been incorporated into the mix. Not just the usual bird and mouse bones. If his mom had ever found those...

The chaos that would ensue would be epic. His mother hated this stuff.

He loved all of it.

And he had spent substantial funds on all if it. Cash he should have been saving for more important things. Like preserving his mental health by stashing away enough money to get an apartment of his own.

But that had not happened, and instead, the hard-earned dollars all went to this. After years and years of dedication to the craft, not a single fucking thing had ever happened. No ghosts. No prophetic dreams. Not even a single tarot reading had been remotely accurate—and Dev kept a journal of every reading. He'd read his diary so many times the pages were damn near memorized.

And still, nothing.

Being shunned by the Shadow Realm might have made him angry, but in fact, the lack of supernatural anything left him with a sense of rejection. Like every good-looking guy had given him the cold shoulder.

One time. That's all he'd ever asked for. Once.

Pursing his lips, Dev reached over and swiped his phone off the nightstand, flicking his wrist upward to wake up the screen.

"Shit." 8:15am. His first seminar started in one hour. If he didn't hurry, he'd miss the last bus that would get him to campus in time to get a coffee and get to class. He'd have to miss *the most important meal of the day,* as his mother always said, and he smelled the tangy aroma that could only be a plate heaped full of scrambled eggs and cheese on toast. The way his mom made eggs was his favorite breakfast food, but not today. No time.

The cacophony from downstairs reverberated up the stairwell, down the hall, and into his bedroom. The whirlwind of his twin sisters had apparently sucked in his parents. They were debating, of all things, marmalade. The constant arguments and noise and lack of privacy made everything feel tight, uncomfortable, and inescapable. If Dev dwelt on those feelings, his body responded in kind.

It made his ears ring, for one, kind of like they were right now. Nothing terrible or annoying. The tone, a high-pitched squeal rang far off in the distance. The ringing always went away as soon as he removed himself from the house or a tense situation.

The chaos left him jittery and nervous. And when Dev had all those nerves driving him crazy, he'd tap his feet or fingers. The movement drove his mother nuts. Once agitated, Dev's body was constantly in motion, looking for an outlet to all the negative energy.

Dev shook his head and stretched out an arm, his hand grasping for the yoga pants hanging from the hook on the back of his door.

Slipping them on proved difficult as the stretchy fabric always caught one foot or another and as predicted, his left foot got stuck about half way down when his toe caught the inseam. Losing balance, Dev pitched forward, hopped on his right leg a couple of times and ended up kicking the copper cauldron still sitting in the center of the summoning board on the floor at the foot of his bed.

The metallic bowl clanged and spun, hitting a nearby bookshelf base and twirled several times, rocking itself to rest.

"Dammit!" Dev collapsed onto his bed, trying not to catapult himself into any bedroom furniture.

He pulled the rest of the pant leg on, grabbed a sweatshirt emblazoned with the University of Alberta's crest from the pile of clothes that lay discarded at the foot of his bed, and slipped the garment over his torso. Dev reached over, stretching as he did, and with the tips of his fingers managed to snag the metal bowl.

He brought the cherished item in to his chest and held it close. Dev caressed the rim of the shiny cauldron, while his thoughts drifted away to questioning his dedication to the occult.

He was twenty-three years old. Graduation with a degree in Sociology occurred in two weeks. Why Dev continued to believe in magical creatures and spirit realms confounded any sense of logic.

Maybe he'd arrived at the end of his journey with the occult. Dev spared a moment to look around his room. So many things. Maybe after class he should get some boxes and start packing everything away. Maybe if he sold some of the stuff on eBay it would at least return some of the money he'd spent.

After all, he had made himself a promise with the summoning board. Nothing had happened...yet. Maybe it was too soon? But surely *something* should have already come to pass?

He gripped the vessel tighter to his chest. Perhaps he should keep a couple of things, you know, the expensive items and the things that meant something to him. Like the bone bag, the summoning board, and definitely his quartz crystal collection. But the rest should go.

Well, the books. Dev should keep those too.

Dev studied the hammered copper dish he now cuddled. He would keep this. He *had to* keep this.

"What are you doing?"

Dev whirled around, still clutching his cauldron. Amna stood in the doorway.

"Nothing."

Amna studied him, then shook her head. "Dad's giving us a ride today. Do you want to tag along? It'll get you half way to the 'U'. Are you sure you're okay? You look weird."

"I'm okay. Just thinking about packing up all this stuff. Maybe selling it."

"What? Really? That's a sudden change of heart, no?"

"Yeah, maybe." Dev gripped the hammered bowl tighter yet.

"Well, if you do, I want your bag of bones. They're awesome!"

"How do you know—?"

"Downstairs in five if you want a ride." Amna twirled and then disappeared down the stairs.

Ugh, nothing was sacred in this house.

Something ticked in Dev's brain.

The cauldron he clung to gleamed. No ashes remained from Cam and his summons the day before. He surveyed the floor—maybe his kick had ejected the contents.

Nope. Nothing.

Dev's mother. Dev scrunched his lips together with suspicion. She constantly barged into his room to "tidy" up.

"Mom!" he snarled in frustration. Once again, he assumed, his mother had been trying to "care," but instead she'd violated his space—his bedroom—and "helped" by neatening and cleaning up. That was the only possibility for the bowl being spotless and gleaming.

A perfect portrait of his mother, constantly cleaning, cooking, and praying to the multitude of Hindu gods. It had to be her.

"Ugh!" Dev raised a fist in the air. Surely the removal of the burnt offering would negate the summons. This wasn't the first time his mother had ruined a spell.

It was time to move out. Cam and he had talked about it. When Cam's parents had begun their ugly divorce, they had talked about getting their own apartment. But months later, Dev still resided in the family home, and Cam had settled for living with his mother.

Besides, good Indian boys didn't move out. They stayed at home and helped. Sure if you were going to university in another city, living on your own was expected, and normal, but if you didn't? Well, then you were abandoning or forsaking your own. Nobody did that. What was wrong with Dev for even considering this course of action? These were the sentiments his parents reinforced after he'd casually brought up the idea.

"How would you pay for rent? You work for us. You help us out, because together we keep the family going." Dev's Dad had declared. He lifted the remote and turned on the TV. Conversation over. Matter solved.

Dev's shoulders sagged, a little less full of life as he closed his eyes. As the world around him became loud, too stressful, tight and close and just too fucking much.

The squeal in his ears got louder.

And now the time had crept to 8:33am.

"Shit, shit!" Dev put the cauldron down on his unmade bed, grabbed his laptop and shut the door as he exited his room. He vowed to himself this time was the last time.

The last time to give in to hope. Clearly he would be spared from anything otherworldly.

But also the last time he'd give in to his parent's wishes and demands about staying home and helping out.

The absolute last time his wants and needs would be placed on the back burner.

He had three classes today, and then there would be free time. He was prepped and caught up on most of his notes and in a good space for finals. Tonight he would pack up all this occult crap and call it quits. And while he crammed all his treasures into boxes, it only made sense to include his clothes and music. Tomorrow held possibilities. Dev would find himself his own place, with or without Cam.

And a job.

Yeah. An apartment and a new job. He could do that.

No.

He *would* do that.

EVEN THOUGH THE fresh and cool spring morning air created pockets of fog, and dew dappled the new grass, and despite the fact Dev only had on a sweatshirt, he was getting warm with his brisk walk to the bus stop. He only had a few minutes to get there, or he'd miss the last bus. Jarring Dev from his planning, the Psycho shower knife scene clip chimed, somewhat muffled from his yoga pants pocket.

It was Cam, who hadn't been impressed Dev had assigned him *that* particular ring tone but then in the space of a heartbeat changed his mind, deciding he quite liked it. From that point forward, Cam mimicked the same noise whenever he got off a resoundingly good burn on someone. Cam had turned Dev's jab into a "thing." Cam's thing. Whenever his friend produced the annoying peal, Dev had to admit Cam's impersonation perfectly matched the real thing. Be damned if Dev understood how Cam made his vocal cords emit such a dreadful squeal. But as much as Dev may have been put off by the wretched noise, he admired Cam's resilience. There wasn't much that stymied Cam. He always managed to turn a negative moment around into something positive, or something about him.

The phone went off again.

Cam detested mornings and therefore never woke up before 9:00am, never mind this early, so what the hell was so urgent? Dev's ire simmered from his mom's cleaning, which had ruined his summoning spell. Waking up to complete chaos between Amna and Bhanu made Dev yearn for solitude and quiet, not having to deal with anyone other than himself.

But again, the phone. Dev grumbled to himself while fishing out his cell. He unlocked the phone with his thumbprint and opened the texting app.

*Dude!*

*Where are you?*

*You HAVE to come over. NOW.*

Dev locked the phone and shoved the device into his pants pocket. Finals. Two more weeks until his career as a student came to an abrupt end. These last few classes were always the most important ones to attend. The profs always gave away hints and pointers on what pieces of their semester's material might appear on the final exam. Dev had to go to class.

Again with the Psycho knife. Dev cringed and dug the phone out again.

> *Dev, are you there? Dude, you have to come over. PLEASE?*

Cam never uttered the word please.

Dev typed a quick response.

> *Going to the U. I have classes.*

The three dots appeared at the bottom of the screen indicating Cam had seen the message and was typing a response, which popped onto the screen in record time, and all in caps.

> *YOUR SPELL! GODDAMMIT. Please?*

Dev stopped cold. What did Cam mean? Had something happened? Did the fact his mom had cleaned out the bowl not negate the spell? Did Cam get one of his desires? Why Cam and not Dev?

Dev might have been angry about the order in which wishes were being granted for a second, but his brain spurred him off in a more positive direction.

It. Had. Worked!

Dev's heart sped up, and feathers tickled the inside of his belly making him feel all giddy. He damn near danced down the sidewalk. The crisp morning air tasted sweet on his tongue as he inhaled deeply. *Finally!* Sure, the summoning had materialized for Cam first and not Dev. Dev weighed whether or not he would consider this a disappointment. But if Cam had got a wish, a desire fulfilled, maybe Dev's were just around the corner. Perhaps the two of them actually summoned their desires into existence.

Bursting with enthusiasm, Dev centered himself. No point in getting too excited, but conflict reared its head.

Which way should he go? Toward classes? That would be the more responsible thing to do. Should he head to Cam's? The more rational part of Dev's brain took over. Nothing had ever happened before. Why now? Facts being facts, Cam's penchant for melodrama over something stupid or perhaps an opportunity to play upon Dev's hopes seemed like the most plausible scenario. It wouldn't have been the first time Cam had pranked him.

Dev got all squinty-eyed, wondering why he and Cam had been friends for as long as they had been. Cam knew every button to push to rile Dev up, and he did so with alarming frequency. Why did he like Cam, exactly?

Bastard. This probably had nothing to do with the summoning. More than likely Cam had figured out another way to toy with him.

Another message appeared.

*Dude are you coming? Seriously, man, you have to see this. OMG.*

To hell with responsibility. The mere possibility the board had worked won out.

He typed out a quick response.

*Coming.*

Dev did a one-eighty and started toward Cam's house. He didn't live far. After his parent's unpleasant separation, Cam had opted to live with his mom, but as his mom regularly prowled for something younger and "Not like your dad", as she had put it, Cam found himself alone more often than not. And that suited Cam who had no patience for dealing with his mother's mid-life crises and sexual escapades. Cam vacated the house whenever one of the new boyfriends was invited over, and there had been a steady string of them. But Cam had divulged that his mom had jetted off earlier in the week for a "business trip," although he had also shared his doubts with Dev on the validity of the purpose when she had left her work laptop at home.

It was only a block and a half walk, and as he headed up the street, his last possible bus to the "U" passed him. Dev's gaze followed the bus, but his feet kept walking toward Cam's.

"Dammit, Cam, this had better be good." Dev muttered to himself.

Around the corner and halfway up the street, Dev arrived at Cam's place and knocked on the door.

Cam answered, wearing a black baseball cap studded with a skull and crossbones in fake rhinestones. Cam grabbed Dev's sweatshirt and yanked him into the house closing the door behind them fast.

"Ouch, dude! The chest hair," Dev exclaimed.

Cam grimaced. "Sorry, man, I know that stings."

Dev rubbed the spot where Cam had managed to pull a clump of fur. "It's okay. So what's the big problem? Did the summons work? What did you wish for? Tell me!"

Cam ramped up the swinging hand gestures, "What took you so long to get here? What did you do? Crawl? Good god, Dev, why? I'm never letting you talk me into one of your hocus pocus shit things again!"

"What the hell happened?" Dev fed off Cam's excitement. "What did you wish for? Did you move something with your mind? Or, maybe set something on fire? Cam...you didn't write down something stupid or flippant, did you?"

Cam's eyes popped open, glaring at Dev like he'd said the stupidest thing in all the years they'd spent together. "Don't be insane. Light something on fire? What? Just... no." Cam wagged a finger at Dev, which made him feel about five. "Never again! I can't believe this is happening to me. You're the one that's all cray-cray about this shit. This should have happened to you! Not me. Oh my god."

Dev frantically grabbed Cam by the shoulders and shook him as he begged, "What happened?"

Cam stepped back a few paces.

"Look. At. This."

Cam removed his cap. Dev braced himself.

Cam stood there, eyes wide, tapping his foot.

"What?" Dev asked as he squinted, searching. His insides were in knots.

"Ugh!" Cam pulled his thick wavy hair away from his forehead. "That!" He pointed toward a reddened bump a thumbnail above his eyebrow.

"What?" Dev's eyebrows pinched together. "A zit?"

Cam rushed over to the mirror with a South Pacific–style carved frame. He took the index fingers from both hands and squeezed the bump. "I have a goddamn date tonight, you asshole. Look at this! It's a fucking antler! How am I gonna get laid looking like this?" Cam spun on his heels and glared at Dev. Accusations sat unspoken and heavy in the air between them.

"If you quit playing with your zit it won't be all red. Besides, I'm sure you have a billion skin products and foundation you can use to hide your little monster for your terribly important date tonight." Dev fumed. Cam had pranked him. Well, maybe not. Maybe Cam believed the zit was a direct result of the spell, but who was spouting the stupid shit now? "Jesus Cam, I missed my first class for you to go off about a bloody zit!"

"It's a horn! The thing is ginormous."

"I've had it with you. I need to get to class."

"Dev, this is your fault."

"For fuck's sake Cam, grow up. It's a pimple. Deal." Dev spun away turning his back on Cam and stomped toward the front door. "Have fun on your date." Dev spit out between gritted teeth.

He slammed the door as he left, to make a point.

His ears were ringing again.

The board hadn't worked.

Cam had, once again, tricked him. Dev had once again fallen for Cam's tomfoolery. He stomped his way down the walkway of Cam's front yard. "You're twenty-three. Grow up, Dev. This shit doesn't work."

Dev pulled out his earbuds from the side pocket on his carrier bag, stuck them in his ears, and cranked the loudest System of a Down song on his phone.

As he walked toward his original intended destination, his steps slowed, the excitement leaching out of him with every step he took. His rage slowly subsiding.

Honestly, what should he have expected? He knew better.

Magic and reality were incompatible. The Shadow Realm had abandoned him once again.

With zero enthusiasm, Dev made his way to the university, contemplating his emotional stock in life.

DEV SAT IN the front row of his Advanced Methodologies of Sociological Research class. Staring at his professor helped to temporarily forget about the crap storm his life had spiraled into. Standing at the front of the class, leaning casually against his desk, Professor Byron Radcliff wrapped up one of the last lectures Dev would ever have with him. Radcliff was his favorite instructor.

The man exemplified the hyper masculine male. His very presence fueled the erotic scenes of Dev's midnight fantasies. Radcliff led a starring role in most of Dev's dreams ever since he had inadvertently signed up for Introductory Sociology, lucked out, and ended up with him teaching the course. Dev had fallen so hard for his professor, it had been a major contributing factor in his continuation of Sociology as his major.

So Prof. Radcliff wasn't a redhead. Still, his hipster-style blond beard, with a touch of grey at the chin sent electric impulses through Dev's groin, making the facial fur nothing short of an aphrodisiac. His close-cropped hair with the crown grown out long, brushed back, expertly styled and gelled inspired Dev to get the same haircut. Highlights of silver at Radcliff's temples sparkled when the overhead fluorescent lights illuminated the side of his face whenever he stood at the podium. The man's shirt clung tight, emphasizing his muscled frame. Radcliff's apparent familiarity with a set of dumbbells had sent Dev to the campus gym, and he had even purchased a membership, but he'd never seen the man there. Biceps bulged every time he wrote more snippets of wisdom on the SMART whiteboard. All these sexy qualities contributed and completed Radcliff's DILF status.

Radcliff's leather suspenders framed his bearish torso, and Dev followed every motion he made as his professor's pectoral muscles jumped and flexed while writing. Dev should have been paying attention to the lecture, spending more time writing down notes than memorizing the tight fit of Radcliff's olive khaki's. Of course, all this daydreaming led to fantasizing about Radcliff.

*Dev unbuttoned Radcliff's shirt in front of the entire class, wanting to expose the giant muscles that lay concealed by his starched white dress shirt. When he'd reached the top of his trousers, he peeled the shirt apart and ran the tips of his fingers over the thick, but trimmed, chest hair. Dev grabbed his teacher's suspender with his other hand and pulled him forward, lips puckered, wanting to taste his instructor while getting to feel the bushy beard...*

"And you pleasantly surprised me with your last assignment. To think most of you will be Sociologists within a few short weeks! Well done." Radcliff shattered Dev's imagination into pieces.

Radcliff grabbed an overstuffed manila envelope sitting on his desk.

*What damn assignment?*

Professor Radcliff began handing the papers out, calling each student by name and making a comment, "Joe, well done! Excellent take on the Conflict Theory. Allison, good work, nicely written, but next time, perhaps reference more than one online article? Devon, watch your spelling, mate." The papers continued to go out, and as each student received their work from Prof. Radcliff, they exited the classroom.

Dev sat glued to his seat his gaze darting to each student as they received their papers. Nerves got the best of him and all Dev wanted to do was leap out of his chair, grab his carrier bag and run out of the room. He hadn't handed in any assignment. Instead of giving into the flight response, he clicked open his file explorer icon on his laptop and searched for the course syllabus in a vain effort to see what he'd missed.

His ears were squealing.

"Dev, can you come see me?"

Radcliff's folder, clutched in his meaty paws, was empty, which is exactly how Dev imagined his heart. Hollow. The back of his neck heated as did his cheeks. Sweat trickled down his spine.

*Dammit, Dev. Your favorite professor. You look like an idiot!*

"Dev, what happened, man? You've never not handed in an assignment. For that matter, your papers are usually better than all these others," Radcliff waved his hand toward the door, as the last students were filing out.

"I... I'm sorry, I don't know what happened. I'm not sure how I missed this."

The high pitched ring muffled Dev's ability to listen to Prof. Radcliff's scolding. Dev put a hand on his forehead. The intense heat and gut wrenching belly twists made him feel hollow, and on fire. He'd never been so embarrassed in his entire life.

"It's worth twenty-five percent of your mark, Dev. You'll need some points on this to pass, and you'll have to do really well if you want to maintain your honours standing." Radcliff crossed his arms, looking more disappointed than angry, but the motion also flexed his biceps.

Maybe Prof. Radcliff would let Dev make up for the missed assignment in other ways, he hoped, but the heat from his shame snapped him back to reality.

"Can you give me an extension? Just a couple of days? I'll have something in to you by Friday."

Prof. Radcliff tilted his head to one side while his mouth twitched into a half frown. "Okay, Dev. But only till Friday. I wouldn't do this with many of my other students. Don't screw this up. I know you're graduating this year."

"I won't. I'm sorry!" Dev turned away from Radcliff and walked, quicker than normal, toward the door. As much as he liked Radcliff, right now he didn't want to be anywhere near him.

He hurried out through the door of the classroom, shutting the glass-paned door quietly behind him. As he did, he noticed Radcliff, who appeared as if he'd already forgotten the episode. The gorgeous teacher sat at his desk busily typing out something on his laptop. Dev's face continued to burn.

*Idiot!*

Dev kept repeating that word to himself as he raced to his next class. The squealing in his ears almost unbearable. A dull throb behind his eyes promised to bloom into a spectacular stress headache.

His life had really gone to shit.

# Chapter Three

CAM STRUGGLED TO get a grip on the edge of the sofa from where he lay on the floor. He sucked in a gasp of air. His lungs felt scorched, burning hot and tight as he struggled to breathe in oxygen. With the last ounce of energy he had left, he pulled his dead-weight body up onto his feet. He reached up to his slick forehead and wiped away the layer of sweat that had formed, then wiped his hands on his designer jeans.

Within moments of Dev leaving, Cam's body had turned on him. Nausea took over as the room spun and tilted. His vision blurred as he threw up all over the hardwood floors. His mother was going to kill him. The roll of the room prevented Cam from steadying himself. The pile of puke at his feet would have just have to wait. The exclusive T-shirt he'd spent sixty bucks on clung to his body, soaked through with perspiration. Standing upright became precarious, but he tried valiantly. As soon as he did though, he wobbled. Taking a deep breath, Cam filled his lungs. But the momentary reprieve only lasted a second before another violent tilt forced him onto all fours. This had to be the worst case of food poisoning ever. Maybe the milk had gone bad. All he'd eaten this morning was the usual bowl of Cap'n Crunch. The sugary puffs had been a mainstay since kindergarten and some things, like delicious sugary breakfast cereals, should never change.

Well, he'd had his usual and coffee. Honestly, if Cam didn't get his coffee first thing in the morning, Camila the Super Bitch arrived and she was nobody's friend, at least until noon when Cam returned and the world became a more hospitable place.

Staggering over to the entrance way, where Cam's mother had hung a monstrous mirror, Cam braced his teetering body by gasping the foyer cabinet beneath the reflective surface. Studying the reflection in the mirror in front of him, he hesitated until he summoned enough bravery to touch the reflection in the glass. His skin was pale and clammy, his eyes shadowed by the black circles under them, and the zit that had formed above his temple on his forehead now had a matching twin on the other side. Both grown to monstrous proportions. A bony protrusion poked through their centers. The pain in his skull pulsed with every heartbeat. Like a migraine. Any light penetrating his eyes stung like thousands of angry wasps.

His skin crawled. Cam dug nails into his flesh, desperate to sedate the itch. And the sensation tormented him further by travelling to new spots. At first, he had damn near scratched his ribs raw, but once the maddening prickling subsided from one area, the itch moved. This time to his shoulders.

*This is what you get for manscaping.*

Still nauseated, he hunched over and threw up again.

*Damn. Cap'n Crunch didn't really dissolve much in half an hour. Gross.*

Cam continued to scratch, but now the tingling had centered near his spine between the shoulder blades, and try as he might, despite twisting and turning, stretching and grasping, the maddening itch continued. Grabbing the knitting needles out of his mother's hobby basket and sliding the half-finished project off, he shoved the points down the back of his collar and went to town, utilizing the sharpness of the metal needles, wanting to excavate a channel into his hide.

That's when he hit something hard, and as he did, a spike of pain like a knife being plunged in between his shoulder blades created fireworks of bright white lights in his vision.

Cam threw up again.

His belly muscles pulled and stretched throughout the retch session. His body eliminated whatever liquid may have been left in his stomach, along with green bile from his gallbladder. The mixture poured out all over his mother's imported wool Persian rug. As his stomach relinquished its hold on Cam's bodily functions, he noted the rug.

"Oh shit. I'm a dead man. That's never coming out."

The itch started again. This time, Cam ripped off his tee and grabbed the knitting needles. Turning slightly, he craned his neck in a most awkward angle to glimpse his back in the mirror. Red marks marred the skin from his assault on it. His shaved torso had stubble growing on it, but the bristly new hair growth wasn't what bothered him.

Two small bumps had formed between his shoulder blades and on each side of his spine. As the itch continued, Cam tried to touch the newly formed nodules. They were each the size of his fist.

He jerked forward, his stomach retched again. Cam had to grab the couch to steady himself.

*What the fuck is going on?*

"There's no way the milk went this bad. I'm hallucinating." Cam tried to finger the newly formed lumps, but it was impossible to reach them. He would have sworn they were larger.

Cam's eyes went wide, with shock tinged in horror, as an idea formed in his head.

This was the result of Dev's goddamn spell— summons—whatever fucking witchery the two of them had done. The very first thing he'd written on that sticky note was coming true.

*That wish!*

"Oh shit. No!" Cam grabbed each edge on the side table positioned beneath the mirror, opposite the front door entrance. His eyes were wide with panic. Cam's mind reeled as his pupils stretched into cat's eyes. The iris shimmered, iridescent gold and green, sparkling with glints of metallics. A far cry from his normal dull cloudy-day blue. "God dammit. I'm gonna kill you, Dev!"

BYRON RADCLIFF STUDIED his students from his desk, making sure he appeared to be busy on his laptop. In reality, he was spying on Dev.

He'd been observing Dev for four years.

Torture would have been easier to tolerate than to stand in front of him three times a week and lecture. Dev's intense gaze fixated on him during each class, making teaching almost an impossibility. Even with his body turned during his lessons, Byron swore those deep-chestnut eyes were burrowing into his back. With the thick ebony eyelashes framing Dev's eyes, the irises appeared black. Black and relentless. And his hair. So thick, always styled to perfection, much like Byron's current cut. If he hadn't known any better he'd have guessed Dev had his hair cut to mimic his own.

Byron remembered two well-known sayings, *mimicry was a form of flattery*, and *flattery will get you everywhere*. Byron raised an eyebrow as one side of his mouth pulled up in a mischievous grin.

Byron stood, smoothing his khakis as he started his lecture, walked over to the podium and leaned forward, talking all the while, pressing his hips into the wooden structure, attempting to stifle the growing erection. Dev's eyes were locked on him. More than once, he'd had to resort to standing behind this pedestal, because he had failed in taming the lascivious thoughts. Dev was so damn good-looking. And smart! Easily the star pupil in every class the man had signed up for. And Byron wasn't sure which he found more attractive, his smarts or the fact Dev adulated him. But as much as he anticipated Dev's presence, the arousal in his groin while Dev silently worshipped him from the student desks made him uneasy.

Acting out his desires with Dev would be a small piece of heaven, but not a reality. Not yet, at least.

What made Dev tantalizing, even more than his studious nature and undivided attention, was his latent supernatural ability.

Being the local high priest in the Coven of the Night Grove, the all-male witch guardians of Edmonton, meant Byron, along with holding a doctorate in Sociology, also had a vast array of other measures available to evaluate potential Shadow Realm newcomers. And the coven at this very moment desperately needed a new novitiate.

Dev succeeded in his academic specialty, but his dormant witch abilities had piqued Byron's interest on more than one occasion.

Witch law meant adhering to tradition. Traditions were never broken. *Latent abilities were not to be recognized and no apprenticeship could be initiated until the individual had demonstrated a harnessing of their personal power.*

Byron hadn't expected to see a complex magical cast from Dev. A geyser of uncontrolled raw energy, yes. And *that* vitality his coven currently lacked. They had lost two witches this year and the group was in a weakened state. Dev's potential would more than make up for the missing members.

Byron needed Dev to come into his own. But laws were laws. No tampering allowed. The witch had to learn how to channel their own energy first.

And Dev had not shown any yearling witchy explosions.

Byron had sensed Dev's potential years ago. Discerning if someone had the prospective to channel ethereal elemental energies was easy enough. More often than not, the students who waltzed through his classrooms were nothing more than a walking husk of skin. And then Dev had shown up.

As soon as Byron had a tingling, a notion of Dev's ability, he performed the ritual. He'd done it many times before, usually at the beginning of each semester, to the whole class, utilizing some devious and questionable items, the least of which required a few white lies in order to obtain a sample of handwriting from everyone. After all, what professor accepted hand-written assignments these days?

His coven had put up arguments though. There were substantial amounts of energy and resources required to execute the spell.

Werewolf intestines were common enough to obtain, but semen from a fae elder? Admittedly, supplies were running low. But Byron forged ahead regardless. One ancient spell completed with a wave of the hand, a sample of handwriting, and a handful of ingredients, and *voila!* Witches, humans, fae and others were revealed.

Dev was all witch.

Despite the arcane knowledge of Dev's true nature, his witch future lay undetermined. Until that changed Byron would have to deal with how frustratingly mundane Dev would remain until he learned how to release his abilities.

Poor kid would explode soon, which wouldn't be good either. Hopefully Byron's coven snagged him before he did harm to himself or others. But it meant Dev had to display *something* magical on his own.

After his class was completed, Byron made his excuses to exit the room faster than normal, placing enough distance away from the classroom and out of earshot of any potential eavesdroppers. Slipping his cell out of his pocket, Byron glanced over his shoulder to ensure his conversation would be private, then pressed a few buttons and held the phone up to his ear as he stroked his beard.

"Hey. Yeah, class just ended. Yup, he was here, and yes, I cast the illusion." Byron listened to the voice on the other end and then responded. "I hope this works too. The spell would be a bloody waste of energy otherwise. Yes, he fell for it, hook, line and sinker. Dev turned the deepest red I've ever seen on a student in fifteen years of teaching. If missing an assignment and suggesting he'll lose his honours positioning doesn't stress him out, not much else will. He's so close. I know, I know. No tampering. But nothing says I can't create some additional life anxiety to see if he'll manifest on his own."

Byron switched positions with the phone, holding his cell to his ear with his shoulder.

"Agreed," he replied. "I think that might be best. He's so close. Honestly, you can almost taste the energy." Byron uttered the last sentence with a hushed voice. "Of course, I'm right. I've been right with every other novitiate in the past. Are you questioning me?" Byron wasn't used to be second-guessed. He changed tactics. "We should make sure he's being watched. Send Tully; he'll use his Gaelic touch. That boy can charm anyone. Did you manage to collect the remnants from their summons? I'm surprised that didn't burst the dam."

Byron paced the empty hallway as his conversation continued.

"So were you able to restore the notes? What did the two wish for?"

Byron stopped, holding the strap on his worn leather satchel, and mused while examining the glass cabinet holding the department's educational display on "What is Sociology?" The presentation was a horrid compilation on information meant to entice first-year students who were taking Sociology 100 into making the discipline their major.

"Really?" Byron's eyes widened as he chortled. "That had to be his friend's, what's his name? Yes, right, Cam. Were you able to recover all the desires written? Perfect. What else? Mmmhmm, yes, well that wording sounds more like our Dev. I can't say I'm surprised Dev wrote what he did, but if those boys managed to summon Mazear, they are in for a world of trouble. You know the Djinn will have to realize the wishes, especially the wishes of a supernatural being. Hopefully all of this will make

Dev spill his pent up load. Then we can step in, and presto...we have a new coven member."

Byron turned away from the cabinet and continued to walk down the hall, "Say that again? What were the other wishes? Oh shit. Well *that* definitely had to come from Cam. Dev would never have written something so stupid. Of all the things...We will need to watch over the idiot. Was there any residual magic on his friend's papers? No. Hmph. Well, it is guilt by association. The Djinn won't care. He'll likely want to play and grant all of their wishes, and let's face it, "Make me the fairy I truly am," is exactly the kind of idiotic request Mazear will love to deliver on. We'll need to make sure the genie remains chained to the board. We can't afford to have him loose again."

Byron shook his head. Why did people play with the supernatural realm when they had no idea what they were dealing with?

"Yes, binding the board again might be a good idea. Now. Send someone to check on his friend, and have Tully watch over Dev. This has to happen soon, we need to replace our lost members. I can already tell our power is waning. We don't have enough energy to fight off the wolf pack. Without the thirteen, we can't protect the ley lines, and without those, we lose the power to control your situation. I'm still waiting for the book from the French coven. And Raphael assured me the ritual in this tome was the answer. If we don't get this done, it's bad news for you.

"Don't worry. You know I'll do whatever I can to protect you. I should be done here after the thesis review this afternoon. We only have one Masters candidate this year, so I won't be long. I'll be home as soon as I can, Addas."

Byron hung up and proceeded to his office.

*Soon, Dev. Soon.*

Byron's eyes grew dark as he grinned, picturing Dev amongst the others of the coven.

# Chapter Four

DEV SETTLED HIMSELF in his bedroom, booted up his laptop and with furious determination clicked through his files trying to find Prof. Radcliff's class syllabus, or an email or a text or a class note that outlined what he should have completed and already handed in to his professor.

He hadn't been studying for five minutes when the melodious songs of Justin Bieber bled through his walls. Bhanu had her stereo cranked up to maximum volume. Dev banged his fist on the wall separating his bedroom from hers. After seconds of no response, he grabbed his earbuds and stuck them in each ear, scrolled for Nine Inch Nails on his phone in one hand while he continued his virtual search on his laptop with the other, getting frustrated at not finding the info he needed.

A nice lady's voice from the earbuds said in a British accent, "Please charge device." The eerie wails of Trent Reznor faded into non-existence.

"Dammit!" Dev pulled the buds out and placed them on the charger, making sure they were firmly connected into the USB port hub plugged into the wall.

After setting them aside to do their thing, he began a frantic search through his desk for his headphones—at least those would connect into his phone through a wire and drown out the cooing and whining of Justin. The headphones were big, like ear muffs, and he often wore them during the winter to keep his ears toasty while listening to his particular brand of gothic, indie, and metal music playlists. The headphones were a soothing moody shade of gunmetal blue. They were comfy, and truth be told, his favorite, but they were bulky and didn't fit into his carrier bag, which meant he usually settled for the ear buds that came with his phone.

"Where the hell did they go?" Dev flipped the pillows on his bed looking for the headphones as his door swung open and his mom came in carrying a load of laundry, just as Amna walked past wearing his headphones heading downstairs.

"Amna!" Dev shouted over his mother's head. Height didn't run in Dev's family, but out of all of them, he was the tallest.

"Dinner's ready in a few minutes. Put these away and come down. And stop yelling at your sister. She can't hear you with those things on anyway."

"They're mine!" Dev flipped his hands out to his side. "Besides, I can't. I have a massive assignment I need to get done for Prof. Radcliff." Dev's mind rushed. Too many things were going on all at once and as per usual, the members of his family were bent on their own selfishness. Zero support for Dev. His ears were still ringing. They'd started at the end of the most embarrassing class he'd ever had with Prof. Radcliff and they hadn't stopped.

"Dev, you've not come to dinner now for over a week. Please come down."

"Mom—" Dev started.

"Nope. Not with me. Not tonight. Downstairs. Now." Being an adult of twenty-three or significantly taller than your mother had no value or weight in the matter. Dev rolled his eyes, gritted his teeth, and marched out of his room.

Once downstairs, he confronted Amna. Dev ripped the headphones off his sister's head, as Carrie Underwood sang "I took a Louisville slugger..." Dev pulled the wire out of her phone. "You are not allowed to go into my room and take my stuff."

"What the hell, Dev!" she shouted at him.

"They're not yours, and no, you can't borrow them," Dev snapped.

"She didn't take them. I went into your room and got them so she would quit moaning about having to listen to Bhanu's music choices," Dev's dad replied from his permanent position in front of the TV, "two days ago."

"Why are you going into my room?" Dev attempted to scold his father.

"Your room?" His head swiveled away from the large-screen plasma TV as his cheeks reddened and his face morphed into the *Don't you dare take that tone with me, boy* expression. "May I remind you who pays for *your* room?" His words had the distinct undertone of ire, an annoyed state Dev recognized from many childhood misadventures which had led to discipline.

"Never mind all of this. Dev, set the table, please. Dinner's ready." Dev's mom placed a stack of dishes on the kitchen counter as Dev's phone chimed, Psycho Knife theme, and with a quick glance, he confirmed it was Cam as a preview of the text sprang to life on the screen.

The ringing in his ears blurred out everything around him. Dev stared blankly at his phone.

> *Dev, please, I'm sorry about earlier but you have to come. NOW.*

That sealed the deal.

Home life had spun out of control into an all-out disaster.

His best friend was still being a demanding diva.

His favorite teacher believed him to be an incompetent ass and consequently his standing within the faculty would suffer. Dev didn't necessarily want to pursue a Masters, but even a letter of recommendation if he wanted to go on to Law...that all hung in the balance.

Dev's ears had escalated to an all-time high. Pent up anger and frustration had been building for months of constant household chaos.

"I can't!" Dev shouted. "Don't you people get it?" He spun toward his dad. "Stay the hell out of my room!" He turned to his mom. "No, I do not want dinner," then cranked his head so he stood face-to-face with Amna, "and you can't use my shit." Heat from his rage flared up his neck and across his cheeks. "I am graduating in less than two weeks! Is it too much to ask for some quiet and respect so I can study? What is wrong with all of you?"

"It's an undergraduate degree, Dev. And besides, it's only Anthropology. It's not like you're becoming a doctor like we'd hoped."

"It's fucking Sociology!" Dev's head swirled. His hands, clenched at his side, were tingling. Every muscle in his body strained with stress. If he stayed in this room with these people for another second, something would slip from his mouth he would regret.

The kitchen lights flickered, and everyone present stopped and noted the weird electrical blinking.

Dev ignored the idiosyncratic lights, stormed upstairs, grabbed the laptop from his bed, and his denim jacket. He stomped down the stairs, almost slipping on the carpet, snatched his carrier bag from the coatrack, shoved his laptop inside, but as he grabbed the front door handle, his father yelled at him.

"Don't you dare leave this house after talking to your mother and me like that!"

Dev turned, glared at his father, and bit his tongue. He bit down so hard he tasted the coppery tang of blood.

Without breaking his stare, Dev reached around, twisted the doorknob and flung the door open. He spun around and stormed outside, leaving his family to stew and probably argue. Dev marched into the darkening shadows of early evening. He had no idea where to go, but anywhere would be better than here.

IT TOOK A solid thirty minutes of walking alone in the cool evening air to attempt to regain any measure of composure. Emotions were reeling, and the last encounter with his family life replayed over and over in his head.

He was such an asshole. With his last words echoing in his head, the embarrassment and guilt weighed heavy in his soul. He had never exploded so unexpectedly toward his family. Regardless, he retained the anger.

"Why can't they give me space?" he mumbled while he shrugged in incomprehension.

Dev's phone went off—Cam. He glanced at the text app, focusing on the red number indicating the number of unread messages. Sixteen of them.

*Oh my god.*

He slipped the phone into his pocket. Dev sucked in a lungful of air, trying to calm down, but everything in the world shifted and swirled. The ringing in his ears had subsided, but the constant buzzing grated on his nerves. If he didn't know any better, he'd swear he might be on the verge of a breakdown.

Looking up past his own two feet, Dev realized he'd managed to walk as far as Whyte Avenue and decided to stop in at his chosen coffee shop for a cup of caffeine-filled deliciousness. The stimulant wouldn't do him any favors, but the rich velvety sweetness of his favorite beverage might make him feel better.

As he opened the door, he was surprised to find the coffee shop almost empty. He expected far more students ingesting coffee and similar beverages while cramming for exams.

As Dev approached the front counter to order, he glanced around the store. Three or four tables were occupied, one with a small group of forty year olds who were all laughing, a woman in the back, half hidden in the shadows and reading a book, and a young couple who mooned over each other. Dev assumed they were out on a date.

As Dev opened his mouth to specify his drink of choice, the glass door opened, a small bell chimed and in walked a drop-dead-gorgeous redhead.

As he stood staring at the most delicious example of the male species, the guy glanced up and caught Dev's eye.

Dev's gaze darted away, but not before the redhead grinned at him.

"Of all the nights. Why?" Dev mumbled as he slumped standing at the counter.

"Sorry, what was that?" the barista behind the counter asked. Both her eyebrows raised as she asked the question, being polite and too customer service-y.

"Nothing. Thanks." Dev paid as she handed him his coffee.

Walking over to the sideboard, Dev poured the required half and half cream and several packets of sugar into his coffee, grabbed a spoon from a metal jar containing a couple hundred of them, and stirred his drink, making sure all the sweet crystals of joy had melted.

The ringing in his ears still hadn't diminished, nor the knots of guilt and anger which had nestled firmly in the center of his stomach. He'd never treated his family so poorly before. Sure they were difficult, but they meant well.

Dev turned and found a quiet table that would have been for two, cuddled up in the front of the shop, right next to the window.

Dev removed his coat and slung the garment over the back of the chair. Rummaging through his carrier bag, he pulled out a notepad and his laptop. All the while, he kept close tabs on the redhead who ordered a half-caf Cappuccino, no foam. The guy's facial hair had the same deep red hues as his head hair, which didn't always happen. A lot of guys' beards were different colors than what was on top, if they even had hair on top. Dev ran fingers through his own thick beard and wondered what this guy's fur would feel like.

Soft and silky, or rough and stiff?

You couldn't see skin beneath the hair, and Dev hoped that meant he had as much fur beneath his layers of clothes. Even from where Dev sat, the man's glacial-blue eyes stole his attention. His straight-edged nose had clearly been broken at least once, making him appear even more masculine and rugged. Thick, dark-red hair with tussles and curls needed a haircut but kind of made him sexier. His blue plaid jacket had a fluffy sheepskin collar, but the arms were tight, indicating there might be big biceps hidden beneath the clothes. Body-hugging, cream-coloured jeans, a white T-shirt, and hiking boots completed the ensemble. The redhead turned, coffee in hand, and caught Dev looking at him, again.

*Dammit.*

The white T-shirt stretched across his chest and showed off the fact the guy had pecs too. Damn. The tightness in the coat sleeves did mean he had big biceps.

*This is killing me.*

"Not the night, not the night. Got to find this assignment and get at least half of it done," he whispered. After all, he didn't want to appear completely insane, especially in front of Mr. Sexy-Redhead, who had taken a seat a few tables away, facing him.

But despite Dev's best intention to look cool in front of Mr. Sexy-Redhead, he battled with his laptop to connect to the shop's free WiFi, repeatedly clicking on the tiny icons, smacking his mouse on the table top, and smashing the space bar.

The ringing in his ears wouldn't go away, and the claxon screeched like an ambulance siren

Dev fought with his laptop, the network, and the internet settings.

"Nothing. Nothing is going right," Dev grumbled as he continued to click like a maniac. And in a moment of complete frustration, he grabbed thick clumps of hair into clenched fists, all of Dev's emotions boiled up to the surface.

The ringing eclipsed everything.

The last words his father had yelled replayed in his head.

Amna walking past him with his gunmetal-blue headphones.

Cam's texts flashed over and over on his phone.

Prof. Radcliff's disappointed face loomed in close.

Dev wasn't a violent person. He was rarely angry. If anything he was passive, and normally, shit like this would have washed across him like the proverbial water off a duck's back. Not tonight.

At that very moment in time, he lost control.

The argumentative network connection became the last straw.

Dev smacked the keys of his laptop, slammed his fist on the table top sending a shockwave of energy through the table he sat at, jarring the spoon still resting inside his coffee cup. The utensil clanked and spun and bounced inside the cup.

The tables and chairs around him all skittered a few centimeters outwards as a tremor of raw energy rippled throughout the coffee shop. All at once the entire store sat silent and every set of eyes were on him.

Dev put his head in his hands, closed his eyes, and attempted to push away the entire world. He hadn't noticed everything around him had moved on its own.

"Hi, having a rough night? Mind if I sit here with you?"

Dev pulled his hands away, turned and stared into those icy eyes of the gorgeous creature who had been sitting so close. His voice, deep and seductive, melted Dev's insides. He sat there, speechless, although his brain no longer fumbled with feelings of rage and chaos. Instead, it filled with the rush of outrageous actions. Pushing this guy up against the nearest wall and ripping his shirt off would be a good start.

"Anyone in there?" The guy chuckled. "So, normally I wouldn't come over and bug someone who was clearly so angry, but the Naiad in the corner over there is getting pissed at you for doing magic in public. Generally we try to keep that shit under wraps, yeah? That was quite a burst of energy."

*What the hell did this guy just say?*

"I'm sorry...what?" Dev stuttered, then bit the inside of his cheek as punishment for being so stupid.

"The spoon? The chairs and tables?" Sexy guy tilted his head and his gaze flicked toward the coffee cup and then back toward Dev.

"I'm sorry. What?"

Mr. Sexy-Redhead put his hand in front of his mouth and chortled. Not loudly, or in a mean way, but Dev couldn't tell if perhaps he was the butt of the joke, or...did Cam put this guy up to some kind of prank?

"Dude, look at your coffee."

Dev ogled his cup, sitting at the edge of the table. The spoon Dev had left to rest against the rim silently stirred itself in counterclockwise motions around and around and around sloshing liquid out and spilling coffee onto the tabletop. The puddle pooled enough to run over the edge of the table and drip onto the floor.

The cup happened to be at the exact same level as Mr. Sexy-Redhead's crotch.

Dev's eyes went wide and his mouth formed a small *O*.

"What the hell? I'm not doing that."

"Well, even though I'm a metallurgist and that spoon is made of metal, the telekinetic part is not part of my talent pool. Although I keep trying to manipulate metal and use telekinesis at the same time, I've had zero luck. But I know there's no way I could ever move everything like you just did. The Naiads are generally more apt to manipulate living things like plants, so I doubt she's doing it." Mr. Sexy-Redhead glanced toward the woman sitting in the darkened corner of the store who glared at them. He tilted his head as he returned his warm welcoming bearded face to Dev. "And other than you, there are no other magical creatures in this store right now, so..."

"What the hell." Dev's eyes darted back and forth between the still-stirring-spoon and the stranger.

The beautiful man leaned forward toward Dev and squinted, studying his confused and shocked look. He pointed at Dev as his perfect smile got a bit bigger.

"Oh my god. Is this your first time?" Sexy guy showed his gleaming white teeth, "It is, isn't it? This hasn't happened to you before!"

He sat down in the chair opposite Dev, their knees touched under the table. Dev didn't move.

"Okay, well I think that's enough of that." Dev's new guest reached over, plucked the spoon out of the coffee, grabbed a napkin, and set the spoon down on it. He grabbed a few more napkins and sopped up the spilled beverage. Once done, he stared at Dev and cracked a smile so large Dev fell entranced.

"Hi, my name is Toliver, but my friends call me Tully. I'm a witch too."

He stuck out his hand for a shake.

Dev's mouth hung open as he stared.

*Holy Shit! It had worked!*

# Chapter Five

TULLY DECIDED DEV did a very good impersonation of a mannequin. He left his hand extended and hanging, palm open, above the tabletop. He wasn't sure what to make of the man. One thing he did know, Dev's dark features and incredible eyelashes made things stir.

Dev sat in his chair, stock-still, wearing a shell-shocked face. Witnessing magic for the first time does that to a person.

Dev's expression told Tully the poor guy was lost. That made Tully want to wrap an arm around him and make everything better, show him the vast world of magic that lay before him. The journey Dev had the opportunity to embark on would be filled with astonishing wonders, both dark and light should he wish to do so.

Slowly, painfully, Dev took Tully's hand, giving it a tentative shake.

Dev's smooth, soft, and warm skin made Tully display a monster-sized grin as he reveled in Dev's hand interlaced with his own. Stroking the back of Dev's hand with his thumb, Tully employed his favorite ability—

charming others—a slight bending of their will. Tully had a little fae ancestry in him, Sidhe blood, *Irish People of the Mounds*, on his mother's side. Not much, granted, but enough to be able to put people at ease and enchant the hell out of them. Witch laws and traditions held twisted beliefs on mixed race creatures. They were frowned on, and matings were always discouraged, but almost every family line had a tale of some wayward relative's dalliance with a fae. And the resulting offspring always absorbed the best qualities of their ancestors. Tully chalked up his family's good looks to this tidbit of folklore. Tully's mother had been a Gaelic knockout.

Along with using the fae blood to bewitch folks every now and then, Tully often sensed another person's emotions through skin on skin contact. Dev's moods were yanking his brain in a nasty tug-of-war. Not surprising given the situation and this gave Tully another reason to want to comfort Dev. He glanced at the handshake with Dev, which was still going on. The contrast between his pale be-damned-Irish-ancestry skin next to Dev's delightfully darker tone was stark.

Tully glanced back at Dev who still had a stunned glare. His deep-brown eyes were framed by the longest, darkest eyelashes Tully had ever seen.

Without warning, the Naiad stood in front of the two of them, hands on her hips, scowling. Tully released his grip on Dev, and put his hands in his lap.

"Well, that was completely uncalled for! You want to tell your boyfriend to cease and desist? Or should I call in the Magistrates?"

"I'm sorry. Apparently it's my friend's first time, so please accept my apologies and we beg your forgiveness. Won't happen again." Tully winked at her.

The Naiad wasn't impressed. "I've cleaned up your mess and spellbound everyone in the shop to forget what just happened. Maybe you should take your newbie out back and explain the rules."

"I'll be sure nothing else happens. Again, our apologies, and thank you for attending to matters." Tully put on his best diplomatic hat. Naiads were notorious for being difficult creatures with short tempers, but she wasn't wrong. Magic in public was strictly forbidden. Accidents and slips happened, of course, but the supernatural community preferred to keep their presence a mystery. Keeping the Shadow Realm as hidden as possible made everyone's life safer. Humans were terrible creatures, capable of mass destruction and torture, and they didn't deal well with changes in their stagnant mundane worlds.

The woodland fae turned and stomped out the door, the overhead bell chiming as she left.

"Whew, well, thank god that went well." Tully rolled his eyes but kept an eye on the creature. A smart witch ensured a Naiad wasn't present before speaking ill of them, Tully returned his bright smile to Dev. He placed his hand close to Dev's, which were fidgeting on the surface of the wooden tabletop.

"Who was she?" Dev nodded toward the coffee shop's front door, still wide-eyed.

"No idea. But a Naiad just the same. They're woodland fae, a particularly challenging species to deal with. Don't worry, I got you. You'll be fine with me." Tully gave Dev a wink.

"I'm...just...wait, fae? What?" Dev's head canted as he furrowed his eyebrows, like when you say something incomprehensible to a dog.

Tully chuckled but attempted to contain his amusement so as to not attract too much attention. He loved the look on Dev's face. What was the expression? *Seeing the world through a newborn's eyes is one of the greatest joys on earth*? And here poor Dev had experienced magic for the first time. A fledgling witch had been born. Tully decided he could look at Dev like this for a long time before becoming bored. Dev may not be able to wield his magic yet, but Tully had succumbed, enthralled and bespelled by Dev and his naivety.

Another chuckle, but from the acknowledgment Tully was a titch jealous. He'd never experienced magic with such innocence. Tully had come from a long line of witches, so magic had always been around. If Tully had to guess, Dev didn't have a similar background. Thinking through his own childhood to when he'd first manifested and how the world opened up to him Tully sympathized with Dev. Changes were afoot, big ones.

Thank goodness Tully's mother had known of Byron Radcliff. Byron had saved him, had wrapped him under his wing and shown him how the world worked within the laws of witches. Bryon's mentoring, and the brotherhood of the coven, left Tully with a dutiful sense of obligation to both, which was why he had gratefully accepted Byron's request. He'd been given instructions to watch Dev, and he'd followed them to the letter the whole afternoon. After spotting Dev sprinting across the campus, Tully had followed him, and now with coffee in hand, and a good-looking dude by his side, Tully witnessed the first exhibition of supernatural abilities from a newborn witch. Who'd have guessed Dev's manifestation was going to happen so quick? Byron, that's who.

What an honour. Tully was thankful for the experience, as it was not one he'd ever had before. Even better, when Tully spied his intended target, the sight of Dev tickled other interests. Dev's dark complexion aside, the man held enigmatic and mysterious qualities, and with his lithe and toned body, the newbie witch stirred up erotic notions. Maybe Byron would pair Tully up with Dev. Perhaps he'd be his witch tutor.

"Why would she have assumed I was your boyfriend?" Dev asked, snapping Tully out of his thoughts.

"Oh! Right, okay, well, ah that's a good newbie question. I hope you're not offended, it's just most male witches are gay, so she assumed you and I were, you know," Tully waggled his eyebrows suggestively, "together."

"I'm not a witch." Dev barked. "Gay, sure, but no witch."

"Ahuh," Tully noted, with a hint of teasing. At least Dev was gay and comfortable with being out. Excellent. Tully didn't know any straight male witches, but apparently there were some. Imagine the journey required to come to terms with your sexuality *and* being a witch at the same time! That would make anyone's head spin. Dev had already conquered one of those. "But you are a witch. A fledgling, granted, but oh yeah, you most certainly are one of us."

"No, you must be mistaken. I—" Dev rose from his chair, but Tully grabbed Dev's hand.

Dev's eyes focused in on the touch, staring hard at their conjoined hands.

Tully had to calm the situation down, otherwise Dev might blow again. He had walked into this situation with all the facts. Byron had told Tully all about Dev, who had no clue his Sociology professor was the high priest of the local coven. And he certainly had no idea Byron had asked Tully to tail Dev. So, perhaps introductions were in order.

"Don't leave. Stay here with me. I'll answer any questions you might have. Let's start with something easy?" Tully recognized the look Dev had plastered all over his face. Suspicion and incredulity. He had to give Dev some credit. Most humans after seeing magic would have bolted in fear, or resorted to violence. Dev's steady gaze told him he was leery and questioning everything. "What's your name?" As much as Tully wanted to meet Byron's expectations on carrying out his assignment, he didn't want his first encounter with Dev to end on sour notes.

Dev, head bowed, eyes darting in every direction, and hesitant to answer a simple question told Tully he was struggling. Tully's heart ached, and he wanted to reach out, put his arm around the guy, and tell him everything would be okay. Maybe even kiss it all better. Damn, the man was a looker!

Exploding a telekinetic wave of supernatural energy would disturb most people.

"Dev. Devid Khandelwal." Dev stuttered as Tully pulled on his hand, gradually drawing Dev to sit back down with him at the table. He didn't let go of Dev, but used his thumb to continue caressing Dev's hand.

"Well, Dev, it is a pleasure to meet you, especially at such a fortuitous time. Tell me, what's going on in your world right now? You blowing off a magical explosion like that usually means you're stressed out? Yeah? I did that once. Mother knocked me into next Tuesday with a backhand right in the middle of the supermarket, then promptly had me sent me off to the local coven for instruction."

"Tully, I'm sorry." Dev pulled his hand away, looking panicked. "I think I need to go. This is all...um, this is too much."

Tully frowned noting Dev hadn't calmed down. Interesting.

*Note to self, Dev's immune to fae charms.*

Realizing he probably looked unhappy, Tully explained his grimace, "I get it, Dev. I'm sorry. Tell you what—" Tully reached into his pocket and pulled out his wallet. He flipped the leather cover open and pulled out a business card. "—it's old-fashioned, I know, but I keep these on hand for instances like this. Take my card. You can ask me anything you want, or call me at any time.

"I know this isn't easy. I'm sure you're world has been turned on its head. But I can help, if you want. Take it." Tully placed the card into Dev's palm, folding his fingers over top.

"Okay. Thanks. I'm sorry. I ...I think I need to go now."

Tully's confidence plummeted. He'd been so certain his fae charms would settle the newbie nerves and Dev would sit with him all night, asking all kinds of questions. Tully hadn't contemplated a negative reaction. Perhaps this whole scene had been too much.

"It's okay, Dev, really. Think things through, go for a long walk, or sleep on it. But give me a call, and we'll meet again. We can have a coffee, or if you're up to it, even dinner. I'm here to answer whatever questions you might have."

Dev's head bobbed in agreement, however hesitantly, at Tully's offer. He packed his laptop and notebook into his carrier bag, whipped his coat on, then slung the sack over his shoulder. As Dev left the shop, he glanced over his shoulder at Tully.

Tully gave him the warmest happy face possible, a gentle wave, and nod of his head. But Tully had to wonder if maybe he'd come on too strong. He was like that sometimes. Confident and enthusiastic could easily be mistaken for overbearing and cocky.

Tully remained hopeful though. With Dev as his charge, he'd see the stunning dark-eyed man again. After all, when something new happens in someone's life and there's someone they can talk to about it, they go and talk to the person who has experience with it.

Tully watched Dev walk down the street. More than once, Dev glanced over his shoulder.

"Damn, he is adorable." Tully cocked an eyebrow as one corner of his mouth pulled up in a boastful show of being impressed with himself. Tully took a sip of his lukewarm coffee, gagged, and set the cup down, pushing it away. Coffee that wasn't hot wasn't worth drinking.

Digging in his interior breast pocket, Tully pulled out his cell and punched a few buttons. Holding the device up to his ear, he waited for the person on the other end to answer.

"Hi Byron. Yup, great news!"

DEV WALKED AS fast as his two feet would carry him without running, although he had no destination in mind.

*What the hell just happened?*

*That spoon.*

"Did you see how cute he was? My god," Dev exclaimed to himself as he walked down the street, but the two teenage girls who were within earshot at the bus stop, waiting for the #4, glared at him.

"It actually happened." Dev's head swam with emotion. He couldn't tell if his queasy stomach churned from excitement of otherworldly occurrences or if he was terrified the summoning spell had worked. Or maybe he was reeling because Mr. Sexy-Redhead had revealed his status as a witch.

Damn, a musclebound redhead. Tully epitomized Dev's every fantasy.

But Dev made a spoon move without touching it!

"I should tell Cam." Cam had been there for everything, so why not this? Never mind Dev was still mad at Cam for his pimple prank. But what if Dev couldn't make a spoon move again? If he failed to repeat the show to Cam, he'd never believe him. Not in a million years. Dev would have to float into Cam's house opening doors with his mind and a whirlwind of designer clothes swirling behind him before Cam would sit up and take notice.

Telekinesis wasn't something you bragged about and expected someone else to believe. You'd have to be able repeat the event over and over again. Dev's head swam with questions on how to replicate the feat, and until he had mastered his newly found talents, there was no way he would go to Cam's, who would never believe him otherwise. Confiding in Cam about his recently discovered ability was out of the question. Making a spectacle of himself at home saying, *'Hey, look what I can do!'* was absurd. No one there would understand. Especially his mom. She'd be horrified. Nope, Dev's witchiness had to be a secret for now.

Dev stopped in his tracks.

What the hell had Dev done? Dammit. He should

have stayed with Tully. The numerous questions running through his mind were fast and furious. Can I do it again? What am I? Who are you? Can I do anything other than move spoons? And what the hell was a Naiad?

"Geez, you're so stupid! Why the hell did you leave?" Dev's mind raced, thinking about Tully, witches, the spoon, and the girl who said she'd spellbound everyone. For the second time in one night, his little corner of the world had condensed into a ball of heaviness, which was becoming too tight and too much. Except now life wasn't fraught with pressure and stress. No, the exact opposite. Dev tingled with excitement. Even the night air was ripe with fresh possibilities.

And his ears were silent. No ringing at all.

Dev shook his head and rolled his eyes. His biggest desire had just come true. The Shadow Realm had shown itself, and like a fool, he'd run, tail tucked, away from it.

"God, you're such an idiot." Dev reprimanded himself. "Maybe he's still there?" Dev spun in the direction of the coffee house, but he'd already walked a long ways away from it.

But if he returned to the coffee shop, what would that look like? Desperate. Extremely desperate. Dev didn't want to appear silly or childish. He wanted to be an adult. Adults took their time and thought about implications and consequences. Dev might also have wanted to impress Tully by exhibiting adult characteristics. Damn the man set the butterflies to swarming in his stomach. So many muscles. So much red fur. Dev would go home, sit in his bedroom, and think about all of this. Tomorrow morning, on his way to class, he'd call Tully and make a date with him to have coffee. Or maybe even dinner.

Besides, nothing guaranteed Tully was even still at the coffee shop.

Wait. A Date? Dev struggled with the concept of a date with Tully. Tully hadn't called it a date, had he? Would Tully even be interested in going out on a date? Dev didn't think his current excitement levels would tolerate being pushed, but the prospect of a date with Mr. Sexy-Redhead *and* talking about the Shadow Realm with witches and other creatures?

Was Dev more excited about the Shadow Realm revealing itself or Tully? Redheaded, muscled, bearded, and delicious Tully. Maybe Dev's butterflies reflected all the excitement of the night.

Dev's mind didn't slow down. He walked home, lost in endless thoughts, chasing one possibility with another and playing out a dozen different conversations in his mind.

For the first time in Dev's entire life, he might have found a place in the world. A magical world, one he always believed existed. And even better, he had a power, an ability. He could move spoons! Maybe he belonged in the Shadow Realm.

And maybe, if the redhead was a witch too, Dev would have some fine scenery along his new journey.

As Dev continued the walk home, he pictured going on a coffee date with Tully, talking about the Shadow

Realm, witches, and magic. For the first time in weeks, Dev beamed with happiness. The ringing in his ears had dissipated. His life looked pretty damn good right now.

# Chapter Six

CAM FLITTERED UP the stairs, his feet inches off the ground, testing his speed and agility for the hundredth time. Gossamer-like wings had grown from the nubs on his back, and they sparkled an iridescent green as sunlight beams refracted off the see-through membranous sections as he zipped past the window. The shafts of light were the same emerald as the iris of his eyes. Never mind the sparkles of gold or the fact his pupils were now stretched like a cat's.

Everything burst forth with vitality and life. Colours were dazzling and vibrant, sunlight, a rainbow of glee, and the shadows were amorphous and animated. There were tiny creatures who lived in both. Some of them were small and delicate, while others were fat and hairy. All of them had teeth. The teeth were disconcerting.

But Cam's new wings were the coolest. He did a quick zip around the house again. The appendages didn't appear as if they would have been able to carry him, but they did. And in keeping with Cam's furball status, the base of his wings were hairy, as were the outside edges and if Cam didn't know any better, he'd swear he'd gotten shaggier all over.

*If that was even possible.*

Cam ran his fingers through his beard. The hair had grown thicker and denser. The occasional whisker sporting the weirdest highlights of grass green whenever sunlight lit up his face.

Cam snorted out a laugh in amusement. This was the craziest and best shit ever. He spun around and flew toward the full-length mirror in his bedroom. Maybe Dev had slipped him some ecstasy, not that Dev ever had, but what else explained the best trip he'd ever been on. But this had lasted way too long and despite all the sparkling colours and shadows he swore were moving, this couldn't be a hallucination.

Cam held out his hand, fascinated as a shimmer of sparkles fluttered into the air in front of him.

"Ha ha! Fairy dust. So cool!"

Despite the continued exuberance with his current situation, Cam would be having words with Dev. Honestly, when he sent him a message and text after text after text and a selfie that bordered on lewd, he expected a response. He'd been naked when he snapped the photo, and the photo contained more flesh than Cam would have normally sent off to his best friend, but it's not like the two of them hadn't seen each other naked, and after all, Cam *really* wanted Dev to see the changes.

Like this tail. Holy shit! Cam whirled in the air trying to catch the spinal extension, and when he did, he stopped, enthralled with its beauty. The appendage was slender, and long, and covered in coarse fur. Cam stroked his new body part for a bit.

And then the ivory horns absorbed his attention. They jutted out from those two damn pimples, the two zits that had started this nonsense. He had an ample rack now. Those pointy bastards had grown every hour until the hard bone had wrapped along his skull and gently curved toward his ears. Even the tips of his ears had gotten hairier and pointed.

Cam pinched the pointy end of his ear and then fondled the tiny hairs running along the outer edge. His ears reminded him of a lynx.

Oh sure, at first Cam might have been mortified with the whole transformation. But not now. After passing out in the initial stages of his alteration from the pain and vomiting, which had been worse than a week-long flu or his last hangover, the rest of the change had been easy. The first few hours had been gut-wrenching agony. But now? Dammit. The suffering had been worth the transformation!

Cam ran his long fingers over his furry torso. He'd magically grown pecs and abs.

"Eat that jocks!" Cam snickered as he spun in the air, floating before the mirror, his tail twirling behind him in an undulating motion. "To think of all the running I've done when all I needed was a summoning board and a wish! Ha!"

Cam's attention redirected to his growling stomach.

The sandwich he'd eaten earlier hadn't stayed down. His yearnings were making him crave things more primal. Flying with speed and accuracy, Cam zipped his way into the kitchen and opened the fridge. He floated in front of the open door, shivering from the cool breeze wafting out.

He riffled through the fridge bins and picked up an apple. The deep red fruit shone at its peak ripeness, cold, crisp and vibrant.

Cam took a bite.

The sweet juices ran over his tongue, spilled past his lips and dribbled off his chin.

Cam gagged.

He dropped the apple and spit the chunk of fruit flesh out.

"Oh my god, that's disgusting." After several other attempts at bread, a carrot, and a slice of cheese, nothing wanted to slide down the ole gullet. There wasn't anything in here satiating the hunger pangs.

Cam opened the freezer door and inspected the first thing accessible. A frozen package of hamburger.

"Well that's gonna be hard to eat." His stomach complained with a growl and churned. "Hmmm, maybe..." Cam grabbed the package and threw the whole thing in the microwave on high for five minutes. The plastic shrink wrap pulled and stretched as the Styrofoam container bubbled and deteriorated.

This wait had gone on long enough. "Come on, hurry up." Cam, still floating several inches above the tiled floor, his gossamer wings vibrating at a steady beat, gave up on his waiting. After two minutes he ripped open the door to the microwave and grabbed the still cold package.

Peeling the cellophane away, Cam leaned in and inhaled in the aroma of the cold ground up flesh.

"Oh, yes, sweet baby, delicious." Cam's tongue, pointed and rough, slithered out and licked the slab of meat.

At the taste of the blood, Cam's eyes grew momentarily wide, his mouth twerked up, and then he squinted as he licked his lips and heaved a giant sigh.

His craving had found satiation.

Cam opened his mouth and pulled his lips tight revealing rows of sharp pointy teeth on both the upper and lower ridges of his mouth.

He smashed his face into the frozen ground meat and chewed through the barely warmed up top layer and the frozen middle.

He gnawed and crunched as a rivulet of blood escaped his lips and ran out the corner of his mouth.

His tongue lashed out and caught the leaked juices.

"Can't spill a drop. That would be bad." Cam took another bite as his eyes closed and his face relaxed, chewing, savouring every morsel, delighting in the texture of the raw meat inside his mouth.

"Best snack ever."

BYRON SLID THE key into the deadbolt and twisted. He pulled open the storm screen, then turned the knob, and pushed in the back door of his and Addas's house. He hung his corduroy spring jacket on the first free hook lining the wall in the entrance and placed his sandy-coloured leather satchel on the floor, but only after he'd fished out an old tattered-looking scroll and a thin oxblood-leather-bound manual.

"Hi, honey, I'm home," he yelled up the stairs.

"Up here, making dinner," Addas replied.

Byron kicked off his shoes onto a rubber mat, climbed the stairs, and walked into the kitchen. The air sat heavy with both heat and fragrance, sweet and savory aromas. He placed the scroll and book down on the counter.

"Smells delicious. What are you making?" Byron said as he came up behind Addas and slid his arms around him, latching them together under Addas's belt. Byron was a head shorter than Addas, but his man had grown over the course of the last year into a beast. Byron wasn't what you'd call short at six foot even, and now he had to stand on tippy-toes to nuzzle his cheek on Addas's shoulder blades.

"Hmm, I love it when you do that. Sweet and sour pork."

"My favorite."

"I know."

"I've got great news. I found additional written documentation we can use to fix you. This," he tapped on the leather-bound book, "is the quintessential guide on ritualistic purification!" Byron squeezed Addas tight, thrilled with his discovery.

"Well, we have lots to be thankful for! I figured I should make your favorite dinner to celebrate your new found witch. Another addition to our monstrous little family. But a spell to help me? I'd say that's real cause to live it up!" Addas, who stood in front of the sink rinsing off the frying skillet, turned the faucet off and set the pan down into the soapy dishwater to soak, then picked up the hand towel and patted his hands dry.

Byron hadn't moved.

Addas grabbed Byron's hands and shoved them down further, so Byron's fingers fondled the thickening shaft of his boyfriend's growing erection.

Byron grinned. "Well, now that's a whole different kind of pork. I swear, everything on you is getting bigger."

"That's no pork; that's your dessert."

Byron gave Addas another squeeze, then redirected his hands toward his boyfriend's belt buckle, fumbling, trying to get the latch undone. He wanted his dessert first.

"Ah, ah ah..." Addas slapped his hands away and turned to face Byron. He placed his thick hands on each side of Byron's neck and pulled him in for a kiss.

Byron tasted the sweetness of the dinner's sauce followed by the spicy tang of the sour as his tongue explored Addas's mouth. He ran his hands up under Addas's shirt, feeling the landscaped torso. The stubble made Byron even more persistent to get his sweets before the actual meal.

Addas pulled away but let Byron continue his under-clothes exploration. Byron's slacks were tented.

"I said, dinner first," Addas admonished Byron, growling, a low rumble vibrating his chest.

Byron licked his lips. "You are a tease."

"I believe you started the shenanigans first, now come on, go wash up—" at that moment Byron's phone rang, the sound muffled. Byron patted his back pocket where he normally kept his cell.

"Oops, left the damn thing in my coat pocket."

"And the damn thing should stay there."

"You know I have to answer. Responsibilities. Being the high priest comes with some sacrifices." Byron leaned forward and, up on tippy-toes, gave Addas a quick kiss, but Byron noticed from the look on his lover's face he wasn't too pleased. His light hazel eyes stared at Byron while one eyebrow arched in disapproval while he got kissed. There deep in the iris a flash of yellow radiated behind the glare.

"Addas," Byron warned with a finger waved at Addas's chest, "you keep that wolf of yours quiet. Remember, you're a witch first. The wolf's not allowed to come out. We don't know what will happen if you shift and we can't have the rest of the coven knowing."

"That's not how this works. I'm almost at the end of the year. The infection has taken hold."

"I know, but we haven't figured out how to reverse it... yet," Byron yelled the last word over his shoulder as he stomped down the stairs and fumbled with his jacket, trying to wrestle his phone from the interior pocket of his blazer.

As he pulled the device out, the call went to voice mail.

"Dammit." Byron waited for a few seconds, watching the screen as he walked up to the kitchen until a red dot notified him of the recorded message.

After a minute or two of staring at this phone and Addas staring at him, the little icon appeared.

"Finally." Byron pushed a few buttons, summoning up the message.

Addas leaned against the counter and crossed his arms over his massive chest. The muscles in his trunk-like forearms stretched and flexed, his light-green T-shirt, which matched his eye colour, pulled tight across his chest and biceps.

Byron had to readjust his crotch while watching Addas. His lover hated the constant interruptions from technology, but he had nine coven members to babysit, and one new witch fledgling to contend with. And the entire coven still scouted for any potential new members. They had two additional spots to fill. Hopefully Dev would be one of them.

As the message played, Byron's face grew dark, his brows furrowed together.

"What happened? Do I need to keep dinner warm?" Addas sighed. Byron pressed his index finger to his lips, asking Addas to be quiet.

"No. Shit." Byron mumbled but kept listening. After a few moments, he pulled the device away from his ear and pushed a button to erase the message. "No, we can eat dinner. Gus, who is keeping an eye on Dev's friend, is quite concerned. He sent a picture." Byron poked a few more buttons to open the text app to see what Gus had sent.

"Oh, fuck. Well, that's not good." Byron showed Addas.

Addas laughed out loud.

"It's not funny."

"Yes, it is. Look at him. How the fuck did a Muggle manage to transform themselves into a deep-forest fae?" Addas asked, eyebrow still arched, arms still crossed.

"Harry Potter reference? Really?"

"If the shoe fits, but you haven't answered my question."

"Summoning board of desire," Byron grunted.

"Mmmhmm. I told you those things were a bad idea. Mazear is a vengeful bitch."

"But they make us some great cash, and besides, this is only one of the many schemes we set in motion as part of the plan to get Dev and other initiates pulled in. I didn't think he'd include someone else in the ritual. That was dumb on my part. I should've anticipated him including another. And if you were Mazear, you'd be a little pissed too."

"Leading on a Djinn, making him think the two of you were an item, tricking him and ultimately binding him into the board was, I'll admit, a somewhat legendary maneuver, but mark my words, it will come back to bite you in the ass."

"Addas, are you being jealous?" A corner of Byron's mouth pulled up as one of his eyebrows arched.

"Hell no. I got to have a piece of him, and that ass was pure perfection. But you manipulated his feelings. That's not gonna end well. And you know how the old fables go. Djinn are not creatures who liked to be used as toys."

Byron had tuned him out and studied the picture Gus had sent.

Addas stepped in closer and took another look. "You know, horns, wings, and a tail, that's upper echelon of the fae. You're gonna have a problem there. Once he figures out meat is all he can eat—"

"Yeah I know. He'll start hunting people." Byron tapped a few more buttons which sent off a call to Gus.

"Hey," Byron started when the call connected, "yeah, I saw. That's not good, and Addas thinks he's morphed into one of the upper ranks, which means trouble. You should bring him in."

The room sat silent as Byron listened.

"So? Use the iron shackles and call in a few of the other knights to help. He can't be left on his own. You know what will happen. We had to dispose of the others who came into human territory. The one we set free last week left here on its last legs. I don't want to have to do this again, but we will if we have to."

Addas listened while dishing up the meal and placing the plates on the table but continued to watch Byron with his arched eyebrow, shaking his head.

"Yes, bring him here once you have him, and we'll keep him downstairs in the cells." Byron put his phone up against his chest and raised an eyebrow at Addas. "What? Why are you shaking your head?"

"Dispose? This is your new witch's friend? Killing his best pal might not be smart."

Byron scrunched his forehead, creasing his brows. Addas was the only one whose personality could deliver the flaws in his thinking in such a way Byron would actually consider them. "Yeah." He cleared his throat. "Just bring him here. Maybe we can reverse it, or something. Hopefully."

Byron hung up.

Addas gave him a disapproving look.

"What?" Byron rolled his eyes.

"You're a monster, you know that, right? What do you think is going to happen when your new witch finds out you've locked his friend up in the dungeon, with the intent of disposing him if you can't fix the problem?"

"It's not a dungeon, more like a holding pen."

"That's better?"

"I suppose not. Okay, fine we won't kill it." Byron sighed.

"Not it. Him," Addas corrected. "We'll figure this out. You figured me out, sort of, I'm sure you can come up with something." Addas stepped forward so he touched chest to nose with Byron. He slid his hands down so he held a butt check in each of his large paws. "And I'd say your ass is far more legendary than the Djinn's."

Byron stretched up and kissed Addas taking his time to taste his lover's lips.

Addas pulled his hands up to the waistband of Byron's pants and slid his hands down, but this time inside. Addas pulled away with a feigned look of shock on his face.

"No underwear? Why Professor Radcliff, you naughty teacher." He shoved a big paw down, feeling Byron's furry ass cheeks.

Byron shrugged, trying to look coy.

Addas continued to manhandle and knead Byron's muscular bubble butt while Byron concerned himself with getting Addas's belt unlatched.

Addas grinned. "Okay, maybe dessert first. Because once the faerie comes over, it's gonna be a long night and not full of the fun I had in mind."

Byron succeeded in getting the belt undone and unzipped Addas's jeans. Pulling the denim apart, he discovered Addas had also chosen to not wear underwear.

Byron's hands were now full of a hefty amount of dessert.

"I should make you eat dinner first, but maybe an appetizer instead?" Addas offered an alternative as Byron stroked him, which had an immediate effect. He had gotten larger in every respect, and now Byron's dessert stood at full attention. Addas placed his big paw of a hand on the top of Byron's head and pushed him downwards.

"Nope, like I said, dessert first." Byron licked his lips as he knelt on the floor.

DEV HAD TAKEN the long way, not making a priority of getting home. He berated himself for leaving. He should have stayed and asked Tully all the questions he'd been accumulating for years, but he'd performed telekinesis and met the most gorgeous man he'd ever seen. The entirety of the situation blew his mind. With each step he took, Dev replayed the events of the coffee shop.

Either would have been a momentous occasion. Okay, so the fact the spoon had stirred on its own took the award for coolest moment ever.

But Tully was cool too.

Damn if the summoning board hadn't worked.

But as much as he replayed the stirring spoon and the stern words from the Naiad, thoughts of Tully wouldn't leave him alone. Dev had almost forgotten about the strife he'd left behind before ending up at the coffee shop. Right now his feet were inches off the ground in elation. Well, not really, but still.

Dev arrived at the front door of his family home, turned the knob, and opened the door.

Sitting in the living room, waiting for him, sat his father. The stern expression on his face had impregnated the room, and the overbearing anger leached all the happiness Dev had harnessed since the coffee shop.

"Where have you been?"

"Out." The floating sensation disappeared, replaced with resentment and a touch of anger.

"You don't get to talk like that to your mother and me. It's disrespectful." His father turned red, his rage returning. He'd pissed off his father, something he tried hard not to do. The man wasn't happy, but Dev didn't care.

"Well, I'll tell you what. You remember what kind of a degree I'm getting, maybe put some importance behind the fact that I'm graduating in less than two weeks with full honours, stay out of my room, respect my stuff, and then we'll call this family melodrama good and I'll coo and fawn all over everyone in this house. How does that sound?"

Dev's father stood up, his fists balled, gyrating with fury.

"I think maybe you should go to your room."

"Yes. *My* room. I think that's the perfect place for me to be."

Dev walked past his father, and as he did the palpable wave of heat infused with stifled rage wafted off his father. Dev's ire matched his father's, after all, an apple from the tree didn't roll too far away. Dev's nerves were shattered. He'd never pushed these limits before.

In fact, this confrontation pretty much solidified his decision to pack everything up and move out. This was it; they had pushed too far. He needed his own space. He loved them all, family always meant well...but, shit. Why couldn't they understand and respect him and his needs?

He glared at his father, ensuring his face didn't give away any emotion, while his brain twisted in a writhing snake-ball of emotions. Dev took the stairs to his room, one at a time thudding down on every step. If he had run up the stairs like he wanted, he may have relayed fear. Dev's jaw clenched tight to the point his teeth hurt. This display of defiance took control he didn't know he had. As he walked into his small sanctuary, he slammed the door to prove a point.

He'd been slamming a lot of doors lately.

Someone walked down the hall stomping down the stairs to the living room. Within seconds, Dev made out his mother chatting with his father. The words were stifled, but this was a common scenario whenever Dev had caused trouble. Mom would always intervene.

In less than a minute, the talking erupted into yelling and another loud chorus began. The same blaring chaos dominated this house. Mom had failed to de-escalate the situation, and that had never happened before. When Mom stepped in, things got straightened out, right quick.

Dev lay on his bed, hand covering his eyes.

As if on cue, and to no surprise to Dev, Amna and Bhanu's voices soon joined the song of disruption.

Dev sighed. It might be a long night.

His memories of the day went to Tully, his creamy skin and bearded face. And those glacier-blue eyes. They were soothing, if not exciting, sparking electrical jolts in his tummy. He remembered the card Tully had given him. He pushed his fingers into his jean's pocket and fished the embossed paper out.

The card was black with silver lettering. A raised Celtic knot in red ink centered and drew the focus into the middle of the card. Dev ran his finger over the shape, and Tully's name.

*Tolliver Mack*

*Brother of the Night Grove*

*293-562-6666*

The argument downstairs raised another notch on the decibel rating.

"This is ridiculous." The noise in the small and tight house had, within minutes of returning, constricted his entire being. Family life was choking him.

A light bulb turned on in Dev's brain. A solution. A way out.

Dev wondered aloud, "He did say to call anytime."

Dev pulled his phone from his back pocket and let his fingerprint open the device.

"Seventy-three texts! Jesus, Cam." Dev pressed the text app, and went to Cam's string of texts. He scanned them. They were row after row and pretty much the same.

*You've got to come over.*

*You have to see this.*

*You're not gonna believe this.*

*Dude, where are you?*

Dev scrolled through the lines. There was one picture, blurred and out of focus. He opened it, zoomed in, and out, turned his phone sideways...

"Is that?" Dev scrunched up his face. "Jesus Christ, Cam."

Dev dropped his phone when he realized he'd been looking at Cam's ass. There was a lot of hair and skin.

"Ugh." Dev picked up the phone and closed the texting app getting rid of Cam's lewd photo and hit the button for a number pad.

His stomach knotted up with nerves. Excitement for sure, but also nerves.

"I should wait until tomorrow." Dev set the phone down at his side.

He continued to caress the business card reading the name again and the title beneath it. The racket coming from downstairs filled his head and shattered any chance of focusing on anything else. Something crashed followed by a loud *bang*.

"Fuck it." Dev picked the cell up, punched in the numbers, and held the device up to his ear.

It rang. His tummy churned as anxiety bloomed. He shouldn't be calling Tully this late. He almost hung up, but the phone rang again. A rush of heat unfurled across Dev's chest and cheeks—

"Hello?" Tully's voice, deep and confident, spoke in Dev's ear and the butterflies took flight in Dev's stomach again.

He put the phone to his ear.

"Hi, uh, Tully?"

"Dev? Is that you?"

"Yeah, sorry, I hope this isn't too late?"

"No, not at all. I'm a bit of a night owl." Tully stopped there. Dev remained silent. "You okay, Dev?"

"Yeah, sorry."

"Oh, okay. Ah...you want to chat?" Tully's voice had Dev giddy and on edge. His feet were tapping together. He always fidgeted whenever he got uncomfortable.

"I...damn. I'm sorry. I can't stop thinking about what happened tonight."

Dev wanted to start asking some of his questions about the Shadow Realm, but a loud commotion began outside his door.

"What's going on over there?" Tully asked. "Are you sure you're okay?"

"It's my family. They're a little over the top, and today hasn't been the most peaceful." As he finished the sentence, Dev's father banged on his bedroom door.

"Dev, come out here, your mother and I need to talk to you."

"For Christ's sake. I'm sorry Tully." Dev's stomach sunk.

"Don't be. Families are sometimes complicated, but are *you* okay?" Tully asked.

"Not really." Air hitched as he breathed in. His world began to implode. His face contorted with the number of out of control emotions. A lump formed at the back of his throat, and his mouth went dry. He was on the verge of losing a tear or two as the swell of everything filled the bottom lids. The past couple of days ran through his head. Missing assignments, idiotic friends, feeling closed in and trapped. His ears had a distant ring, like it echoed through a tunnel.

"Are you in danger, Dev?"

"Oh, god, no. No, nothing like that. I just—" More ringing.

"Dev. Come out here now," his father yelled.

"Tully, I'm sorry to be so forward, but I need to get out of here. Can I meet you for a beer?"

"Sure, but I have a better idea. How about some peace and quiet. Why don't you come over to my place?"

Dev's eyes widened. A million ideas ran through his head, including one which ended up with him and Tully naked. The ringing dissipated a tad.

"Ah, you sure I'm not imposing?"

*Bang, bang, bang.*

Dev's father had resorted to smacking his fist on his door. Dev's father had a temper, but in all his years, he'd never seen him be violent. Tonight Dev had pushed his father beyond the man's limits.

Dev, on the other hand, sank into an uncontained puddle of anxiety, stress, anger, and elation from talking to Tully.

"Wow. It is loud over there. No, you're not imposing. I wouldn't have invited you if I didn't want you to come over. I'll text you my address."

"God, you're a life saver. Thanks Tully. I'll see you in a bit."

"Yeah, no worries. See you soon."

Dev disconnected the call, stood up, grabbed his jacket and the carrier bag he went nowhere without, and opened his bedroom door.

There stood everyone.

All of them glaring at him.

"What?" Dev mustered all the hostility he'd absorbed since returning from the fateful meeting with Tully and threw it all in his father's face.

"Downstairs. Now. We're all having a family meeting."

Dev's phone buzzed. He glanced at it. A message from Tully.

*10125 84 Avenue*

"You all have a fantastic meeting. I'm going out."

And with his declaration, leaving everyone stunned and slack-jawed, Dev pushed past his parents and his siblings, while slinging the strap of his bag over his head and arm so the bag rested on his left hip. He stomped down the stairs, slipped on his worn out runners sitting on the floor mat in the foyer, and escaped through the front door.

Dev delighted in picturing the looks of shock and bewilderment on everyone's faces, which would last for all of a few seconds, until they burst out in loud voices, all talking over top of themselves.

Dev however, focused on his destination. Turns out Tully didn't live far away, and he promised a night of magical conversation.

Dev smiled, and the swirl of everything stilled.

Things might be looking up.

# Chapter Seven

DEV STROLLED DOWN the sidewalk, earphones in, music blaring, but watched his step. The Old Strathcona neighbourhood, despite its hundred years of age, had stood up relatively well, boasting both sizeable mansions and student domiciles in the same block. But it did show signs of its history and the sidewalks were in need of repair. Cracks had split the cement in many places, heaving portions up enough to snare a less than watchful traveler.

Streetlights beamed down, illuminating the ancient and towering tree-covered street, but as the spring leaves hadn't burst forth yet, the skeletal branches cast shadows on the ground which would have made most folks spooked.

Not Dev. He relished the darkness. The night promised quiet, solitude, and stillness.

His carrier bag bounced on his hip as he walked toward his destination, which he kept careful track of with his maps app. He knew the area relatively well. After all, only a couple of blocks away the bustling hub of Whyte

Avenue beckoned the university students with countless bars and trendy restaurants. These were the hotspots he often frequented with Cam. But he'd never ventured much north of the Gen Z hotspot.

Glancing at his phone, he deduced Tully's place to be only meters away. Looking up, Dev squinted as he focused in on house numbers, most of which were not well displayed especially in the long shadows of night. A couple of houses down from where he stood, loomed a monstrosity of a mansion. There were a few of these castle-like beasts in the area. Most were leftovers from a bygone era, where wealth had once inhabited. Despite the difference in demographic populations, the neighbourhood contained mostly University students and the vast majority of old houses had become Greek fraternities. The odd apartment building or high-rise condo existed, as did ancient monstrous houses chopped up into individual stylish condos. The latter always cost a fortune to rent. Most students couldn't afford them.

Dev walked closer to the mammoth house, complete with a third floor turret containing a massive round window, numerous peaks, and an ancient tree in the front yard. The old rusting wrought-iron numbers nailed into tired and worn red brick stood out.

Dev checked the text message on his phone and compared the two.

*10125*

They matched. He'd arrived. Standing dead still, Dev studied the titanic beast of a structure and decided he liked the house. It reminded him of dilapidated castles and the Addams family. But as much as the house may have bid him welcome, the realization Tully lived within the bones of the structure gave Dev pause.

Tully was a witch.

*Huh, well, apparently I am too?*

Tully was also gorgeous. Like drop-dead handsome, the stuff of Dev's dreams. Husband material handsome. Thinking about Tully sent shivers down Dev's back, and the spontaneous eruption of feathers in his tummy gave away his nervousness. He didn't know Tully. Maybe the invitation to come over was a clever ruse to get a human sacrifice in through the door? How should he know? The whole scenario freaked him out.

Dev stood in front of a stranger's house, a man who proclaimed he lived in the Shadow Realm—Dev had had no proof of Tully's magical abilities. This visit could be the end of him, or perhaps the beginning of a whole new way of life.

Dev had dreamt of this, hunted and sought it out. He wanted this to be true so badly, and now, a handsome man he didn't know from Adam agreed to show him.

He'd wanted the Shadow Realm to reveal its presence. Check.

He'd also wished for some kind of supernatural ability himself. Check that too.

And now it was time to throw all caution to the wind, believe in his dreams, and trust a total stranger.

*How did I get here in such a short time? This is so not me.*

Dev stepped another foot closer to the mansion.

He hoped Tully had been truthful with him and coming over this late at night constituted the beginning of a friendship. Maybe he hoped for too much. The thrill of being away from Amna and Bhanu's constant loud voices and the puffy red face of his father made him almost giddy. Having Tully suggest this alternative spurred his brain into thinking of possibilities for the night that were too good to be true. And if a situation was too good, it wasn't meant to last or, perhaps, not as good as it first appeared.

With a slight hesitation in his step, Dev walked up the stone pathway leading to the huge wooden doors sporting more wrought-iron in the shape of a lion-headed door knocker. Intricate carvings of rabbits at the base of an old tree and tiny birds perched in branches adorned the surface.

Dev took the ring dangling from the metal lion's head and banged the clacker a couple of times, but not too hard or too loud.

Seconds went by, but for Dev, time strung out.

Big empty seconds.

*Should I knock again?*

Dev glanced at his phone, checked the number on the front of the house with his text message from Tully.

*Yup, that's right, maybe—*

From behind the closed door, the muffled *clomp, clomp, clomp* of someone coming down the stairs lit Dev's excitement. It had to be Tully.

When the footsteps stopped, the room fell quiet for a second then the metal *snick* of a deadbolt sliding back shattered the calm.

The door creaked open.

Tully stood there barefoot, in a tight grey T-shirt and a pair of baggy sweatpants.

"Hey!"

"Hi." A swell of uncomfortable heat blossomed in Dev's chest which rapidly spread to his neck and face. "You're sure this isn't too late?"

"God, no. As long as you don't mind me in comfy clothes?" Tully flashed a big red-bearded grin, showing off his pristine white eyeteeth. Dev swore they gleamed and sparkled, which of course made him melt. "Come in! Damn, it's still cold at night. You'd think by this point in April it would be warmer."

Tully took a step back, giving Dev an extra inch or two to walk into the foyer of Tully's home. But once he'd entered, Dev figured from the cramped vestibule the house had been chopped up into many apartments, like so many others in the area.

"How many units are there?" Dev asked, trying to act casual and grownup and not desperate to talk about magical witchy things.

"Oh, not that many. My uncle owns the house. He has the main floor and basement. I live above and there's another smaller studio on the third floor, but it's empty right now."

"Really? I would have imagined there were more suites. This place is huge." As Dev said "huge," he happened to be looking down at Tully's sweat pants.

*Damn, I love guys in sweatpants.*

Tully chortled. "Well, come on up. Uncle Bart's already asleep and once he's out, the dead could dance on his forehead. He'd never know."

"Oh, well, all right then." Dev wasn't sure what to make of that.

"We can talk for hours. He'll never even know you were here."

"Oh, gotcha." Dev took note of the "talk for hours" and hoped he'd be spending the whole night here. Tully closed the door, turned, and walked up the stairs. "Leave your shoes on. You can take them off once we get upstairs."

The stairs were steep, and everything had been layered with wood. Not the thin veneer hardwood so popular with builders now, but the old large plank hardwood. There were scuffs and marks embedded deep into each tread of the stairwell. The place had history. Dev decided he loved the house, even if it contained a thousand ghosts or a history of grisly murders. If the walls were able to talk, they'd entertain him with stories for days. The banister had a carved solid wood handrail, with flowers and vines etched into the spindles. A touch of mustiness permeated the air. The smell of old houses. The stair boards creaked as Dev climbed.

At the top of the stairwell, Tully turned to the left and opened another huge wood door leading into his apartment. To Dev's right, the ascension continued on up to the third level, ending in another big wooden door, he assumed to the empty apartment.

"Come on." Tully gestured Dev to follow him, still smiling ear to ear.

*Man that smile. That face!*

As Dev entered, butterfly wings tickled the inside of his chest and stomach. If this wasn't a first date, it sure reminded him of one. It definitely erased the chaos of home.

"Let me take your coat." Tully walked behind him and held out his arms. Tully grabbed the collar and Dev sensed the heat coming off Tully's hands against the back of his neck. He shrugged his jacket from his shoulders, excited that Tully stood inches away from him.

Tully helped peel the garment off, as Dev slid out of the sleeves. Tully moved with the grace of a well-rehearsed dance move, smooth and elegant. The gesture spoke to Tully's ability to take lead and make Dev feel comfortable.

Tully took the jacket and opened up slatted folding closet doors where a myriad of other coats and sweaters hung. Dev's joined the others. From where he stood, the smell of days old cologne wafted off Tully's hung clothes, and Dev hoped his jacket would rub up enough against the other occupants to have a scented reminder of Tully to take home.

Dev slipped his worn runners off and shuffled them off to the side of the area rug lining the floorboards at the door's landing.

"Great, what can I get you to drink? Wine, beer, tea? Pick your poison."

"Oh, um...you know it's been forever, but I think I'll have a glass of wine."

"White or red?" Tully asked. Dev raised an eyebrow, impressed. Dev's only guest over to his house had been Cam, or other family relatives. Tully exemplified such a perfect host, Dev had to wonder if he did this often.

"Doesn't matter."

"I think I have an open bottle of red." Tully walked down the a hallway separating the main entrance from the rest of the apartment, but as Dev followed the short distance, the wall gave way exposing a massive living room and kitchen, with a fireplace in the corner, a real one, currently displaying a crackling fire. A huge picture window exposed the darkness of the front yard and the tree-lined street. Soon, the leaves would hide the street, and this room would feel like a tree fort hanging in the branches of the massive elms lining the boulevard.

"Wow, this is beautiful!"

"Thanks! Yeah, Uncle Bart had this place fixed up nice. Rent is cheap, but we're family, and he's pretty old, so I have to spend some time looking after him. But he's a funny guy and has so many stories. I don't mind." Tully grabbed a bottle out of the wine cooler tucked into the side of the kitchen's peninsula island and popped the cork that had been wrestled into the bottle's opening. "Hope you don't mind, this was already open." Dev shook his head.

Tully poured two glasses and, with one in each hand, walked over to the large creamy coloured sectional hugging the outer wall.

As Dev glanced around the room, he took in the space. Tully's entire apartment reminded him of his own bedroom. There were book cases lining almost every wall space, packed full of old books, and modern ones. Dev glanced at a few of the titles, *The Witches' God, Spiral Dance,* and *Psychic Self Defense.* All works Dev had familiarity with. There were some leather-bound tomes that appeared to be from centuries gone by, most of them with script Dev couldn't read. At least one of the books was in French. Pointing with one finger, Dev caressed the spine of a particularly ancient-looking tome. The embossed and etched spine defined a sense of elegance or importance, and if to emphasize that, the supple leather gave way to his touch. This book had to be expensive.

"I'll let you read anything you want, but come sit with me for a while first."

Dev glanced over his shoulder. Tully had pulled himself up into the corner of the sofa and held a glass in his hands, taking a sip. The other glass waited for Dev, perched on a coaster on top of an old weather-beaten wooden coffee table. The slab of wood, scarred and dented, had seen at least a hundred years of use.

Tully patted the cushion right next to him.

"Come, I don't bite. Sit. Chat. Tell me why you didn't wait to call me like I told you to."

Dev rolled his eyes. "I probably seem desperate." He sighed.

"Ha. Not at all." Tully chuckled. "Okay, maybe a little, but from the ruckus and commotion coming through the phone, I figured you needed some respite. Come on, handsome, sit next to me. Tell me everything." Tully grinned as he raised the glass to his lips and took another sip.

Dev wandered over and sat on the cushion next to Tully, glanced at him and his glacier-blue eyes and half grinned. He reached for his own glass and had a sip.

"Oh. That's really good." The wine was chilled, but the alcohol burned his throat pleasantly. Sour cherries made his cheeks pucker, but a hint of spicy black pepper warmed him. Dev took another sip.

He set the glass down on a coaster and sank into the cushions of the couch, his head resting on the cushion. Tully waited, eyebrow arched as he studied Dev.

"Thanks."

"For what?"

"Rescuing me. Don't get the wrong idea, my family is everything, and despite the constant chaos, they mean well. It's just...they don't understand."

"As I said to you earlier, families are complicated. Mine is. Why should yours be any different?" Tully chuckled. "So is anyone in your family magical?"

Dev nearly spit his wine out, being mid sip when Tully asked him. "No, they think my interest in all of this is nuts. They have no idea."

"Well, if I'm being honest, magic is nuts. Wait. The more you learn and experience the better it gets, I promise."

Dev hung on every word from Tully, staring into his incredible eyes. He struggled to find the courage to tell a stranger about the love of his life—magic. After a couple of silence-filled minutes, he summoned up the nerve to respond. "I've been reading and practicing runes and tarot and...well everything for years. You know," Dev started and then stopped. He studied Tully's face, trying to determine if baring his soul, sharing his hopes would be handled with care. For so many years, Dev's interests had been branded as silly and a waste of time. The only person he ever opened up to was Cam, and even his best friend often made fun of him. Building up trust and courage to tell a stranger he had just met? A huge leap of faith would be required. Was Dev ready to let it all fly?

Tully picked up on his hesitation, put his hand on Dev's thigh, and inched closer. "It's okay. You can tell me as much or as little as you want. I'm not going anywhere, and I'm not going to think you're crazy."

"This is all so weird." Dev took a deep breath and exhaled. That simple gesture released so much stress. A weight he'd been carrying around for years. Dev glanced at Tully, an awkward grin plastered across his face. If he kept this awkward behaviour up, Tully would think him a basket case.

"Have you tried to release another burst yet?" Tully asked, his hand still on Dev's leg.

"God, no. I wouldn't even know where to start. I don't know what happened to begin with."

"Well, we can work on that." Tully winked. "It's tricky, this magic stuff, and you know it has a cost, right?"

"No, I..." Dev tilted his head. "What do you mean 'a cost'?"

"Nothing comes for free in this life, including magic." Tully grinned, leaned forward, and placed his glass down. "So, there's energy everywhere, right?" Tully's hands waved in front of him. "Every single living thing has pulsating energy. Animals are different from humans, plants are way down the evolutionary totem pole, so to speak, but they all still contain that zap. A buzz, a spark of life. That energy? As a witch, you'll come to sense it, be able to harness it, and eventually wield it." Tully waggled an eyebrow and put his hand back on Dev's thigh. "But you have to be careful. All life forms have an expendable amount. A finite resource, if you will. So you can't cast spells or use your abilities endlessly. You'll drain yourself and everything around you if you're not careful, and then...well...that's lights out for you, and anything else around you."

"Jesus. Really? That's...frightening. So, blow a fuse and you die?" Dev's eyes widened.

"Well, all energy is eventually replaced. So you cast a small spell, you're drained a little, but by morning your reserves are back up. You cast a bigger spell and you lose more energy. Energy takes time to replenish. But despite the recovery, the leaching takes its toll. A witch's lifespan isn't long. We tend to deplete ourselves. We're lucky if we live to seventy. Uncle Bart's an exception. He's eighty!"

"Uncle Bart is a witch too?"

"Yeah, runs in my family, on my mother's side. Hard. I didn't stand a chance."

"Huh, cool. I wish. So your entire life you've had abilities?"

"Nah, not until shortly after puberty, but everyone's different. I met one guy once, he didn't manifest his powers until his thirties. Which, you know, good for him. He'll outlive all of us. Not me. I started early, so, ya know, not a good prognosis on the age front."

That was a punch in the gut.

"Well shit, that's a shame." Dev didn't want Tully to think the concept of witches draining themselves to death might be somewhat frightening, so he resorted to making it into a flirty thing with a wicked smirk and a bit of the devil in his eyes as he stared into Tully's. He swore immersing himself in those blue eyes would never get tiring.

"Look at you, taking this all in stride." Tully winked. "If I didn't know any better, I'd say you were flirting, Dev."

Dev laughed. His foot tapped under the worn and weathered coffee table. "I might look calm on the outside, but..." Dev rolled his eyes. "But my stomach is in knots, even now."

"Why? Good lord, why?" Tully squeezed Dev's thigh and leaned forward. "I hope I'm not adding!"

"No! No, not at all. If anything..." Dev blushed and turned away as he continued, his foot beating out a furious rhythm. "No, you're the hunk who flew in and exposed a hidden world I had hoped and believed existed, but couldn't find—"

"Oh, you've not seen anything yet." Tully's lips formed a half-knowing smile. "Hunk, huh?" Tully moved his hand closer to Dev's crotch.

"Ooooh, yeah." Dev noted the movement. Part of him said, *No, no, not yet*, but a larger part of his brain screamed, *Farther, go higher!* Dev grabbed his glass and took a large swig, then put the stemware down. His movement was clunky. Heat flushed across his chest making him all flustered. Dev needed to get a hold of his emotions.

"Well, that's flattering, thank you, but the feeling is mutual. You're damn handsome. So beautifully dark in comparison to my pale-ass skin."

"Okay, now I know you're putting me on."

"No, I'm not. Geez, Dev, you kidding me?" Tully took a sip, swirled the wine in the glass then set it down. He glanced up at Dev with his crystal eyes. "You've got the darkest, thickest hair I've ever seen, and your eyes are mesmerizing." Tully leaned in closer. "May I?" Tully asked.

"Uh, sure," Dev granted permission, but to what, he wasn't sure.

Tully leaned in and rubbed his face against Dev's beard.

"You're beard drives me wild," Tully whispered while cheek to cheek with Dev, then returned to his own spot with a beguiling grin.

"Oh boy." Another wave of heat flushed over Dev's face. This couldn't be happening. It was a stomach churning thrill to be sitting here with Tully. But, wow, all of this? Within one night? How'd Dev get so lucky? His pants were so tight right now.

Magic. Tully. Wine. Sitting with Tully on the couch right now, Dev didn't care, but he wanted this night to go on forever. Dev cleared his throat and sat there, staring off, trying to focus and put things right in his head.

"Dev, everything okay?" Tully asked.

"Oh yeah, sorry, more than okay." And from out of nowhere, Dev found an ounce of courage, something he didn't have in situations like these, and he asked, "Can I kiss you?"

Dev's cheeks blazed with fire, astonished at what came out of his mouth.

*What are you doing?*

"I thought you'd never ask." Tully inched forward.

Dev leaned in and Tully met him half way. Dev closed his eyes as his lips met Tully's. The rough rasp of Tully's beard against his own, the heat, and warmth from Tully proved too much.

Dev let out a repressed moan. Months had passed since his last date, and that ended with a good night kiss after an awkward and silent dinner. Being close to another guy, especially one so good-looking had a hardening effect down under.

Tully took charge, grabbed Dev's face in his hands and pulled Dev in close.

Everything on the coffee table slid away from them as their kiss deepened.

Tully pulled away first, his cheeks flushed.

Dev's eyes were half-lidded.

"Wow, another burst."

"Sorry, what?" Dev glanced around, confused.

Tully chuckled. "Look at the coffee table." Tully nodded his chin toward the old rustic plank of wood. Everything sitting on its surface had been pushed outwards. The glasses hadn't tipped over, but the wine sloshed around their insides. "Just like our first encounter at the coffee shop. Can't you feel the energy when you release?"

"I don't know what you're talking about." Dev furrowed his brow, causing lines to crease his forehead.

"You did that, man. You're telekinetic." Tully squinted. "Let me try something?" Tully's eyes were bright and excited, and he still had a grin from ear to ear.

"Ah, sure?" Dev asked, insecure and embarrassed, yet his heart thumped in his chest, and his palms had gone hot and sweaty. He rubbed them on his jeans.

Tully gave Dev a wink. "Trust me. Okay?"

"Okay." Dev, overexcited, struggled to inhale.

Tully picked up the two wine glasses and walked them over to the kitchen counter. He went over to one of his bookcases and pulled out several books, placed the stack on the coffee table close to where Dev sat.

"Now, where were we?" Tully turned, facing Dev. He placed one knee down, next to Dev's side, and then spread his legs wide, stretching the fabric of his sweat pants tight as he placed his other knee across Dev so that he straddled Dev's lap, facing him.

"Oh boy," Dev whispered.

Tully grabbed Dev's face again. Dev's heart continued to beat, but the rhythm pumped so fast he swore the organ would burst out his chest. His cock pulsated and throbbed, pushing up against his denim pants to the point he was uncomfortable. The heat and warmth from Tully's thighs against his own and his hands on Dev's cheeks kept him focused on the electrical sensations coursing through his body.

Tully's lips pressed against his. They were warm, and Tully's beard scratched against his skin, which accelerated Dev into overdrive. He grabbed Tully's waist and pulled him in closer, pushing Tully's mouth open with his tongue wanting to taste more.

Dev slid his hands up underneath the tight grey T-shirt and ran his fingers over Tully's furry stomach. He didn't have any extra around his middle, but he also had enough meat to cover up a defined set of abs. Dev loved it all. Dev continued to push his hands up to Tully's chest. His pectoral muscles were well developed, and the fur continued. Unlike a lot of men these days, Tully hadn't trimmed anything, and Dev laced his fingers through the hair covering Tully.

*Oh my god, I could never get bored of this.*

Dev lost himself in his own exploration and hadn't noticed Tully's hand had slipped between his legs until his crotch got grabbed, giving Dev's concrete-hard erection a gentle squeeze.

The heat raging from Tully's hand pressed up against his groin set fire to Dev's inhibitions. He desperately wanted Tully to rip his pants open and free him, stroke him, touch him with no clothing as a barrier. In that moment, petting Tully's hairy chest, while Tully gave his dick another squeeze, Dev's mind exploded.

The books on the coffee table flew off in all directions.

Tully pulled away but kept his hand on top of Dev's groin. He smiled with a lopsided grin, his eyes sparkling with excitement and his lips moist from Dev's tongue.

"I thought so. So, you're an aurologist."

Dev sucked in air and then exhaled, shuddering. Making out with Tully made his head spin.

"I'm a what?" He continued to stroke Tully's fur.

"Your energy comes from your soul. For me, I get energy for magic from the earth, specifically metal. You however, you take the vigor from the very essence of your life. Your soul. Aurologists are triggered by emotions. Not exactly common, mister. Like one out of every hundred or so. Me, I'm a dime a dozen."

Dev pulled Tully in again and gave him a deep, wet kiss. Dev turned so his mouth was a hair's breadth away and whispered into Tully's ear, "I don't think you're common, not even remotely." Dev beamed as he sat against the fluffy cushions, panting, and gazed up at Tully.

Tully's bewitching grin never waned, his hand still rested on Dev's boner.

"So, wanna get naked?" Tully asked.

"Dear god, yes."

Dev wasn't going home tonight.

# Chapter Eight

"LET'S GO." TULLY cocked his head toward the hallway and got up from his position straddling Dev. He pushed himself off the couch and Dev, turned, and grabbed one of Dev's hands. Tully smirked, feeling Dev's clammy skin and his heartbeat through the meaty flesh of his palm. "Bedroom's down the hall."

Tully wanted to run there.

As they entered the room, Tully went to the nightstand and flicked on the lamp. The light, warm and inviting, cast long shadows in the room. Tully went around and lit a couple of candles and drew the curtains.

Standing on the far side of the room with the bed between them, the radiance of the candlelight bathed Dev in a glow of soft incandescent light. His shy grin from the other side of the bed smacked Tully's desire button hard. Tully grabbed the bottom of his T-shirt and pulled up revealing his muscled torso covered in hair. He pitched the shirt on the floor beside him.

"Oh my god, you're so good-looking." Dev's eyes were half-lidded, as if the undressing motion had hypnotized him.

"Your turn." Tully arched an eyebrow, studying Dev half covered in shadows. He mimicked Tully's action and pulled off his T-shirt and let the article of clothing drop in similar fashion.

"Damn." Tully stared for a few more seconds taking in Dev's trim, taut body, while finding the ties to his sweat pants. He pulled the strings out and undid the bow he'd tied to keep them snug on his hipbones. Now they were loose and fell a few inches, exposing his bush and the top of his hardening cock.

In one swift motion, Tully jumped onto his bed, the cream-coloured and puffy comforter absorbed his body's impact. After such a graceful landing, he reached forward and grabbed the top of Dev's jeans and pulled Dev on top of him.

"No hocus pocus. I don't want my room decimated."

"No guarantees," Dev replied while taking the opportunity to run his hand over Tully's chest. Tully got harder feeling Dev's skin against his own.

"You keep your abilities in check or I'm going to have to punish you. Got that, mister?" Tully copied Dev's initial reaction to them being so close and half-naked. Stroking Dev's chest, Tully kissed him in between words. He kissed his lips, then placed one on his cheek. Grabbing and turning Dev's head, Tully nibbled his ear, whispering, "Your. Pants. Need. To go."

"So do your sweats." Dev tweaked one of Tully's nipples.

"Hmmm, yes, do that again." Tully arched his back and hummed with closed eyes enjoying the sensation. "Take them off, Dev."

The heat from Dev's hands burned delightfully into Tully's waist as Dev placed a hand on each side of Tully's hips. The waistband of his sweats ran across his hips and down his thighs as Dev pulled.

Tully's cock sprung out as soon as the material which kept his manhood hostage had been removed. But once the treasure was exposed, Dev didn't stop.

"Damn. Damn, damn, damn." Dev licked his lips. Tully watched as Dev's hand began to explore.

Tully shivered as Dev's fingers caressed his skin from the knee up his inner thigh, over Tully's creamy skin and red hair. Dev's fingertips grazed ever so lightly across the bottom of Tully's balls, the sensation making him suck in a hiss of air. Dev repeated the ghostly touch over the length of Tully's rigid dick.

In response to the slight but intense sensation, Tully clenched, which tightened his nuts, bringing them closer to his body, while his dick bounced and bobbed.

"No fair. My turn." Tully may have been bigger than Dev in height and muscle mass, but he hid an additional talent. He excelled in agility too. In the space of a heartbeat, Tully grasped Dev, twisted and flipped him to get Dev naked as fast as possible.

Tully fumbled with Dev's belt until Dev helped him, but he shooed his hands away. "Mine. Let me do." Tully leaned over and licked the treasure trail leading from Dev's pants waistband to his belly button. Dev's skin turned to goosebumps as Tully saw Dev's stomach muscles twitch.

Tully took his hand and pushed his fingers under the top of Dev's pants, seeking his own reward. The pants were the right amount of loose to allow Tully to inch forward enough to grab the base of Dev's erection. Dev's shaft radiated heat, pulsating in Tully's hand. Dev gasped at Tully's touch, but his hands were busy fondling anything he got a hold of on Tully's body.

Growing more excited, Tully pulled his hand out and unzipped Dev's jeans. Using brute strength, he tugged both Dev's underwear and jeans off, making sure all appendages were free, he dropped the denim and boxers to the floor.

"That's more like it." Tully grabbed Dev's prick and stroked him a few times. "You're bigger than me. I've not met many who are. This will be fun." Precum oozed out, and Tully's eyes lit up. "I love a man who leaks."

As Tully kept stroking, he sidled up beside Dev, and leaned forward to kiss him. Their mouths opened as eager tongues ran across each other. Tully marveled at how sweet Dev tasted.

Tully kept the hand motion going, Dev grabbed Tully's boner and reciprocated as their kissing continued. Where ever Tully's skin connected with Dev, little bursts of energy zapped and hummed through his skin. Months had passed since Tully had had anyone in his bed, and even though this night moved far too fast with Dev, he wasn't regretting a single moment.

Lost in the joys of touching each other and exploring a new body, Tully didn't notice when the two of them began to levitate off the bed, lifting up by only a foot, steadily rising to two.

When Tully pulled away to breathe, he opened his eyes to see he and Dev were close to the top of his four poster bed. Dev's eyes remained closed, unaware, but from the look on his face his bliss had enraptured him.

"Dev!" Tully whispered.

"What?" Dev opened his eyes to stare at Tully, all smiles, until his current surroundings registered. "Woah." His eyes grew wide in disbelief.

"I told you no funny business. Bad witch." Tully gripped Dev's erection at the base and squeezed tight, but the action didn't have the intended punishment effect. Instead, Dev rolled his eyes up into his head and moaned. A rivulet of pre-cum ran down the side of his cock and over Tully's fingers. "Oh, I see." Tully gave up on the idea of reprimanding his deviant warlock and, instead, decided to pleasure him.

Tully moved toward Dev's erection and opened his mouth wide.

"Oh god!" Dev exclaimed as Tully swallowed the entire thing.

TULLY FELL ONTO the bed, sweaty, spent, and sticky as the down pillows fluffed, catching his fall. Glancing at the alarm clock next to his bed, Tully noted the time. They'd had several rounds of sex, four hours of skin, fur, muscles and cock. The alarm clock read three in the morning. Dev followed suit and fell on top of Tully.

"Oof, sorry." Dev huffed as limbs tangled together, but he grinned lopsidedly. Tully rearranged his arms until he had Dev snuggled up close and tight against him. He took the quiet of the moment to check out the state of his room. Books were scattered, as were both of their clothes, a lamp had turned over, and the sheets to the bed were tangled and strewn about. The room had been hit by a tornado. Dev, unable to control his abilities had released wave after wave of telekinetic energy. Each orgasm had been explosive, in more ways than one. At one point, Tully expressed concern over their rambunctious activity which might have woken his near-dead sleeping Uncle on the first floor.

"Wow," Tully whispered, his eyes widening as he licked his lips. He groped between Dev's legs and ended up with a palm-full of Dev's nuts. He gave a gentle tug.

"You keep that up we'll be going another round," Dev replied, nipping at Tully's nipple with his teeth.

"Oh, god, you have to stop." Tully pushed Dev's head away. "You know I love when you use your teeth to tease me. And as much fun as you are, I'm not sure my room would withstand another Hurricane Dev. Besides,

I'm starving. Want something to eat?" Tully asked, glancing down toward Dev.

"I could eat." Dev laughed as he peered at Tully. "You sucked all the vitality out of me."

"Twice." Tully chuckled.

"You vampire!" Dev laughed.

"Hey, I know I'm redhead pale, but I ain't that pale. Besides, my heart still beats." Tully grabbed Dev's hand and placed his palm over his chest. Tully lost grip though, and Dev's hand glided over Tully's hairy pecs, down his stomach until his hand gripped something else of Tully's that was still thick from the last erection, but started leaking like a kinked garden hose as Dev's hand continued to remain there. "You're bad and I love it, but come on, let's go. I have leftover pizza in the fridge. We can have more fun after."

"Man that sounds perfect." Dev bounced out of the bed and went for his clothes.

"What do you think you're doing?"

"Getting dressed?"

"Like hell you are. I don't want you to cover up. It's too gorgeous." Tully winked and Dev blushed.

"Okay, a little weird, but okay."

"Weird? How so?"

"Tully, I live with my family. It's not like I walk around naked. Ever. Even in my own bedroom. My sisters, or worse, my mother could walk in at any moment." Dev explained with a horrified look on his face. Tully mirrored the reaction.

"You need to move out."

"Yes, I most certainly do." Dev agreed as he let his boxers drop from his hand, granting Tully's wish. "But I don't have the resources to do get my own place, as much as I'd like to."

"Pizza, now." Tully grabbed Dev, kissed him on the lips, and slapped his ass. He grabbed Dev's hand as Tully's tummy growled. "See? Hungry."

They walked hand in hand, naked, down the hallway to the kitchen. Tully opened the fridge and pulled out a box of Funky Pickle Pizza.

"No way, I love their stuff!" Dev licked his lips in anticipation.

"It is good, isn't it?" Tully popped open the box and grabbed a slice, then turned the box around for Dev. "You want yours heated up?" he asked, being the gracious host, but stuffed his piece into his mouth.

"Nope, cold pizza is the best." Dev took a huge bite out of his own slice.

Tully nodded in agreement leaning against the counter, studying Dev in all his birthday-suit glory, eating pizza.

"Well, I have to tell you, when I first saw you, I'd hoped we would end up here, but I didn't think this would have happened so fast. We're still good, yeah? You're going to respect me in the morning?"

"Are you asking me to stay the night?"

"And all day tomorrow if you want." Tully winked again.

Dev stopped chewing and stared at Tully, matching his deep penetrating gaze. "I think I'd like to spend the entire day with you. Maybe you might demonstrate some witchy stuff?"

"I could, as long as you promise to not put a single stitch of clothing on." Tully waggled his eyebrows.

"I don't think I've ever spent this much time naked, never mind an entire day." Dev grabbed another piece of pizza. "Okay." But as soon as he spoke, Dev frowned and rolled his eyes. "Ugh, but I can't."

"Why not?" Tully furrowed his brows together. Putting his slice of cheesy goodness down on the counter, he walked around to Dev, slid up to him, and pressed his naked body against Dev, their groins grinding together. "Anything I can do to change your mind?"

"No! I mean, yes, but..." Dev dropped his pizza slice on the counter too and sighed. "I desperately want to. This has been amazing, and you saved me from certain insanity having to deal with my family—"

"But?" Tully interrupted.

"I have classes tomorrow and a huge assignment due for one of my professors I haven't even started yet." Dev's shoulders slumped forward.

"I'm surprised. You don't strike me as the procrastinating type." Tully cocked an eyebrow.

"That's just it, I'm not. I'm graduating in a couple of weeks and I have to get this assignment done or—" Dev stopped, his face a mask of desperation and disappointment. "Or I might not graduate. My honors standing is currently in jeopardy. I can't let that happen."

Tully leaned away from Dev, running the tips of his fingers from the nape of Dev's neck all the way to the base of his cock, where he playfully grabbed Dev and gave a gentle tug and squeeze. "Do you trust me?"

"Well, I mean, sure, but—" Tully stopped Dev's words by gripping him tighter. "Ugh, you're killing me."

"Trust me. Stay with me tonight. I want to take you somewhere tomorrow morning before your class."

Tully leaned forward and kissed Dev, his tongue licking Dev's lips. A request for Dev to allow him entrance, which Dev allowed. Dev's hands slid around Tully's waist and pulled him in tighter.

The pizza would have to wait.


BYRON SUPERVISED THE Coven of the Night Grove's upper ranks, longstanding knighted members, as they manhandled the wild fae into an iron-barred cage deep within the bowels of his cellar. The lair lay concealed from the upper stories through a series of heavy metal doors and a steep winding stairwell. This far beneath the basement of the old house, soundproofing was guaranteed. Addas stood by his side, but he didn't look happy. The faerie hissed and barred its teeth as Gustave

Nightshade used his elemental magic—air. The atmosphere of the confined dungeon thickened as Gus called forth the element. Air shimmered, condensed in front of him, swirling until it formed a mini whirlwind. As he pushed the vortex forward, turbulent winds caught the forest fae and spirited the creature further into the cell. Gus's long red hair billowed out behind him, an after effect of his magic, which made him appear regal and powerful. Truth be told, he liked to stir up trouble, had a tendency to be crude, and would bed anything that paid him attention.

The fae flapped its wings, desperate to break free of the magic, but the night had already been a long battle getting the creature wrangled and over to the coven house's secure holding cells. The beastie had put up quite a fight, which had worn him out. The wrestling and tussling against the knights had dwindled in strength and ferocity. As the magic enveloped the fae, Gus easily pushed him into the cage.

Once inside, Eduardo Blackwood dug into the voluminous cloak he often wore and pulled out several ball bearings. Byron respected Eduardo, who should have been the coven leader. No one matched his magical skills. He excelled in ancient languages and his dark Hispanic heritage made him damn-near irresistible. But Eddie lacked diplomacy, and he needed some political inclinations to lead the Night Grove and manage the tenuous relationships with the other covens, clans, and groups within Edmonton's supernatural community. Eddie tossed the tiny spheres into the air. As they began their quick descent to the floor, he lifted his hands, and twitched his fingers making symbols with each flexed move.

The bearings came to a jarring stop several inches from the floor, hovered, and then spun around one another like orbital moons of a faraway planet. With more gestures, he sent the metal globes into the holding cage, where they melted, turning into ribbons of liquid. They weaved and bobbed through the air, undulating like airborne snakes. As they neared the fae creature, the multitude of ribbons combined into four streamers, two of which dove fast and quick toward the fae's hands, the others at its feet.

Targeting each of the beast's appendages, like snakes chasing their own tails, they wrapped around an ankle or wrist, and with a vicious snap and bite, the streamers of metal became solid shackles.

The creature howled, throwing its head backward, curling its claws and stretching its wings out. The metal cuffs hung off its limbs, heavy and pulling the airborne fiend down to the ground. The shrieks emitted by the beast were unholy, and where its flesh touched the restraints, smoke rose in sinewy rivulets, undulating and infusing the chamber with a scent of burnt flesh.

Addas snapped, "I don't think any of this is necessary, Byron. Look at him. He's in pain and scared."

"I know Addas, and I don't like this either, but if we don't suppress the fae and bring Cameron back he'll lose whatever humanity he might have left. We had to do something similar with the last one. Remember?" Byron cupped Addas cheek. "I don't like this any more than you."

He turned around to face the fae, who knelt in the center of the cell, sobbing. "Now, my little forest creature"—Byron kneeled near the writhing and squirming fae, its wings stuttering and flapping involuntarily. Its glance zipped from one person to the next, tears streaming down its face, all while he pulled at the bindings—"if you want the shackles removed, you'll be good and remain calm and stay in your cell until you can glamour into human guise and we can have a reasonable chat. Look, my boys even brought you some clothes from your house. You be nice, you get to put them on." Byron turned and pointed toward the leg of a work table which had been pushed up against the far wall. On the dank concrete a pile of neatly folded and stacked clothes sat taunting Cam. They were his, including his new rainbow snakeskin boots. The furry beastie continued to paw at the manacles, leering at Byron in a way that would have made a serial killer wary.

"Fuck you," Cam hissed baring his pointy teeth.

"All right, you leave us no choice. Eduardo, if you would please?" Eduardo thrust his arm high into the air, whispering words in a long forgotten language.

"Byron, please, don't." Addas begged. "Think of what's going to happen when your new novitiate finds out what you're doing to his friend."

"Addas..." Eduardo's spell completed its purpose with rapid ferocity. This allowed Byron to focus his attention on the cell's new inhabitant. Addas turned and left. The fae's arms were thrust upward as the fetters on each hand sprouted and grew chains. Links birthed from links until an entire cable had grown, like a snaking vine in fast-forward motion. The chain wound itself through the top of the cage, and around the bars. More erupted from the metal cuffs on each ankle, and within a minute, the minion of the forest jerked spasmodically as the metal cables locked tight, constricting the fae within the iron cage. Cam pulled on his restraints, spread eagle, locked in iron bracelets and strung out to look like a fly caught in a spider's web.

"When you're cooperative, we'll let you free. I know the iron hurts, but you have to regain control of yourself, Cam." Byron stared eye to eye with the beast. "I wouldn't take too long. That iron will burn right through to the bone. You'll heal, but the burns will leave some nasty scars." Byron's face left no room for interpretation. He meant business. Remorse or empathy for the feral being did not exist. These fae were wild, and if left untamed, Cam would become a danger to humanity. Byron had suppressed others, he'd control this one too. Hopefully he'd find a way to reverse the summoning board's work and revert him back to human or, at the very least, turn the high ranking, horned and winged, cannibalistic forest fae into something passing as human.

Cam hissed again, lunging forward, trying to bite Byron.

"Eduardo, bring me the syringe." He glanced over his shoulder. Eduardo turned and walked toward a cabinet, opened it, exposing several medieval looking weapons and torture devices. Grabbing a large hypodermic, one with an oversized barrel, and a wicked looking needle, he handed the device to Byron.

"I don't want to have to do this to you, Cam. If you calm down and glamour into a human, the restraints wouldn't be necessary and I wouldn't have to use this."

Cam, the forest fae, snarled, its eyes glinting red while he focused on Byron. "I will kill you," he hissed with a forked and bumpy pointed tongue.

"I see. Well then, for now, you can stay shackled like this. And I'm afraid I'm going to have to prove to you who's in charge."

Byron took the torture device, walked around the other side of the creature and with no hint of mercy, plunged the tip of the hypodermic in between the fae's wings.

Cam flapped his wings in an effort to beat away Byron, but Byron closed his eyes, and let the membranous and hairy wings slap him, mussing his hair and sending staccato jolts of pain through his face. He pushed the needle deeper, aiming to get into the spinal column.

Cam shrieked again, but this time in pain, and writhed, struggling to get away from the syringe. The smell of burnt flesh permeated anew as Cam tugged and yanked on his restraints. He begged Byron to stop.

"Please."

Byron pulled the plunger on the needle extracting a most vibrant green and effervescent liquid. Muscles along each side of the creature's spine twitched and flexed, trying in desperation to move away from the violating spear. Byron didn't stop until the syringe's chamber had filled with fae juice.

He pulled the needle out and lifted it up to his face as he tapped the container. Bubbles floated to the top.

"Now this here boys, this is gonna give us the best boost we've had since the last fae." Byron walked around to face Cam. He showed the bubbling emerald juice to his captive. "Cam, this is your essence. I drain enough of it, and you cease to exist. I extract just the right amount, and you become more human than fae. I can do the procedure so there's next to no pain, or I can do this so you squirm the entire time. Your choice. Cooperate, or suffer." He turned to others. "In the meantime, this will suit us well." Cam let out a whimper. Byron half turned toward him. "Behave and you won't ever have to go through this again."

Cam fell forward, fainting from exhaustion and agony.

# Chapter Nine

TULLY WOKE UP, the sun shining in through the edges of the blackout blind. He had one leg wrapped around Dev's, and his arm held Dev's torso tight against his own.

*I want to wake up every morning like this.*

Meeting Dev and ending up here had happened so fast. Much too fast. But Dev's big brown eyes, so full of wonder and excitement, were hard to resist. His lithe body and thick beard got Tully riled. And he may not be experienced with men, but he sure figured out what to do between the sheets. Last night amazed Tully. He had come more times than he thought possible, more than he ever remembered. Dev excited him. Something magical about Dev's wonder, the sparkle of seeing everything for the first time, made Tully feel like a new witch himself. And Dev was brainy. The boy had smarts. The guy had it all, and Tully hoped Dev liked him too.

But wow, all those feelings in one night.

*Brakes, man. Put the brakes on. Slow it down.*

He barely knew anything about him. But Tully hoped to change that.

Enough day dreaming. He'd promised to take Dev somewhere special before his classes, and Tully bet after he revealed his surprise, Dev would want to spend the rest of the day with him. Maybe lounging here, in bed. Naked.

Tully leaned over and placed a kiss on Dev's neck.

"Hmm, morning. I thought I felt you stirring." Dev stretched his arms out and yawned, then arched his back, and ground his butt into Tully's morning wood.

"You're terrible. And I love it." Tully stroked Dev's thick matt of chest fur, and nibbled on his ear.

Dev grabbed Tully's hand and pushed him toward his groin.

"Well, damn, it is a good morning." Tully grasped Dev's hardening cock and stroked him a couple of times. "And as much as I would *love* to continue this, it's almost nine o'clock, and if I'm going to take you where I promised, we need to get going."

"It's what time?" Dev bounced out of bed as he searched the room for a clock.

Tully chortled and pointed to the watch on his wrist.

"Shit, I'm going to be late!"

"No, you won't. I'll drive you."

"No, dude, I have like twenty minutes."

"Dev," Tully sat up in bed, grasped Dev's hand, and laced his fingers through his overnight guest's. "Seriously, trust me, this is all going to be okay." Tully winked at him, got up out of bed, pulled the blind, and released it. The fabric flapped its way up as it rolled away revealing a sunny spring day through the window. Tully reached for his phone, and typed out a text.

> *Hey, need 2 come see u. I have Dev with me. I think u should meet. Coven maybe?*

Dev was frantic. Running around the room, picking up his clothes and hurriedly wrenching them on, the dance lacked a certain gracefulness, but the absurd antics made Tully smile.

Three dots appeared at the bottom of Tully's phone.

> *You SLEPT with him already?*

Tully laughed, then replied.

> *Maybe. Wouldn't tell you. But he's worried about his assignment. You know, the one that never existed? ;) Should meet before he loses his mind.*

Tully glanced up to see Dev, disheveled, but dressed, a look of absolute panic on his face. Tully just shook his head. "You're gorgeous when you're flustered."

"You're stunning when you're naked, and I would love to do nothing more than have my way with you right now, but," Dev tapped his wrist, "I. Need. To. Go."

"Okay."

Tully's phone chimed.

> *Okay. We have class in 15. You can make it?*

Tully pulled on his pants, skipping underwear, then hoisted a T-shirt over his head. He didn't expect to be in these clothes for long, and hopefully he would be out of them and with Dev by the afternoon.

Tully typed back a response.

*Yup. On our way. Be there in 10.*

"Okay, let's go. I'll drive you to class." Tully threw an arm around Dev's shoulder and the two walked out of the bedroom with Dev hurrying Tully along the way.

"HEY, WAIT A minute," Dev furrowed his brows when he realized he hadn't told Tully where he needed to go on campus, yet Tully had pulled up to the parking lot nearest the Sociology building.

"I'm a witch. I know things." Tully chuckled, parked the car, then grabbed Dev's hand, pulled his fingers up to his mouth, and kissed them. "Trust me. Okay? I know, it's all weird n' shit. All shall be revealed." Tully winked.

"You're freaking me out."

"You'll be okay. I promise." Tully opened his car door, exited the vehicle, then closed it. He waited for Dev to do the same. Tully pressed a button on the car's fob to lock the vehicle.

"Nice car, by the way." Dev ran his hands along the silver Audi TT.

"Gift from Uncle Bart." Tully rolled his eyes. "It's way too nice. But he wouldn't take 'no' for an answer."

"Damn. Okay, my class is up here. Maybe you can take me to your surprise after class? Will you wait?" Dev pointed toward an entrance.

"Mmhmm." Tully let Dev take the lead.

After ascending a couple of floors and rushing toward a class with a glass door, about half way down a lengthy hallway, Tully pulled his cell out and typed a short message.

*We're here.*

Less than a second later, Tully got back a "thumbs up" emoji. The high priest had been watching his phone.

As they arrived at the classroom door, Professor Byron Radcliff, donning a sports coat with elbow patches, his typical suspenders and tight, but well-fitting slacks opened the classroom door and beamed at Dev who, being late for class, was running on a crash course toward his professor.

Tully's chest expanded with a swell of pride as he witnessed Byron open his arms accepting a new witch. He couldn't help but smile from ear to ear as Byron Radcliff, professor of Sociology, and high priest of the Coven of the Night Grove grabbed Dev's shoulders and pulled him in for the biggest bear hug of Dev's life.

DEV DAMN NEAR ran head first into Prof. Radcliff and had no time to react as the bear of a man pulled him into a massive hug.

"Oof." Byron squeezed hard. As much as being wrapped up in his professors arms reminded Dev of many a fantasy, breathing became a serious issue. Dev squirmed to get space.

"I'm so happy!" Byron exclaimed, hanging on tight.

Dev's head swam, in part from lack of oxygen.

"What? I don't understand…" Dev choked out.

Tully, standing behind him, dropped the biggest bombshell of Dev's twenty-three years.

"Dev, I'd like to introduce you to Byron Radcliff, also known as the 'Professor,' and high priest of my coven."

"What?" Dev wriggled out of Prof. Radcliff's strangulating bear hug. He stood in front of the two men, slack jawed and wide-eyed. Had he heard everything correctly? Did he …wait…did that mean—

"You mean you're a witch?" Dev spoke a little too loudly.

"Yup." Byron bobbed his head enthusiastically, motioning for Dev to be quieter, but grinned all the same, teeth gleaming and eyes sparkling, "I've been waiting four years for you to manifest, Dev."

Dev shook his head. He hadn't heard any of this right. "Mani what?"

Tully interceded, "Your telekinetic burst of energy? Last night in the coffee shop and then multiple times last night?"

"Jesus, Tully. And I know what manifest means... I've just never had occasion to use the word in reference to myself." Heat flushed through Dev's neck and cheeks radioactively pulsating as he glanced between Tully and Byron.

"It's okay, Dev. I already know about last night." Professor Radcliff patted Dev's shoulders. "Tully, maybe we should take the guy out for a coffee after class? Can you stick around?"

"What do you mean you already know?" Dev cast a suspicious glance at Tully while heat from embarrassment made him instantly sweaty.

"I'm a witch; I know things." Professor Radcliff, still smiling, winked at Dev.

"For fuck's sake." Dev's glare bounced between Tully and Byron. "Is that a coven saying?"

"I used the same expression out in the parking lot." Tully chuckled, pointing over his shoulder toward the parked car.

Byron and Tully stared at each other, then laughed.

"Yeah, sort of." Byron rolled his eyes. "Look, class is about to start. Dev, go take your seat. After, the three of us will go out and you can ask all the questions you want. Fair?"

Tully waggled his eyebrows.

*How the hell am I going to concentrate for an entire hour* in class?

Of course coffee with his favorite professor and a gorgeous redhead was definitely all right. And talking about the Shadow Realm, and Dev's newfound abilities was the conversation of a lifetime! The relief and excitement had Dev on pins and needles, and terrified. What did all this mean? With one wish he'd become a witch. And his favorite Prof had supernatural abilities too? All this from one wish?

The summoning board had worked.

Damn.

The whole damn thing worked.

After all those years of searching, he had arrived.

He needed to call Cam.


CAM LAY FLAT against the cool concrete, his cheek pressed against the damp cement, contained within an iron-barred cell. The shackles around his wrist hurt like hell, but as much as he wanted to be free, he couldn't control his rage whenever one of the men came to check on him. He'd bit, hissed, and spit as they'd come close, inspecting him, and each time, he got the needle.

His back ached and spasmed, from the violent stabbing of the oversized syringe.

So instead of fighting, because he didn't have anything else in him, he lay still against the coldness of his cell floor, in the dark, both of which were oddly soothing.

Cam wondered if Dev had gotten his wishes. He sure as hell had got one of his. He moved his head to another spot on the floor cooling the other side of his face. His horns dragged against the concrete.

"I'll never be flippant ever again." Cam, realizing what he'd mumbled, instantly took the careless statement back. Of course he would. Sarcasm, flippancy, and wit, that's what he did. He sighed.

Inhaling the dank air of the chamber, the rank odors of musty old books, dust, mold, and...

Wet dog fur.

"What the fuck?" Cam raised his head and tried to determine where the odor originated. His tail twitched. Twisting and turning meant the iron manacles bit into his flesh. "Ow, dammit." His wings flapped a couple of times in irritation. Smoke curled up from the charring flesh.

The movement caused a sharp pain as raw flesh burned when his fae skin touched the metal. The sensation quieted him. As long as he didn't move much, the shackles hung loose and the iron didn't burn as badly. Cam shifted his weight and tried to position himself so the fetters weren't pulling. At least when lying on his side they didn't sizzle his flesh.

Off in the corner of the room, he spied two glowing eyes.

A growl rumbled across the floor.

"Oh shit." Fear crept up Cam's spine, raising every hair on his back. Panic clawed in the depths of his gut. He shimmied away from where he lay, crawling backward as far as possible, which of course shifted the iron rings, succeeding in only more burning.

*Hissssss.*

Tendrils of smoke rose from his wounded wrists and ankles.

Surrounded by bars meant to contain him ensured he wouldn't have to worry about the monster on the other side of the room. Cam didn't want to know what may lie in the darkness. Look at what had happened to him. What other creature was out there? Would the thing want to eat him?

"Don't pull, quit being a shithead, and they won't keep you in the iron cuffs." A deep voice growled out, gravelly and stern. Advice had been given from the glowing eyes. They blinked, momentarily disappearing and then rematerializing in a different spot.

"Who are you? What are you?"

"My name is Ev. Werewolf. If you play nice, you might have a chance of getting out of here." The voice should have been terrifying. The admission of being a shapeshifter didn't sit well, but oddly, the lilt in the testosterone laden tones piqued Cam's interest. But as much as Cam tried to focus on the dark, attempting to discern what lay in wait, it remained hidden. In the depths of the dungeon, against the cool concrete and dank air, shifting shadows and glowing eyes instilled panic within Cam.

"Werewolf? Yeah, right." Werewolves. Ha!

Then again, maybe not so much a laughing matter, as Cam registered the weight of his newly acquired horns and noted his tail, which flipped back and forth on the concrete floor like a cat's.

Maybe werewolves weren't so exceptional or idiotic. The gnawing sense of panic returned as Cam gazed out into the darkness and realized the werewolf's glowing eyes had never disappeared. They floated in the shadows watching him.

"This scene brought to you by a B-rated horror flick," Cam mumbled.

Except this wasn't a movie.

"That's why you're still in chains, idiot. Lose the attitude, play nice, and Byron might let you out of here. Sounds like you have an ace up your sleeve. None of the others had quite a distinctive advantage. Don't screw it up."

"Yeah, and what possible advantage could I have?"

"Not sure how this all fits together, but one of your friends is a new novitiate witch in their coven. They won't hurt you too badly if you've got that kind of connection. But what a fae is doing being friends with a witch is beyond my reasoning. How the hell did that happen?"

Cam struggled against his restraints, listening to the nearby monster. The metal burned again.

"Dammit," Cam snarled, repositioning himself again to lessen the scorching. "Let's just say all of this is rather new. So, tell me, smartass, if you're so knowledgeable, and know how they'll treat me, why are you still in here? Why don't you play nice so they'll let you out?"

"They'll never let me out. I'm a Werewolf. Sworn enemy of witches. All of my kind are. Besides if they did set me free, I'd hunt them all down and kill them, one by one. And I'd make every last one of them suffer." The absoluteness of the statement made Cam shiver.

"Well then, I guess you're pretty much stuck. As am I, and here we are."

"Yes, here we are. Now shut up and do as I tell you. Play nice; they're coming."

"Why are you telling me any of this?"

"Because if you get out, you'll be free of their clutches. Once you're free, you'll go to your own kind. You'll go be fae. You won't be able to resist the call of the forest. And once you reunite with your own kind, they'll tell you what these fucking witches do. Why we all hate them. Fae hate witches. Werewolves hate witches. You'll seek to destroy them as much as my kind does."

"Oh shit." Cam became quiet, thinking of Dev. Was the growly monster across the room right? Had Dev abandoned him and become part of the rank and file who assaulted him? Rage bubbled in the pit of his guts. Cam squinted as he chased a train of thoughts.

"That fucking board really did work. Goddammit Dev, what the hell did you get us into?"

# Chapter Ten

DEV FOUND HIMSELF sitting in the Starbucks where he and Tully had met and his manifestation had first occurred. His coffee, loaded with cream and sugar sat untouched as he listened to Professor Radcliff.

"So, every semester I have a few spells I use to determine if any of my students have latent abilities. About one in a hundred do, but even then only a few will ever manifest. When you walked in to my class four years ago, I knew right away. The energy hummed off you.

"But I did the sigil spell anyways and the cast confirmed what I already suspected," Byron explained.

"Sigil? Like a mark? On what?" Dev asked, enthralled, horrified, but wanting to soak everything up.

"On one of your paper assignments. Why do you think I had you all hand in a handwritten assignment? Nobody does that anymore. Everyone emails their documents."

"But why didn't you tell me? Do you have any idea how many years I've longed for this? How lost I've been, like I didn't belong anywhere?" Disappointment riddled Dev. But at the same time, knowing his beliefs in the Shadow Realm were real and being recognized and counted as one of its members contradicted the letdown. The combination of emotions made for conflicting physical sensations. He reeled from the overwhelming push and pull. He'd finally found where he belonged, but damn it, they had seen him and knew about him all this time, and...why?

"We have rules, Dev. Until you are able to tap into your abilities, we can't touch you. Think of the Shadow Realm as an exclusive club. We can't just let anyone in. There's safety in smaller numbers. Think what humans would do if they found out." Professor Radcliff continued his speech.

"I... you have no idea. For so long, I hoped, I prayed, I practiced—" Dev's foot tapped and he wrung his hands.

Tully reached across the table and grabbed Dev's hands. "Dev, I feel really bad for deceiving you. You know why I followed you, you get it, right? Byron's orders?"

"Yeah, I do, but...damn man." Dev's eyes shot downward, focusing on his feet under the table.

In the blink of an eye, another pair of hands covered his own.

Professor Radcliffe held both him and Tully. "Dev, look at me." Byron's voice held the self-assuredness and authority of a father figure. Dev glanced up at Professor Radcliff's beautiful eyes, but his insecurities didn't allow him to keep his focus there. He looked away again.

"Dev, come on." Professor Radcliffe squeezed his hands. "You've manifested now, and Tully thinks you're an aurologist. That's special. Rare, in fact. But I want to be the first one to welcome you to the Shadow Realm and also to let you know if you want tutelage, I am here to help you. Once you're comfortable, we can talk about binding you, a ceremony making you an official 'citizen' of the Realm. But please, call me Byron outside of class," Byron leaned back into his chair, "And I hope you can accept my apologies for the cloak and dagger behaviour from Tully and myself. I want to be there for you as you walk the first few steps on your new journey!"

Tully cleared his throat as he gave Byron a "and what about me?" look. The gesture didn't go unnoticed by Dev, which made him all giddy on the inside.

*I think Tully likes me.*

Byron let loose a quick snort. "Yes, and I'm sure Tully feels the same way too. I'm kind of glad you two have a connection. It's important to have someone you feel you can trust and talk to for the first few months as you get settled."

"I still have a gazillion questions." Dev scrounged deep inside himself, finding a modicum of courage. "Like, what the hell an aurologist is, what are the other kinds of magic, and what is this binding thingy you mentioned?"

"Oh my goodness, well, that's a lot. Okay, ah, let's see. There's a host of different specialties. Each talent is associated with an element the witch is attuned to," Byron explained. "Like Tully is earth, and is a metallurgist."

"What are you?" Dev asked.

"I'm fire. A pyrokineticist." Dev screwed up his whole face as Byron declared his ability. Byron laughed, deep and throaty, "You'll get used to all the terms. Basically I can summon and control the element of fire."

"Wow."

Byron flipped his wrist over to glance at his watch. "Gah, I'm sorry boys, but I have to run. I have another class. Dev, I don't want to pressure you into anything. I'm sure all of this is happening too fast, but would you like to meet the coven? We're having a gathering tonight. Come, meet the others, and check out our family. You'll love the guys, I know it. Now that you're part of our world, there's no point in you wondering what the Shadow Realm is all about or feeling alone. We've got you."

"Well, I'll just check my calendar…" Which was ridiculous. He had nowhere else to go. But he didn't want to seem too eager or green. Sitting here talking to his favorite professor, a man he'd often lusted over but also respected for years, about witchcraft and the Realm was undoubtedly the most bizarre of fantasies. However, the lascivious daydreams had recently vanished in a puff of smoke after meeting Tully. At least Tully and Dev were closer in age. And damn, can't forget Tully's muscles or all the red fur. Despite the deception from Professor Radcliff, the years of waiting to find the Shadow Realm and knowing Tully had tailed him, Dev discovered he didn't care. He shot a glance at Tully and grinned.

"Yes, Tully will be there too. Look, I do have to go, but take the afternoon, think about it, hang with Tully, and if you decide you want to come," Byron turned and looked at Tully, "Tully will bring you, right?"

"I think you should come." Tully winked and mirrored Dev's happiness.

"Tully, no pressure. Choices, right?"

"Yes, I'm sorry. Only if you want, Dev."

"I do. I want to learn and know everything. I really do..." Dev started but trailed off, revealing at least some hesitation.

"But this is a big decision. Dev, take your time. Think about it. Okay? I'm always here to talk to, and now that we know you are a witch novitiate, you can come see me anytime. Okay? Even after university graduation. My door is always open. If you don't feel comfortable with us, we'll connect you with others."

"Oh shit! Graduation. Damn it," Dev covered his face with his hands, shaking his head, "I almost forgot. I owe you an assignment!" Dev's face flushed as he remembered. He lowered his palms expecting a scolding from Professor Radcliffe.

"Ha! Yes, about that. Confession time on my part. There's no assignment, Dev." Byron arched an eyebrow and gave him a wink. "This past week, you were buzzing. The energy coming off you rippled in waves, much stronger than your normal vibrant self, but almost tangible. I sensed you hadn't released. Looking at you now, I can tell you've let some steam out.

"We're not allowed to tamper with your progression, or lack thereof, at the beginning. You have to discover that on your own. But I may have caused some additional stress in your life. Sometimes a gentle push will send someone over the edge. And my plan appears to have worked." Byron, still half smiling, stared at Dev. "Sorry if I made life unbearable, but I'm not sorry I did it. You're here now."

"Wait, no assignment? How'd you manage...I sat there and watched you hand out papers. Everyone else in the class getting their papers..." Dev stared agape. "Seriously? How?"

"I'm a witch. I know things." Byron winked at Tully and the two chuckled. The professor turned his focus to Dev. "A little glamour spell. Made the situation look to you, as if I handed out assignments, when in fact I did no such thing."

"That's why I couldn't find anything about it! You know, I damn near went insane." Dev's face screwed itself up again.

"I am sorry, but now I have you." Byron threw his sports coat on as he stood up. "Tully, you'll look after him this afternoon?"

"You bet." Tully wrapped his arm around Dev's shoulders.

"Good. I hope to see you tonight, Dev." Byron, smiling, leaned over and patted Dev's hands. "I'm glad you're one of us." Byron turned and walked out of the coffee shop, the bell chiming as he left.

Dev sat there. Life had changed so drastically in such a short period of time.

He was a witch.

His favorite professor had been watching him for four years and had known he had latent abilities all along.

Tully had tailed him, and thankfully had been there for his first manifestation, but by Tully's own confession had been knee deep in all the devious maneuvers. The entire plan had been so secretive, but at the same time, Dev understood why.

Humans must forever be ignorant. This had to be kept under wraps. They had been testing Dev to see if he belonged to them. This planned chaos, so devious, had been a set up. Thrusting Dev into a pit of self-destruction so he'd come into his own as a witch had been the goal. The last couple of days were "cloak and dagger" as Byron had said, but completely necessary.

He got it.

Dev was in.

And he had Tully.

Why didn't he feel better about where he'd landed?

DEV SAT IN Tully's car, still stunned and staring off beyond the dashboard. The quiet hum of the luxury car filled the background with white noise, adding to the Zen of the moment, allowing him to zone out.

"So, um...everything okay in there?" Tully slipped his hand into Dev's lap and gave his thigh a squeeze.

"Yeah." Dev shook his head, trying to focus. "I'm sorry, Tully, I am. You've been so good to me," Dev grinned, casting a sideways glance at his redheaded companion, "in multiple ways."

"Mostly it's been my pleasure, and yours." Tully chuckled. "So, what do you want to do this afternoon? Hang? Go back to my place? Or do you need some quiet time? I can take you to your parent's place."

"Oh god, no!" Dev responded lightning fast as his eyebrows damn near rose right off his forehead. "Ah shit, how the hell am I going to explain this to them. Hey Mom, look at this...I can make things move."

"Well, no you can't until we teach you how to access your abilities." Tully looked over at him and winked.

"You don't get it. They are not going to understand this. Any of it."

"Right, but they can't know though. They aren't magical. You told me so yourself. And if they're not part of the community, they don't get to know."

"Well how the hell am I going to explain—" Dev rubbed his face out of frustration.

"I think you've come to the conclusion that moving out and living on your own might be your best option. Living your magical life will only be possible if you're separated from them," Tully offered.

"Yeah, I suppose. Shit. I've never kept anything from them. Ever. Cam and I have talked about moving out. But I don't have the funds nor do I make enough to afford my own place. Cam and I had planned to split all the costs. And my family will not be good with me moving out. Good Indian boys don't do that."

Tully sat there, quiet for a moment, looking into Dev's eyes.

"I have an idea." Tully nodded as he continued to ponder. Dev raised an eyebrow wondering what plot Tully had hatched. From the look on Tully's face, the idea had taken root and blossomed.

"Mmhmm, what's that?"

"The apartment above me. It's cheap, Dev, like two hundred a month. It's more of a studio than anything else. And I'm pretty sure Uncle Bart would be willing to drop the price down if I suggested you and I were...you know...close. And you're a novitiate who needs to be close to me for...study reasons." Tully arched an eyebrow and smirked.

"What? No, I couldn't ask you to do that. But damn, you can't get anything this close to the university for under seven hundred a month. Isn't this a little too, ah, not sure how to say this." Dev squirmed in his seat. "I mean, we met yesterday. Don't get me wrong, last night was *amazing*, but..." Dev trailed off, not stating the obvious, but he wanted Tully to understand. Despite Dev's hesitation about the studio apartment, he hoped Tully would extend a second overnight invitation.

"Yeah, this is all too fast. Believe me, I've thought the same thing. But this also feels good, Dev. You feel good." Tully squeezed Dev's thigh again. "If you take the apartment, I promise I'll be a complete gentleman. You can come downstairs whenever you want and we can practice magic together, and you can borrow any of my books. And if we want to eat pizza naked together, I wouldn't be opposed to doing so." Tully waggled his eyebrows.

"Oh my god, you're incorrigible."

Tully chuckled, but Dev reeled, trying to figure out how to move forward.

"Can I tell you something? It's kind of personal, if that's okay." Tully shifted in his seat and stared at Dev as the car idled. Dev studied Tully's face, something Dev would happily do for hours. And as glorious as the last twenty-four hours had been, he waited for the other shoe to drop. Life had a way of making sure the pleasure bubble burst. "I like you, Dev. You're pretty cool, and damn your eyes, man. Hot. But I'd want to get to know you better. Having you close means we can take the time to figure each other out, and in return, you get a crash course in the Shadow Realm. Byron will test you. There are exams."

"What? Seriously?"

"Yup. So you're a novitiate, and I'm a brother. I've passed my first set of exams and moved up the ranks. Next is rector, then master, and after many years and a lot of exams and experience, you get to be a knight. Only the best of the knights will become Byron's rank, a high priest. But don't sweat it. Don't even worry about exams, not yet. I'll get you through it if you want.

"Look, I know sleeping together was crazy fast. I'm not an idiot. Horny sure, but I understand. But you know what us gay guys are like. We sleep with people, and become best friends later. I mean, lots of my friendships have developed from a one night stand." Tully stopped then grimaced. "Wow, that didn't make me sound very good, did it? Now I'm fucking rambling. Look what you do to me! It's not like I've slept with tons of people either. Dammit, I'm digging myself into a hole here.

"What I'm trying to say is this. I don't know where any of this will go between you and me, but I think I'd like to find out. I'd be pretty excited to have you so close. I like being around you."

Dev considered Tully's words. He was so handsome and smart. Despite the speed of the last two days, Dev had the same feelings. He put his hand on top of Tully's. He'd wanted to get to know Tully too, but the world spun too fast at the moment. Sure, moving into the studio would mean he'd have his own space, no yelling sisters and no forced family dinners. The apartment would be perfect. Or moving there would be disastrous. He wished Cam was here. Lost in his own winding trail of internal arguments and without thinking too hard about his actions, Dev pulled his phone out from his pocket and checked it.

Nothing. No notifications, no emails or calls. Just nothing.

That's weird. Cam hadn't texted him again, and he never went more than a day without texting *something*.

Dev glanced up to see Tully staring at him. Dev blushed, embarrassed and turned, staring out the passenger window.

"Sorry, I don't mean to be rude. I was looking to see if my friend Cam had messaged me." Dev glanced at Tully and scrunched up his face in apology. "I talk to him about everything, and I kinda wish he was here right now. But we had a fight, and I haven't seen or heard from him in a bit. If you want to get to know me, you'll have to get to know Cam too. We're like brothers, ya know? Always together. I hope Cam likes you as much as I think I do." Dev squinted at Tully, waiting for a response.

"No worries. It's all good." Tully dismissed Dev's worry with a wave of his hand. He smiled, continuing to stare at Dev.

"Tell you what, how about you show me this place?" Dev suggested.

Tully's grin grew massive and his eyes widened in excitement. Dev loved Tully's constant positive attitude, especially when he'd made him beam like this. Dev's chest puffed out, knowing someone else got excited being around him. Obviously Tully wanted him to move into the studio. Tully's reaction made Dev happy. He didn't always get support or happiness from his family, or even from Cam.

"I think that's a great idea!" Tully put the car in reverse and made his way out of the parking lot. At the stop sign, Tully flicked on the turn signal and made a left. "You're gonna love it!"

"I'm going to send a quick message to Cam? Okay?"

"For sure, go for it!"

Dev typed out a text to Cam.

*Dude, you there? Are you mad? Sorry I haven't responded.*

*It worked!*

*Call me.*

Dev had a burst of butterflies in his stomach. Maybe this would all work out.

BYRON MADE HIS way out of the coffee shop and to his car.

*Finally!*

One step forward to putting the coven back together again. Dev would be perfect. But there were other matters to attend to.

A short drive to his university office, Byron slung his coat over the arm of a chair, then unpacked his laptop and booted the computer up. He had lied to the boys. He didn't have another class.

The volumes he had requested from another coven had arrived.

Selecting a key from his key ring, he unlocked a cabinet and pulled out a couple of old books, some lose papers, and a scroll.

Setting them on his desk, he walked over and flipped a whiteboard to the reverse side. With a glance around the room to ensure his solitude, Byron ran his hand over the surface repeating a single word, "Perth".

A wave of flame danced across the board. Perth, the rune of secret things, of concealment, unwound the concealment spell hastened and fueled from Byron's fire. Writing on the whiteboard appeared. A giant checkerboard with various circles inscribed within each square. Each circle though had different symbols. Every possible spot on the board held hex marks and witch script.

Byron walked over to his desk, sat down at the laptop and clicked his way through several documents. After reading a bit, he flipped open one of the old tomes. He shuffled through a few pages until he found the reference he needed.

> *Lycanthropy: ly·can·thro·py—/lī ˈkanTHrəpē/*
>
> *Noun: the spiritual transmogrification of an individual into a lupine form*
>
> *History: Commonly held beliefs state the earliest mention of these beasts is from the Epic of Gilgamesh, a Sumerian poem.*

Byron wasn't interested in the historical beginnings of documented werewolfism. The books had arrived from a French coven he'd been in touch with through internet connections. He'd paid a hefty price to have these relics shipped to him. The high priest had assured him the answer to unravelling a werewolf infection lay within these books, and he had, in fact, seen the ritual performed.

The solution to Addas's problem lay within this tome.

Byron's finger scanned the text as he skimmed over the words, thankfully having been translated into English.

*Infection: The saliva of a lycanthropic host contains the highest viral load possible for subsequent infections. Contrary to popular theories and recitations, the contagion incubates for several months before the primary transformation occurs. Within said time period, observed diseased individuals display secondary wolven characteristics such as increased olfactory abilities, irritability, keen attention to high-level decibel ranges, all expected reactions considering.*

*However, the contamination resides within a dual layer of the corporeal form. The disease permeates the musculature and organ tissues but also invades the individual on a spiritual plane.*

*Undoing the infection is difficult, nay, almost impossible, however our experiments conclude only positive results have been achieved with ritualistic purification before the first transformation and must address both levels of infection.*

Now, we were getting somewhere.

Byron flipped through the following pages, reading and studying, making notes and marking the moon charts. Not surprisingly, the phase of the moon played a paramount role in the ritual. In fact the heavenly orb needed to be given the utmost consideration. After making additional calculations, and creating a list of some key ingredients he didn't have, Byron deduced his time remaining to save his lover waned.

If Byron interpreted this right, he had mere days to pull this off.

> *Side Note: Upon several occasions, we were fortunate to be able to transfer the virus into a witch. One would have expected the magick available to the infectee would have resulted in a hybrid being, one of great power. This was our hope. The trial results have indicated otherwise. The two branches of magick are at odds with each other and all subjects suffered. The situations ended in utter disaster. The two sources of power are not compatible, or perhaps the corporeal structure of a witch is sufficiently different enough than that of a human, thus resulting in a mutated first morph that did not survive their primary shift. We have documented this repeatedly.*
>
> *Conclusion: The two natures are not compatible.*

Byron had run out of time. He pulled out his cell phone and made a few calls. He'd need his knights to pull this off. And the purification ritual would have to happen before the next full moon, which lay only days away.

Byron closed his eyes and held his head in his hands while his elbows rested on the desk.

He had to save Addas.

# Chapter Eleven

TULLY FLEW UP the second set of stairs leading away from his front door. He had driven as fast as possible, breaking a few traffic laws to get Dev here, and the light sheen of sweat on his back gave away his anxiety and nerves showing Dev the upstairs apartment.

He wanted Dev to like it.

Pulling out a keyring, Tully flipped through a few options until he found the skeleton key to open the door.

"Wow, seriously? Who has keys like that anymore?" Dev watched closely, peeking around Tully.

"I know, right? When Uncle Bart did the renovations, they recycled a lot of the original pieces of the house. The doors were one of them, along with the locksets, and so, you rent this apartment and you get to haul around the coolest looking key in the city!" Tully glanced over his shoulder while he fiddled with the key in the lock. He couldn't contain his smile.

The door knob didn't budge.

"Gah." Tully pulled the key out and stepped back, which meant he pressed right up against Dev.

"I think you told me you were going to be a gentleman?" Dev laughed as he wrapped his arm around Tully's waist and pulled him in tight.

"Oh, man, you're making that promise almost impossible to keep. No, silly, the lock isn't giving so, how about I show you your first taste of someone doing a little hocus pocus."

"What? No way...yeah man, do it." Dev's voice, steeped with enthusiasm and excitement, made Tully beam brighter with pride.

"Okay, so this is totally first-year type stuff. You'll learn how to do this. It's pretty easy." Tully, with Dev still wrapped around his waist took a step closer to the door. He cupped his hands and held them up to his mouth and blew, rubbed them together, then shook them out.

With a deep breath in, followed by a long exhale, Tully closed his eyes and imagined the door swinging open, as he pointed a finger he drew a sideways *V*.

The symbol, visible to Tully, burned in metallic copper, and as he listened closely, the rustling of the shifting sand of earth surrounded them. The element had come to aid him in his spell.

The symbol, the ancient Norse rune Kena, disintegrated, but as the glyph faded, the door knob twisted. The door rattled, and as the portal opened, its hinges squeaked, bidding them both inside.

"Wow! That's incredible. What was the letter? Can I do that too?" Dev said as Tully glanced behind him to see Dev's eyes wide and glazed over in amazement.

"Wait...you saw the rune? Wow, I couldn't see anything until after my binding. Cool. You're gonna be one hell of a witch. And you will cast this rune and many others as soon as you learn a thing or two." Tully gave Dev a friendly elbow in the ribs. "Come on, let's have a look at the place." Tully grabbed Dev's wrist and, not wanting to, unwrapped Dev from around his waist and pulled him into the upstairs apartment.

Dev walked into the center of the room, his mouth agape as he rotated, taking in the tiny but unique studio.

"I know it's small, but the space would be all yours."

"Does the furniture all stay?" Dev asked, pointing to various objects.

Tully glanced around him. He'd forgotten the last tenant had left everything. Tully hadn't done anything to the studio since then. A monster-sized four-poster king bed dominated the room, shoved up against the far wall, fitted out with plush pillows and a dark maroon duvet. Little tassels hung from the tops of each of the posts, and a black faux fur throw lay tossed across the corner of the bed. The walls were all lined with bookcases, which of course were dotted here and there with collections of books. A chestnut leather Queen Anne chair and footstool sat on the opposite side of the room, with a side table—one of those wooden creations whose legs have feet on the ends, making the table look like the whole thing would spring to life, get up, and walk away.

A reading lamp with a Victorian-style shade sat on top of the side table. Tully walked over and turned the knob under the lampshade. In the middle of the day, the light wasn't going to do much, but if nothing else, turning on the lamp would prove to Dev the furnishings were at a bare minimum, functional.

"Holy shit, Tully. This place is incredible." Dev ran his finger along the rim of the chair rail which topped the wood paneling covering the lower half of the walls.

"Ah, but you haven't even seen the best part." Tully walked over to a wall of curtains which were partially open enough to let in the midday sun, making the apartment bright and cheery. He rustled behind the material, looking for the pull cords, and when he found them, he gave them a couple of gentle tugs. The curtains parted, as if they were seated in a theatre and the play was about to begin. Once the material had been pulled to each side of the room, a huge round window allowed the day's sunshine to pour in, flooding the room in cheery golden rays. The monstrous window took up the entire outside wall of the one room apartment and framed a massive Bur oak. The tree's expanse covered the entire yard and the heavily gnarled bark gave away its long standing occupancy in the yard. Tully spied a squirrel racing along one of the branches. The oak made the apartment feel akin to a tree fort.

A luxurious Persian rug lay in the center of the floor, intricate weavings of flowers and vines, with small birds and hares scattered throughout the pattern. The carpet covered a lot of the original hardwood, but it was the same wood used throughout the ancient mansion, polished up though and looking as new as possible.

Over in the corner, the small kitchenette had a stainless-steel fridge. Not a big one but large enough to accommodate a single occupant. A sink, a microwave, and a two burner stove top rounded out the area, which provided more than enough for anyone who had never been keen on cooking. The students who had lived here in the past had never complained.

Besides, Whyte Avenue, just a few blocks away, offered a variety of restaurants to a hungry potential renter.

"Just down the hall is a bathroom." Tully pointed as Dev's stare followed. "It's got a great shower."

"I'll take it."

"Take what? A shower?"

"No, silly, the apartment. I'll take it."

"Well that was easy." Tully grabbed Dev and embraced him. "You sure you don't want to think about it? I mean, moving out for the first time, your family, Cam and you had a plan...and well, I absolutely want you this close, but like you said, it's all a little—"

"Hush, I'll take it. This is incredible." Even wrapped up in Tully's arms, Dev's head rubbernecked as he checked out the place.

"Okay, well, I'll talk to the old man downstairs and see if I can get you a good deal." Tully offered. "But it's gonna cost you."

"You can take all of my money." Dev glowed.

"I wasn't talking about cash." Tully shifted so his fingertips touched Dev's belt buckle. Tully ran his fingers along the top of Dev's pants "But you know, if you want to pay me..."

"You trollop." Dev chuckled.

With a quick tug, Tully had Dev's pants around his ankles, and had a handful of Dev's sizeable balls in his hand, the underwear Dev wore an unpleasant barrier.

Dev nuzzled Tully's neck, running his beard up against the bare flesh.

Tully shivered. "Dammit, I love it when you do that."

Not able to continue with the tease, Tully gabbed the sides of Dev's boxers and pulled down, which rewarded Tully with a meaty handful of Dev's hard cock. He pulled it gently a few times, watching as the foreskin peeled back, revealing a plump and swollen head, and then in reverse as the skin covered it up again. Tully was cut, and getting to play with someone who hadn't been altered instilled an exciting variety of magic in its own way. Tully's stroking was making Dev's legs shake.

Tully placed a kiss on Dev's exposed neck, reached around him, and hoisted Dev up off the ground, walked two steps toward the massive bed, and threw Dev onto it.

Tully pulled his shirt off and peeled himself out of his jeans, exposing his own throbbing excitement.

"Well, damn." Dev reached out and grabbed Tully's nuts. "Guess I'm about to make my security deposit."

"Yes, you most certainly are." Tully pulled up on Dev's tee.

Tully wanted him naked and exposed, and once he had stripped Dev and spent sufficient time kissing several spots and lacing his fingers through Dev's chest hair, he settled on his final destination.

With Dev's hard cock gripped tightly in one hand, Tully repositioned himself so he knelt over Dev. He tongued and licked the tip of Dev's sizeable cockhead which leaked with the pulse of Dev's excitement as his member throbbed. Tully stroked Dev a few more times. He inserted the tip of his tongue into Dev's slit, trying to lap up whatever precum might have oozed out.

But there was too much to explore on Dev. And without any further hesitation and too much excitement, Tully opened his mouth, mindful of his teeth, and swallowed all Dev had to offer.

Dev tilted his head and moaned.

The security deposit would be made soon enough.


DEV'S LIFE NORMALLY contained a lot of chaos, so he'd expected a certain amount of resilience to everything that had happened in the last day or so. Not so much. Life had been a bit of a whirlwind. The witch thing. Finding out his professor had been hiding his position as the high priest for the local coven. And Tully. Damn, Tully.

The sexy redhead's confidence, knowledge with the witch stuff, and hairy muscles met every single one of his personal fantasies to a tight "T". And right at this very moment, as Dev grabbed fistfuls of thick, dark auburn hair in his hands, the heat and wet of Tully's mouth sliding down his hard dick brought him close to losing control.

Dev involuntarily thrust his hips forward, wanting to push himself further into Tully.

"Oh my god, Tully, damn, you are so amazing." Dev's eyes rolled as Tully tugged on his sack.

Dev's vision blurred as the room tilted slightly, losing control and focus except for the overwhelming sensation of Tully's lips sliding up and down.

Tully's mouth came off his engorged cock with a *pop* as Tully slid his hand up and down Dev's length, when a new warm and wet sensation gripped him. Dev glanced down to see Tully sucking on his ball sack, his tongue massaging the underside of the tender skin.

"Holy shit." Dev's hips thrust back and forth in short bursts. His tummy clenched tight as his legs began to quiver.

"Ah, Tully...oh god," Dev sucked in air through clenched teeth. The stimulation too much.

"That's my man, give it to me." Tully cocked a half grin while watching Dev writhe in the pleasure he provided.

Dev sat up while his entire body tightened, his balls pulled themselves in close to his body.

Tully placed his mouth over Dev's cockhead again and sucked as Dev erupted. Loud shouts of ecstasy escaped Dev's mouth with each wave of orgasmic pleasure.

Dev grabbed the back of Tully's head and held him as he spasmed and shot the biggest load of his life.

When the aftershocks of his orgasm settled, Dev fell onto the bed. "Holy! Promise me you'll do that to me again." A slick sheen of sweat covered Dev's lithe body.

Tully crawled on top of him, still naked and pressed his muscled furry body against Dev. Dev wrapped himself around Tully in a huge bear hug, one he'd never let go voluntarily.

"I promise I'll treat you like a king every morning you wake up and you're with me." Tully pressed his swollen lips up against Dev's. Dev opened his mouth, wanting all of Tully, and also tasted the remnants of himself in Tully's mouth.

"Your turn."

"My turn what?" Tully whispered into Dev's ear.

"What can I do to make you come?"

Tully giggled. "I already did."

"When?"

"While I was on the floor, swallowing you. And damn, by the way, when's the last time you popped your cork? 'Cause I almost didn't swallow everything."

"I believe that would have been last night. Several times if I recall. And you wasted your spunk on the floor?" Dev slapped Tully's ass cheek.

"I'll clean it up."

"I'll say you will. Can't be coming into my house and making messes all over the floor."

"Listen to you!" Tully chuckled. "You haven't even owned the place for ten minutes and you're bossing me around." Tully sneered at Dev, trying to look all serious. "I kinda like the bossy Dev." Tully's mouth bloomed into a beguiling smirk.

"You're such a goof."

"Yeah, but I get the sense you like it."

Dev laughed in return. "Yeah, I kinda do. So, can we spend the rest of the afternoon in bed like this?"

"Absolutely. You gonna come with me tonight and meet the rest of the guys?"

"I really want to. But..."

"Too much? Too soon? You want to go to your parent's place and get your stuff instead?"

"Yes! And no. Oh my god, they're going to have a seizure when I tell them I'm moving out."

"If you want I'll come with you? Might help with the family drama, you know, they're not going to start a big fight or commotion if there's a stranger there."

"Oh yes they will. You don't know them."

"I think I'd like to though."

Dev flushed. He'd never brought a boy home before. He'd always wanted to, and he had a sense Tully would be a perfect gentleman around them. Well, he hoped. Honestly, he didn't know Tully well at all, but being around him, talking to him, eased him. Tully exuded a sense of calm. And over the last day he'd been so kind and fun and...well...damn sexy.

The last day.

*What the hell was wrong with you?*

*You don't know him at all!*

But a quiet voice in his head whispered, *just give it a chance.*

And Dev wanted to. Everything in his life had changed so fast, but Tully had made everything seem okay. He wanted this all to continue.

"You're crazy to want to meet my family. They're not bad people, over emotional and a tad chaotic, but they're good folk. I feel guilty for wanting to move out, but at the same time, I've dreamt of making this move for so long."

"Seems like you've been wanting a lot of things to happen for a long time."

"I have."

"So come to coven tonight. Byron is exceptional. He taught me everything I know, and the rest of the guys are as amazing. I promise you. You won't regret it. I know I'm not supposed to pressure you, but I want you to come."

"I do too. Okay. I'll come. And maybe tomorrow we can move some of my stuff in after my classes? If you're free?"

"Yes!" Tully beamed bright and gave Dev a huge kiss. "You're gonna love it! Both here and coven, I promise"

"What time is the gathering tonight?"

"Not till seven. We got lots of time."

"Excellent!" Dev let go of his bear hug on Tully and, instead, wriggled a hand in between their two bodies so he had access to grip Tully's still engorged cock. "Seems like you're still raring to go? I think turnaround is fair play, right? On your back mister, I have some work to do."

"Oh... I see!" Tully closed his eyes in anticipation. "We're going to have a fun afternoon."

"Yes, yes we are." Dev shimmied down until his face lined up with Tully's groin. "We most certainly are."

# Chapter Twelve

CAM PULLED HIS upper body up off the cold cement floor and rested while balanced on his forearms. He barely had enough energy to prop himself up. His wings had lost their shine, even in the darkness of the dungeon, they had once sparkled and gleamed earlier. Not now. And if he didn't know any better, Cam would have likened them to a plant thirsty for water.

"God, I feel like shit." Everything ached as he spoke at the damp concrete floor.

"I keep trying to tell you; quit fighting them. Every draw of fluid they take from you leaches a little more of the fae out of you. Unless that's what you want?" Everton growled from his cage. Cam still hadn't seen him, only shapes and glowing eyes, but Ev's gruff voice had at least one positive effect. The animalistic rumblings let him know he wasn't alone.

"I don't know what the hell I want, other than to get the fuck out of here or talk to Dev. Maybe both."

"The one who's the new witch?"

"Yeah, that one. He's the smart one. He'll figure this out."

"Or kill you. That's what they do, you know. They kill, for power."

"You don't know Dev. He'd never do that." Cam sneered. His faith in Dev and their friendship permeated deep into his bones. Dev would never hurt him, or anyone for that matter. Regardless of the fact the damn summoning board had worked, and Dev was now one of *them,* he'd known Dev all his life. Dev had always been nothing if not kind and gentle. Not flippant and mouthy like Cam had a notorious reputation for being. Damn his insolence. Once again his piss poor attitude had landed him in hot water, or in this case, naked, cold, and shackled.

"Well, all I can tell you is this. I've never met a witch I liked, and in the end, they're all killers. They absorb energy to cast their spells, and in order to keep themselves alive as long as possible, they steal energy from anywhere they can, including other kinfolk from the Shadow Realm. They've killed six of my pack this year. We only managed to take out two of theirs."

"Sounds like you've done your fair share of killing too." Cam grunted as he slipped off his forearms and lay down on the hard floor. The concrete was like a cool cloth draped over the back of your neck when you'd been out in the sun too long. But as soothing as the cold temperatures were, the hard concrete kinked his neck, and the dank odors wafting off of the floor made Cam cringe. "Doesn't seem right you judging them for the same actions you've taken."

"You don't know me. You don't know what it's like or how it's always been. You weren't there to watch as your packmates were drained of their lives. And for what? Power? Control? The Coven of the Night Grove has held this region for generations. And the last two high priests have been violent and bloodthirsty, keeping all the mana for themselves. The shifters, the fae, and the undead have been starved for well over a hundred years. We're no longer willing to sit and let the feud continue. The witches are gonna get theirs. You wait."

"I literally understood none of that." Cam breathed out a heavy sigh. Ev had been sort of kind to Cam since he'd been locked up in this hell hole, but the man tended to ramble. And Cam's deduction of Ev had settled on "missing a few marbles".

*Damn, why can't I get up?*

"You'll soon understand. You wait. Your friend will turn on you. He'll be exactly like all those other witches." Cam listened to Ev while he shuffled within his cell desperate to find a comfortable position. "What are you trying to do, kill yourself? Just lay still, your body needs time to regenerate. And if you don't start playing their game, they will drain you dead."

"What the hell are they taking, anyway? What's in those tubes?"

"They're extracting your spinal fluid, which would do anyone harm, but for the fae, it's a certain magical death. That fluorescent green goo is coming from your repository of fae mojo juice. The spinal column is the factory. You need the liquid to be fae. Byron wasn't telling you lies. If they take enough of your mojo out, you'll get to a point where you won't have enough to regenerate and they'll literally suck the fae right out of you. If you don't die, you'll become human again, sort of. Once you've been fae-touched, you never go back to normal. The last one they did this to reverted back, but was only a shell of a person, in the end. She left here a bit off in the end, if you know what I mean." Cam shifted on the floor again, thinking Ev had gone "off". Trying to find any position offering a semblance of comfort was damn near impossible. Ev prattled on. "But if those witches take much more from you, you'll die. I can smell you from here. Believe me, you don't smell great. Your body is at the end of its rope."

"My back hurts so bad," Cam mumbled. A general burning ache radiated out from several spots along Cam's spine.

Ev continued, "But if they don't take any of your mojo juice, you'll become fae, and you'll turn away from humanity. Fae are a whole other level of crazy. No fur off my pelt if that's what you want."

"I'd never turn my back on Dev."

"Yeah, you would."

"Well maybe taking the juice out of me is a good thing." Cam attempted to yell across the room, but then the spinal procedure had sucked more than fairy mojo out of him.

"Tell that to your body right now; you're a mess. You need to sleep. Trust what I'm saying. Play their game. The fact your buddy is one of them might mean they'll let you go."

"If Dev knew I was down here, I'd be out in a hot minute."

"You sure about that?"

"Positive."

Ev fell quiet for a few moments but then broke the silence. "We might be able to get out of this..." Ev's voice rumbled. His vocal tone had a way of crawling across the floor, reverberating through Cam's chest. The growl should have been menacing or disconcerting, but Cam found Ev's testosterone laden voice relaxed him. Maybe Cam had an affinity for the growl as they were both magical creatures? Perhaps a Werewolf didn't compare to what he had morphed into. Or maybe the fact they were locked up together lent a deeper bond between them, considering their unusual circumstance? Cam didn't know nor, at that point, did he care. A small part of him realized being alone in this situation would have been far worse, and for that, he begrudgingly liked Ev.

"I just want out. And to be in a warm and comfortable bed," Cam whispered. He closed his eyes, trying to forget the pain and remembered past summer days. Him and Dev hanging out by the pool in his mom's backyard, lounging and drinking ice cold beers.

"If your friend rescues you, would he take me too?" Ev asked, quieter than normal.

"If I asked him to, he would."

"What do I have to do to make that happen?" Ev demanded.

"Oh man, it'll cost you big."

"I don't care what the price. I'll pay. I need to get out of here and back to my pack. I've been here too long."

"How long have you been in here?" Cam's voice barely registered. Exhaustion had sapped any strength he'd had.

"I don't know for sure. A year? Just…sleep, rest and regenerate. And for all the gods' sake, be nice to them. We can talk more later. I need to think."

Cam's eyes fluttered shut. Exhaustion took over as he slipped away and fell asleep.

TULLY KNOCKED ON a massive steel door. The sleek flat planes were polished and spartan except for a geometrical linear design. Dev stared at the line work until Tully pointed out, "It's a goat's head. See?" He traced the line of the horns and then where the eyes would be and the nose, which was made into a door knocker.

"I see it now, yeah. That's an odd thing to stamp on the front door, no?" The house reflected a minimalistic and modern flair, and didn't seem to fit Dev's perception of what Professor Byron Radcliff would live in. He'd expected more bookcases lined with tomes, old artifacts scattered about and furniture reminiscent of an old English study.

"It's a witch thing. Horned god and all."

Within short order the door swung open, and behind it, the largest muscle-clad man Dev had ever seen stood in the threshold.

"Tully!" The monster grabbed Tully and enveloped him into a massive bear hug. As Tully disappeared into the mountain of flesh, Dev heard a distinct *oof*.

"Hello, Addas." Tully pushed away and grinned, but seeing Tully without one would have been a rare event indeed. The man shone like a positive and optimistic beacon, an all-around happy guy. "Dev, this is Addas, Byron's boyfriend. Careful, he's a hugger." Tully elbowed Dev in the ribs, and Addas laughed at the comment.

"You are exactly how I pictured you, Dev. Byron has done nothing but talk about you for days, and texted, and emailed. I can't begin to tell you how excited he is you're here."

Dev stuck out his hand for a handshake. "Nice to meet you."

"Bah, we're brothers now," and with that, Dev found himself smothered in biceps. He heard Tully laughing behind him.

"I did warn you."

"Mmhmm," Dev managed to squeak out.

Addas pulled away, allowing the two men entrance. "Come on in! Everyone's already here, and I have to say, Byron's not the only one that's excited."

Addas took their coats, and Tully and Dev slipped off their shoes and toed them over to the pile of other shoes discarded by the guests who had arrived earlier.

"That's a lot of shoes," Dev whispered to Tully.

"Only twelve pairs, yours and mine included. A coven is always made up of thirteen people. We're one short. We had a couple of unfortunate accidents last year."

"What does that mean?"

"Deaths. Remember, I said being a witch shortened one's lifespan."

"My god. What the hell did I sign up for?" Dev stared at Tully with wide eyes.

"Well, technically, you haven't signed anything yet. Don't worry about it. Honestly, they were accidents. Unusual ones too."

"Oh, okay." Dev didn't feel convinced. He glanced at the pile of footwear and noticed a pair of boots neatly tucked away in the corner. A pair of rainbow coloured snakeskin boots. *Damn those look like Cam's shoes.* But as soon as that registered, Tully pulled on Dev's arm. As they climbed the stairs to a landing, the room opened up into a huge living room with a massive fireplace against the far wall, and a bear skin rug thrown in the middle of the floor. Dev was taken aback at the gathering of men in front of him. Every single one of them radiated sensuality, power, and although there were a number of different body shapes, each would have been considered eye candy. Short, tall, square-shouldered tanks and lean swimmers builds, all of them had beards, goatees, or some kind of facial hair, even if three-day-old stubble was the extent of it.

"Is being a witch and gay equal to being good-looking, muscled, and furry?" Dev asked Tully quietly.

"What? I..." Tully glanced around the room and laughed. "I never noticed before, but, ah, yeah, I suppose so." Tully furrowed his brows as he scanned the room.

Dev followed Tully's gaze and as he studied the men in the room, self-conscious emotions nagged at him. The demon voice of self-doubt reminding him he didn't belong. He couldn't possibly measure up to these paramounts of male masculinity.

From across the room, Byron turned around to face them. A gaggle of men clustered behind him. He spread his arms out wide as he addressed the assembled crew, "Boys, here's the man of the hour, the latest addition to our Shadow Realm. Dev! I'm so glad you decided to come. Everyone is dying to meet you. Welcome to the Coven of the Night Grove." Byron rushed over and gave Dev another bear hug, equal to the strength and force of Addas's embrace.

Dev, certain his eyes were going to pop out, tried to wriggle out of the bearish grasp.

"Ah, thanks Professor Radcliff," Dev managed to get out as they disengaged from the hug.

"Nope, none of that here. My name is Byron, please call me by my first name." Byron's big hands were squarely planted on Dev's shoulders. "Oh, I'm so glad you're here!" And again, Byron yanked Dev in for another hug.

"Ahem." A brusque voice came from in front of Dev, who had his eyes squeezed shut, enduring the affection from his favorite teacher. The extra attention from his mentor would spur private fantasies later, but if truth be told, the hug lasted longer than socially acceptable. Dev struggled to breathe, and besides, he had Tully now. Still, a voice inside him thought *I'd pay twenty bucks to watch Byron and Addas. Damn, that would be some show.*

"Byron, you going to monopolize him all night? Or are you going to introduce him?"

Byron pulled away, "I'm sorry, Gus, you're right. Forgive me, but I am happy you came, Dev. I guess I can't have you all to myself. Besides, Addas would want some too." Byron gave Dev a wink and a knowing look. Dev's eyes went wide at the mere suggestion of him being sandwiched between Byron and Addas. Byron leaned in close to Dev. "Come on, I know the rest of the guys want to meet you." Byron placed his hand in the crook of Dev's elbow and steered him around to meet three men who were standing in a straight line, all with welcoming faces, if not a tad stoic. "Tully, would you mind getting Dev something to drink while I introduce him around?"

"No, not at all." Tully studied Dev. "You good?"

"Of course, he's okay, don't be silly." Byron chuckled making a shooing gesture to Tully. Tully smiled one of his award-winning grins, turned around, and went off to find drinks for the two of them. "Dev, these are my three knights Gus Nightshade, an atmospherologist, Eduardo Blackwood, a terralogist who has zooempathy talents, and you've already met my boyfriend, Addas, a technomage."

There was a round of curt but strong handshakes, except from Addas, who beamed and winked.

"I'm not going to even guess at what those specialties mean." Dev blushed, his neck feeling warm and once again reinforcing how much he felt like he didn't belong here.

"Not to worry," Addas chimed in as he put a massive paw on Dev's shoulder and gave him a squeeze. "You'll learn. Technomage means I have a certain way with mechanical things. Most technomages are focused on the latest gadgets, computers, technology, computer programming." Addas shook his head. 'That's not me at all. I'm still stuck on old-school things. Motors, engines, circuits, that kind of thing. But my cell phone gets amazing reception where ever I am, and everyone in the coven has the best running cars in town, so I guess there's that." Addas winked at him.

"I get to play with air. Probably the least sexy of the abilities, and perhaps not as powerful as Eddie here, but turning into smoke has gotten us out of a few tight spaces." Gus nodded toward Addas, who smirked in return. "Welcome to the coven, Dev. I understand you're an aurologist. That's really rare. Hope you decide to join us."

Eddie bumped Gus out of the way, extending his hand again. "Dev, a pleasure. I'm like your friend Tully, but instead of being able to play around with metal, I can use any form of the earth. And I have a thing with animals."

"You make your ability out to be some kind of sexual perversion. You're not sleeping with them, are you?" Gus teased.

"Really?" Eddie shot him a dirty look.

"What? I'm just saying..." Gus turned toward Dev to comment, "He can talk to most creatures and they'll do his bidding. Watching their animal eyes gloss over as he charms them is creepy as fuck."

Dev chuckled. For all the introductions and complicated terminology, the guys had all welcomed him with warm words, handshakes, and hugs. Each of them were guys Dev would have liked to hang out with.

"I'm not going to remember any of this tomorrow," Dev confessed.

"It takes a while, and hey, if you stick around, Byron will put you through your paces. You won't have any choice but to learn." Eddie raised an eyebrow. "Let's go around the room, ah, let's see...okay, over there in the corner, the blocky dude with the short-cropped hair? That's Kerr, his thing is with sound, which is weird, and he's new. Only been around for about what?"

"Six months?" Gus added.

"That's about right. And Kerr is talking to Lazaro, and Lazaro is my pupil, and he's like me...gotta thing for Earth, but he's good with plants too. Standing beside them—damn is that boy always on his phone?" Eddie didn't look impressed.

"Give him a break," Gus said. "Guaranteed he's on a dating app trying to organize his next evening liaison. It's not easy being single and a witch."

"Hmph. Yes, well, that's Marcus, he's a water baby." Dev's head swam with information overload, overwhelmed and excited to be standing amongst so many good-looking guys who all had powers and abilities. "And in the other corner is Scott, another Air like Gus."

"And he's my pupil," Gus added.

"And next to Scott, the big guy with the long beautiful wavy hair everyone is jealous over? That's Sparks, and his brother is standing next to him, the one in all black. That's Wiatt. Wiatt is another anomaly. He's...I guess you could say..." Eddie grimaced, sticking his tongue out with disgust.

"Oh, for all the gods' sakes. He's a necromancer. Plays with dead things and spirits. He's one of the nicest guys here. Don't listen to Eddie." Gus punched Eddie in the arm playfully.

"What? He creeps me out." Eddie faked an over exaggerated shuddered to make his point.

"What does Sparks do?" Dev asked.

"Ha. Not obvious from his nickname? The boy likes things shocking. Electricity is his game."

"I'm never gonna remember—" Dev stared right at Sparks as Sparks caught his eye, bowed his head in Dev's direction, nodding in acknowledgement. Dev didn't know what to do but was thankful when Tully arrived.

"Hey, so...did they bombard you with everyone's names and abilities?" Tully handed Dev a beer. "And I didn't know what you'd want to drink, so I grabbed this. Byron's got everything though, so if the beer isn't to your taste..."

"No, this is fine, thanks." Dev took a deep long pull on the hoppy beverage, only to find his nerves had left him thirsty, and so he took another swig. "And yes, that's exactly what they were doing."

Joining an established group tended to be weird until you'd spent enough time with them to have built your own history. Dev knew this, and even still, being jettisoned into the coven, even as a guest, meant all eyes were on him. An underlying current in the room prodded Dev's brain, a notion they all expected Dev to join their ranks.

*And would that be so bad?*

"Come on, Dev, let's go to talk with some of the others. These three will keep you hostage all night if I let them."

Eddie put his hand on Dev's shoulder. "He's not lying. I will say Dev, I like your energy. I think you'd fit in well with us. No pressure though. And hey, if you ever have any questions, hit me up." Eddie turned to Byron. "By the way, that thing you wanted? I found it out on my hike. It's in your private study. I also had to drag the *clothes you wanted* up from downstairs. They're down in the foyer by the closet. They were proving to be a distraction and getting in the way where we had them stashed."

Byron cocked a half grin clasping Eddie on the shoulder. "Always thinking of the coven. Eddie here was my first knight. We go back many years. He's a solid guy, and the best terralogist around." Byron radiated with pride. "How about we give Dev a few days to settle in as a witch first, eh? Maybe we'll talk about him joining the coven after a few weeks." Byron stared at Eddie then turned to Dev. "Eddie's not wrong, though, we'd love to have you."

"Wow, thanks guys." Dev raised his beer bottle toward them in a half-hearted, awkward cheers sort of gesture.

As they took a couple of steps away from Byron and his knights and toward the other men, Tully leaned into Dev telling secrets, "They are pretty cool, which is awesome as they're in charge if Byron's not around. Eddie has been like a father figure, like Byron, he's a great guy. Gus on the other hand, nice enough, but he will try to get down your pants."

"Is that so bad?" Dev asked, playfully.

"Not at all, but if you get the opportunity I want to watch."

"Oh, kinky." Dev grinned. "Don't worry, he's not my type. But there is this one guy…" And Dev stopped and attempted to charm Tully, "Thanks for bringing me, truly, I've been vibrating with excitement all afternoon.

Excitement and nerves though. Still very nervous about it all."

Tully shrugged off the compliment, but Dev noted his typical happy bearded face got a bit bigger and brighter.

"Anytime."

"All right, everyone," Byron's loud voice boomed across the room. Must have been a skill he developed being a teacher. "I think it's time to give our guest here a taste of what coven life is all about. Whaddya say boys? Quick informal circle and we'll call upon the elements and do a blessing?"

There were general nods and murmurs of acceptance around the room.

Tully raised an eyebrow and smirked. "Well, Byron doesn't do this with newbies. He really wants you to join. You okay seeing some more magic? Get a taste for what we're all about?"

"Oh gods, hells yes!" All of Dev's hesitancy went out the window. "Bring on the magic!"

# Chapter Thirteen

DEV INTENTLY STUDIED the room, fascinated as each of the men fussed about, preparing the living room for the "impromptu circle" as Byron had called it. Dev, thinking back to the books in his bedroom, recalled ceremonies for a blessing he'd read about. Being book smart didn't compare to witnessing the real deal. Books, pictures, and internet videos paled. Dev's skin tingled, and harnessing his excitement was almost an impossibility. Tonight he would witness a ritual performed live.

The bear skin rug got rolled up and put away. The coffee table and sofa were moved to the side of the room. And as each of these elements were shifted and the floor exposed, Dev tilted his head as he spied something painted on the floorboards. Lines, writing? What was it? Dev's squinted.

"Okay, I've seen that look on your face before," Tully remarked. "What's up?"

"It's nothing. I'm watching everything and I'm intrigued." With his laser-focused eyesight, Dev made out the outer line of a huge circle. He turned to Tully. "Is there a pentagram on the floor?"

"You shouldn't be able to see the writing. At least, not yet." Tully shook his head. "That's twice now. You noticed the rune when I opened the door with magic, and now you're seeing the coven circle? Wild."

"Well, can't you see it?"

"Yes, but I've been bound and given over to the Shadow Realm. Remember? I told you the other night...you'll see things you never imagined."

"So, I'm a witch. I've manifested my abilities, several times." Dev smiled, thinking about how those instances had happened. "What's this binding thing?"

Tully responded with his own mischievousness, "I hoped maybe we could set your powers loose again tonight, you know, if you want. But to answer your question...the binding thing is sort of like...baptism for Christians?" The way Tully made the comparison led Dev to believe the parallel echoed a similar enough sentiment.

"Oh, okay. When does a binding happen after manifesting your powers?"

"Well, I suppose the induction could happen anytime. I mean, if you want, I'm sure Byron would agree to do it tonight. But you don't know what's involved or the purpose behind it all."

"I'm giving myself over to the Shadow Realm? A place I knew existed since I can remember, have searched desperately for but never found until now? The place I've longed for and dreamt about my entire life?"

"Ha! Okay, well, maybe you do. You want me to go talk to Byron?"

Dev's head canted to one side and a wry smirk formed as he contemplated the possibility of being bound to the Shadow Realm. "Yes. I do. I ran away from you the other night because I was overwhelmed. I'm not doing that anymore. I know this is what I want."

Tully bobbed his head once in acknowledgement and went off, cornering Byron at the other end of the room. He had a discreet and quiet chat while Dev continued noting the scurrying about by the rest of the coven members. The transformation didn't take long, but the minimalistic living room which had been magazine-spread decorated and the perfect entertaining space morphed. The vibe of the room had subtly altered, and Dev's senses picked up on the tense expectation and the low buzz of side conversations from the men as they continued their ritual tasks.

Byron came over with Tully and stopped in front of Dev as Gus and Eddie helped bring an ancient looking sideboard and positioned the antique at the front of the room. Sparks, Kerr, and Wiatt were busy putting items on its surface, and as Dev studied the added objects. He counted off a bundle of sage, crystals, an athame, and other occult items, many of which he had at home.

"So, Tully tells me you think you're ready for your binding? Are you sure? That's a pretty snappy decision, no? Wouldn't you rather wait until after you see us perform a simple circle, call upon the elements, and do a coven blessing?"

As Dev weighed Byron's words and witnessed the brotherhood between the men as they carried out their duties, he only had to think about the ceremony for a second.

"No, I don't think I need to wait. I've been wanting this my entire life, and here I am. I'm not sure I want to wait anymore. I was so hesitant and flabbergasted when I first met Tully, I had to walk away. Witches and magic, and all those muscles and red hair." Dev bit his lip in a grimace of angst. "And after, I felt foolish and childish. I don't want to walk away from this again. I know this is where I belong."

Byron peered at Tully as Tully acknowledged Dev's response. "Sounds like the man knows what he wants."

"Okay. You know once you bind yourself to the Shadow Realm, that's it. Right? There's no backing out or undoing what is done. The choice to give yourself over is always yours, but once done, the ritual is final."

"Am I'm selling my soul to the devil?"

"Well, not the devil, but you are committing yourself to the supernatural community. You'll have to follow our laws and you'll be held accountable for your actions. Don't get me wrong, Dev, I'm *thrilled* and honored to be the one to do the ceremony, but I want to make sure you are committed."

"You'll be with me the entire time?" Dev turned and asked Tully.

"Yup. I'll be right here."

"And my soul is still my own?"

They both laughed. Then Byron spoke, "Absolutely. Yours to sell to the first fiend you come across if you so wish."

"I'm in," Dev barked with a most decided look on his face.

This was it.

Byron's face altered from a concerned father figure giving advice to a beaming proud parent. "All right men, slight change of plans!" Byron yelled out to all in the room, "Dev has decided he wants to do his Binding Ceremony tonight. All here in favor?"

A resounding war cry of triumph bugled from all in attendance.

"Any naysayers?" asked Bryon.

There wasn't a peep, other than the pop and crackle of the fire still raging in the fireplace.

"Very well. Gather the right stuff for me Eddie, Gus, and Addas. We're going to welcome a new brother into the Shadow Realm."


"TULLY, TAKE DEV into the other room and have him change into some robes. Make sure he's wearing the black one, after all, black will be his color if he is an aurologist." Byron turned and gripped Dev's shoulders again. "I'm so proud of you right now I could burst. But I want to ask you one more time... You sure?"

"You make it seem like I'm making a bad decision." Dev furrowed his eyebrows. His shoulders tensed beneath Byron's warm meaty hands.

"Think of the binding this way. You're about to get tattooed. The ink is needled into your skin. Once injected and the ink settles, the mark is permanent. There's no 'I didn't mean to,' there's no washing away the tattoo. I just want to be one hundred percent sure you're sure."

Dev half grinned and tilted his head, looking at his favorite mentor for all the years he'd gone to university. "You know I've respected you for a long time. I also thought you were one of the smartest people I had ever met and, well, still do. To find out who you actually are came as a shock, but I trust you. I can't believe you would be doing anything to harm me in any way. So yes, I am sure."

"Atta boy." Byron pulled him in for another bear hug.

Squished and barely able to breathe, Dev mumbled through Byron's thick chest, "You guys really like your hugs."

Byron chortled and released Dev, turned him around, and gave him to Tully. "You know what to do with him." Byron gave Tully a wink and sent them off into a side room.

Tully led them to a spare bedroom for guests. An opening in the far wall had the promise of an en suite bathroom. Doors to a monster-sized walk in closet took up another wall, but the bed surprised Dev in only being a double. Tully opened up the closet doors, and rifled through the astounding selection of hanging garments.

Dev didn't see a single normal shirt or pair of pants. Every hanger held a robe, of varying lengths and colours, and every one had different stitchery embellishing the hems and collars.

"Wow, that's some collection."

"Impressive, isn't it? Some of the robes are over a hundred years old. There are ones for each of the various witch festivals, and for different kinds of ceremonies, like tonight. They are also colour coded. Each witch has their own natural talent and demands a particular style and colour spectrum," Tully explained.

"And I get my magic from my soul, so I get a black robe?" Dev asked.

"Yup. Blue for water, yellow for air, or sometimes purple, green or brown for earth, red and orange for fire...you get the idea. Black is for spirit."

"Delightful." Dev grimaced. He would have much preferred a more festive colour.

"Okay, strip."

"Naughty boy. I don't think Byron would appreciate us getting freaky in his spare bedroom."

"No, silly. Out of your clothes. You're naked under the robes."

"You subscribe to the skyclad theories? I've read about this before, but —"

"When you're doing spellwork, you don't want any interference with the energies. So, when we're participating in a magical ceremony as a group, we all wear our robes with nothing else. The robes are all made of cotton, silk, linen, or wool. Natural fibers. And nothing mixed either. The natural fiber makes for cleaner, more focused energy. Plus the stitching is spellwork adding more oomph." Tully waggled his eyebrows.

"Okay. I guess that makes sense." Dev proceeded to remove his clothing, folding each item and placing them in a nice pile on the bed. Tully followed suit.

Dev watched Tully; a gorgeous creature like him stripping wasn't something you passed on. His shoulder and chest muscles rippled and bulged as he pulled off his jeans. Dev's cock twitched, excited at the sights. He tried to study Tully with a nonchalant side glance, but Tully caught him and winked. "Pretty sure you don't want to walk out in front of the guys with a big boner. They would appreciate it but, perhaps, not on your first night?"

Dev glanced down at his thickening and lengthening shaft. "Dammit, sorry. You do this to me. You know that, right? This is basically your fault."

Tully laughed, faced Dev, and pointed to his own nether regions. "Like this is yours." Dev got a good eyeful of Tully's hard cock, which had a slight bend up, almost as if the stiff shaft stared Dev in the face.

"Okay, well this is distracting. It's not like we can do anything about it." Dev willed himself to think of puppies and horror movies and vacuuming. Anything to tame the beast and not think about doing erotic things with Tully.

"Here, throw this on." Tully pitched a long dark charcoal robe at Dev. The colour wasn't the inky jet Dev had been expecting. The material didn't shine, but the deep shade shifted, appearing dark as night, then dusky.

The edges were stitched in silver thread in an intricate pattern of curlicues and wisps. Tully gripped a steel-grey robe. As Dev flung out the large expanse of material, he noted where the hood and sleeves were, slipped an arm through one hole and brought his other arm through the other armhole. Flipping up the cowl-like hood, Dev realized the front panels only covered his shoulders. There wasn't enough material to cover his entire body.

Dev pulled the hood off, laying it across his shoulders. "Ah Tully? "

"Yes?"

"Really? This is nothing more than a cape with sleeves and a hood."

"Yeah, no barriers for the energies, right?"

"My junk is hanging out."

"That's kind of what skyclad means."

"You mean to tell me I'm going out into a crowd of men I barely know, and one I've known for several years, flaunting my wang for everyone to see?"

"Everyone else will be in the same state. No one cares." Tully shrugged. Nudity held no hesitations for him.

"I do." A knot of worry tightened in the pit of his stomach. Whatever chubbie he may have sported had long gone.

"Dev, come on. We're all big boys. We all have a penis; it's no big deal. When we work, we do it skyclad so nothing interferes between our bodies and the Shadow

Realm. We are open and available to receive and expend energy. The robes are all spelled to aid and assist, but they don't cover everything so we are open to the environment."

"Oh boy, I don't think I can do this."

"Dev?"

"Tully, remember at your house? You said to leave my clothes off when we ate pizza at the kitchen counter? This is not me. I don't run around naked."

"But you live with your family. You've been restricted. Being naked is natural. It's a body, and you have nothing to be embarrassed or concerned about. And, if I may, you have a beautiful body."

"I don't know..."

"Okay, look, I think I know the problem here. You're making this sexual. Right? Being naked is the same as having sex or being pleasured. That's not the case here. There is nothing sexual about this ritual. And this summer, we are going to the nude beach. A lot."

"Ugh," Dev grunted. "I have to?"

"No, no one would ever force you. Ever. But this is how we practice. And if you decide to wear your clothes, no one will judge you, but so you know, all the others will be wearing robes like this."

"Fuck me. I'm going to see Byron's schwang."

Tully threw his head back and laughed, loud. "It is a nice schwang too, but I'll tell you a secret so you're not gawking during the ritual...Addas is huge. I swear to all the gods he must pass out when his cock is erect."

Dev gaped, "Oh my god, I didn't need to know this."

"Seriously, if Byron is bottoming in the bedroom, he'd better be doing Kegels to keep everything tight."

Dev's mouth dropped open as he attempted to suppress a laugh, which didn't work. He bit his lip, sniggering at the image in his head of his favorite professor bent over.

"There, that's better." Tully pulled Dev in and gave him a quick kiss. "Remember, I'm here for you. No one is forcing you to do anything. You are safe, and no one is going to go for your junk, except Gus, and he won't *dare* do anything inappropriate during the ceremony. Maybe after."

"Not helping. But okay."

"You'll do great."

Tully pulled Dev in for a hug, skin meeting skin. Tully's muscled body radiated warmth and fuzziness and comfort. Dev's reluctances swept away with the comforting touch of Tully's skin and fur.

"Tully?"

"Yeah?"

"This isn't helping."

Tully pulled away and made a funny face at Dev, who glanced down toward his groin.

Tully laughed again, then swatted Dev's re-aroused penis.

"Quit showing off. I don't want anyone else to be enchanted by your masculine ways!"

"Not possible." Dev kissed Tully, a quick kiss on the lips. Anything else would have spelled disaster.

A knock on the door interrupted them.

"You guys ready?" an unfamiliar voice came from behind the closed door.

Tully glanced at Dev.

"Breathe. You'll be fine."

Dev inhaled deeply and let it out through pursed lips. Dev nodded.

"Yup, come on in Sparks." Tully gripped Dev's hand.

The door creaked open and Sparks walked in, wearing a robe like Tully and Dev, but his blinded Dev with pure white. Sparks's long locks had a slight wave to it, reminding Dev of Cam. Sparks's muscles competed with Tully's and certainly outdid Cam, despite his best friend's stocky appearance. Apparently harnessing Electricity equated to going to the gym on a daily basis.

*They must all have gym memberships. Maybe there's a witch gym. Damn.*

Spark's chest had a dusting of hair on the lower part of his enormous pecs. His tummy twitched as he moved, etched with tight muscle, and a thin line of light brown hair crept up from his groin to his belly button but didn't go any further. Dev peeked. Sparks's robe revealed his nakedness. Dev closed his eyes momentarily, trying to focus on something other than the generous amount of testosterone in the room. Like every other man in the coven, Sparks had model worthy looks.

"Dev, you look awesome! A black robe suits you." Sparks's boisterous voice matched his enthusiasm.

"Ah...thanks, Sparks." Dev's cheeks reddened. Here he was, pretty much naked in front of a stranger, and he conceded to Tully's statement. Nothing in this moment held any sexual tension. If anything, his self-consciousness came to the forefront. The ritual about to occur promised to be a real head trip. "I like your robe too."

Sparks pat Dev on the back, then wrapped his meaty arm around his shoulders. "Let's go, brother. I've not seen a Binding Ceremony yet, other than my own, and the experience is different when you're the center of attention. I'm excited for you."

"Ah...thanks again?"

"You'll be awesome," Sparks added. His excitement obvious.

Tully leaned over to Dev's ear. "We like Sparks. He's a good shit." Sparks turned, blushed, and winked at Tully.

So far, the Coven of the Night Grove had been warm, welcoming, and just about everything Dev had ever hoped for. He understood from his personal studies not everything about the Shadow Realm would be awesome, but up till now, the head-spinning journey had been nothing short of amazing. The events of the night replayed in his mind, and nothing had been remotely like what he had pictured.

But thinking about the coven's members, and despite hugs and acceptance from all of them, the undertones of what Dev expected from a witch coven were there.

Secrecy, selective membership, and power.

And maybe the guys were a little sexy too.

Sparks led Dev out the bedroom door with Tully following behind.

# Chapter Fourteen

CAM'S EYES POPPED open. He lifted himself up from the coolness of the floor, and as he did so, the shackles bit into his flesh. He barely registered the pain anymore, but looking at the wounds the iron had burnt into his ankles and wrists made him want to puke. The blackened flesh festered and reeked.

"Dev," he whispered, sensing his best friend in the entire world.

From across the room, Ev growled deep in his chest.

"Cool it, wolfman. I can feel Dev." The wings on Cam's back sputtered and flapped with excitement. Cam's brain tingled and energy hummed underneath the surface of his skin. "Oh man, this is like...this is like eating edibles. My whole body is tingling. What the hell is going on with me?"

"Faerie shit." Ev chuckled deep in his chest, and if Cam hadn't spent the last few days with him, he'd swear the rumble had been a growl. "Faerie magic. Evidently Byron and his boys didn't take all your mojo. You're starting to develop abilities all of the fae have. You're sensing other magical beings nearby, and if you've known Dev for a long time, you'll be attuned to his vibrations."

"Known him for a while? He's like my damn brother." Cam became excited. If there was a way, any way, to let Dev know he lay down here, chained and held hostage, tortured and humiliated, Dev would rescue him. Dev would save them both.

Cam's wings involuntarily beat, which raised Cam off the floor, but the shackles and chains kept him restrained. Cam stretched up toward the ceiling, pulling even with the bite of the claddings. He wiggled his fingers, desperate to feel more of his friend. His entire hand vibrated.

"Dev." Cam's eyes watered as a tear fell. "I can feel him!"

"You know, if you're already getting fae powers, that means –" Ev stopped speaking and whistled, "Damn, I've not seen that before."

"Seen what?"

"You're glowing."

Cam glimpsed down, arm still outstretched toward the ceiling, sensing his best friend in the whole wide world. The electrical tingles of *knowing* trickled down his arm and into his shoulder, dancing across his chest, making his heart pound faster. But the light he emanated took him by surprise.

Cascades of sparkles floated like snowflakes within the beaming bluish light of his aura, as his diaphanous wings kept him alight. He wanted so bad to get to Dev. The want transformed into a need. The glow intensified and lit up the room, chasing the shadows away into the far corners and illuminating everything.

Cam stretched toward the ceiling, certain if he extended a little closer he would touch Dev. Cam closed his eyes, losing himself in the sensation, letting the prickle run through the layers of his skin so the itchy sensation dominated. Dev became the only thing that mattered. Cam centered himself in the unmistakable sensation of Dev. He could see his best friend, standing in the middle of a room, surrounded by others.

"Dev!" Cam yelled out. "Argh!"

"Cam, easy man, you'll wear yourself out." Ev squinted. "And that light, think you can turn the brightness down a notch or two? You're hurting my eyes."

Cam glanced over toward Ev's voice. He'd not seen anything of Ev other than his glowing eyes. The shadows were deep and long in the dungeon.

For the first time, Cam laid his eyes on the monster called Ev.

And for a brief moment, the sight of the werewolf blacked out all memories of Dev.

Everton, the werewolf, was massive.

One witch who had been present on the first day Cam had been abducted nearly matched Ev, but not quite. The frame of the werewolf, the sheer breadth of his shoulders encompassed the entire cage.

The man was a monster.

Ev shielded his eyes with a thick hand, a paw so big the palm would have covered Cam's entire face. Muscles rippled all over Ev's body with every movement. Being caged, held captive, and kept weak had leaned him out. His naked body allowed Cam the lascivious opportunity to leer at him, all of his cut and shredded muscle covered in fur, not to mention the dangly bits, which weren't bits at all.

"Cam, please? My eyes. That hurts."

"Oh, yeah, ah…sorry." Cam forgot about Dev as he focused in on the shapeshifting beast. Huge, naked, bald on the top of his head, but furry in all the right places. "Damn," Cam whistled.

His wings slowed and beat less as Cam stared and studied Everton, he descended until his feet touched the hard cool floor. The glow subsided a bit, and as the light lessened, Ev dropped his mitt of a hand.

"So, Ev, tell me"—Cam had at one point been concerned about being eaten by the werewolf in the corner. Now Cam pictured himself being eaten by the werewolf, in a not-as-dinner manner and concluded the act might not be such a bad thing—"how much more of this faerie magic do you know? If I can sense Dev, can I communicate with him?" Cam gave Ev his best come-hither look, batting his long eyelashes, folding his wings together and tilting them to side, trying his best to look coy. Cocking an eyebrow and glancing at Ev, Cam flirted with the beast in the corner—the musclebound, furry werewolf—and regarded him in a whole different light.

Faerie light, as it were.

DEV WALKED INTO the living room, eyes closed being led by Sparks. His guts were writhing, nervous about the ceremony, more nervous about being exposed. Being nude was a bizarre sensation. To have even the cool still air of the room up against his bare skin down there sent some thrills of excitement to his groin. But he tried his best not to focus on it.

The room lay in silence, deathly silence. He kept his eyelids shut as he'd been instructed.

Sparks clasped his hand. "You can open your eyes now," he whispered.

Dev peeled open a slit of one eye to see Sparks. His new friend had led Dev into the center of the circle, in the middle of the pentagram drawn on the floor. The one he shouldn't have been able to see yet. Sparks positioned him so he faced Byron, then wrapped him in his burly arms and hugged him, skin pressing against skin. So much skin. And yet for another fleeting moment, Dev delighted in the feel of Sparks up against him. His body tighter and harder than Tully, not as furry, but the soft touch of groin against groin may have started a touch of electric arousal.

Dev opened his eyes, surprised by the sensuality of the hug, and peered deep into Sparks's eyes.

The gesture implied nothing but warmth and welcome from him.

Sparks released his embrace, grinned and winked, grabbed Dev's head, gave him a quick kiss on the forehead. He turned and walked to an empty spot within the circle. Obviously his appointed position.

Byron faced away from Dev.


BYRON'S HEART THUNDERED in his chest. His back hot, despite the fact his bright red robe like everyone else's didn't cover the front. He had rushed down to his study in order to grab a syringe of the fae juice and bounded back up the stairs. He wanted this ceremony to be extra special, and this juice would be just the thing. He grabbed the edges of his cloak emblazoned with black metallic thread, making flames all around the bottom of the robe, and fluttered the material, creating a bit of a breeze in an attempt to cool him down.

Arranging the tools on the altar, Byron placed his hand over the large syringe filled with effervescent dayglow green juice and the reason he dripped sweat. He closed his eyes and mumbled a quick prayer to the gods.

Faerie mojo liquid. The potency of this stuff had been documented in the coven's history books for eons. Tonight the coven needed an additional boost. They were still missing a member, and in order to sway Dev into joining an additional *show* might push him into becoming their newest brother. Besides, they didn't have an aurologist, and neither did any of the other male covens in the city. This enhancing boost to their magic would be a tantalizing display to ensure Dev would want to join his group of men.

Byron ended his personal prayer, turned and regarded the assembled group and raised his arms.

"Brothers of the Night Grove, we welcome young Dev into our arms. A revered guest and welcomed fledgling witch. Brothers, let us open the door to the Shadow Realm and bathe our new member of the community in the magic that surrounds us all. Let us introduce Dev to our world and make him one with the gods' powers.

"Dev, you stand in the center of a pentagram, surrounded by kin who welcome you with open arms.

"Let us call upon the elements and build our circle of power and protection. Let us also invite our gods to witness this induction to the shadows."

Byron acknowledged Eddie.

Eddie stepped forward, his long olive-coloured robe swirling out behind him. His long hair undulated outward as he spoke. "I call upon the element of Earth. Majestic, grounded, stoic, and turgid. Unrelenting in strength, stable and reliable, I ask you to consecrate our circle. Create us a wall of protection to keep out anything seeking to harm us."

Swirls of sand snaked their way across the floor, winding and twisting throughout the legs of the brethren, until there were dozens of writhing sand serpents looping about. "Power of Earth, come to our circle, lend us your power." The last sentence Eddie bellowed as he raised his hands in a quick movement to clap above his head. But when he made contact, the smack of his two hands reverberated energy akin to two boulders crashing together. At that moment, the sand serpents halted and formed a perfect ring on the outside of all the men gathered.

Eddie stepped into his designated place at the northern point of the circle. Gus took a step in. His robe flapped out behind him, the sleeves billowing; the air in the room became unsettled as gusts whipped through the small gathering, swirling everyone's robes.

"I call upon the element of Air. Unpredictable, invisible, ever-present, and life giving. Powerful with force but grants us the power of speech and language, I ask you to consecrate our circle. Lift our prayers and energies to the gods, through you, let us sing their praise."

A gentle swirl of air rotated around the group. The breeze warm and soothing, forceful enough to maintain a constant movement, rustled of all the robes. Hair became tussled and the candle flames on the altar danced. Gus returned to the outer circle.

Byron peered at Dev with squinted eyes. The wonder plastered on his face unmistakable as the guys brought forth the two elemental energies.

*Wait 'til he gets a load of this.*

Byron stepped forward, raising his arms outward, hands outstretched like claws, fingertips up.

With his teacher voice, Byron called upon the third element, "I call upon you, element of Fire. Illuminating, forging, stoker of passion and creativity. Your touch will burn, but your presence grants us warmth and security. I ask you to consecrate and cleanse this circle of any ill will. Be our inner light and let us shine in front of our gods."

Flames erupted from Byron's fingertips. The sting of their touch didn't bother Byron, not after this many years. As the blaze grew into pillars of fire they descended from Byron's hand until they touched the floor. Each column of flame moved outwards, dancing and flickering until they passed the ring of coven members and butted up against the wall of sand surrounding them. The fire heated the sand until they merged, and the hue of pale tawny grains turned molten, glowing hot red. The circle pulsated, embers flickering within the granules. The crackle and hiss of heat added to the *whoosh* of the gentle breeze still rotating around the coven.

Byron stepped back.

Marcus took one step in, his slicked dark-brown hair glistened with wetness as he crouched to the floor. Splaying out his arms he commanded the element in a hoarse whisper, "I call to you, element of Water. Fluid and deep, moon-bound and mysterious, you hold our deepest memories and are the vessel of our dreams. I ask you to consecrate this circle and wash our sacred space with the purity of your ancient, thirst-quenching vitality."

In front of Marcus, a pool of black liquid bubbled up from the floorboards. Ripples in the puddle ringed outwards and as each ring hit the edge, the size of the pool grew larger and larger, until the water dispersed as large as the circumference of the assembled group. As the liquid touched the heated edge of the sand wall, a hiss erupted and steam formed. The gentle breezes caught the vapour and distributed dew around the room. The air reminded Byron of his last tropical vacation. Humid.

Good thing the robes were fluttering still, else they would have sopped up moisture on the floor.

Marcus rejoined the others.

Byron turned toward the altar, bowed his head, and for a moment stood silent. All the other men also let their heads down, as the subtle rustlings of wind, water, fire and earth surrounded them.

Breaking the silence, Byron spoke, "Mother goddess, we bring to you a man, grown, yet a child to the realm. We humbly invite you in and ask you to sanctify this circle with your presence. Bless our initiate, consecrate him, and welcome him into the realm of hidden knowledge, the ways of old. Grant him his unique talent and power. Show him your youthful beauty, your motherly compassion, your sage knowledge. Take him as he is now, a human, and rebirth him into our world as a witch. Show him your world, the Realm of Shadows.

"Father god, lord of light, see your son. Acknowledge his kinship and fealty to you. Let him know your kindness, your wrath, your sex and wildness. Bestow upon him your blessing and watch over him all of his days. And when his time comes, gather him up, and bring him to the eternal grasslands and enchanted forests. Let all your creatures regard him as a brethren in the Realm of Shadows."

Byron lit two tall white candles. The candle sticks holding them were each carved differently. The goddess, represented with three faces—maiden, mother and crone were engraved onto a single feminine body with long flowing robes. The god's had massive antlers and a scruffy tail with furred legs. The feet were cloven hoofs.

In order to bind Dev to the realm, Byron needed to insert a shard of Shadow Onyx into his body. The first step and notably the most disturbing part of the ceremony of becoming a citizen of the realm. Picking up a long strand of thin silk thread and a box containing several shards of marbled shadow onyx, Byron walked over to Dev.

"Left or right handed?" Byron asked.

"Ah, right?" Dev shrugged. "Does it make a difference?"

"It does. Your dominant hand projects, your subordinate hand receives. We need you to receive and be bound into the Shadow Realm. Give me your left hand, palm up." Byron instructed.

Dev complied, lifting his left hand up, palm splayed.

Byron grasped his wrist to hold him steady, displayed the shards to Dev. "Pick one and only one. Your first instinct is always right."

Dev studied the stones. A stone caught his eye with one end pitch dark, but had several veins of grey running its entire length until the shard turned pure white at the other end.

Dev pointed to the stone he resonated with.

Byron plucked the chosen stone out, handed the box with the remaining shards over to Gus. Byron placed the stone shard so the crystal lay flat against Dev's forearm. With one hand, he began to wind the long red thread clockwise around Dev's arm, ensuring the gemstone stuck tight to Dev's skin.

"Dev, this stone is shadow onyx. This gem is the gateway to the Shadow Realm, symbolizing initiation and change. The stone, created of the earth within tumultuous gas cavities of a volcano will free you from your fears, for not everything in the Realm is good. The stone represents a balance between all that is good and evil. The black in the gem represents the pit, the void, and all that lurks there. The grey is the world between, where we walk. The white is the never ending sky and the hopes and dreams of all.

"The thread is made of the purest silk, left to bask in the glow of a new moon, and charged with the energy of the sun during the first day of the summer equinox. Stronger than any other fiber, silk is as tough as iron. Silk is also hypoallergenic, cleansing, and non-toxic. Between these two qualities, the thread will keep you bound to the Realm while protecting you from all sorts of poisons and diseases. After tonight, you are free from all ailments, except those of a magical nature.

"The colour of red represents passion, energy, and vitality. The thread is durable and long lasting. It is motivation.

"Now, don't move."

Byron released Dev's arm and studied his eyes. Dev nodded, accepting his instructions.

Byron returned to the altar and picked up a large wooden stick, carved with runes and symbols. The wand had several encrusted gems but ended in a pointy, tetragonal crystal.

Byron stood in front of Dev and instructed him, "This gem, this thread binds you to the Realm, and makes you forever a part of it."

He grabbed Dev's wrist, pointing the wand overtop of the thread and stone, and drew a single line.

Dev's flesh opened. Muscles, veins, tendons all moved to the side. Dev squirmed and hissed.

"No movement, Dev. Do not even inhale."

Dev's face scrunched together, and Byron noted the twitch of his jaws muscles clench tight as the stone sank into his arm and nestled itself within crook of the ulna and radius bones. The thread pulled tight and coiled itself until it ripped through Dev's flesh, sinking deeper and deeper until the thread wrapped around his arm bones, and the stone.

With a flip of his wrist, Byron waved the wand and the open wound stitched itself together.

"Like I said earlier, it's kind of like a tattoo."

Dev smirked, but the gesture was lopsided. If Byron didn't know any better, he'd have sworn the panicked gaze Dev displayed meant he'd second-guessed the entire ritual. Too late now.

Turning away from Dev, Byron went to the altar, put the wand in its place and grabbed the small cauldron containing the ash of many sticks of incense the coven had used over the years. As he walked up to Dev, who rubbed the arm now containing a shard of onyx embedded within it, Byron stuck his thumb into the ash and used the dust to mark Dev's forehead.

"Dev, this ash is a symbol of earth. May the element ground you and make you as strong and stable as a boulder."

Byron returned to the altar, placed the cauldron in its spot, and grabbed the incense burner. When he stood in front of Dev, he held out the burner. Thread-like trails of smoke wafted out and lingered in the air. Byron waved his hand through the smoke, grabbing the tails. They wriggled as if trying to escape. He pushed his hand and the smoke against Dev's bare chest. Byron rubbed Dev's chest, ensuring the smoke seeped into his skin.

"Dev, this smoke is a symbol of air. May the element grant you eloquence of speech and allow you to stay invisible as a creature of magic."

Byron returned to the altar, put the incense burner down, and grabbed the candle of the god. He brought the taper to Dev.

"This might sting a little, son." Byron gave Dev an evil leer and then winked. "Dev, this flame is the symbol of fire. May the element give you desire and lust, and burn in you for all time."

Byron cupped Dev's cock and balls in one hand, held them firm, as he tipped the candle, letting a single drop of wax fall which landed right at the base of the shaft on Dev's manhood.

Dev hissed, "You coulda warned a guy!" His eyes were wide and his jaw tightened again. Byron snickered at Dev's reaction and judged from his expression when the burn of the wax had subsided. The paraffin wouldn't harm or scald, and Byron smirked with pride that Dev stood stock still throughout another intense portion of the binding ceremony, absorbing the blessing of the element.

"Good boy." Byron winked but stood there staring at Dev.

"You've still got my junk in your hand," Dev whispered through gritted teeth.

"Relax Dev, have a little fun. You're becoming a witch." Byron gave Dev's parts a squeeze whispering, "Nice nuts." He released him, returned the candle, and grabbed a crystal pitcher holding the moonglow charged water. Every coven had ample supplies of it. The enhanced liquid was used in most potions and tinctures and held more potency than plain old water.

Byron poured a small amount on Dev's feet, watching as the rivulets ran over the skin, but instead of pooling onto the floor, Dev's skin absorbed the water like a sponge.

"And lastly, this splash is a symbol of water. May the element grant you access to the deepest mysteries, may this liquid cleanse away your human life and prepare your way into the Shadow Realm."

Byron went to the altar and returned the pitcher. He picked up the athame. The pointed ceremonial knife had been in the coven since its inception. The blade had been forged by a blacksmith and wrapped in thick leather, carved with runes and christened by numerous witches' blood throughout many years of ritual use.

The blade commanded attention. Its age reflected its power.

Byron took it, point down, and inserted the tip into a bronze chalice carved with various arcane symbols and encrusted with semi-precious jewels.

"We invite the gods to be with us now. Bless this sacred wine. Imbue it with your grace, your power, and your fortitude."

Byron placed the athame in a sheath strapped to his wrist, flung out his robe so the voluminous material billowed out, he grabbed the syringe full of the faerie's spinal fluid held the cup high for all to see. A collective "ooh" sounded from the men in the room. This liquid, rare and powerful, would grant them additional abilities for a brief time, but no one had any inclination of its contents. Save for the knights, Byron had never disclosed the source of the fluid, or how he'd obtained it.

Byron depressed the plunger into the vessel. As he replaced the needle on the altar, the last of the bright green, effervescent liquid lingered on top of the sacred wine. The mixture in the chalice bubbled then stilled.

Byron hoisted the spiked and blessed wine in his ornate goblet toward the ceiling, leaving his hand held high while he recited an ancient pagan prayer.

"We your brothers, welcome your rebirth,

As you leave the mundane world behind,

Come step into the Earth.

We your brothers, trustworthy and fair,

Invite you past the veil. You'll breathe for the first time,

Come step into the Air.

We your brothers, stoke your passion and desire,

Beckon you close, to feel hunger and ire,

Come, step into the Fire.

We your brothers, won't let you falter,

Your path now decided. Dark and dream-filled,

Come step into the Water."

Byron pulled the chalice to him, walked toward the first coven member to his left, and going clockwise offered the vessel to each witch. They held the cup in one hand as Byron took their other and stabbed them with athame. A single blood drop became a personal gift donated from every witch into the chalice. Eddie and Byron switched so the coven leader added his own blood drop. The goblet made its second round, and as it passed from each member to the next, all took a single sip.

After everyone had had their taste of the blessed wine, Byron walked to the center and gave the chalice to Dev.

"Drink." Byron commanded. "Receive the gods' blessing, and as the wine becomes part of you, so shall you be inducted into the Shadow Realm."

DEV GLANCED OVER at Tully.

Tully nodded and smiled.

"Well, here goes everything." Dev hoisted the chalice to his lips and drank the remnants, which turned out to be more than a swallow. As he emptied it, he began to feel hot. Sweat broke out in beads on his forehead and back.

Fire blossomed in his brain. His eyes went wide as he stumbled.

Tully, looking concerned, made a motion to grab and steady Dev, but Byron held out his hand to stop him.

Tully glanced at Byron. Dev panicked as he saw Tully's worried expression.

The air around Dev thickened, became almost viscous, and at the same time, the colours in the room intensified. The pentagram at his feet, barely visible before now glowed bright red. Orbs of light danced around the coven members and Dev sniffed hints of sulfur from Byron who grasped his arm and steadied him.

"It's a bit of an adjustment. You okay?"

"I...I think so," Dev stuttered. Byron's face swirled as Dev lost focus. He shook his head, trying to readjust the world.

Byron took the vessel from Dev, let go of him, and walked to place the chalice on the altar. He returned to Dev and grasped him by the shoulders. "Welcome, brother, to the Shadow Realm."

Dev beamed. His second wish had turned into reality, becoming a full-fledged citizen of the Shadow Realm.

But then the happy sensation vanished, replaced with a need to vomit.

He lurched forward. His stomach flipped, and for a moment, bile rose in his throat. Everything became a blur.

Dev's eyes rolled up as the vision of Byron's face swam in tilted directions.

Dev's legs gave out from under him.

He went down fast.

His face slammed up against Byron's chest as strong arms wrapped around him. His vision tunneled until everything went black.

# Chapter Fifteen

THE PERIPHERAL EDGES of Dev's vision plunged into darkness while everything else slammed out of focus, like a brick had been taken to the side of his head. Numb. Disoriented. Blurred. The ringing in his ears returned with a vengeance.

Steadying himself to stand upright was almost impossible.

In the distance, a distorted vision of a woman walked toward him. She had a seductive sway to her hips as one foot stepped in front of the other. A white cocktail dress clung tight to her curves, adorned in tiny white crystals which sparkled and threw beams of light into his eyes, which stung. Her long blonde hair had just the right amount of curl, and they bounced liked springs in time with her strut. Dev made out the *click-clack* of her high heels as she continued to approach.

She grabbed his chin, which forced Dev to stand up straighter, and turned his head one way, then the next.

She snapped her fingers in front of Dev's face a couple of times.

"Come now, boy, snap out of it. I don't want to slap you, but I will. I need you lucid for this." She glanced over her shoulder. "I swear, they interrupt me, beg me to make an appearance, and then they leave me with this. What am I supposed to do with him? It's always the same." She sighed.

As she leaned in close to Dev, he smelled an entire summer festival on her. Candy floss, popcorn, night-blooming jasmine, the thrill of a rollercoaster ride and sex. She peered into his eyes, harrumphed and let go of him.

*Holy mother of...these are the gods?* Dev's insides tightened with excitement and fear as the realization cemented itself into his brain.

"Bah, he's one of yours."

From behind Her, a dark shadow emerged, antlers filling the space. The rack of pointy tips stretched out toward the sky. They were gargantuan. But the horns were nothing in comparison with the massive presence of masculinity filling the space around him. Dev became small, insignificant, like he should shrink or bow. Instead, dropping to his knees and flailing before his deity was all he mustered.

"What are you going on about? Honestly, you need to be nicer. This one has just become one of ours. Can't you sense the newness?" a deep voice rumbled. The Horned One slid powerful arms under each of Dev's armpits and hoisted him up onto his feet. "There you go, young one. No need to fall all over yourself." He stepped back and pushed the woman forward. "Do your thing."

"Don't tell me what to do, and look at him. He won't remember any of this. You deal with him." She sneered at Him with a quick glance over her shoulder.

The Horned One shooed Her forward, gesturing toward Dev. "I will, but he still requires your blessing. He is one of mine, I can see that now, so I'll take care of him, but you still have to do your thing. So—"

"Ugh, fine." The goddess threw Her hands up in the air and twisted Her lips into a quizzical visage as She stood there contemplating the freshly inducted witch into Her Shadow Realm.

Dev's vision cleared as the woman approached again. She grasped each side of his head, pulled his head down as She kissed his forehead and then each cheek.

"There. All blessed. Happy?" She retorted loud enough so the The Horned One would hear.

She pulled away though, looking disgusted with Dev. Using one hand, She wiped her lips as if She had residue from Dev's skin on them. Still grasping Dev's head in Her hands, She tilted Her head as She squinted, Her eyes studying him.

The ringing in Dev's ears had stopped, and his vision cleared. A kiss on the forehead from this woman had righted his head.

"Finally. I do believe he's coming to. Look, the light in his eyes has returned. And...well, he tastes..." She smacked Her lips together a few times. "That's curious." She released Dev's head and put a finger to Her lips and the other hand She crossed over Her chest.

She tapped the digit against Her pout a few times.

"Something is not right. Maybe I was too abrupt. He's still definitely one of yours. None of my wiles will work on him. Yet, I can see he's clever. Big heart, with an imbalanced obligation for helping others. To the point where he neglects to care for himself. He could prove useful."

The Horned One stepped forward, His deep-brown eyes, darker than Dev's, stared intently. The Horned One peered into his soul and ripped his spirit apart. Dev lay bare before his god.

"I see other things in there too."

"Shush." She flicked Her hands at the god, insisting He back away. "I'm not done yet. You'll get your chance."

She took Dev's head into Her hands again. Her face reflected confusion and yet, curiosity as well. She leaned in close to him. Dev summoned up all his courage and strength to stand stock still and not move. After all, She was a goddess. This time, She licked him.

Dev stood mortified.

"Hmph." Her brows furrowed, and Her mouth pulled into a frown as She licked Her lips.

She leaned in again and tasted Dev a second time.

Her face tightened. "He's been tainted." She appeared shocked.

"What?" The Horned Man cocked an eyebrow and appeared worried. "As in poisoned?"

"No. No, not that. He's not..." She crinkled Her face, licking Dev a third time.

She dropped Her hands and as Her eyes widened. Her mouth went to the shape of an *O*. Then She scowled. Her face morphed from a summer beauty to a haggard winter crone. The wrinkles on Her face deepened. Her cheeks became sallow. The flesh turned grey. She pointed a crooked and withered finger at Dev.

"He's got magic that does not belong to him."

"What, in all the tall trees and never-ending grasslands are you going on about?"

"There's witch magic in there, but I sense a touch of the fae as well. That's not right."

"Maybe he's of mixed blood."

The goddess glared at the god, "Don't you think I would be able to see that just by looking at him? No... that's not it."

"I sense no wrong-doing on his behalf. His heart seems pure. You said so yourself. His purpose is to assist, not to steal. Have you deciphered this correctly?"

"You question me?"

"Always, as you question me."

"Hmph," She repeated. "I'm not sure I like this one. He has extra magic. He's powerful. You're going to have to watch him. Carefully. We can't have him skewing the balance." She turned and glared at The Horned One. "And we all know your male witches tend to screw things up marvellously."

"Says you. I think they're quite delightful."

"You would. Remember the time—"

"Please, none of your stories. They go on forever." She raised one eyebrow so high Dev considered the possibility a fight to end all fights would erupt. The Horned One ignored her. "What blessing shall you give him?"

The goddess pursed Her lips and shook Her head. "Honestly, you make me crazy."

The god leered with a wicked glint in His eye.

"You taunt me on purpose, don't you?"

"You're beautiful when you're annoyed."

"Flattery will get you nowhere, Old One."

"And yet, I know you love it. Crave it, actually." He nodded toward Her, a gesture that told Dev this would never end in a fight. The banter likened the two as an old married couple. "So, my queen, what blessings shall you give this strange one who has witch and fae abilities?"

The goddess sighed and gave in to The Horned One. "One where I can supervise him. I can't afford to have this one out of control." Her sage voice crackled as She spoke, but She moved forward again and as She did, time reversed. She outstretched a hand, older but not withered, placing her palm on Dev's bare chest. The Crone had disappeared, in Her place a motherly face, full of love and concern spoke. "You, child, are powerful yet you have no knowledge of your capabilities. You have been enhanced, yet this is magic not native to you. This is wilder, ancient, and complicated. You will have a difficult journey moving forward, and I will need to be a constant presence in your life to ensure you do not abuse this power.

"I think I shall make you my emissary. People will seek you out for direction and purpose. You will assist them. When they do, you'll come to me with their problems and I shall direct you in guiding them. Through this, I can ensure you are using your abilities as you should."

"Well done, Mother." The Horned One nodded in approval, His massive grizzled arms crossed across the great expanse of chest muscle. The sprawling antlers swayed as the god's head moved, and Dev became concerned He'd gore the woman with them.

"I'm done. He's yours now. I take my leave." She glanced at Dev one last time, raising one finger and wagging the digit at him. "Don't disappoint me, child. The consequences will be grave." With the gentleness and rustle of a summer breeze, She wafted away with the winds.

The Horned One stepped forward and put His arm around Dev's shoulder. "She's dramatic, that one." He chuckled. Dev became ramrod still. The Horned One had tucked him under his arm.

"Easy now, son, nothing to be afraid of." The Horned One gave him a squeeze.

"Well, I wasn't going to say anything." Dev stuttered still wrapping his head around the fact he had been in the presence of such greatness, but shut his mouth. He shouldn't have said anything, especially something so flippant.

"Ah!" The Horned One laughed. "There you are!" The beastly god pat Dev's shoulders and pulled him even closer, chortling to Himself as he did so. "Tell me, quietly, did you feign your unawareness? Were you toying with her?" He had a mischievous grin on His bearded, but kind face.

Dev glanced at the god, knowing he should tread ever so carefully. "Goddess no! The terror struck me dumb."

"Smart man. She is terrifying, I promise you. You would do well to not anger Her. But She is your mother, Dev. She means well, and sees much more than She ever lets on. And as much as She might foresee trouble within you, I can tell there are other things in your heart, Dev."

"You know my name?" A shiver ran down Dev's spine.

"I know the names of all my boys. My male witches are unique creations, rare beasts, beautiful, wild, and powerful, yet all of you have a tenderness that makes you vulnerable. The druids now, they are different. Both sexes are equally powerful, stoic, and hard. They are forces to be reckoned with. The animals which run free in the forest each have their strengths and weaknesses, and a purpose, but they are wild and their minds are not complicated. But there's always been something special about the witches that warms my gnarled old heart." The god leaned in closer and pulled Dev around so He looked at him eye to eye. "And I have a soft spot for you." The great god smiled. His face warm and welcoming, and Dev calmed while standing in the radiant light of The Horned One's grace. "There you go, son. That's better. Respect for us and reverence is appreciated, but I get anxious when my boys are scared. Please don't feel that way. The fear on your face ruins your good looks."

"But you are a god!" Dev whispered.

"That I am. But you know as a witch, there's a bit of us in you too, right? Even more than the humans. You might not know that yet, but as your powers mature, you'll feel me inside you. I promise." The god waggled an eyebrow at him, and Dev understood The Horned One was flirting with him. "You know She gets all the female witches, and there are plenty. But I get you, Dev, and that makes me happy." He leaned over and kissed Dev on the forehead. Dev smelled His musk, the scent of an old forest grove, the moss growing on trees. As The Horned One gazed into Dev's eyes, a captivating grin blossomed. "May I kiss your lips?"

Dev, nervous but excited, agreed.

The Horned One leaned forward. His bushy full beard and moustache surprised Dev in being much softer against his face than he anticipated. The god's lips were warm and tasted like the sweetest of spring water. And as the kiss lingered, a bouquet surrounded Dev as he smelled rushing rivers, leather hides, spice, and wet fur.

Dev's mind stilled for a moment. His muscles relaxed as a wave of safety and serenity washed over him within the arms of his horned god, this wild beast. Dev might have been a tiny bit afraid. He pulled away, glancing up into His eyes. Dev found the courage to ask, "You mentioned there were other qualities in me. What do you see, if I may?"

"You may." The Horned One sat, pulling Dev down with Him, and leaned against a tree trunk Dev hadn't noticed before. The god helped position Dev so he settled between the god's thick legs, which were so hairy Dev would have sworn they were furred. "I see the things she recognized in you. A big heart, a tenderness, a willingness to help. But I also see purpose. You are driven. Like a dog with a bone, or a wolf with its kill. Neither would relinquish their conquest unless it's unto their master. You are much like that. You have dedication and perseverance, and because of those qualities, I want to make you a protector, Dev."

Dev, stunned at the revelation, wasn't sure he agreed. "I don't feel like I fit your description. As a protector and an emissary, what am I supposed to do?"

The god chuckled again. "I think you will figure that out. But I shall give you one other talent as well. Often times being a protector comes at great risk and cost to personal safety. You have the magic within you to protect yourself, but protecting others often means helping them find a way to help themselves. Sometimes you will need to seek out answers. You will need to stalk down threats and expose them, and for all that, I shall also make you a tracker." The Horned One wrapped one giant-sized arm around Dev's chest and pulled Dev back so he lay against the god's body, which warmed him. There had never been a single other time in his life where he'd been at such ease. Which considering his company, a god, and The Horned One at that, he should have reacted differently. Scared, timid, unworthy. Terrified, perhaps? But Dev found no sense of those emotions.

"So I am to be an emissary, a protector, and a tracker."

"Yes, I think so. I believe that is a good combination."

"May I say one more thing?"

"Of course, Dev. What is on your mind?"

"Thank you."

The god pulled away as if the words affronted Him.

"I'm sorry, should I have not said that?" Dev asked.

"My son, you honour and bless this old one's heart." The Horned One snuggled in closer to Dev and continued, "It is not often these days our presence is accepted, acknowledged, let alone thanked. Your graciousness is appreciated, young one. I think as much as the goddess is hesitant about you, I like you." The god rolled over, grasping Dev in His massive arms, then grabbed his wrist. The same wrist where he had worn his kalava. Bright light shone out through the god's fingers that had wrapped around Dev's arm, and when He removed his hand, the red thread had been replaced by a woven, leather band, with a small silver charm hanging from it. The metallic talisman glinted in the sunlight. Dev had to squint, holding his arm up to his face to determine his gift mimicked the shape of The Horned One's antlers. Dev gazed at the god's face, only to see The Horned One radiating love and light toward him. However, the comfort Dev found in the god's gaze morphed into something else. The god rolled taking Dev with Him. In a short tumble, Dev lay pinned to the ground. "I like you very much, indeed."

The Lord of the Forest lay atop him, yet His massive size didn't crush him, instead Dev became immersed in musk, muscle, and fur. They were lying in tall grass, enjoying the crystal blue sky above. The summer air ghosted warm breezes across Dev's skin and the perfume of prairie flowers was adrift.

The Horned One beamed with happiness at Dev.

In His eyes, Dev stared at the rawness of lust and wildness. The Beast lifted Dev's legs and put them over His shoulders.

Dev, still wearing the ceremonial robe, surprisingly found he had been exposed this entire time, and more so, it gallantly displayed his arousal. The Horned One waggled His furry eyebrows upon seeing Dev, and then motioned to His groin which also stood engorged. Dev's eyes went wide looking at the size of the god's erect cock. He remained intact, hooded and natural, and Dev spied the tip peeking out from the foreskin, oozing precum. His balls were heavy and swung.

Dev wanted to touch Him, explore the size and girth which was larger than anything he'd ever seen before.

He checked himself. He gaped at a god's erect penis, and as much as he didn't want to, he pulled his eyes away from the beautifulness of god and peered into loving eyes.

The Horned One chortled.

"I see your desire, young witch. Please me as you wish."

Dev reached between the god's legs, a bit of a feat as his legs were still slung over the god's shoulders. But he let one leg slide down The Horned One's arm, which gave him access to touch everything he wanted.

And the shaft was firm, and thick, pulsating with divine passion. Pulling down on the god's cock, the velvety skin followed Dev's motion, exposing a massive head. Precum ran down, over the head and shaft, coating the member, and Dev's hand. The Horned One trembled as Dev stroked the length of engorged flesh. His penis was so thick Dev's grip lacked the ability to wrap his entire hand around it.

"You know how to make an old goat happy." The Horned One grasped Dev's cock in his massive hand and ensured Dev's received pleasure as well.

Dev let his hand slip from the god's shaft and cupped His enormous balls, feeling the fuzziness of them and the heft.

"I want to bestow your gifts to you. Are you ready?"

Dev wasn't sure what the god meant, but with a jerk and a shrug, the god repositioned Dev so his leg perched on top of the god's shoulders again, and the giant mushroom head, which had leaked so much the glans glistened, pressed up against Dev's backside.

The monster member would never fit. But the god pressed forward. Dev opened up for The Horned One as his fists grasped clumps of grass and moss on each side, expecting pain. His stomach twitched in excitement and fear.

But instead, Dev relaxed in the sensation of being filled with pleasure, almost to the point of brimming over. The horned god began to pull out and push in again. The massive head brushed up against Dev's prostate. The sensation stoked pleasure so great Dev would have never imagined getting fucked would be so heavenly. Losing himself in the rising swell of desire, Dev arched his spine, granting The Horned One all the access the god would need.

"Enjoy, little one. Do not be afraid. How else did you expect your god to bestow your blessing?" The beast's voice rumbled.

Dev let go of the earth he'd gripped in fear and, instead, ran his hands over the furry muscular chest and thumbed the hard nubs of the god's nipples.

And with no pain, and endless pleasure, Dev rocked in time with The Horned One as He continued to slide in and out of him, swept up in powerful arms and held close. The scratchy beard sent tingles of pleasure across the skin where the god nuzzled his neck, and giving into the heathen sensations, Dev let go of everything and floated with the intense sensations of being enveloped by his god.

He wrapped one arm around the thick shoulders, and with his other hand, grabbed one of the god's worn and rough horns and held on, for dear life.

The Horned One continued to thrust into Dev, as Dev rode the waves of delight and matched the god's movements with his own pushes. The Horned One pulled up so He stared eye to eye with his newly consecrated witch. His eyes turned red, His teeth became the fangs of a wolf, and His thrusting became wilder. Dev orgasmed without ever having touched himself, ribbons of white cream coating his chest and stomach. Over and over he shot, and Dev didn't think his orgasm would ever end as he shook and shuddered in utter pleasure.

In response, The Horned One howled as He slammed into Dev indicating the god's eruption inside him. The god, still buried deep within Dev when He shook off the last throes of pleasure, focused in on Dev and warned, "Be sure, little one, you never disappoint either of us. There would be hell to pay."

And with that, there were no more words. In the still of the forest, Dev found himself alone. Small birds chirped and hopped from one branch to another above his head. A rabbit chewed in a patch of clover while a fox slinked through the tree trunks deeper in the forest.

Dev closed his eyes and snuggled into the memory of being held tight in the arms of his god, but the red eyes remained fast in his mind as he fell asleep.

# Chapter Sixteen

TULLY RUSHED OVER to Dev, scooped him up into his arms and away from Byron.

"Dev, are you okay? Dev?" Tully shook him.

Dev's eyebrows lifted, and Tully got a sliver of a glimpse of his eyes.

"I think he's coming 'round," Sparks reported from behind Tully. He had laid a gentle hand on Tully's shoulder.

Dev murmured something incoherent.

"I'll go get him something to drink." Addas disappeared into the kitchen.

"Dev, wake up." Tully shook him again.

Dev grumbled and moaned, peeling his eyelids open. Tully watched Dev's pupils enlarge and shrink.

"Hey, handsome," Tully whispered.

Dev blinked, several times, then shifted to look up into Tully's eyes.

"Hey, yourself."

"You okay? You had us all a little scared."

"Why?" Dev's voice rumbled as if gravel had been shoved in his throat.

"Because people don't pass out from being bound to the Shadow Realm. That's why."

"I had the most amazing dream." Dev made a motion to sit up. So Tully assisted him.

Dev leaned forward and put his head in his hands, rubbing his face and shaking his head.

"Here." Addas reappeared with a tall glass of water dripping from condensation. "It's ice cold, which will help, and I want you to eat this." Addas handed Dev half a sandwich and the water.

"Okay." Dev chugged back a good third of the water and took a couple of bites of the sandwich.

The entire coven had circled in tighter, concerned about their new Shadow Realm brother. Byron had crouched in front of Dev, and as Dev finished off the food and gulped the last of the water, he took the empty glass from Dev and handed the vessel to Addas.

"So, feeling better?" Byron asked.

"I think so."

"We've broken rules. Once the circle is cast, no one leaves the sacred space until we dissolve the elements and clear the area. But that all goes out the window when one of us attempts a nose dive in the middle of a ritual. You up for completing this? Or would you like to take the rest of the night off?" Byron placed a hand on Dev's thigh.

Dev grinned and shook his head. "No, let's finish. I've come this far. Not sure what happened, but my body burned from the inside, and the air around me got way too thick. Everything went black. Then I had the craziest dream."

"Well okay, let's finish? Maybe you can come visit me tomorrow and we'll talk about the dream." Byron gave him a wink, looked up at everyone, and gave a curt nod.

"I'll bring him by." Tully puffed his chest out.

Dev stared at Tully and bobbed his head once in acknowledgement.

The men reassembled themselves to their appointed positions around the circle.

Tully waited in anticipation as Byron, Eddie, Marcus, and Gus, raised their hands in unison, all standing behind everyone else, and as they did, the energy in the room shifted returning the magical buzz. They reinforced the protective circle.

This would always be Tully's safe and calm space. He glanced over at Dev, whose eyes were still glassy, but the grin on his face as he glanced over his shoulder at him created waves of happiness and exhilaration deep within his chest. He couldn't help but smile back.

BYRON RESUMED THE ceremony, although he had to admit, Dev passing out concerned him. No one he had ever bound had lost consciousness. Got tipsy, stumbled, even had to take a seat to adjust to the transition, sure.

But passing out? Never. And although Byron had wanted to give Dev a real magic show, the rest of the Coven would have had his hide if something bad happened to Dev. Fireworks and spectacle would have to wait for another day.

"Only one last thing to do," he boomed with his teacher voice. "I ask for any volunteers to step forward and become Dev's blood brother. The companion who will share in his footsteps, will guide and instruct, befriend and share knowledge so our new brother never missteps or feels lost along the shrouded path. Who will walk with Dev in the Shadows?"

Tully stepped forward, and Byron nodded his approval.

But Sparks stepped forward too, and as he did, he glanced at both Tully and Dev, as if asking for permission. Tully grabbed one of his shoulders, giving his traps a squeeze. Dev, still glassy-eyed, grinned from ear to ear.

"It's not unusual to have two blood brothers. Dev, what say you? Do you accept the company of these two men who will aid you in your journey?"

"Ah, sure." Byron would have to tell Dev the significance of this part of the ceremony. It didn't appear to Byron that Dev understood the role these two would play. He'd have to explain how important Sparks and Tully would be for him at a later time.

Byron waved toward Gus and Eddie, who both came forward to the altar, each grabbing a long length of rope.

Byron grabbed the athame and walked toward the three men. Tully and Sparks held their arms out.

"Dev, I want you to hold out your palms next to each of your brothers." Dev did as instructed.

Byron made quick cuts in the center of each palm that was presented to him. Gus took Dev's right hand and placed his hand in Spark's left and bound the two of them together. Eddie did the same with Tully and Dev's left hand.

Byron held each of the bound hands and spoke.

"What is your blood, is now their blood. What is their knowledge, is now your knowledge. You are tied to one another, as they are tied to you. Your brothers will never forsake you, they will uplift you, and carry you, as you will do for them." Byron studied both Tully and Sparks. "Do you accept this responsibility and promise to uphold your brother at all costs, fearing the wrath of the gods should you fail?"

In unison, they said, "We do."

"Dev, can you place your trust and faith in these two men?"

"I can." Dev glanced at both of them, one after the other.

Byron called forth his fire and set the ropes binding the three alight. Flames burst and Byron contained a grin as Dev pulled away expecting to be burnt. Tully and Sparks held him fast as the combustion engulfed their fists. Within seconds, all that remained of the ceremonial ropes were there disintegrated remnants. Blackened ash rained down like snowflakes. No burnt skin, no blisters, just fists clasped together covered in the charred remains of the rope.

"So be it," Byron stated.

Byron turned toward the altar as the gathered men cheered.

Tully wrapped one arm around Dev's waist, and Sparks placed his arm across Dev's shoulders.

Byron placed his hands on the altar, thanking the gods, and beamed.

Other than Dev's blackout, this couldn't have gone any better.


THE COVEN CIRCLE dissolved after Dev gained two new brothers. His whole life he'd always been the eldest sibling at home, and as much as he loved Amna and Bhanu, he'd always wanted a brother. Someone to confide in. And now he had two. Although he hoped Tully had other intentions than being just a witch brother. In fact, Dev wanted to continue doing things with Tully that would be deemed distinctly unbrotherly. Glancing around the room, he spied Sparks, as he talked to some of the other Coven members. He shook his head, sending his long hair rippling. The man was stunning. Dev couldn't say why Sparks had stepped up as well, but the more the merrier, and Dev would probably need a lot of guidance as he stepped through the Shadow Realm. The idea of having two brothers excited Dev, and if truths were being told,

Sparks ignited a little more excitement than just brotherhood for Dev.

"Dude, are you okay?" Tully asked.

As Dev focused on the voice and came out of his mire, he glanced at Tully. Lights swam in front of Dev's eyes, orbs of colour bobbed and weaved around Tully's head. Dev tried to swoosh them away.

"Truthfully? I don't know. I'm seeing shit."

"Oh, that's sort of normal for a while after." Tully grabbed his hand and squeezed. "Little blobs of colour? Right?" His face appeared apologetic.

"Why didn't you people tell me some of this shit?" Dev giggled.

"It's supposed to be your own personal journey, Dev." Byron spoke from behind him. Dev did take note everyone stood around socializing still in their robes, even though the ceremony had ended. Several of the guys were drinking and chatting, a few had plates of food. This nudity thing blew his mind, and it would take Dev a while to get used to it. "Everyone's experience is different, and if we tell you what to expect, you'd go into the whole thing with expectations. Did *they* come see you?"

"They? They who?" Dev asked.

"The gods. When you blacked out. You said you had a dream. Most people don't lose consciousness, but almost everyone has at least some vision of *them*." Byron stated matter of factly.

"Oh. Them. Ah," Dev strained to remember his dream, which like all dreams eluded his memory and appeared as fragmented and broken short clips of images that made no sense. "I think so. Yes?"

"Do you remember what they said? Or would you prefer to talk about your god encounter tomorrow?" Byron inquired with a slight lilt in his voice.

Dev turned around to see Tully better, but instead, he caught sight of Byron.

Where Tully had spheres of brightly coloured light floating around him, which uplifted Dev's happy feelings being cheerful and fun, Dev studied Byron, wrapped in swirls of blackish-blue and muddy red. Dev had no idea what those colours or shapes meant, but the vision didn't *feel* right. Something about those colors left Dev with a grimy sensation on his skin.

Dev pulled his gaze off of Byron and focused on Tully, "I can't remember, or, at least, what I do remember doesn't make any sense."

"That's okay. Over time snippets will come and you can come talk to me when they do." Tully winked.

Byron came around and stood in front of Dev, put a hand on his shoulder and patted him a few times. "I'm so proud of you. You did so well. When you're ready to go, I'll have Tully take you home, but would you come see me tomorrow? I want to set you up with some books and give you your first magical task. It'll also give us an opportunity to talk more if you want."

"See, I told you. Exams are next." Tully gave Dev a knowing glance.

"Stop it. You'll scare him off." Byron chuckled. "But he's not wrong. There will be tests."

Dev stood hypnotized as the shimmers of muddy red and dark blue snaked around Byron. The undulating ribbons of smoky colours put Dev off and made him feel icky. Dev half grinned and gave Byron a short bow. Byron accepted with a pat on his shoulder, then walked away to go join the clutch of men who had gathered near the kitchen.

Dev stood close with Tully. After a few moments of silence, watching everyone else in the room, he leaned in to Tully's ear and whispered, "Can you take me home? I think I need some time to think."

"Of course! You're sure you're okay?"

"Yes, definitely. I think? Just, you know, the whole ritual thing turned into a bit of a night."

Tully pulled Dev in for a hug, which Dev accepted. Dev closed his eyes and let go of all the excitement of the evening, feeling safe within Tully's strong arms.

"It's okay, Dev." Tully nuzzled Dev's neck. "Let me go talk to Byron, and then we'll go home." Tully stiffened a little after saying *home*, He grabbed Dev's hand, stared into Dev's deep brown eyes, and asked, "Which home?"

Dev grinned.

"Take me to my shiny new apartment, and stay with me?"

"That's a date."

AFTER TULLY AND Dev had bid their farewells, changed into their street clothes, and walked outside, Dev let out a huge sigh.

Tully glanced over at Dev and his expectations of snuggling together in Dev's studio apartment disappeared into a puff as Dev screwed half his face up into a grimace. "Dev, are you sure you're okay?"

"Yeah?"

"That's not encouraging," Tully chuckled. "Did something bad happen?"

"I don't know if I'd say bad." Dev tried to put the pieces together as Tully opened the car door for him. "I'm not sure what to make out of all of it."

Tully got into his side of the car, reached across the console, and grabbed Dev's hand. He gave Dev's sweaty palm a gentle squeeze, but kept his hand attached as he started the car and put the vehicle into drive. "Don't worry, we can chat about anything that happened tonight, but only if you want. We can stay up all night if needed."

"Thanks, Tully."

Tully smirked mischievously in an attempt to lighten the mood. "Wanna spend the night naked?"

Dev let out a burst of a laugh as he turned to stare at Tully, a smile from ear to ear. "You're horrible and incorrigible. I spent the entire night naked around a bunch of strangers. I think my naked quota is good."

"You know I was joking, right?"

Dev tilted his head and cocked an eyebrow. "Are you rescinding your invitation of naked cuddles?"

"Ah, well, no, but..." Tully's gaze darted around in confusion; understanding he had a propensity for being lewd at times, Tully wondered if maybe he'd gone too far with the whole naked thing.

Dev's grip on Tully's hand tightened. "I have a lot of questions, and I sort of wish all these floating colours would fuck off. Damn it's distracting, and why does everything feel ten times more intense than before the ritual tonight? Everything is so amplified. You know?"

"I know. You'll get used to it."

"I'm not sure I want to get used to it. It's amazing, but disconcerting too. But if everything feels this over-the-top, I can't imagine what you're going to feel like while we knoodle."

"Knoodle? Well now, there's a term I haven't heard in forever."

"I could use some cuddling wrapped up in big strong arms. You know anyone like that?" Dev glanced to the side at Tully.

"I might. We can call him when we get to your place." Tully mimicked Dev's cocky attitude, but with a grin, and winked.

"Perfect." Dev rolled his eyes. "And thank you. Thanks for being there, thanks for stepping forward and volunteering to be my blood brother, and thanks for coming over to me that night at the coffee shop. So much has happened in the space of a couple of days. So thanks for...damn..." Dev couldn't capture his gratitude. "Just thanks."

Dev glanced out the window, hiding his face from Tully, who took his eyes off the road for a second as he grabbed Dev's chin and turned him to stare into his eyes. He brought Dev's hand up to his lips and gave his fingers a gentle kiss.

The rest of the short drive lay in silence, but Dev never let go of Tully, and Tully rubbed his thumb against the back of Dev's hand the entire way home.

# Chapter Seventeen

IT MIGHT HAVE been deep into the night, time stood still when you couldn't see the sun, and now that Cam had sensed Dev so near, his scheming kicked into high gear. Everton had spilled the magic beans, so to speak, telling him all about fae powers. Abilities he now possessed.

Granted, he had no idea how to use them or how to make any of his abilities work, but he would if it killed him. He'd do his damndest to figure this fae magic shit out. He had to get the hell out of here. Knowing Dev had been so close and Cam being stuck in his current predicament solidified the void of his best friend not being by his side. This whole captivity thing fueled violent fantasies against the witches who had captured him.

*Fury hath no wrath like a fag scorned.*

"Watch out bitches..." Cam spat. He had screamed at the top of his lungs all while Dev had been so close, which only earned him snarls and growls from Everton. Ev's reaction only ramped up Cam's determination, but in the end, Cam hadn't gotten anywhere with his temper tantrum. With a scratchy throat and nothing but a hoarse voice left, Cam concluded he couldn't rely on his ever dependable best friend, Dev. Not this time. As much as Cam wanted to be the damsel in distress, he had to get himself out of this shit pile of trouble.

The shackles around his wrists and ankles had burned so deep the bone had become visible. The pain had been constant and intense, but now, he barely acknowledged the sensation. He had grown numb to the burning. Cam would break free of his prison, and if a few witches got hurt along the way, so be it.

One thought kept swirling around Cam's brain. Why had Dev been in this building, socializing with the very people who held him hostage? Cam needed to see Dev. There were conversations to be had, questions to be asked. Cam swam in guilt thinking about the years of ribbing over Dev's infatuation with magic and stuff. How could he have known this shit was real? Apparently, Dev had.

But getting out of this prison eclipsed everything. Well that and food. No one had fed him yet while imprisoned and Cam's tummy rumbled and growled.

"So, let me see if I have this right. The upper tiers of the fae are akin to something like royalty?" Cam asked.

"They are referred to as royalty, so, yes."

"And you think I'm royalty?"

"Absolutely."

Cam huffed, "Why? What the hell makes me so special?"

"The horns."

"Really?" Cam tried to run his hand over his horn, but the chains restricted his movement. The best he could do was to tilt his head toward his hand and touch the tip of one of his newly formed horns. They were rough but solid, and even though the base had at one point hurt where the horns broke through his skin, now the rough bone had a sensual quality to them. In fact, the bone didn't seem like an intrusion or an imposition, despite how clunky they were. The giant curled horns lay against his skull as if they had been there throughout Cam's life. Truth be told, he'd grown fond of them.

"Yes. Only the most high-ranking males have horns. You realize you'll be expected to mate and produce children?"

"Sorry, say what now?"

"Only royalty can breed. So, with the horns," Ev pointed in Cam's general direction, "that means you."

"Hell no. With a girl fae? No, uh-uh. Not gonna happen. I'm a gold-star gay. We're keeping the status, thank you."

"You're a what?"

"Never mind. Just no. Breeding is never going to happen. I don't do girls." To hell with expectations, he'd been bucking them his entire life, and he had no desire to change his ways to please anyone now. He glared at Ev, but he couldn't stay mad at the man.

But after staring for more than a few seconds, Cam became flustered. The werewolf, lean, scarred, muscled, and furry met all the qualities Cam gave to an extreme few men. Everton earned Cam's DILF status. Despite his current situation, and the pain of the iron around his extremities, Cam changed tactics and raised his eyebrows suggestively at Everton. "Now, if you want to talk about doing big furry werewolves, you know, I could be convinced."

Everton snarled at the change in Cam's demeanor. Fangs extended and protruded past his upper lip.

"See, now you do shit like that and it's getting me horny. Stop it."

"You're utterly bizarre." The fangs retracted, but Ev smirked at Cam. "But I like a little crazy. So you... boys?" Ev inquired.

"No, not boys. Men. Big, musclebound, hairy, bearded men. Like you. You'll do."

"Really?" Ev licked his lips.

"You just wait. I'm going to get us out of here. Either Dev will come find us and rescue us, or I'm going to master this fae magic crap and bust us out. So, invisibility, luck, talking to animals—which makes sense now," Cam cocked an eyebrow toward Ev and gave him an attitudinal, know-it-all grin.

"I'm not an animal," Ev snarled.

"Yeah, sure, sure. What else am I missing?"

"Agility, resistance to most poisons, somnolence, charm, illumination." Ev counted on his fingers, then shook his head. "There's a lot."

"What's the middle one?"

"What middle one?"

"You said som...sonnel...what the hell was that word?" Cam furrowed his brows.

"Somnolence? Sleep spell. If you cast the spell correctly the magic will put people to sleep."

"Well, now, why didn't you mention that before? I do believe you've figured out our ticket out of here!" Cam had an idea.

"I only know of one fae who can pull off magic so powerful, and she outranks even you."

"Again, with the rank thing."

Everton pursed his lips. Cam had figured out this happened when Ev fell into deep thought. Not much passed by Cam when Ev spoke. The monster of a man captured his attention. Ev let his expressions play out across his face. Poker would never be a good game for him to play.

Ev nodded while raising a finger and shaking it at Cam. "But maybe you could do it? Magic abilities depend on the type of fae. Some are better at illusions, while others are nothing more than tricksters. You might as well give the fae magic a go until we know what you can and can't do."

"What do you mean?"

"How can you be royalty fae and be so damn dumb?"

"Kind of thrust into the position, here." Cam's wings flapped as he threw his hands out to his side, and sneered at Ev, "Not like I studied up first. Geez." Cam gave Ev a dirty look.

"I only witnessed the sleep thing once. Aine held her hand up and blew dust out and into her enemies face. The human went down in seconds. Total coma. I'll tell you whatever I know, but you need another fae to show you. But if you don't figure out how to harness at least one of those abilities, we're never getting out of here."

"Okay, okay. Shush. Let me think." Cam's stare gazed up toward the ceiling as he scrunched his lips together.

"Does it hurt when you think? It looks like it hurts," Ev asked.

"Shut up, asshole. Honestly, if you weren't so cute..." Cam's wings fluttered at the notion of running his hands over Ev's muscular chest. His tail dashed back and forth.

"All right, I'll tell you what. You figure out how to become invisible. If you can pull it off, we should be able to trick these damn witches and get us both the hell out of here. You break us out of here and I'll give you a night you won't forget." Ev leered at Cam.

Cam canted his head to one side. "You'd let me –"

"If a heavy petting session gets us out of here, oh yeah. But no glamour, you gotta bring the horns."

"You kinky wolf." Cam blinked a few times, almost at a loss for words. Almost. "My gaydar is never off, and I had no clue you were into guys. Must be the monster thing that's screwing with the spidey senses."

"I wouldn't box me in to a single category."

"Really?" This confession stopped Cam for a moment. He tilted his head and raised an eyebrow. "Whatever makes you happy beast-man. Just as long as I get my five minutes in heaven. Scratch that. I want a couple of hours." Cam squinted at Ev, attempting to discern if the man would make good on his promise. A werewolf bang might rattle off the icky residue his current situation had created. The prospect of Cam getting his rocks off with the werewolf created enough sexual tension to make him figure this magic shit out. Well, sex with a werewolf and freedom. And food. Okay, and question time with Dev. But if truth be told, his hormones were winning and the idea of a night of fun with the hairy beast in the corner won out over all the other motivators for busting free.

"Okay, so, magic...how would one do magic?" Cam would have been pacing if the claddings were looser and weren't causing his flesh to sear.

Cam remembered all the times he'd sat in Dev's room watching him play with his Tarot cards or his bag of bones or casting some spell. He always sat cross-legged on the floor, still with his eyes closed. So Cam figured he should do the same.

He positioned himself so the iron cuffs were somewhat comfortable—which they never were—and sat like Dev, closed his eyes, and became statuesque.

And he waited.

And waited.

"What the hell are you doing?" Ev barked.

"Shhhh, I'm doing magic."

"Oh my god, I'm going to die in here." Ev slunk down into a corner of his cell. "You want to turn down your light show? I'd like to get some sleep."

"You're not going to die in here. I'm going to figure this out."

"Right."

"You know, if you quit being such a negative asshole, good things might happen once in a while."

"Nothing good ever comes from having witches around."

"What the hell did they do, anyway? The hate is pouring off you. Why the blood feud?" Cam stood up and focused in on Ev, who had lain down on the cot in his cell. At least Ev had a cot. Cam didn't, and he'd already given up on the *act like Dev* thing to do magic.

"Well, there you go. There's another one of your fae abilities. Reading emotions. god, you know nothing!"

"No, I don't! If this was Instagram I would have posted a selfie and tagged it 'woke up like this'. Which isn't untrue, but...ugh, forget it." Cam's frustration neared explosion status.

"Calm down. Okay, history lesson time." Ev sat, rubbing his eyes as he balanced on the edge of his cot, which he'd rammed up against one end of the cell, close to the bars. Cam had noticed Ev never touched the bars on his cage. "Witches are supposed to be guardians to the ley lines."

"What the fuck is ley line?" This magical crap made his head spin. Too complicated.

"They're the conduits of magical energy and they crisscross all over the world. There's a power center close to here, which means there's more magical energy around these parts. As you move away from the center, the energy dissipates, but as long as there's at least one line there's magic trickling out. For as long as anyone can remember, the witches in this area have lay claim to the power center and have used the ley line for themselves. They were sworn to help balance the magic and ensure all of the supernaturals in the area had equal access to it, but also to keep the humans safely ignorant. Instead, the Coven of the Night Grove have overpowered all the groups, funneled the magical energy to themselves, and captured our kind to drain their captive's magic to use for their own purposes. It's what has kept them in power for a long time." Ev let out a heavy sigh.

"So what happens when you drain the power out of these beings?" Cam asked, feeling uneasy.

"How did you feel as they sucked the spinal fluid out of you?"

"Like I was going to die."

"Exactly."

"Bastards." Cam's tail twitched on the damp cement. The residual sting of the needle being stabbed into his spine along with the uncomfortable pressure when Byron pulled the plunger, sucking the fluid out of him, remained etched into his brain, and most likely his body too. He had blacked out several times during the process. How many other fae had he done this to? From deep within, his rage brewed, and his ire climaxed. Cam turned the anger into a tingling sensation, like a thousand bubbles were making his blood boil. His tail lashed from side to side and his eyes narrowed. He got lost in the emotions of anger, hate, and vengeance. Cam's teeth sharpened into points as he sneered, exposing a row of vicious teeth.

The light around him intensified, but the rest of the room darkened, forewarning doom.

Cam lost himself in his rage storm until Ev's voice boomed out from the other side of the room.

"Ah, Cam, I think you figured your fae magic shit out."

TULLY AND DEV lay exhausted, sweaty, and spent on Dev's big king-sized bed in his new apartment. The sheets were tangled around them. The big curtain hanging from the ceiling to floor hadn't been drawn, so the massive circular window beamed bright with the moon casting its white light into the room.

Dev let his arm flop down onto the bedspread, his hand still clutching his cell.

"Nothing?" Tully asked.

"Not a thing. Just went to voice mail. Again. This is so not like him." Dev had tried calling Cam multiple times over the course of last night and this morning. Cam hadn't picked up.

"Can we go over there later? Just check on him? He's probably mad at me for not responding to him..."

"Sure thing."

Dev rolled over, closer to Tully, and ran his hand over Tully's massive hairy chest. He stopped when his fingers discovered wet spot. He leaned in and licked the fur clean.

"If you keep tonguing me, we'll have to go again." Tully kissed the top of Dev's head.

"Gee, that would be terrible," Dev chuckled. "Can I ask you something?" Dev snuggled in close to Tully.

"Of course."

"What happened when the gods showed up during your binding?"

"Well...not much. I remember some blurry visions and a feeling like they were inspecting a prize bull, but I do remember the whispers in my ear of what my blessings were." Tully wrapped his arm around Dev, stroking the top of his shoulder once he had Dev nestled into his side.

"That's it?"

"Yup. Okay, so other than the fantastic sex we just had, you've been...what's the word?" Tully pondered for a second, raising his eyebrows. "Pensive. I'm going to go with pensive. If smoke poured out of people's ears when they were in deep thought, you'd be a factory."

"Sorry. Too much to think about. And I've pieced it all together. You know, I got more than blurry visions, although that's how everything started."

"You want to tell me? I mean, you don't have to. What happens during your binding is all yours, but if you want to share, I'll listen."

"It was all overwhelming. Fuck. Where do I begin?" Dev perched himself up on an elbow so Tully's eyes were in his line of sight. "I watched the goddess shift in between all three forms, Maiden, Mother, and Crone. Crone isn't something I care to see again. All skin and bones, She reminded me more of a corpse than a Crone." Tully's eyes were as wide as saucers, and Dev noticed. "Oh wait, gets better. Apparently I have magic I'm not supposed to have, She doesn't trust me, needs to keep an eye on me and so I'm going to be Her emissary. I should expect She'll pop in and out of my life to make sure I'm behaving. Oh, and She looked at me and said 'He's definitely one of yours,' to the god."

"No way! She called you out for being gay?"

"Yeah. And then told me to behave otherwise there'd be consequences. The god told me I had other qualities, that He liked me, and gave me the blessings of being a protector and a tracker."

"Shut the front door! You got three? No one ever gets three. Fuck me."

"Yeah, so about the three," Dev began but didn't know how to finish. How was he supposed to tell Tully about the god bestowing his blessings? Tully and he were dating, right? Sort of? They hadn't had any conversations or had made commitments to each other. They had only known each other for a few days, but those short handful of hours had been an amazing. Would Tully be angry if Dev told him everything? Didn't everyone get their blessings in the same way? Dev had to fess up. And besides, he wanted to know if Tully had had the same experience. "Tully, would you be angry if I had sex with someone else?"

"Ah, well, maybe a little jealous, but you know, we're not committed to each other. I mean, it's only been a couple of days. I—" Tully stared at him as he narrowed his eyes. "Do you mean to tell me you had sex with a god?"

"Maybe?" Dev grimaced.

"Shut the hell up! Geez, Dev." Tully whirled around so he touched nose to nose with Dev. He latched onto Dev's side and had the most mischievous grin. "Tell me everything!"

"You're not mad?"

"Why the hell would I be mad? It's not like you're going to deny a god. Come on."

"He was so good-looking." Dev confessed. "Not like you, but," Dev bit his lower lip, "Tully, he smelled like leather. And, you know, horns."

"Oh well, I know what I'm getting you for your birthday."

"Horns?"

"No! Well...how about something in leather? Although now that you mention it, some horns might be fun." Tully's smile was nothing short of lascivious. .

"Shush, honestly." Dev swatted Tully. "Tell me the truth. You're not angry or mad?"

"You are so cute. No, I'm not mad. I'm thrilled for you. Not everyone gets to say they fucked a god!"

"Other way around."

"I hate you. You know that, right?" Tully pinched Dev's nipple.

"But you and I hadn't fucked yet, and...Tully, I had hoped you would be my first."

Tully grabbed Dev and wrapped him up in his arms and pulled him tight, "You lucky son of a bitch. No one is ever going to compare to getting laid by a god."

"But I wanted it to be you."

"Oh my, you are adorable. Look, I am fine with playing second fiddle to a god. Do you know which one? Did he tell you his name?"

"No, but from the horns and the mannerisms I'm thinking, Cernunnos. But I'm not sure."

"Damn. And you're a protector, a tracker, and the goddess's emissary. Holy shit, Dev."

"You sure you're not mad?"

"About what?"

"I had sex with someone else."

"Dev, are we dating? Is that what you're asking?"

"Well...I don't know, what is this? Are we?"

"Do you want to? Can't say I'd mind." Tully pulled Dev's head up. He had buried himself into the side of

Tully's chest, fearing the worst. Dev glanced at Tully and he could tell from one look that this naked, muscular, hairy redhead with the dopey expression, stroking Dev's cheek was as smitten with him as he was with Tully.

"Maybe."

"Okay. So, let's be boyfriends." Tully kissed Dev. Tully's tongue pressed against his lips and Dev parted them allowing Tully's tongue to wander wherever it wanted to go.

After a few minutes of some passionate making out, which had Dev erect again, Tully pulled away but still had Dev locked tight within his arms.

"Let me ask you," Tully got a serious look on his face, "do you want a monogamous relationship? Just you and me? Or do you want open? Or something in between? Cards on the table, tell me honestly."

"I don't understand." Dev's eyes almost popped out of his head.

"What's not to understand?"

"Tully, I've never had a boyfriend before."

Tully's eyebrows raised high on his forehead. "Explain to me, how someone as damn good-looking and wickedly smart as you has been single all this time?"

"Well, other than a couple of dates, I didn't put myself out there. So, yeah. Here I am, with my first boyfriend." Dev kissed Tully.

"I'm going to need a lot of those. But seriously, you're so new to all of this. The witch world, not having had a boyfriend before. I've been around a bit longer. I've had some fun. I don't want you to miss out."

"Not sure I'm missing out on anything." Dev ran his hands across Tully's massive muscles.

"Trust me, you are." Tully laughed. "And I'm not saying this to be mean or as a dig, I want to make sure you don't feel stifled in this, us, as boyfriends. That's kind of fun to say. Boyfriends. How about this—you and I are dating, seeing each other, and if you get an opportunity elsewhere, I'm okay with whatever you decide to do."

"I don't know. I think I'd feel weird. I'm not sure I would be comfortable without you being there."

"Okay, what about if we find a third? Or a fourth?"

"Group sex?"

"Don't knock it till you've tried it." Tully raised one eyebrow and grinned. "Also, male witches, most of us are gay...sex magic is a thing, and then there's Beltane, and the spring holiday is coming up in a couple of weeks."

"Woah, too much." Dev put his hands up in front of him.

Tully laughed again, kissing Dev's head.

"You don't have to answer, but I want you to think about it. We get to define our own parameters for what this 'dating' thing means. Fair?" Tully asked.

"Okay, that's fair."

"Okay." Tully squeezed his massive arms, and Dev melted.

"Groups, huh?" Dev asked, sheepishly.

"Oh yeah."

"That's kinda hot." Dev pondered.

"I can tell you think so. There's a steel pole rubbing up against my leg." Tully pushed his thigh into Dev's erection, teasing him. "Again?"

"Yes, please. But would you do that thing with your tongue and the whiskers on your chin?" Dev cocked an eyebrow while gazing and, getting lost in Tully's glacier eyes, this time Dev's tongue wanted to explore.

"BYRON, WHERE THE hell are you?" Addas called out from the basement stairs.

"Down here, in the north section." Byron yelled. He had to raise his voice over the shriek of the Spriggan he attempted to harness to the table. The vile lesser fae clawed at him with its twig-like arms, but its fingers barely made a scratch. The sentient twig chomped with tiny teeth, but even when the row of wooden nibs bared down on the webbing in between Byron's fingers, he didn't even notice the creature's desperate attempts to get away.

The fragile, thin body, covered in fuzzy moss, undulated and writhed, bucking and thrashing in an attempt to break free from Byron's fist. Placing the micro-monster onto a large wooden slab, Byron pinned the creature down to the plank and managed to place several straps across the tiny forest fae. The Spriggan was the lowest life form in the fae species. Once secured, he grabbed a pair of tweezers and snapped off a twig making up part of the beast's leg. Dropping the body part into a test tube, he secured the vial with a cork. Tiny leaves began to sprout from the severed limb and thread-like tendrils erupted and swirled around, almost as if they were trying to find a way out. Byron placed the glass container on his work table, a stainless steel wheeled cart which belonged in a surgical suite, not in a basement. Byron tightened the straps to secure the wriggling plant to the tabletop. Lurching and fighting against the restraints, the Spriggan continued to screech as Addas came up behind Byron.

"Where did you get the Spriggan?" Addas's eyes went wide. Spriggans weren't seen often and never in the city.

"Eddie went on a hike." Byron grabbed a different pair of pointed tweezers and a long thin needle.

"Byron, stop." Addas put gargantuan calloused hand over top of Byron's.

"Please, don't." Byron stated, again calm, with a hint of anger buried underneath.

"Look at the poor creature, Byron, it's terrified." Addas's eyebrows pinched together in concern. The smallest and weakest of the forest fae clamored and scrambled to break free.

"Addas, we need it. I need the thing to try to fix you. Spriggan's have regeneration properties you need. It's one of the ingredients listed in the book I brought home. This is for you. And we have to do this tomorrow or else I won't be able to save you."

"Not like this. No more, Byron. I can't let you do this. Look at him. Look in his eyes. You can't use these creatures to try to experiment on extracting an infection we all know can't be reversed. I'm cursed. It's been a year. I'm going to lose control and soon."

"I will not let you turn into one of those dogs." Byron spat. "And besides, this thing is barely sentient!"

"We're all creatures of the gods." Addas placed another hand on Byron's shoulder and pulled him away from the still writhing creature. The living twig had resorted to making weird grunts and squawks. "None lesser or greater than the other. Each with a purpose."

"And this thing's purpose is to make you healthy."

"No, hun, it's not. We have to find another way. Come on, come upstairs. It's time for bed. We've had a long night. Dev's binding went well. Let's focus on the successes."

"I have to find a way Addas. You're out of time."

"I know, but not tonight, and not this way. Okay?" Addas pulled Byron in for a hug. "Promise me?"

"Mmhmm. Okay." Bryon mumbled, but he didn't mean it.

He had to save his Technomage.

He couldn't let Addas shift into a Werewolf. Not even once.

He'd lose him.

And Byron loved him too damn much to let Addas morph into a damn dog.

# Chapter Eighteen

UPON WAKING, DEV stretched in bed, listening to his shoulder and spine crack as he extended his arms above his head. His toes pointed as his legs tensed under the covers. In one graceful motion, he tucked one hand underneath Tully's pillow, and wrapped his arm around his chest. In return, Tully snuggled in closer.

"I could stay here all day." Tully grasped Dev's hand and pulled Dev in tight against his skin.

"Well, sure, that'd be good, but I hoped if you were free, maybe you would help me bring some stuff over from my parent's house?"

"You mean I get to meet your parents? I'm in!" Tully rolled over. Dev, excited for the day, recognized a similar emotion in Tully's morning eyes.

"Careful what you wish for. It's bound to be uncomfortable and chaotic. Remember, nice Indian boys don't leave the family household."

"Oh, pshaw. It'll be fine." Tully kissed him, running his fingers through Dev's beard. "I'm sure after I meet your parents they'll be so smitten with me looking after you, they'll let you go and help you pack."

"Oh my, you are in for a treat." Dev shook his head in disbelief.

WALKING UP THE front steps to Dev's family home, Dev shivered, and nothing around him had the familiarity it once held. He'd been gone mere days, and yet, his entire world had changed. This inner city, modest two-story house wasn't part of his world anymore.

In reality, within Dev's heart, he'd already left. The ingrained tradition of sticking around and helping out his family had died. He had no idea how he would tell his parents though, and as frustrating as they were, Dev still loved his family. The closer the front door loomed, the slower Dev's feet moved.

"You look terrified." Tully grabbed his hand.

"Yes, but it's worse. I can't stay here anymore. Not with us dating, not after the binding. I can't." Dev glimpsed down toward the cracked and broken sidewalk. The walkway stretch of concrete had been where his sisters and he had played for many years. A footpath he'd walk a million times, and now he walked toward his family home for the last time. "I don't belong here anymore, but they're not going to see my leaving as a good thing. My mom and dad are going to think I'm betraying them, the family."

"You know, I might be able to help." Tully gave Dev a sly glance. "Witches and all, right? What's the point if we can't use some hocus pocus to make the painful things less so?"

"What are you going to do?" Nerves bundled up in his tummy, making him queasy, and rather hot.

"Maybe a touch of the Sidhe." Tully gave his hand a squeeze. "Trust me, it'll be okay."

"I don't know –" The front door burst open and Amna came rushing out. Wearing a bright red sari, an odd sight as Amna abhorred wearing traditional clothes. She swept in and grabbed Dev.

"What are you wearing?" Dev shook his head confused. Bhanu was more apt to dress up to please their parents.

"Oh my god, you're okay." Amna ignored Dev's question sliding her arm into the crook of Dev's and pulled him onto the front stoop. The open door, like an exposed maw, waited to ensnare him. "Quit resisting! Geez, Dev. Who's your friend?" Amna whispered to Dev, "He's gorgeous!"

"Amna, let go." Dev pulled free and turned toward Tully. "Tully, this is my sister, Amna. Amna, meet my boyfriend Tully."

Amna gave Dev the stare to end all stares. "Is this what all the drama's been about? Why you've been missing for two days with no calls?" Amna waved her index finger around in circles. "Why didn't you say so?" Amna placed herself in between both Tully and Dev, linked her arms through the both of them and escorted them into the house.

As they entered through the front door, Dev's mom and dad were sitting in the living room, his father perched where he always sat, in front of the TV.

"Oh!" Dev's mom gasped, stood up, and ran over to her eldest son, enveloping him in a massive hug. She buried her face in Dev's chest. She looked so small. Dev let go of his sister and hugged his mother.

"Where have you been? I've been so worried!"

"I'm sorry, Mom. I..." Dev picked his next words carefully, "I needed some time to myself."

"Well, I wouldn't say *that* exactly." Amna snickered. Dev shot her a death stare.

"Mom," Dev tried to pry his mother off him, "Mom, please...I want you to meet my friend, Tully."

Dev's mom pulled away and glanced at the stranger in her house, glared up at Dev. "I think we need to have a talk, as a family."

"No, Mom. Tully is going to help me this morning. I've found an apartment. Tully lives close to my new place, and he's going to help me move some stuff over there."

"You're not going anywhere." Dev's father stood up. His fists balled, and his cheeks reddening with anger.

"I'm not arguing with you." Dev locked his glare to match his father.

"Dev, come have coffee with me." Amna pulled Dev away. "Mom, Dad, I think you should take a few minutes to meet Dev's new friend."

Tully smiled, bright white teeth shining, as he stuck out his hand. "Mr. Khandelwal." Tully grasped the man's hand from his side. As he slid his fingers into Dev's father's hand, Dev let out a hushed "Oh" as he figured out Tully had resorted to using magic.

Tully's thumb rubbed the back of Dev's father's hand, and Dev relaxed as he noted the physical transformation of his father as he succumbed to Tully's Sidhe touch. A little touch of the Irish Mound People indeed. Before Amna had taken Dev into the kitchen, Tully had both of Dev's parents sitting on the couch, each of his hands were busy, one interlocked with another from both Dev's mom and dad. Tully's thumbs worked overtime as he rubbed both of their hands. Dev only caught a fragment of the next sentence. "Dev's going to come live right above me, and…"

Amna yanked him into the kitchen.

"Well done, big brother. He's a real charmer." Amna giggled but got serious as she steered Dev to the small kitchen and forced him to sit. Dev blinked a few times as streamers of royal blue and deep violet swam around her. "Next time you decide to disappear for a few days maybe give me some warning? Look at what I'm wearing! I had to do this to please Mom and calm her down. You owe me. I've made coffee for you." Dev sat at the kitchen table, his leg bouncing with nervousness, and he strained to hear the conversation happening in the living room while Amna fixed him a cup. He waited as his sister put the exact amount of sugar and milk he would like. She handed him his cup, poured herself one, leaving the beverage black.

"Wait, you made coffee for me? How'd you know I was coming—" Dev grasped the coffee, the earthy rich scent smelled so good. "And since when did you start drinking coffee?"

"For about the last year, but you've been pre-occupied." Amna stood at the edge of the counter. She took a sip, then frowned. "Still not quite used to this. I prefer my tea, but you know, you either like ground dirt or cut grass." She shrugged, holding her hand out behind her.

The sugar bowl jittered and shook slightly, then slid from where Mom had always kept the container on the other side of the counter. The bowl spun as it moved into Amna's hand, jarring with a little thud as it hit her palm.

Dev's jaw dropped. He pointed at Amna.

"Yes, big brother, you're not the only one in this family."

"But...how?"

"Well, how, I don't know. I suspect it's genetic seeing as how great-great grandmother was a *dayaan*, and auntie too, now I think about it."

"What? There've been others?"

"Well, not that Mom is going to tell you, but yes. So," Amna raised an eyebrow and squinted at Dev from over her coffee mug, "you're finally bound and bringing home a metallurgist part fae witch boyfriend? Might as well get all in with one good push, right? Which shade of shadow onyx did you select?"

"You know about binding?"

"Dev, please, keep up. We have limited time here while your boyfriend bespells our parents."

"I got bound last night. Geez, Amna, I don't remember—"

"Do you remember the shade? Was the stone dark? Or white?"

"Marbled, I think. Black with white veins through it. There might have been some gray."

Amna nodded. "That's good. I chose solid black. I wish now I'd selected something like what you did. You'll at least have access to more energies. Good, bad, dark, light."

"Are you saying you're dark?"

"Not a white witch, no. But it's all good. Nothing for you to worry about."

"When were you...I can't believe this." Dev ran his fingers through his hair in exasperation. "Why didn't you say something?"

"Come on, Dev, you know the rules. Not until a witch has manifested their power are they even eligible to be bound to the Realm. I couldn't say anything to you until you did. Rules are rules. Anyway, it's all happened. You're on the right path now." Amna peered out through narrowed eyelids again as she concentrated on Dev's face, took another drink of her coffee and grimaced. "Aurologist, right? Not bad, Dev. That's a rare alignment. Watching you these last few months, I thought for sure you were going to lose your mind. You've been such a bitch."

"Amna!"

"Well, you have. It's been awful. You've been awful." Amna dipped the spoon into the sugar bowl still cradled in her hand. She put several heaping spoons of sugar into her cup and stirred it. Lifting the cup, she took another sip, then grinned. "Better. Looks like we're not too different, you and me. Sweet tooth must run in the family genes too." She hoisted her cup in a sugary coffee cheers.

"I can't believe it. Does Bhanu know?"

"Rules, Dev! Of course not. She's blissfully ignorant and totally mundane. She's as dead as Mom and Dad."

"How can you tell?" Dev sat still, wide-eyed at this family revelation.

"My talent. I can see those who will become part of the Shadow Realm and identify those who already are. And what they are."

"Cool! What complicated name comes with that talent?"

"Sensate. It's also part and parcel of an aurologist branch of specialties. And it's only cool some of the time. There's more supernaturals wandering around than you'd think. And the creatures! Walking around and seeing all the fae for the first time disturbed me and my dreams for weeks. They're amazing creatures, and there's so many of them. I still don't understand though, how they glamour themselves into something looking human."

"I haven't been out in public. Like I said, the binding happened last night."

"Wait till you go to the "U". There's three supes in my class at the high school!"

"How many? That seems, I don't know, a bit much?"

"Well, there's a power center close by, so, higher concentration of magic. But you're right. There are an awful lot. Which coven?"

"Guardians of the Night Gr—" Dev didn't get the whole name out.

"No." Amna frowned. "Really? Damn it, Dev."

"What?"

"They don't have a good reputation in the city. There's some shady shit going on there. You be careful."

"That's where I met Tully, and my favorite professor turned out to be the high priest."

"Is this the professor with the beard? The blond? You always got gooey-eyed and stupid with a hairy, bearded boy around. Dev, please be extra careful. There's something not right in our neck of the woods. An imbalance of sorts. My coven sisters think your group is hoarding the energies from the ley lines. Which is why there are so many supes around. Normally energy would trickle out and dissipate far and wide. But if your guys are stopping the energy, the community will migrate as close to the power center as possible in order to have access to the magic.

"Without access Dev, they can't maintain a glamour and without their glamour ability they become exposed to humans. We can't have the humans knowing we exist. You know what would happen? Nothing pleasant. Not to mention some fae will simply wither and die without magic." Amna's face had tightened and her jaw clenched. "I don't like this Dev. If I have to, I'll introduce you to others, but I'm not happy with you being involved with this group."

"Great. I find what I've been searching for my entire life and you tell me I've got myself mixed up with the wrong types of people."

"I'm telling you the rumors." Amna put her coffee cup down. "Promise me you'll at least look at other covens in the city. There are a few."

"I will. I promise."

"Okay, good. It's quiet in there. I think Tully may have put them to sleep with all the Sidhe magic."

"He wouldn't!"

Tully popped his head around the corner. "Your parents are having a nap on the couch. They look peaceful and comfy!"

"You were saying?" Amna cocked an eyebrow with a deadpan serious glare. "How much Sidhe is in you Tully?"

Tully's mouth dropped open. "You know? Dev, you can't tell."

"No, it's okay. She's one of us."

"What?" Tully's face mimicked his own from moments ago.

"Runs in the family. So, how deep of a sleep are they in? Like Sleeping Beauty? Rip Van Winkle? Or will they wake up this afternoon?" Amna had her arms crossed over her chest and her lips pursed together as she finished talking.

"Is that bad? I'm sorry, I can go wake them up. I hoped with them asleep moving your stuff out would be easier for you, Dev."

Amna glared at Dev, walked past Tully and placed a hand on his shoulder. "I know you were thinking of Dev. I'll make sure they don't wake up with a hangover. Dev, think about it. Please."

Amna disappeared upstairs.

"What was that all about?"

Dev shook his head. Amna had to be wrong. Tully wouldn't do anything shady. Being selfish and mean wasn't part of his nature. In fact, none of what he'd seen of the guys the other night indicated any such horrid behaviour.

But he'd only known Tully for a few days. A fast, furious, sexy hot, incredible, mind-blowing two days. Well okay, maybe more like three.

Dev wondered if perhaps he had missed something, anything implying the Guardians of the Night Grove were a nefarious coven.

DEV AND TULLY each pulled one last box out of Tully's trunk.

They had managed to pack a dozen boxes of occult supplies and grabbed as many coat hangers out of the closet as possible. Garbage bags held T-shirts, socks, and underwear. The last few hours had turned into a long afternoon, but Dev was at least thankful he didn't have any big furniture to move.

Tully had helped him every step of the way, and several times, Dev had stopped and scrutinized Tully when his boyfriend hadn't been looking.

He didn't see it. The sexy redhead with the glacier eyes championed the arena in gentility and kindness. There wasn't anything about Tully anyone would consider questionable.

They lugged Dev's treasured possessions up to the apartment and put them on the floor. Tully fell backward on the bed while Dev sat and grabbed a box, unpacking its contents. The rest of the afternoon and early evening Dev spent sorting out everything and putting stuff away. All the while, the seed of doubt lay embedded, starting to sprout and taint everything he'd been so happy about the last few days.


AS DEV PULLED out his bag of bones and a remaining tarot deck out of the last box. Amna's warning still sat weird in his belly. He wasn't sure what to make of her gossip about Tully's coven, and the news had flavored the whole moving out process into a clingy cloying taste in his mouth. The kind where you have to brush your teeth a few times to get rid of the bad taste. Except every time Dev tried to rationalize what Amna had told him, voices inside his head were saying otherwise. The voices were the proverbial red flags, and they were waving against a clear blue sky.

What Dev needed to do was to talk to Cam. Cam had always been his sounding board, his confidant and partner in crime.

Dev pulled his phone out of his pocket and flicked the screen on.

No texts, no calls. Nothing. After three days of silence from Cam, Dev began to worry. This behaviour didn't match Cam's natural patterns.

"Hey mister," Tully came up behind him, putting his arms around Dev's waist and nuzzled Dev's neck as he whispered into his ear, "all the empty boxes are broken down and packed into the trunk of the car. You done with this one? We can take the box down to the car and stop by the recycle station to dump them all off."

"Sure." Dev glared at his phone and hadn't even glanced at Tully.

"I tried so hard to make that sound sexy. Guess I failed."

"What?" Dev snapped out of his trance as he turned to face Tully.

"Occupied much? You've been off the whole day, ever since the binding. Are you sure you're okay? Please tell me. I'm starting to get concerned having you bound to the Realm so early was a huge mistake." Tully's brows were pinched in the middle, signaling his apprehension, but all Dev focused on were fuzzy long red caterpillars across Tully's brow. That and bright floating orbs of colour.

"There's so much. I think I'm feeling everything times ten. These swirling colours around everyone are driving me nuts and frankly, I haven't heard anything from Cam in days. It's not like him. I'm worried, Tully. Something is wrong.

"I mean, I got my wishes from the summoning board, so far. It must mean his wishes came true too, but there's been no texts, no calls....nothing. It's weird."

"All right, let's go to his place. Let's go check up on him." Dev understood Tully was trying hard to be supportive, reassuring and acting as his Shadow Realm blood brother. He was also being a good boyfriend.

"You won't mind?"

"Not at all. He's your closest friend. I'd like to meet him." Tully picked up the last empty box. "Come on, let's go."

"Be careful what you wish for. Cam can be a real whirlwind."

"I believe you said something similar about your parents, and that turned out fine. This will be fun." Tully beamed then grabbed Dev's hand, tugging him toward the door.

DEV WALKED UP to Cam's front door and rang the doorbell. Tully stood close behind him. From behind the door, voices giggled.

*Maybe Cam is home? Why hasn't he called or texted?*

The door whisked open, startling Dev.

Mrs. Habersham stood there, in a short cover up, the same colour as the day's sky, which at this hour darkened and melted into the shadowy purple of twilight. The woman beamed at the sight of Dev showing her oversized whitened teeth.

"Dev! Oh my goodness, it's been a while. How have you been?"

"I'm fine Mrs. Habersham –"

"Oh, don't be silly, call me Carrie."

A rustle from the kitchen indicated Carrie had company. The fridge door slammed.

"Carrie, I found the whip cream! Who's at the door?"

"One of Cam's friends, Benny, come meet him!"

Benny emerged from the kitchen, wearing nothing but revealing silk boxers close in shade to Mrs. Habersham's ensemble.

"Well, hey there!" Benny had a little less than ten years on Dev and Tully, which meant he was twenty years junior to Cam's mom. Muscled and taught, not an ounce of fat anywhere, in another circumstance, Dev might have been turned on. "You didn't tell me Cam had such good looking buddies."

"Yes, Dev, how rude of me, who's your friend?"

"Ah, sorry," Dev closed his eyes in shock with the entire awkwardness of the situation, a subtlety lost on Mrs. Habersham. "This is Tully, my boyfriend."

Benny moved forward and extended his hand in greeting, shaking both of their hands. Dev watched his wang wiggle with the shaking action.

"Boyfriends? That's fantastic. Carrie, why don't you invite the boys in?"

Another voice echoed from down the hall, this time, a feminine voice. "Hey guys, where'd you go?"

Dev turned to look at Tully, whose eyebrows had shot so far up they were lost in his tussled red mane.

"Ah, yes. Well, sounds like you're busy, Mrs. Habersham. We came by to see Cam."

"Oh, Cam's not here. Didn't he tell you?"

"Tell me what?" Dev frowned.

Benny had draped his arm around Cam's mom and his hand slid down to one of her breasts.

"Cam left a note saying he left to spend time with his father. That bastard." Her mouth sneered as she mentioned her ex-husband. "But it's his father, so what can I say? Right?"

"Do you still have the note?" Dev asked.

"Sure thing honey, let me go get it." Carrie turned, slinking away from Benny. Once she had disappeared Benny cocked an eyebrow at Dev and Tully.

"You sure you don't want to come in? It'd be fun to have some guys here too." Benny leaned forward and in a hushed tone whispered, "I go both ways." He winked and grabbed his crotch.

Carrie reappeared. "Benny, for god's sake, stop pestering the boys." She laughed and smacked Benny's rump.

"Hey," but he chuckled sticking his rump out further, "just having a little fun."

"Guys? Where the hell are you? I need the whip cream." The woman yelled from somewhere within the Habersham house.

Carrie handed over the letter to Dev. "Here you go honey. You can keep it."

"Thanks, Mrs. Habersham."

"You sure you don't want to come in?" she asked.

"Ah," Dev blushed, turning his light-brown skin a shade darker and rosy, "no, we're good. Thank you."

"Suit yourself! Have a good night, boys." Mrs. Habersham closed the door, and the giggling on the other side resumed.

"Oh. My. God." Dev stared at the closed door. "Did we get asked to an orgy with my best friend's mother?"

"I do believe that's what happened." Tully mashed his lips together, but Dev noticed Tully biting his lips in a desperate attempt to not bust a gut laughing.

"It's not funny; it's gross!"

"Why? She's having a good time."

"Yeah, but I don't need an invitation for front row seats to see it!"

Tully shrugged. "Good on her. So, what does the note say?"

Dev walked down the cement steps toward Tully's car. He grabbed his phone out of his pocket and punched the button for the flashlight app. The bright light flooded the page with artificial light. Dev studied the note but made a face while doing so.

"What's the matter?"

"Well, the note says '*Mom, gone to visit Dad. Will call in a few weeks. Don't worry, I'm fine.*'" Dev glanced away from the note and toward Tully.

"Cam would never leave for *that* long and not tell me. He also would never stay with his dad. As much as he detests his mom while she's...entertaining...he hates his dad even more."

"That's odd. No?"

"What's weirder still, I can tell Cam didn't write this."

"You said Cam wouldn't do something like this."

"No. Not what I meant. I mean I can *see* Cam didn't write this. The lettering is moving and shifting around. It's almost as if the words were put there by force and they're trying to escape."

"What?"

"Can't you see this? Look at the note. The letters are moving."

Tully peered over Dev's shoulder. "Looks like handwriting to me."

Dev's gaze darted around the paper trying to watch everything as the letters shifted around and words moved. A bunch of letters slid off the paper. Dev sucked in air through pursed lips as another sentence formed.

"Tully, look, what does the letter say now?" He showed Tully the reformed letter. Tully's eyes rounded out as he reread the note.

*"Mom, get Dev. Wiccan goats Den."*

"What the hell does that mean?" Dev asked.

Tully shook his head and shrugged, canting his head slightly, "The god made you a tracker, right?"

"Yeah, so what?" Dev shot Tully a disdainful look.

"I might be wrong here, but this looks like you just got a clue, Mr. Tracker. Maybe you're right, Dev. Maybe Cam's gone missing."

# Chapter Nineteen

IF CAM HADN'T already been stark naked and cold from the dankness of the cellar dungeon, he'd have been hot and sweaty for all the effort he exerted attempting to recapture his Fae abilities.

"Nope. I can still see you." The tone in Ev's voice would have been humorous if the situation wasn't so dire.

"You're not helping," Cam growled. His tongue ran over the sharpened edges of his teeth.

"We're going to die down here."

"Will you shut the hell up?" Cam had grown beyond tired with the ribbing. Then he remembered the times he'd done the same thing to Dev. Guilt wormed its way into his stomach. Cam sneered at the wolf-man. Ev stood close to his cell's bars, naked, swinging his meat back and forth taunting him. As much as Cam wanted to run his tongue all over the wolf man, this current display hadn't added anything to assist in their great break-out-plan. Cam's wings beat several times giving away his emotional state.

"Ah, see, there you go! Your legs are gone."

"What?" Cam barked out in frustration, gritting his teeth. Ev pointed at Cam's lower half, which made him look down. Sure enough, the shackles holding him in place appeared as if they were floating in midair. From the waist down, Cam was invisible. "Well, damn." Cam's mood shifted from pissy because of the werewolf's taunting to stunned over making himself invisible. But in that moment of hesitation and shift in his mood, the mystic invisibility shroud peeled away. His legs reappeared.

"You're getting better!" Ev's voice lilted, an odd bit of encouragement from the surly beast. "Maybe I need to tease you more."

"I don't think my nerves can handle it."

"Maybe I should taunt you with other things?" Ev, ran his hand down his furry torso, over his shredded abs, and then manhandled his wolfy bits, stroking himself a couple of times.

"I think we already determined that didn't get the right emotions flared up to make me invisible."

"No, but stroking the beast and getting you riled makes me all warm inside."

"I hate you a little, you know that, right?"

"Mmhmm." Ev continued to play with himself.

Cam took random peeks at Ev and would have been excited over watching this bit of exhibitionism, but between being held captive and the shackles burning his flesh, he wasn't feeling it. Cam had real work to do. Although Ev tried valiantly to piss him off. Anger apparently triggered invisibility.

The clanking *thunk* of a deadbolt being turned made him refocus. They were about to get a visitor.

Fresh air from the upper levels wafted down to Cam's cell. Food cooked in the kitchen above them. The aroma smelled like eggs and bacon. It must have been morning. And the glorious scent of brewed coffee hit his nose.

"Oh damn, what I wouldn't do." Cam had lost track of time locked away in a basement surrounded by bars and not a window in sight. Footsteps thudded on each tread of the stairwell as someone made their way down.

Ev snarled. Visitors meant only one thing. A stabbing session.

Byron rounded the corner from the stairwell. He wore tight blue jeans and a white T-shirt stretched across his muscles.

"All right, boys, I need things. Ev, assume the position please."

Cam's heart lurched in his chest as he watched Ev, who had been captive for months, do precisely as asked. So much humiliation and mental anguish wafted through the room. There would be consequences if he didn't acquiesce. Byron bypassed Cam altogether heading straight to Everton's cell. Since Cam had arrived, Byron had ignored the wolf man until now.

Ev kneeled on the cement, bent forward until his check rested against the stone floor. He placed his hands on top of his head.

"Good boy." Byron took a key from his pocket and unlocked Ev's cage. A flickering spark of ire inside Cam's chest exploded as Byron opened Ev's cell door, and the accompanying squeal of metal grinding against metal set his nerves further on edge.

Cam watched everything.

Byron grabbed Ev's hands and hoisted them above his head, stepping on them to pin him to the floor.

Ev whined.

"You don't have to be such an asshole," Cam blurted out.

"Cam, remember what I said? Control your anger—that goes for your words too." Byron glared at him. "Otherwise I'll get the syringe and withdraw some more juice. From the looks of things, you still have too much fae left in you. I expected you to develop some of their characteristics, but frankly, you've gained too much. Truthfully, I'm surprised you're still as fae as you are. You should be more human by now.

"Maybe I should take more juice for good measure. You'll be next."

Byron kneeled over Ev, grinding his foot into the back of his hand.

Ev didn't move a muscle, but Cam spotted the veins popping out on his neck and forehead from the strain of the pain and anger.

With a smooth motion, Byron produced a syringe from out of nowhere, dug the needle into Ev's neck and thrust the apparatus into a vein with enough force to make Cam grimace. Dark blood pumped and squirted, filling the vial.

Ev continued to exude a high pitched whine while one of his feet tapped the ground repeatedly. Cam's memories flashed to earlier, when he'd been tied down and stabbed with the fucking syringe. The needles always hurt, both his flesh and his pride.

"Atta boy." Byron petted Ev's head as if his hostage was some lap dog.

Byron's authoritative attitude pissed Cam off. Nobody should be treated so poorly, hostages or otherwise. Cam strained against his shackles and ground his pointed teeth, watching Byron torture and degrade Ev.

"Now, stay put until I'm on the outside of the cell." Byron stepped off Ev's hands and backed out of the cell. Once past the door, he slammed the swinging cage door shut, yanking on the bars a few times to ensure the cell had locked.

"Byron," Cam burned on the inside, but with all his strength mustered he kept his emotions in check, "why are you doing this? Why hurt him, or me? Is this for fun?" Information would have been nice, but Cam wanted to lure Byron closer.

"Different reasons, none for you to be concerned about."

The sheer pomposity Byron displayed boiled Cam's blood. "Well, how about something to eat? I'm awfully hungry." Cam asked. "I promise I'll be nothing short of high society polite. Scout's honor, swear on bibles, and all that sort of thing."

Byron laughed out loud. "Well, if that actually meant something to you, I might have put some stock into it. Addas keeps telling me I should feed you, but I'm not so inclined. Food gives you energy. I don't need fae and werewolves strong while in captivity."

Cam sneered, all toothy, but trying so hard to be nice. "Addas seems to be more human than you," Cam hissed but checked himself and turned his evil face into the warmest smile he could muster, all nice and polite like. "Please? A nice big thick juicy steak would be awesome. And maybe one for my friend here?" Cam tilted his head toward Ev, who picked himself up off the floor.

Byron sighed. "Addas isn't human, but he is kind. Much more than I am." Byron rubbed his face. "Do you promise to behave?"

"I promise. I'll even roll over so you can come stick me and take some faerie go go juice. Honestly, anything for some food right now." Cam stomach twisted and yowled in hunger, but he wanted Byron closer to him. He needed him close.

Byron's gaze held no promise of mercy or kindness. Distrust marred his good looks. "If I give you something to eat, Addas will be happy, and I'm more inclined to ensure his happiness than yours. But fine, I'll be back."

Byron disappeared up the stairwell carrying the syringe with him.

As soon as the metal grind of the door closing stopped, Ev snarled, "What are you doing?"

"Oh, trying something."

A few minutes later the door to the dungeon swung open again with the same slight groan of metal on metal hinges. The whine and screech the door always made set Cam's teeth on edge.

Cam heard footsteps on the stairwell. He focused all his energy into one singular thought.

*Sleep.*

Byron appeared with a couple of raw steaks bites. "Addas insisted you each get bigger chunks of meat, but I persuaded him otherwise." Byron sneered in disgust as he got close to Cam's cage. "I swear, you try anything..."

Byron placed his chest up against the bars, put his hand through them and swung, throwing a chunk of meat over to Cam. The meat fell a ways away, which meant Cam would have to stretch in order to grab his morsel of sustenance. Stretching would cause the shackles to touch fresh flesh, and that meant more pain. Byron was such an asshole.

Instead of focusing on his dinner, Cam activated his alternate plan. Pouring all his energies and emotions into one action, Cam exhaled, thinking the same word over and over again.

*Sleep.*

A light sparkle of dust motes, unseen to the naked eye, floated across the distance from Cam to Byron. As Cam exhaled, slowly, calmly and imperceptibly to anyone else in the room, the microscopic specks glittered and shimmered in the space between them. The distance between him and his captor wasn't that far, and Cam spied a few of his sleep minions which had floated across the distance and landed on Byron's shoulder. Byron needed to be closer in order for him to gulp a whole fleet of these tiny particles.

When Cam hadn't moved, Byron scrunched up his face, then sneered and threw another chunk of steak. The meat landed with a slap against the cold concrete, closer to the intended target, but Cam sat there, continuing his train of thought. Focusing on a single idea had to be the hardest thing he'd ever done. Ignoring the food became an additional struggle.

Byron took the few steps over to Ev's cage and repeated the process, throwing raw, dead flesh toward Ev.

The tangy coppery scent of residual blood in the meat whet Cam's mouth. The disappointment ebbed from Cam to have to watch the precious liquid seep onto the cold stone of the basement floor.

*What a waste.*

Byron turned away from Ev's cell and blinked several times. He glanced at Cam, and Cam noted how unfocused Byron acted, his eyes blinking, gaze darting in different unfocused directions. Byron shook his head, then yawned.

"Didn't get enough *sleep* last night, Byron?" Cam emphasized the one word, embellishing the notion with calmness, serenity, and warm blankets fresh from the dryer. Those fluffy warm snuggles where the sweet fabric softener smell caressed you like a comforting hug.

Byron focused in on Cam, his gaze veered and teetered. He wobbled, taking a step away.

"It's been a stressful couple of days, and I haven't slept well, but..." Byron squinted and pursed his lips, glaring at Cam. "Nah, you wouldn't be able to."

"Able to what?"

"Never mind," Byron quipped and yawned again. "Eat your food. You won't get any more. You can expect me to take some more of the fluid later. Can't have you going any more fae on us."

Byron sauntered toward the stairwell, but as Cam listened, each plod of Byron's steps were heavier than normal. Cam's gaze intensified while staring toward the stairwell. He didn't dare say anything until the door ground shut. "Well, look at that, Ev. Not so bad, huh?" he whispered.

Cam had followed Byron's exit from the dungeon as he replayed the last few minutes in his head, staring toward the stairwell where Byron had disappeared. "Ev?" Cam turned to look at the wolf, but Ev had curled up in a ball in the corner of his cell, and the rumbling snore told Cam everything he needed to know.

"Well, look at that indeed." Cam's eyebrow arched as his mouth ticked up in a crooked grin.

His grin continued to expand until his face morphed into an open mouth. Wide, toothy, and with several rows of sharp fangs.

Cam bent over and snagged the raw meat from the floor, brushed off some imagined dirt and sank his teeth into it.

Blood trickled down his chin.

BYRON CLIMBED THE last of the stairs, turned into his study, and put the syringe of werewolf blood on his desk. He would deal with it later. He stretched his arms out and yawned for a third time. His sudden tiredness struck him as odd. Sure, he'd been busy and stressed, with Addas's predicament and all, but he shouldn't be this sleepy.

Byron wondered, tapping his fingers on the desk near the vial of blood. Maybe this exhaustion had a direct relation to the human-turned-fae downstairs, but he shrugged off the probability. Somnolence was a talent only female fae could employ. And besides, life *had* been rough the past few days.

He shook off the grogginess and turned to his bookshelf filled with trinkets and amulets.

After picking up several charms, some strung through on leather straps, others with thin flexible wire, Byron found the right one.

The talisman came apart in two pieces of wood, which when separate didn't look like much, but when put together, they formed a heart. There were holes drilled into the wood, and wire had been used to sew the heart together, one piece attached to a much larger one. Rough bark surrounded the entire edge of the heart. This would be the perfect gift. The heart, a symbol of desire and passion and the oak wood represented strength and knowledge.

Byron held his fingers out and closed his eyes.

From within his core, he called out to the fire element. Thinking of the crackling of a hearth, the smell of wood smoke, and the heat of embers, Byron brought all of those sensations out through his fingers, where they made quick shapes in the air. Contracting and dancing, interlacing and splaying, his quick finger work emblazoned the tiny stitched up heart with a number of tiny sigils, all of them combining to form the symbol for the Coven of the Night Grove. A full moon with a goat's head within a pentacle.

Byron's fingers rested, and he let out a deep sigh, opened his eyes, and studied his work.

Perfection. The amulet, the size of a silver dollar, rested in the palm of his hand, intricately decorated with runes and humming with power. Byron found a leather strap with a strong clasp and wove the thin leather strip through the amulets hook made for this purpose. He secured the clasp and then pulled forward a small box.

Byron opened the lid and placed the charm in the wooden vessel. With a wave of his hand, he uttered a single word.

"Conceal." The box slammed shut while fire danced off Bryon's fingertips, descended to the box, and enveloped the wooden casing as a complex rune burnt itself into the side of the box. Symbols and glyphs superimposed themselves over one another, contained within several concentric circles, while other witch marks burst forth from the center in long spike-like spears. When he finished, the wooden box appeared as if there were no openings, lids, or any other way to recover the charm inside.

This would be Dev's first task.

Find a way to open the box. His reward would be the object hidden within. A gift of passion, strength, and knowledge from the coven, which Byron hoped Dev would soon become part of.

Now he had to figure out what to do with the creatures he held captive beneath him. The Spriggan lay in the next room still strapped to the wooden table. He had checked on the pitiful thing earlier, but the sentient twig had faded, losing vitality and glow. Without Addas knowing, he had harvested the items he needed from the wretched beast.

Between the wolf's blood, the Spriggan's inherent healing abilities, and the royalty fae's mojo juice, Byron had the right combination of herbs and magical ingredients to create the alchemical vaccine to save Addas. Well that and the access to all the energy in the ley lines, along with a few other key witchy ingredients. With the assistance of his knights, Byron would rid the wolf infection from Addas and complete the rituals he'd studied from the imported spell books. The ritual had to happen today and before the last partial moonrise. Tomorrow evening the moon would be full . If they waited any longer…

He couldn't lose Addas to the werewolf inside his lover, and if Addas were to turn, he would die.

Witch wolves didn't exist.

Byron yawned again. "Damn, maybe you do need a nap," he mumbled to himself. Turning, he left his study and climbed the remaining stairs up to the kitchen where Addas, the brute, the big loveable oaf, had whipped up an amazing spread.

A huge bowl of scrambled eggs lay in the center of the table, and Byron identified flecks of green and red, which meant diced up peppers, and Addas would have ensured the eggs would be cheesy. His favorite. On another plate a stack of pancakes awaited, with blueberries, and of course a monster plate of both bacon and sausage. All the accoutrements were on a set table.

"Coffee?" Addas already had a mug in his paws pouring the cup full.

"Yes, please!" Byron leaned over and kissed Addas. A lingering kiss.

"I've been keeping this warm. You need to eat. Big day today. Dev and Tully are coming at ten, they just texted. Gus and Eddie are scheduled for noon as you requested. What do you have planned?" Addas passed the mug over to Byron, which he accepted and took a quick sip of the steaming hot, earthy liquid.

"I think I might have finally cracked that alchemical vaccine for you. And the full moon is tomorrow. That means today's the day."

"Byron, I wish you'd let this go. You know no one has ever reversed this. And as much as I don't want to shift, the infection is already starting to manifest itself. I can feel the wolf inside you know. The dog is not happy."

"We can't have you shifting. There's nothing written anywhere of a successful wolf-witch combination. There's lots written about those who have tried. The two powers are from separate branches of magic and if combined, it's deadly. I can't lose you."

Addas stepped in close to Byron, grabbed his coffee, and placed the cup on the table. He wrapped his massive arms around Byron and held him close. "I don't want to lose you either."

"You know, a year ago, you and I were the same height. Look at what the wolf's infection has done to you."

"I don't know, I kinda like being bigger than you."

"Addas..."

But Addas kissed him again. "Eat up, this is getting cold." Byron's shoulders slumped forward as Addas released his hold.

As Byron sat at the table and stared at his mate, his eyes glassed over and went watery. The additional lines around Addas's eyes, the down pull on the corners of his mouth, the haloing of yellow around the iris, and pointed eye teeth were all physical changes the infection had incurred. He also noted the emotional and spiritual alterations. Addas had never growled or snarled at him. But now? The outward acts of defiance occurred daily. Not to mention the increased sexual drive, and his jumping at every noise.

This afternoon's attempt, this last combination of ingredients, was Addas's last chance.

# Chapter Twenty

"WE'RE LATE!" DEV ran up to Byron and Addas's front door.

"Relax." Tully sauntered up the front walk.

"Easy for you to say, you've never been late to one of his classes!" Dev rapped the door knocker in the center of the door, which happened to be the nose of the goat.

As the stylistic lines etched into the door tugged at Dev's brain, something about the linear minimalistic design set him on edge. As Dev reached out to touch the patterning on the door, the portal opened and Byron welcomed them with outstretched arms. Byron stood tall and proud, a big man whose frame filled the doorway. The dressed-down style of faded and worn jeans with a V-neck, tight white T-shirt made Dev's heart pump a little faster. The high priest, also his favorite professor, epitomized a fine specimen of masculinity.

"You're late." Byron squinted.

"See!" Dev turned and glared at Tully.

"My fault Byron, sorry. I kept him in bed too long this morning."

Byron chuckled. "No worries. We've been busy here, and it's going to be a full day. Come on in. I've got things for you Dev."

Dev and Tully removed their shoes and coats, walked up the flight of stairs, and down the hallway, following Byron. They passed the living room where Dev had been bound to the Shadow Realm two nights previous and entered the kitchen. Addas, with his monstrous size, blocked out the kitchen window as he stood in front of the sink washing up an enormous pile of dishes. Enough plate ware for a buffet for twelve.

Addas turned sideways, his hands still over the sink, scrubbing. "Hey guys! You hungry? I have leftovers from breakfast."

"I'm good, thanks anyway." Had Addas grown in size since he'd seen him last?

"No, thanks, man. But, you got coffee?" Tully quipped.

"Yup, grab a mug, pot's on the stove." Addas lifted his chin in the direction of the cupboard holding the cups. Tully made himself busy.

Byron had wrapped an arm around Dev. "Well, you ready for your first lesson?"

Dev's heart stuttered and his stomach churned as he watched the sickening muddy colours circulating around Byron. Addas, on the other hand, was a sight to behold.

Dark shadows warped a bright-blue aura, making the colors shift to green and topaz.

"Ah, yeah," Dev replied, distracted.

Tully came over with two cups, handing one to Dev.

Dev smiled. "Thanks."

"I know you live for your morning caffeine rush. And there's cream and lots of sugar in it."

"You're the best."

"All right, boys, enough cooing at each other. Let's go to my study. Addas, you good?"

"Yup, I got this. You going to be a while?"

"No, I think I'll get the boys set up and then I'll come up here and help you. I have to get ready for Gus and Eddie, but they shouldn't be here for another hour and a bit."

"Have fun!" Addas winked at Dev, then turned back to scrubbing his pan.

Dev gripped the handle of his mug too tight and followed Byron down the stairs leading into the bowels of the house, careful to not slop his coffee during the descent. They came to a landing where to the right a closed door blocked their path. Byron snapped his fingers, muttering a spell. A ripple of heat brushed past Dev's cheeks. After the door opened, Byron crossed the threshold, and as Dev entered, he stopped with a jolt, slack jawed, and ogled the room before him.

A huge wooden desk sat off to one side, complete with computer screen and keyboard, but the technology accounted for the most modern thing in the room. An assortment of ancient-looking items were scattered on the desk, including an old wooden box. The room was lined with bookcases, all of them packed tight with books. Leather spines with gold lettering, binders stuffed with paper, shiny paperbacks with colorful covers, and old scrolls stacked in a honeycomb pattern were in every direction Dev glanced.

"Are all these books on magic?"

"Some, yes. Others are coven histories, species description documents, and alchemical recipes. There's different sections as well. Here's one for divination," Byron pointed, "then over there are books on crystals and rocks, and this wall is dedicated to the elements. It's partly my collection, but also all the resources for the Coven of the Night Grove which has been around for a long time."

In the center of the room, a large globe sat perched on a mechanism allowing the sphere to spin, which the ball currently did. Instead of the usual country boundaries and color-coded maps, the continents were in a dark taupe, and the world's oceans a deep brown. The colour scheme, in similar monotone shades, reminded Dev of sepia photographs. Gold lines crisscrossed all over the planet, converging in epicenters forming hubs. Sporadically, a burst of energy would fire off where several lines converged making the connected lines all grow brighter for a brief moment.

Dev leaned in and watched, fascinated by the display.

"Those are the ley lines. Our coven's main purpose is to make sure the line that passes through Edmonton is kept safe. The supernaturals around here get greedy and absorb too much of the energies, so we've kept a throttle on the ley line for many, many years. We only allow small bursts of energy out at a time, then harvest and save the rest."

"What do you mean 'get greedy'?" Dev glanced over his shoulder to Byron, Amna's comments bubbling out from his memory and recent conversation.

"There are a lot of different species of supernaturals, Dev. Some are quiet and content to blend in to the environment, others are bent on destruction and chaos. Remember the Shadow Realm is equal dark and light. We strive to maintain the balance."

Dev weighed the comment. What Byron had confessed made sense. It's not like you'd want a werewolf pack running rampant through the city, or a nest of vampires taking up residence.

*Was that a thing?*

Dev recalled all the TV shows and movies he'd seen over the years and wondered how much of the supernatural world had been depicted true or what had been exaggerated or an outright lie.

"Okay, enough. You'll get to know the ley lines and how to tap into the energies later, but for now, I've compiled a bunch of texts I want you to read through and study. There's a workbook on top. You'll need to go through your books and perform each of the exercises contained in them. Plus I need you to start keeping a journal. Every day you should be writing, documenting anything you've gleaned from your reading, spells you cast, successful or otherwise, encounters with other species. It will help you learn, note the differences between the mundane and the magical, and most of all, get you in tune with the energies surrounding our immediate area. From there, we'll make sure you learn how you can use them.

"We still need to test you to see what specifically you're talented in as an aurologist. Each classification is a large family of abilities. Some you'll be able to do, others, not at all. I'd have liked to do those spells with you today, but I have other commitments I need to attend to. Until you are tested though, you'll need to be careful. As I'm sure Tully told you, witch lives are short. Every spell takes a little of our life force. Some of us learn how to borrow from the elements we're attuned to, but the expenditure of casting spells and weaving magic always costs. As much as that will happen to you too, you may have the ability to leach life forces. Your natural attunement to the spirit will aid you in absorbing those energies." Dev stared at Byron. Out of nervousness he picked up a palm-sized piece of amber sitting near the globe. "So we need to get you trained up to avoid depleting everyone around you."

"Damn." Tully put his mug down on a side table. "I didn't realize Dev had the ability to leach from others."

"Possibly." Byron stated, "Don't worry, that's advanced skills, something you shouldn't be able to do right now. The faster we get you competent, up to at least the skill level of a brother, the safer everyone is, including you."

"I don't want to leach from anyone." Dev fingered the crystal he'd picked up, tracing the sharp edges and running his finger over the smooth sides.

Byron walked over and took the crystal from him, replacing the gemstone down on the table, near the globe.

"This is a soul trap. Probably not something you want to play with." Dev's eyes widened even further as he chanced another quick glance at the stone he'd absentmindedly fondled. "There's lots to learn, and I'm here to make sure you survive all your lessons and remain in one piece. Tully and Sparks are also responsible for your well-being, so spend as much time as you can with them, and do magic with them. As your blood brothers they'll guide you. Remember there are as many dangers as there are wonders in our happy community. Okay?"

"Okay." Dev nodded, but shivers ran across the tops of his shoulder as the skin on his head tingled.

"All right, here's your stack of reading material," Byron hoisted a small pile and placed them off to one side of his desk. "There's Understanding Auras—most important for your attunement—, Basic Divination, Intro to Runes, Beginners Guide to Witchcraft, and a novel on the Shadow Realm the general public believed was great fiction." Byron glanced over at the two in front of him and chuckled. "The book is amusing, but also one hundred percent true. These here are your workbook and a few scrolls. I expect you to master these simple spells."

"Is there a due date for all this?" Dev asked, forever the perpetual student.

"Well, as fast as you can. I'd say you should have this done within a couple of weeks, but sooner would be better. You're strong, Dev. I need to get you up to speed."

"Okay." Dev glanced at Tully feeling exasperated.

"I'll help. Don't worry."

"And there's this. A small test." Byron pulled the sealed box into the center of his desk and tapped the top with his finger a couple of times. "There's a gift in here, yours from the coven. When you open the box, you can have the gift. I hope you like it."

"Sure."

"Great. I have some things I need to take care of. I'm going to leave you boys to it. Oh, and the box is secured. Your test is to figure out how to open it. Tully, you're not allowed to do it, but you can stay for moral support." Byron picked up the small container and tossed the box toward Dev. He caught it, turning the object over several times inspecting all sides and running his hands over the smooth surfaces. "I'm also sealing you two in the room as well. Once you figure out how to open the box, you should be able to figure out how to open the door as well. Practice, right? I have things to do with the knights this afternoon. We'll be in the sub levels, but we're busy with coven business, so let yourself out once you get your first test done."

"Wait. You're sealing us into the room?" A twinge of panic knotted Dev's stomach. One of those red flags waving somewhere in the distant recesses of his mind. Tully didn't look too concerned.

"Yup. Think of this exercise like an escape room. Don't worry. There's a bathroom in the corner and there's a water cooler over here. If you're not out by dinner, I'll come get you." At that, Byron turned, shut the door, and within a few seconds, Dev's confidence levels plummeted as he watched the door disappear, the seams and hinges melding into the walls.

"Well, I guess we're all by ourselves!" Tully waggled his eyebrows.

"You're terrible."

"We're alone." Tully jumped up and made his way over to Dev, wrapping his arms around him and nuzzling his beard into Dev's neck. "What do you want to do first?" Tully let his hands slide down so they cupped each of Dev's butt cheeks as he nibbled on Dev's neck.

Dev pulled away and stared at Tully, shaking his head. "You are terrible. I'm not so sure I like being locked away."

"You're fine. I'm here. I had to do this on my own."

"Really?"

"Yup. So, I already know the answer, but so do you." Tully let go of Dev, raised his hand to his temple, and tapped his finger there. "Think about it."

"Ugh." Dev wriggled free and returned to stand in front of the stack of tomes stressing him out with more homework to complete in addition to the finals he still had to write in order to get his degree. "I'm not sure I can get all this done in time, Tully. I still have my last set of exams at the 'U'. I'm not throwing all my hard work and education away."

"Nor should you. Don't worry. You got this." Tully slumped into one of the overstuffed reading chairs. "So, what are you going to do first to open the magical box?"

"Fuck me. I have no idea."

"Think Dev, you've already seen this."

Dev glared at Tully. Frustration flared, stirring Dev's anger at himself for not being able to figure this out. He didn't like being put on the spot or the claustrophobic sensation of being trapped in such a small room. Tully, present or otherwise, didn't help. Dev sorted through the books Byron had left him, looking at them one by one. Surely there had to be something here.

Tully chuckled, picked up a book himself, and leafed through it, glancing at Dev every so often.

The morning slipped away.


BYRON GLANCED AT his watch. Time had snuck away. One o'clock had come and gone already. Gus and Eddie had shown up an hour earlier than expected, and were in the bottom levels of the house making preparations. Setting up the subterranean expansion holding the werewolf and the fae for this afternoon's exercise would be a major undertaking. The deepest level of the house had been built over a hundred years prior, and used for captives many times over the century or so the Guardians of the Night Grove had held their sacred space here, but more importantly, the subterranean room lay over top of the coven's most precious resource.

He had checked on the boys in his study a couple of times, standing still in front of where the door had once been, but only the odd rustle of papers broke the silence. They hadn't emerged yet, which in some ways signaled compliance. If Dev struggled to come up with the solution on his own, it meant Tully was playing by the rules and not giving Dev the answer.

"You in there? We could use your help." Gus startled Byron from behind.

"Yeah, sorry. Dev's sealed into my study. Just checking on him."

Gus chuckled. "Kena? You used that one?" Gus pointed to where the door to the study had been.

"Too obvious?"

"Not if he doesn't know a thing about runes. Glad you weren't my teacher. That's mean."

"I have faith he'll figure his first test out. The book with the answer is in the stack I left for him."

"Well, here's hoping he figures the rune is Kena" Gus shouted the rune's name out loud, while giving Byron a shake of his head. "You really can be an asshole, but it's one of the things I love about you. Come downstairs. We need you and the two...ah...guests are not liking the current arrangements. And it's time for Addas."

"Not surprising neither of them would be happy about their forced involvement, but we need them. Or more, we need the energy their species contain."

"You sure this ritual won't kill them?"

"Well, not that we'll say anything to Addas, but there's no guarantee. In the end though, does their survival matter? It's a human-eating fae and a werewolf."

"Good point."

Gus turned and headed down to the depths of the dungeon while Byron went the opposite direction and poked his head into the kitchen. Addas sat at the kitchen table with a large leather-bound book of his own, a cup of tea at his ready, and a couple of gears which hovered above the surface of the table, winding and grinding all on their own.

"What are you doing?" Byron came up behind Addas and slipped his hands down his front, feeling the massive chest of his lover.

"Oh, searching, like you. Hoped maybe I could find something in the technomage texts. Maybe there's a code or browser search we haven't come across. But I'm not getting anywhere fast." Addas sighed, glancing over his shoulder. "As I haven't for the past year. You know, Byron, we haven't talked about what *might* happen. I'm terrified, but trying to keep my shit all together. I don't want to go yet. I'm not done." His breath hitched.

"We're not going to lose you. I promised you after the incident we'd fix this, and that's what we're going to do. I have something concocted in the bottom level. We're going to try out the purification ritual this afternoon. But I need you down there."

"Is this what you and the boys have been up to?" Addas grabbed Byron's hands, squeezed them, then stood, and faced his mate.

"I think I may have a way to pull the wolf energy out, using healing fae vitality, the usual alchemical anti-werewolf ingredients, and a recipient for your wolf infection. After all, wolf should attract wolf, right? In addition, we'll have all the energy we'll need from the battery and the ley lines."

"Byron, you're not using the two guys downstairs as guinea pigs, are you? I won't let you."

"Look, if all goes right, and I have every reason to believe this will work, the only thing that will happen is the fae and dog boy will be super tired when we're done. I can't kill the fae. If Dev ever found out, I'd lose him before I ever had him initiated into the coven. If the werewolf doesn't survive the procedure, well, no loss there in my books, but we don't need any more reasons for the wolf pack to come knocking. If this all goes to plan, by tonight, you'll be free of the wolf, and I'll let the other two go. Besides, we have to use up some of the faerie power. I can't send him out into the world like he is now. We'll draw more of his fae out so he can be more human."

"That didn't work the last time."

"It worked well enough."

"The girl is living in the mental ward at the university hospital." Addas tightened his grip on Byron's hands. "Please, don't do this."

"I promise, this will work." Byron brought Addas's hands up and gave them a kiss. "Now, can you come downstairs and activate the globe?"

"You need a conductor or you'll blow the whole place up. And besides, the globe is in your study, no?"

"Yes."

"Aren't the boys locked in there?"

"Well, you know, you can do your technomagy stuff."

"Jesus, Byron." Addas shook his head but, in the end, threw his hands up in surrender and followed his lover to the bottom level where few people were ever invited.

# Chapter Twenty-One

DEV POUNDED HIS head on the desk surface several times. They'd been in the room for well over two hours and he hadn't come up with anything.

Tully twiddled his thumbs, looking about as bored as any witch had ever been. But despite his boredom and frustration, he had tagged along to be support for Dev. But even support had its limits.

"Okay, this has taken too long. I can't stand this any longer." Tully closed the book he'd been leafing through for the third time, stood up, walked over to the desk, put his hands on the surface, and leaned over. Glaring at Dev, he said, "What happened the first time you got to see me use magic?"

"You're not supposed to help." Dev glared in response.

Frustrations had bubbled to a breaking point.

"I don't care. You should have figured this out already. Besides, I'm getting hungry, and if I know Addas, he'll have sandwiches ready for us as soon as we're done." Tully's stomach rumbled in objection to being empty.

"I repeat, you are terrible."

Tully chortled, "It's all good. I'm not giving you the answer, but I might lead you toward it. Focus. Do you remember?"

"Of course I remember. Drawing the symbol and hearing sand rustling as you tried to open my new apart—" Dev's eyes expanded as the memory hit him. He face-palmed himself. "I can't believe I didn't think of that."

"Sometimes a new witch needs a hint or two. It's okay."

"Byron gave me a book of runes." Dev sorted through the tomes given to him to study. "Yup, this one." Dev flipped through the pages and within a few minutes exclaimed a cheer, "Kena! The rune of opening. But the symbol has other meanings as well, like clarity, sincerity, and concentration." Dev's brows furrowed as his finger followed the lines in the book, reading as fast as his brain assimilated the words. "Does that matter?" Finally. Patience and kindness had persevered and Dev had his answer.

"Runes are versatile. I do believe you have figured out the solution to your problem." Tully exhaled.

"It's the same symbol you drew on the door."

"Exactly."

"So, I just draw the symbol on the box!"

"Try it." Tully took a step away.

Dev stood up, grabbed the box, and placed the cube in the center of the desk. He took a couple of deep breaths and drew the symbol for Kena. The rune replicated a sideways *V*, or maybe more like the lesser-than sign used in mathematical equations.

The symbol Dev had drawn appeared black, like ink tattooed into pale skin, different from the one he'd seen Tully invoke. His had been a tawny colour, which might have been the difference between their different attunements. The rune stayed there for a few seconds and then disappeared.

"Okay, so...why didn't that work?" Dev picked up the box and inspected it. He flipped the box over several times and pushed at a few spots on the smooth woodgrain surface.

Nothing happened.

Tully leaned up against a bookcase spoke up, "You need to tap into your own element. You can't draw a symbol and expect magic to happen. You have to power the symbol with energy. So, I call on the power of earth. You have to figure out how to gain access to spirit."

"Ugh." Dev threw his head back. "How the hell do you do that?" Dev growled in frustration.

"And here we sit for another three hours." Tully hung his head. "Try to find the energy within you. This is the first lesson. Not the rune. Byron is asking you to figure out how to trigger or use your own well of power."

Dev stared at him blankly.

The afternoon drug on, Dev staring at the box, while Tully's stomach grumbled again, this time in protest.

BYRON, MADE HIS way through the heavy metal door, closing it, soundproofing the subterranean level from the rest of the house. Gus and Eddie were already down here, and he hoped Addas would join them soon. As he rounded the corner at the end of the stairwell, he observed Everton, who paced in his cage, and then noticed the floating shackles from Cam's cell.

"Well Cam, that's impressive. I think you've become too much fae and we need to tip the scales." Byron grabbed a chair and swung the seat around to sit in front of Cam's bars.

"Fuck you," Cam's voice uttered from within his cage, but came from nowhere in particular. Byron squinted, trying to discern where Cam's head might have been. The ownerless words reminded Byron of a haunting.

"Now, now. Remember what I said about anger and words? You want to be set free, you have to show me you're more human than fae and that you can control your emotions. So far, you're not doing either." Byron positioned himself in the chair, crossed his legs and arms. Eddie and Gus were busy doing other things in the room. "So, Cam, we have a ritual we need to do down here, and I need your help. I'm going to make a deal with you."

"Pretty sure I said 'Fuck you." More ethereal words from the air. The claddings moved as Cam's body shifted, giving away Cam's actual position.

"Leave him alone," Ev snarled.

"Ev, enough from you."

"Why do you treat him like shit? God, you're such an asshat," Cam shouted.

"He's the reason I have to perform this ritual," Byron snapped.

"He had it coming! Filthy witch. You steal what is not yours!" Ev barked and growled. Low, deep and loud. The rumble sent shivers down Byron's spine. Everton Lilch had to easily be the largest wolf Byron had come across, and he'd seen his fair share. The beasts were not something to be trifled with. Capturing him had been one hell of a task and a regretful night where the coven had lost brothers.

"You attacked him. You are responsible for the mess we're in right now." Byron raised his voice, which ricocheted off the concrete walls and floor of the basement dungeon. Losing control of his emotions meant Byron had lost control of the situation, something which rarely occurred. He needed to get himself in check for this afternoon's ritual. Embarrassed by his loss of control, Byron's cheeks and neck bloomed with heat. "And unless you want me to remind you of what witches will do to punish bad behaviour, you'll hold your damn tongue." Byron's jaw clenched tight, lips pursed, brows furrowed thinking of his Addas.

With a threat of impending torture, Ev quietened, although he continued to mumble to himself.

"What does he mean?" Cam materialized, like someone had peeled a blanket off him, glancing at Ev, concern and worry in his eyes.

"Everton was the one who infected Addas. We were ambushed while tapping a secondary ley line. In the fight that night, we were taken by surprise. We lost good men for no reason other than some stupid vendetta. Addas nearly died he'd been mauled so badly. But in the end, we overpowered the bloody mutts. This one here tangled with Eddie, and rocks hurt like hell when slammed into a skull. Knocked him the fuck out. We should have killed him, but Eddie wanted a subject to study, you know, all part of the zooempathy in him. So Everton got sedated and brought here. We lost coven brothers and we didn't know what to do with Addas. We knew he'd been infected. Once bitten, there's no reversing or curing lycanthropy. Or so everyone believes. But I've got a spell figured out. And today we're going to fix Addas."

"No shit," Cam stared at Ev. For the few days they'd be locked up together, Everton had failed to mention this tidbit of information.

"All's fair in war. If you bastards weren't hoarding all the energy from the ley lines, maybe we'd have some peace and equality around these parts."

"That's an interesting take on it," Byron scoffed.

"How so?" Cam glared at Byron. If anyone should be believed, the credit went to the caged animal, not the witch who'd tortured Ev for the last year.

"This is not your battle, Cam, and the dog is wrong. We keep the balance by ensuring there's enough energy for everyone but less for the darker forces." Byron threw a thumb in Ev's direction. "Can't have them running wild and crazy. We've been tasked with ensuring the protection of the Shadow Realm in this area for hundreds of years. And during our reign, we've kept the peace. You don't see demon possessions here or fae uprisings or spree killings by werewolves. Why? Because we keep the energy levels locked down. The result? Balance." Byron puffed out his chest. Gus and Eddie had taken position behind him, their arms both crossed as well.

"That's some lofty goals, mister." Cam questioned him. "You're playing Mother Nature? God maybe? You get to decide who gets what? That doesn't equate to balance for me. That sounds like you have all the power and you decide who gets a meager stipend and who doesn't." Cam glanced at Everton with sympathy for the prisoner. Cam's lips thinned as his anger stirred. Sharp pointy teeth poked out of his mouth as his eyes shrunk into his head and the skin around them went black. Cam's wings sputtered several times, his tail lashing back and forth. "I think I get why he's so angry with you."

"Cam, not your worry. Besides, I have a deal for you. But you need to check your anger. You help me perform this ritual to rid Addas of the hound infection and we'll let you go."

"Sorry, what now?" Cam's teeth grew longer as his anger swelled. "You need me for exactly...?"

"Fae have healing ability. Look at the skin near your handcuffs and ankle restraints. The iron burns all fae. The flesh might sting for a bit, but your body heals itself. I need more of your mojo juice. You give me more fae fluid and we'll let you go after our spell work as long as Addas is cured."

"Really?" Cam tilted his head and sneered. A long pointy tongue flicked out, like a snake sensing the environment. "That's a fantastic deal. I'll let you suck out more spinal juice from me, which by the way, stings like a mother fucker. So, you do your hocus pocus and you'll let me waltz out of here."

"As long as Addas is healed. And with what I have planned, this will work."

"And if I agree to this, you let Everton go too."

"Nope. Can't do that. He's a filthy beast, and I can't risk releasing him and having him infect anyone else or kill anymore witches. No. He stays here."

"But you said you can't have me wandering about either, so how do I know to trust you?"

"If I take enough juice out, you won't be able to do any fae shit. I figure a good six vials should do the trick. Apparently we haven't taken enough yet. Look at you."

"Six? Do you know how many you've already sucked out of me? Seventeen. Believe me, I kept count." Cam hissed as his eyes popped open and widened, looking like giant-sized cue balls. "Do you have any idea how bad one vial hurts? And you want to take six? You'll kill me."

"It might feel like it, but I swear, the procedure won't kill you. Just keep you human."

"I don't think I want to be human anymore. So, that's a no from me."

Byron glanced over his shoulders at Eddie and Gus. They changed their stance from backup on guard to poised and ready to strike, arms outstretched and magic ready to cast. The air in the basement dungeon thickened and became electric.

"Nice. Who's the animal now? You have me shackled and caged, and you're the one bringing additional goons to the fight?"

"Look, all we need is the fae juice. I'll be gentle. It'll be easier if you just let it happen."

"Once again, fuck you." Cam raised the middle finger on each of his hands and jerked them both toward Byron. His wings beat fast and furious and his tail switched to and fro like a metronome.

"Being angry won't help, Cam."

"I think it's going to help me fine." Cam, uncontrollably angry, began to disappear again.

Byron shook his head, then turned to face his knights. "Boys, it's time."

Eddie raised his hands and with a flick of his wrist, the bars on the cell collapsed into piles of iron fillings on the floor. Byron stood up and pushed the chair off into the corner. Gus created whirlwinds that shifted the metal flakes from many small mounds into several big ones. Eddie made strange gestures with his fingers. The metal flakes were reforming into snakelike ribbons that lashed out toward the invisible Cam, trying to snare him.

"I need you to be still, Cam. Let this happen," Byron commanded.

As much as Cam crouched and darted to dodge Eddie's magical metal ropes, the shackles prevented him from going far. The clanking of the iron links moving rang throughout the basement like out of tune gongs. Byron moved forward, extending his hand as his fingers burst into flame. The heat never bothered him, but the magical pyre would subdue the faerie. He placed his hand where Cam's chest should have been. Byron had to guess where Cam's body parts should be based off the floating handcuffs.

An ear splitting shriek pierced the chamber as Cam's flesh seared in the heat. Fur singed and melted into the fae skin. Cam became momentarily visible as his eyes rolled into his head.

Everton yelled out, "Stop it! Leave him alone."

Byron grabbed Cam's arm with his flaming fingers. Cam lunged forward and attempted to bite him, but one of Eddie's ropes wound around his neck.

Gus, using his air vortexes, pulled a new contraption out from the recesses of the room. A corner that had been so dark Cam had never been able to see into the shadows and his fae aura had never illuminated.

A huge 'x' made out of wood with a wide plank in the middle and a slim board across the top skittered into the room and in behind Cam.

Eddie moved closer, and as he did, the iron rope around Cam's neck tightened. It swung around the top board on the big X, and with one tight pull, Eddie had fastened Cam to the rack.

With fiery hands, Byron positioned Cam, skin blistering and popping, while Eddie's ropes ensnared his arms and legs. Despite the violent struggle Cam ended up spread eagle, ramrod straight, back exposed, and unable to move. The iron ropes tightened again, biting into his flesh, and the sizzle of his skin dominated the small concrete room, as did the aroma of burning fae flesh.

"Grab the syringe and the tubes, Gus." Gus did as told, returning with a rolling stainless steel cart complete with several instruments, all of which were designed to inflict pain. Byron leaned in close to Cam's furry pointed ear. "We'll get our juice whether you cooperate or not, but I had hoped you would've made this easier, Cam. Addas's life depends on this."

"What about mine?" Cam screeched as the first needle dove into his flesh and punctured his spinal column.

"Stop it!" Everton yelled as he pounded on is bars. But silver against a werewolf stings as much as iron on a fae.

The knights of the Coven of the Night Grove always got what they needed to keep the balance.

# Chapter Twenty-Two

CAM FOUGHT VICIOUSLY.

His wings had given the men a sound beating, but to no avail, and one of the appendages hung loosely, ripped part way through.

His tail had lashed out several times, slicing the darker-haired witch and inflicting a deep cut across his cheek, but after several violent flicks, an audible crack occurred, alongside a sharp pain near the base and now the appendage hung lifeless from his body.

Beaten, bruised, and burned, he'd been stuck with the syringe multiple times. Several vials of effervescent fae juice lay on the table pushed up against the wall. On the surface lay more devices of pain and torture that had been used on him. They had injected him with several other potions as well, any of them should have made him sleepy, according to Byron. But none of them had worked. Maybe his fae resistance to poisons had kicked in.

But with the removal of all the fae goo, he shouldn't have had any abilities whatsoever. For whatever reason, Cam's fae powers simply didn't wane.

Three experienced and adept, muscular witches with near limitless amounts of magical energy still had difficulty in taking the royal fae down. Despite Cam's staying power, he didn't stand a chance as a newly formed fae. He acted out of instinct and fear, not from calculated and practiced combat maneuvers. After a long battle, Cam lost.

Byron, Gus and Eddie were in the last stages of completing the set up for what appeared to be an important ceremony. The cages holding Cam and Ev were gone, and in their place were two St. Andrew's Crosses, one on each side of the room, Cam strapped to one, with iron cuffs around his wrists and ankles, tighter than the shackles they had used in his cell, and a new one around his throat, holding his head back slightly. If he attempted to adjust his view, his neck came in contact with the metal. But his arms and neck were in unnatural positions, which made his muscles tired and strained from attempting to keep the skin away from the tortuous metal.

His head dipped forward and exposed flesh seared as it touched the metal. Everything hurt. Cam had fought valiantly, to no avail.

But despite the excruciating pain, he had one grain of hope he clung to. After succumbing to the knights' torture, he had sensed Dev.

The familiar and comforting vibration of his best friend taunted him. And as much as he hoped for the possibility Dev would come to save him, the fact that it hadn't happened yet was another puncture of the syringe. Except instead of sucking fae fluid out of him, the betrayal drained the bond of his relationship with Dev. Knowing Dev kept the company of these men who would inflict such pain upon living creatures made Cam tear up. He had shed several in anger, pain, and sadness. Rivulets ran down his cheeks, washing away the grime from being held captive, the soot from Byron's fire, and the blood spray from several wounds. Whose blood Cam didn't know.

Why hadn't Dev come to find him? Why hadn't he'd been saved? A lifetime of memories flashed through Cam's mind of him and Dev. Memories now hurt more than the sting of iron or syringes.

Ev had been similarly restricted. As if the dungeon needed another rank odor, the nose-wrinkling scent of burning werewolf hung in the air. The metal restricting Ev had to be silver, and magically the element did as much damage to him as the iron did to Cam.

Eddie, the witch Cam had slashed with his tail, grabbed his head and wrapped a thick strip of material across his eyes. But with all the fighting and tussling about, a corner of the fabric used as a blindfold had lifted giving him a small window to see the actions of the upper ranks of the Coven of the Night Grove.

In between him and Ev, a massive circle had been chalked out, and Byron walked around the area several times sprinkling moonglow water. Gus had already called forth the element of air, as wisps of smoke circled and intertwined around one another creating a hypnotic counterclockwise motion around the magical area.

Eddie manipulated the salt crystals, building up the circle's outer rim, following the intricate diagram written out on an old tattered scroll. The illustration's complexity proved difficult to set up. Circles within circles, and hex marks were written between two concentric rings, but there were gaps in the center of the sphere outlined with two thick lines. By the time Eddie finished his work, there were four circles within the larger magical outer circle, and adjoining lines shooting out from the main area, with additional rings drawn around him and Everton. There were symbols and witch script, and things Cam had no knowledge of in terms of what they were supposed to do. The entire set up escalated his gnawing fear, making Cam weep. Death was certain.

If Dev were here, Cam might have made reference to a certain summoning board that had similar markings. Etchings placed around the outer edges to "make the board look all gothic and shit". Cam had seen some of these symbols before and now recognized they weren't for decoration. The ones from the infamous summoning board that had started this nightmare hadn't been either.

"All right Addas, time to do your bit." Byron rubbed his hands together. Addas had joined only a few moments before. He had hung in the shadows of the room and paced.

"I don't want you to do this. Is this necessary?" Addas pointed toward Cam.

"Did you want him running around free?"

"Honestly? Yes."

"Addas, we've been through this. We need their energy, their essence. Cam's fae healing abilities, supernatural luck, and anything else his wild magic will lend will be beneficial. Ev will attract the wolf out of you. The beast inside you will recognize its own kind and will want to be near it. This will work. It *has* to work." Byron's face flushed as he spoke, and his voice got louder. "I love you. I am not willing to let you go. Please. I need you to bring the battery here. Call the sphere to you."

"Have you got a conductor as well?" Addas's shoulders slumped in resignation as he reminded Byron of the electrical need.

"Yes, Eddie ensured there are silver filings mixed in with the salt. We used the material from the werewolf cage. The metal will act as the conductor and disperse the stored energy."

"Did you want direct access to the ley lines?" Addas asked with an edge of reluctance in his voice.

"If you can pull that off, yes! The more energy the better. This will come off without a hitch."

Addas shook his head, pursed his lips, and frowned. "I hope you're right." Addas shook his hands a few times, exhaled and inhaled deeply, then closed his eyes. He held his arms out in front of him, and turned them so they looked like they were getting ready to catch an enormous ball.

The air around Cam thickened and filled with an intense hum, as if a massive summer electrical storm were coming. If he had been able to shift his head and view his arms, he'd know the hair would be standing up on end.

*Zap!*

Addas held a large brownish globe with golden lines wrapping around the sphere in all directions.

ANOTHER THIRTY MINUTES had passed with Dev closing his eyes and focusing hard on trying to tap into his natural abilities.

Tully became more and more impatient, and not from a disbelief in Dev, but from his plummeting blood sugar. He was starving. Hangry didn't even sufficiently describe his current mood. But he tried with all his might to muster the patience necessary to get Dev to succeed in this first challenge.

"Dev, you're thinking too much. You're not feeling." Tully held his head in his hands, then let his hands drop, not wanting Dev to pick up on his disappointment, frustration, and impatience.

"I'm sorry! I don't understand why I can't get this." Dev peeled his lips back exposing clenched teeth.

Tully got up and walked around the desk and stood behind Dev, wrapping his big muscular arms around his boyfriend. Dev rubbed his bearded cheek against the fur covering Tully's arms and sighed.

"Don't be discouraged. That won't help. Have confidence in yourself. You're a witch! You can do this." Tully squeezed Dev in a hug.

The electronic *zap* caught Tully's attention as he honed in on the source of the noise. Dev followed Tully's motion and both focused on the globe as the sphere shimmered for a second until the ball crumpled, disappearing while imploding in on itself.

"Holy shit!" Dev pointed toward the empty spot. "Cool as shit! Why can't I learn this!"

"That was Addas." Tully beamed. "Translocation, but he can only manipulate tech-like objects. He's found my phone for me on more than one occasion." Tully chuckled. "I wonder what they want with the globe?"

"I could sit and watch the thing for hours. The fireworks those lines shoot off are so damn cool." Dev stroked Tully's arms.

"It's more than a map. It's a big battery of sorts. Byron uses the globe to store the excess energy from the ley lines."

"I have so much to learn." Dev shook his head.

"Hey, remember? No desperation. It makes worry lines which don't look good on you."

"I should have already completed this task. I don't feel much like a witch right now."

Tully gave his boyfriend another squeeze. Grinning from ear to ear, Tully licked his lips. "I think I have an idea."

"Yeah, what's that? No, don't tell me. You're not supposed to help and you've already done too much." Dev rested his elbow on the desk with the sealed box in front of him. He shook his fists at the object. "Open already!"

Tully chuckled but withdrew from Dev. "I'm not going to give you the answer to everything, but I think I know how to make you tap into your power."

"Mmhmm, how?"

"Trust me?"

"Sure."

"Close your eyes." Tully walked around to the front of the desk. He studied Dev who gave him an "I'm not sure I trust you" stare through squinted eyes. "Close them!" Dev did as instructed, however reluctantly. "Okay, good, now keep them closed. No matter what you hear or feel, keep them closed."

"What are you scheming?"

"Shh. Okay, now pick up the box and hold the thing in your left hand. Concentrate on the weight, how the wood feels balanced in your hand. Feel the grain, notice how smooth and polished the sides are. Picture the center of the box, imagine its hollow center, and visualize what might be contained within it. Think of nothing but the box, the lines of it, the shape, perfectly square, get lost in the pattern of the wood grain. It's so smooth."

Dev held the box, his brow furrowed, creating worry lines across his forehead.

"Now, with your right hand, draw the symbol for Kena on the surface of the box and whisper its name. Repeat the action over and over, get lost in the sound of the rune. Kena." Tully had slipped beneath the desk, positioning himself so he aligned headfirst in front of Dev's crotch.

He unzipped Dev's fly. Within a few movements, Dev's thickening cock greeted Tully. Dev's junk had heft and radiated heat from being packed away for most of the day, but the soft skin and fuzzy balls left Tully salivating.

"Tully! What are you—" Dev's voiced disappeared and transformed into a moan as Tully wrapped his warm wet lips around Dev's shaft. Dev's moan deepened into a growl. Dev's hand hit the desk surface with a *smack*. Gripping the base of Dev's thick cock with one hand and cupping his ball sack in the other, Tully's lips stretched as Dev's member filled. In no time, Tully's mouth was chock full with warm pulsating man meat. As his shaft lengthened and thickened, the engorged penis filled his mouth to the point where he started to gag. Tully had to pull off, but only for a second. And with a *pop* he released Dev's thick mushroom shaped head from his lips. "Don't stop Dev, and keep on repeating Kena. Let me do my thing here. You do your thing."

"Oh!" Dev replied, getting it.

Tully hoped the sexual excitement would release a burst of energy, something akin to what had destroyed his bedroom the first night the two of them had spent together. If Dev focused his excitement into the rune, this exercise would be over as soon as Dev shot off a load.

And Tully gave this task his undivided attention.

Up and down, sucking gently, with his tongue masterfully teasing the head, slipping his tongue underneath the foreskin, ensuring the most sensitive spots were getting the most attention. Tully left a slick of saliva, which he used as slippery lubricant, using the hand at the base of Dev's shaft to stroke and suck at the same time.

Warm, wet, and the right amount of pressure. Tully's head bobbed up and down.

Dev moaned "Kena" more than saying the word as an invocation.

Tully refused to give up. He continued until Dev's balls constricted and pulled up close to Dev's body, and his shaft became rigid.

"Oh, shit..." Dev's one hand clenched the edge of the table tighter as his hips bucked forward, pushing his swollen cock as far as Tully's throat would allow.

Dev was so close.

Tully took note of Dev's balls tightening. The cue urged him to go even faster and suck harder.

# Chapter Twenty-Three

BYRON PULLED THE stainless steel cart toward Ev. Reaching for another syringe, and an empty chamber, he slid the needle into Ev's arm and let the pumping action of his heart fill the tube full of werewolf infection liquid.

"Filthy," Byron muttered to himself. Ev, who had succumbed to all the sleeping agents the knights injected into him, lolled his head to one side and mumbled something unintelligible.

With another tube filled, Byron slid the needle out. A blood drop beaded on the skin, grew large, then rolled down Ev's arm. Byron wasn't worried about putting gauze on the puncture wound. The werewolf in him would heal the hole. Byron shuddered at the sight. Filthy dog blood. With the toe of his shoe, he stepped on the blood smearing it into the concrete.

Byron glanced up to see Gus and Eddie who had taken their positions within the ritual area. Addas had too as his hands rotated and flowed, as if he were performing Tai Chi movements. The ley line globe floated in front of him. Electrical bolts of pure white energy erupted from the bottom and struck the dividing center of the magical circle created on the basement floor.

Eddie flicked his fingers. Where the lightning bolts from the battery hit the floor, Eddie manipulated the concrete floor so the cement crumbled away opening and exposing a thin vein of what resembled white gold. The vein sparked and pulsated. Beneath this floor, hidden under the concrete, a ley line pulsed. The energy source provided the coven with additional power and had been a deciding factor generations ago on placing the house on this patch of land, and why the subterranean rooms were built to accommodate ritual work so close to the energy source.

This ritual would expend an enormous amount of energy, but anything the coven did to protect Addas against his impending doom would be worth the effort.

Byron took his prize tube of blood and set it on the work space situated at one end of the room. On the table sat a mortar and pestle, the vials of fae juice, and a variety of other alchemical properties, herbs, and minerals.

Flipping through the imported French lexicon he had shown Addas a couple of days ago, which had been the only one to have described the purging of a lycanthropy infection, Byron fingered each line of the recipe before him. With quick movements, he measured out the various components, mixing dried and crumbled bark from a Mountain Ash, a couple of desiccated mistletoe berries, and the dried flowers of deep purple Monk's Hood, and placed them into the mortar. He grabbed the glass test tube holding the Spriggan limb. As he opened the cork and slid a long pair of tweezers into the narrow opening, diminutive tendrils wrapped around the end of the stainless steel utensil, attacking it. But the tiny body part's violent barrage barely phased Byron. Hell, the whole Spriggan would have been defenseless. Snapping the twig between the two prongs of the tweezer, Byron's eyes squinted as he dropped the twitching twig into the mortar. He had to hold the writhing plant in the liquid with the tweezers as the tendrils attempted to pull itself out of the bowl. Damn thing kept attempting to escape. With his free hand he sprinkled crystalized calcium into the mix, grabbed the pestle and began crushing all the items with a twisting motion.

As he pressed down on the twig, green sap squirted out. The tendrils writhed in a last burst of life, then became still. He continued until he'd created a glob of greenish paste.

Next the herbal healing properties were added. A clove of dried garlic, ginger, and thyme, all noted for their natural anti-viral and anti-bacterial abilities. Another good mix and the paste took on a more beige colouration.

Byron added a healthy dose of the effervescent green mojo juice, and as the glowing, bubbling emerald goo hit the herbs, a *crackle* erupted from the tiny bubbles, hastened by the additional ingredients. Smoke billowed up from the bowl and ran over the edges, like the pouring of water over dry ice.

Byron stirred the concoction and glanced up. Gus chanted, keeping the element of air circling the outer ring of the ceremony space. Eddie circulated around the ritual area ensuring the salt and silver lines maintained their placements while widening and deepening the opening in the floor, exposing the glowing gold ley line that had lain hidden. Addas, his monstrous and muscular form shadowed against the bright light in front of him, stood positioned in the center of the ritual sphere, setting the battery so the housed energy would power the spell. As he made links between the globe and the chalked out lines, each connection illuminated a quadrant of the larger circle, the magical glyphs glowing bright blue-white.

Nodding to himself, Byron held confidence in his knights. The plan continued according to his perfect coordination. Admittedly, the ceremony consisted of a hodgepodge melding of several schools of theory into one huge infection-ridding, purification ritual.

For the final touch, Byron took the syringe holding the werewolf blood. He pressed the plunger with great care. He didn't want any of the blood on himself, and only a miniscule amount would be required.

A single drop of blood welled up from the tip of the needle, expanded in diameter, and fell.

Byron's excitement level peaked as the blood drop descended into the bowl. The atmosphere of the room thickened with magic and Bryon's anticipations grew. As the werewolf blood hit the top of the concoction the red contrasted against the pale green brew. As the blood dissolved, immersing itself into the roiling potion, coils of deep red swirled out along the surface, like a flower unfurling it's petals in the new light of day.

Like a live vaccine, the single werewolf blood drop should introduce the virus into the serum, but not be enough to make a human seroconvert. There wasn't enough of the virus for full lycanthropy to take hold. And Byron hoped with all the other magical components, this tainted liquid would turn into a vaccine. A tincture of health. Injecting this into Addas, along with jolting him with the energy from the battery and the ley lines would activate the magical properties to expel the wolf out from Addas.

One last problem remained.

Once the wolf had been cast out, the foul creature would want somewhere to go, and that's where Everton came in. If Everton suffered from a mortal wound, the rogue wolf spirit would merge into one body in order to save one of its kind. This sacrificial blending had been written about in all the books he had collected on lycanthropic lore.

So, problem solved.

Byron took a fresh needle, placed the end into the pestle and lifted the plunger, pulling up his created vaccine. The fluid had taken on a slight yellowish cast, making the serum look like pus.

He placed the vial on his work table next to the other syringes, one of blood, several of fae mojo.

Grabbing a large serrated hunting knife, he walked over to Everton.

"Is everyone ready? This is the last step."

Addas turned. "I'm not quite ready, I need a few minutes to— What are you doing?" Addas's hands dropped as he observed the huge blade Byron held.

"He needs to be wounded. Once we get the wolf out of you, the spirit will be attracted to a wounded Everton, who will absorb your wolf and the two wolves will combine in order to heal their host. I have tons of documentation citing the phenomenon. You'll be free. The trick is getting the wolf out of you, and for that, we have this." Byron held up the vial with the pus-like liquid

"Byron, no. I can't let you." Addas took a step out of the circle.

"Stop. Not another step forward Addas. The ritual has to go like this. We're out of time and we've worked so hard to get this far. This is the only way."

"I can't let you continue hurting everything in your path to try to save me. My life is not worth all this pain and blood!"

Byron's lips tightened into a frown as his eyes glassed over. "It is worth it!" Byron yelled. "Why won't you do this? This will set you free and we won't have to worry about the damn wolf in you any longer!"

THE GUT-WRENCHING guilt stabbing Addas's stomach reflected in the grimace on his face. The deep conflict of trusting Byron with all his schemes, or giving in to the werewolf infection and his inevitable doom had tormented him for a year.

Be free, or die. Nestle within the arms of his lover for ever and ever, or suffer a horrible death as two incompatible branches of magic destroyed his body trying to maintain a balance within a human form.

He couldn't abide by all the wretched things Byron had done, and yet, he'd done them trying to save him. He didn't feel worthy of the sacrifices that had been made in order to save him. He was worried the gods would judge them for sacrificing so many victims along the way.

But at the same time, he didn't want to lose Byron. And he didn't want his life to end. Witch lives were short, but he hadn't even reached forty yet. Surely what Byron proposed was the only way.

Cam would still live, despite some scars from the extractions. Everton would experience momentary pain before the wolf spirits would save him. Besides, the drugs they'd used to sedate him ensured he'd felt very little. In fact, he might never know.

Addas had to trust Byron.

He had to do this.

Addas's head hung as his shoulders slumped.


"ADDAS, ALL THE battery connections made?" Byron asked his mate.

"Only the ley line remains to be linked," Addas reported.

Byron began to run through his mental checklist of items. With the vaccine completed and waiting to be administered, his coven knights placed and doing their jobs keeping the circle intact, the energy flowed from the storage globe powering up the ritual area. The ley line had been exposed. All that remained was to connect the subterranean power source to the spherical battery, and wound Everton. The timing of this ritual in combination with the waning of the full moon had worked out perfectly.

"All right, Addas, complete the last connection. Let's do this." Byron stepped over to Everton and stuck the serrated knife into the wolf man's midsection, half way between his hips and his rib cage. The sharp blade sliced through the flesh easier than Byron had expected. Blood seeped to the surface of the wound, but as he pushed the knife in to the hilt more gushed out. Byron wished he had worn gloves.

It wasn't until he cut toward the belly did he encounter any resistance. Obviously he'd hit some critical organs along the way.

Everton made unusual noises. The straps held him tight to the wooden cross by the silver bands, but despite the metal, and his apparent unconsciousness, the wolf inside stirred.

Everton began shifting. But without a conscious human form and the silver restricting the wolf, the morphing became distorted and haphazard. Teeth grew through the cheek, the muzzle distended crooked, shoulder bones popped and snapped, but hung awkwardly. Ev bled out through his eyes and ears.

"Addas, now. Do it now!" Byron signaled to his lover.

Addas twisted his hands, like he was trying to pull something out of the base of the globe.

A thick bright white bolt erupted from the bottom of the globe snapping itself to the ley line.

An eerie hum filled the entire room.

Byron tensed inside. The moment had come. All his research, sacrifice and testing, the blood and tears had led to this moment.

And then all hell broke loose.


DEV'S EYES ROLLED as he lost himself in total ecstasy. The sensation of Tully gripping him at the base of his cock and sliding his hand up and down with his warm, wet mouth slathering his shaft had him about to explode.

"Tully, I'm gonna come." Dev gripped the table.

"Focus on the rune!" Tully garbled out.

Trying his damndest to do as instructed, Dev kept repeating the name of the rune, "Kena, Kena, Kena..." Except his words were getting louder and louder, until his body betrayed him and let loose. Dev's balls tightened up to his body as the first gush of his orgasm spilled. He yelled out, "Kena!"

Tully had mastered the act of pleasuring Dev, and the orgasm ranked in the top five of his life. The ripples of pleasure that washed over him were little earthquakes undulating his stomach muscles and buckling his knees.

Dev felt the semen rush through his shaft, only to burst forth inside Tully's mouth. The sensation of Tully's tongue lapping and lashing over his sensitive head as each stroke of Tully's hand pulled back his foreskin kept the orgasm going.

Dev inhaled deeply. His breath ragged and staggered, but as he drew air, he elongated his back, shivered with anticipation and held his head high. Vibrations filled and excited him.

TULLY KEPT HIS hands working, tongue licking, and his throat swallowing enough to ensure Dev experienced the best blow job he'd ever had.

An odd sensation swam over Tully. Despite giving the best blow job he'd ever performed, and thinking he should be aroused, the room around him tilted as his vision swerved. Tully let Dev slip out of his mouth, as he fell backward, throwing his hands out behind him to catch his own fall.

Energy drained out of him as Dev shook from the force of the orgasm.

Dev had tapped into his powers, but he accomplished the one thing Byron said he wouldn't be able to do.

Dev was siphoning energy.

Tully glanced around the room, trying to catch his bearings. "Dev…" Tully grabbed his boyfriend's leg.

"Dev..." Tully, caught up in the power drain, watched as snake-like tendrils of syphoned power writhed and wormed their way toward Dev.

Dev, lost in the convulsion of his orgasm, had no idea the spell he'd let loose.

CAM, STILL CONSCIOUS and in excruciating pain, writhed with anger toward Bryon. Desperation washed over him as he witnessed Byron plunge the huge blade into Everton. As the rage took over and billowed up inside, Cam became invisible once again, but this time, a new sensation emerged alongside his ire.

At the base of his skull, a tingling sensation bloomed, spreading over the top of his head, and down his face.

*I hope this entire thing goes sideways. Byron doesn't deserve to keep his mate.*

The energy in the room flickered, wavered, and stammered.

Byron pulled the knife out of Everton and placed the bloody blade within a large towel, folding the material over the blade, careful not to touch the blood, when a bright flash of light exploded all around him.

A wave of powerful energy detonated from the battery.

Cam braced himself for the impending explosion as everything in the room was thrown about in slow motion, the center of the blast emanating from the globe battery.

Wisps of white, tails and snakes, writhed and wriggled out from the middle of the detonation. They coalesced on the edges of the room, then twisted their way up the walls, and disappeared across the ceiling and up the stairwell. All of the sphere's energy, and the ley line's pulsating fuel travelled in one direction.

The direction where Cam felt Dev.

INSIDE BYRON'S STUDY the air hung thick. Thick with energy and magic. Tully lay on the ground clutching his chest and whispering, "Dev, stop. Stop."

Dev, lost within the swirl of energies hadn't noticed Tully's plea. So much energy. Vortexes of power twirled around him, sinking into him, being absorbed into his body.

Tully crawled out from under the desk, which took all of his will, rolled over and glanced up at his boyfriend.

Dev's eyes shone gold. A white aura hung around him. His lips parted as he uttered one word, "Kena."

For a second, everything lay in silence. One of those moments where nothing moved and the world stopped.

A bomb erupted. At its center stood Dev. Waves undulated out from the novitiate witch and as each ripple touched various objects in the room, drawers opened, books fell off their shelves and landed on the floor, exposing various pages while tearing others away from their bindings. Cabinets ripped their doors off the hinges, the door to the study burst open with such force the doorknob slammed against the outer wall. The sealed box flew across the room, its top ripped away from it.

The amulet inside spilled out onto the floor.

On the opposite side of the room, a bookcase vibrated and shook, and as the last wave hit, the case sprung open revealing a secret room.

Then silence.

Tully sucked in air, rolled over, and pushed himself up. His legs wobbled beneath him. "Well, we won't be doing *that* again." He swiveled his head to find Dev.

As the gold colour drained from Dev's eyes, he gaped at the destruction he'd created then noticed his limp dick hanging out, which he tucked away and zipped his pants up. When he spied Tully, shaky, wobbly and barely able to get to his knees, he ran over to him.

"Oh my god, Tully, what did I do? Are you okay? I'm so sorry." Winding his arm underneath Tully's and hugging him tight, Dev helped Tully stand up.

"I'm okay." Tully teetered to one side.

Dev helped right him. "I don't think so."

"I'll be fine, give me a minute. You sucked the energy right out of this room, and from outside of this room as well. You did the one thing Byron said you couldn't, at least yet."

"I siphoned energy."

"Hells yes you did."

"But I siphoned from you too!" Dev's eyes went wide and white, his mouth beginning to turn downwards.

"But you didn't mean to. It's okay. It'll take some time for me to replenish—"

"But not all, I stole some of your life force. I just shortened your life!"

"Dev, chill. It's okay. You didn't mean to do it. And I don't think you took— What's that noise?"

Dev swore he picked up on a faint rasping as well. Accompanied by barely audible scratching, a half-hearted whine whispered from the secret room.

"It's coming from the room behind the bookcase. Which, by the way, I didn't know existed. Cool." Tully broke away from Dev and walked toward the secret door. Dev followed.

The bookcase had become dislodged from its hinges and stood open. Dev and Tully had to push on the heavy structure in order to gain entrance to a small antechamber. The room's walls were so close together Dev could touch each side with his arms outstretched. The only light illuminating the room came from the study, and Tully grappled in the dark to try to find a light switch.

Dev took a step into the room, toward the scratching sound, as something brushed up against his forehead and through his hair setting off a panic mode as he brushed away the offending intruder, which Dev pictured as a monster spider descending from the ceiling to eat him.

Instead of a spider, Dev found a cord.

"Oh, Tully..." Dev pulled the cord as a bare lightbulb ignited and illuminated the room.

A tiny yelp called out in front of Dev and Tully as they both peered down to see a fragile creature, strapped to a wooden plank, squinting and trying to turn its head away from the light source.

It whined, and with long twig-like hands scratched the surface of the table. Dev wanted to scoop up the tiny and delicate terrified creature and soothe him.

"Holy shit, Dev. That's a Spriggan. I've never seen one before."

"What the hell is a Spriggan?"

"It's the lowest form on the fae family tree. Literally. An animated plant."

"It looks scared."

"If I remember, they are attached to a specific tree and spend their whole lives living in or on a single tree. This pint-size guy has been separated. It's not going to survive."

"Well, if that's the case, what the hell is he doing in a secret room of Byron's? Wouldn't he know that? Why would he do that?"

Tully glanced around the room. An assortment of tools, vials, and metal appliances were scattered about the work surfaces, all of them raising horrific and torturous images.

"I don't think I want to answer that." Tully glanced around. "What the hell was Byron doing?"

The tiny creature whined again, weak and barely able to move. But as Dev inched close, and leaned in to get a better look, the lowest of the fae reached out, as if begging for help, raising one slender branched arm toward Dev, whimpering.

"I can't stand listening to it, and look, it's missing a leg." Dev pointed. His finger lay close enough to the fae that the twig stretched out and grasped Dev's hand, gazing at him with big pleading eyes. "The poor thing."

Dev moved his hand away from the Spriggan and began undoing the straps holding him to the table top. The creature shuddered and shook. As soon as the last strap came off, the thing crawled over to Dev's hand, its missing leg making the movement jerky and clumsy.

Dev glanced at Tully. "Are they safe?"

"I don't think the poor thing is big enough to do anyone any damage, besides, he doesn't look very healthy."

Dried up micro leaves had fallen where the Spriggan had been strapped down. The sentient plant crawled up Dev's arm until he clambered onto his shoulder. Reaching out a tentative hand, the living plant placed its stick like fingers against Dev's cheek.

"I think he's thanking you," Tully offered.

"How do we help him?"

"It would need to return to his home tree. How would we even know where to take him?"

The Spriggan bent down to its other leg, snapped off a branch that would have been a tibia in a human and held the piece up, offering his body part to Dev.

It shoved the leg bone a few times in Dev's face.

"I think he wants you to take the leg part."

Dev placed his palm close to the creature, as the Spriggan placed the slender branch that had been its leg in the center of his palm, he pushed and pulled on Dev's fingers so the plant part became protected by Dev's closed hand.

The Spriggan placed both its hands over its chest, then reached up and placed them on Dev's cheek.

Dev's heartstrings were tugged. The unfortunate thing. Why he would have broken off a piece of itself and given the tiny plant part over to Dev remained a mystery.

The Spriggan, crawled down Dev's arm and into Dev's hand. Dev lay his palm out flat for the beastie.

It curled into a ball as if to go to sleep.

Dev watched, horrified as the creature disintegrated until only a tiny pool of green, effervescent fluid bubbled in the center of Dev's hand.

It seeped into Dev's skin, sizzling and smoking as the creature disappeared.

Dev's eyes went wide, again, as he turned to face Tully, one hand open, still smoking, the other clenching on to a tiny sprig that had been the leg of the Spriggan.

"That's the same liquid Byron put into the chalice at my binding!"

"Whoa, Dev. Your eyes are sparkling, like the liquid!"

"And all those coloured orbs I had been seeing, the hallucinations that had subsided? They're back. Tully...Do you know what this means?"

Tully went pale.

Byron had been killing these tiny creatures to get their fluid.

"Byron's been making us all drink dead fae."

# Chapter Twenty-Four

BYRON PROPPED HIMSELF up on one elbow and braced himself with his other hand. Blood trickled from a gash on his forehead. He shook his head, trying to stop the ringing in his ears and rid himself of the fuzzy vision.

*What the hell happened?*

The subterranean dungeon had blown up. Everything and everyone in the vicinity had been blasted to the outside edges of the room. The salted circles laced with silver shavings were scattered, the floor still split open, the ley line exposed and pulsated, but the edges where the floor met the concrete walls were covered in salt crystals and debris. The coven knights attempted to regain composure. Only the faerie and the werewolf, still chained and shackled to their crosses, looked unharmed and unfazed.

Addas crouched over, hugging his knees, shaking and rocking on the balls of his feet, huddled close to the wall he'd been blasted toward. Beside him lay the stainless steel cart Byron had left all his utensils on. Syringes filled with the various liquids lay scattered around him.

Byron stood up, shaky on his legs, and stumbled toward his lover. He laid his outstretched palm on Addas's massive shoulder when a warning growl resounded from deep within his mate's chest.

"Addas, are you okay?" Byron leaned in and whispered, "Still that wolf. I know it's getting harder—" Addas whipped his head around to stare at Byron. The look in his eyes told Byron in one short exchange Addas was terrified and panicked. Addas stretched out his hands to Byron, a gesture pleading for help.

"What the hell happened?" Gus yelled. He held his ears. Blood dripping from between his fingers.

In the second Byron took to glance at Gus and return his look to Addas, his lover's fear had vanished, and so had Addas.

Addas's head shape had distorted. The top of the skull had flattened out, and where his scruffy cheeks should have been, where unshaven nuzzles had woken Byron up every morning for many years, an elongated jaw had turned into a muzzle. Addas's once beautiful hazel-green eyes had morphed into a light grey, circled with a brilliant yellow halo around the pupil. The whites of the eyeball were slowing filling with blood.

"No, no! Addas, pull that in!"

"Oh shit." Eddie pulled himself away from the shifting Addas. Eddie's leg bent in an unnatural way. He grimaced as he pulled himself toward the stairwell.

Addas reared on his haunches. The transformation incubating for a year had begun.

"No! This is all wrong. You shouldn't be shifting yet. Not for another night or so."

A fang slid over of Addas's lower lip, extending from his upper gums. Blood trickled over the long tooth and dripped onto the floor.

Addas ascended, standing up to his full height. Byron had to lift his head in order to keep looking at his boyfriend. The monster filled the room.

Byron's lower lip trembled and his stomach dropped. He'd failed. He sank to his knees in defeat. He had lost his lover.

Byron noticed the syringes sticking out from Addas's side. Within one vial a quarter of the bright red contents still sloshed around in the chamber. Several others were partially filled with the effervescent bubbling fae fluid.

"No!" Byron fists slammed the floor as he scanned the vicinity, his gaze darting until he found what he searched for, the one vial that contained the yellow pus-like fluid, the vaccine he'd created.

Scampering toward the syringe and turning away from Addas, he grabbed the vial that had meant to be his lover's rescue. Maybe hope existed within the vaccine. Maybe this would still save Addas.

As Byron's hand grasped the needle, a sharp pain dug into his shoulder and slid all the way down his back. Fire blossomed in his flesh and spread with violent speed across the front of his chest as something wet dripped into the crack of his ass.

Byron turned, syringe grasped in one hand, and swung his arm with all his might toward the snarling and snapping beast.

The needle stuck into what had been his boyfriend.

Byron yelled a primal scream as he depressed the plunger, pushing the viscous fluid into Addas taught neck muscles.

But the stab only enraged the creature.

Its head jerked up toward the ceiling as the wolf opened its maw, exposing a row of razor sharp teeth. Releasing an eerie howl, making the hair on Byron's neck rise.

Skin ruptured and split. Byron stared in horror as Addas's internal wolf emerged from its yearlong dormancy. The human flesh fell off Addas, and the wolf that had lain asleep for so many months awoke, making a brutal first appearance.

Angry and crazed, the beast snapped.

Gus and Eddie attempted to make their way to the freedom of the stairwell, but the wolf leapt there faster than they might have ascended to their escape. In one fell swoop of a claw, long talons ripped through Gus's throat.

Gus grasped his slashed neck, blood spewing everywhere, cascading out from between his clenched fingers. He gurgled, but the wolf swung again. Gus lost one side of his face.

He dropped hard to the concrete floor with a sickening *smack*. He convulsed a few times, then lay still as the blood pooled out from underneath him, blooming and spreading into a large puddle behind his head.

Eddie screamed, clutching the top of his leg as the wolf-man stepped on it, preventing the witch from moving any further. The wolf bent over, its enormous mouth opened to full capacity; lunging forward, the beast took a chunk out of Eddie's side. The flimsy robe proved no barrier. A few snaps of the jaw and entrails lay all around.

One last bite ripped out Eddie's throat.

He lay silent next to his coven brother. No more screams, no more magic. The scent of death thick in the air.

The beast turned toward Byron.

Byron cried out and shook his head in denial. He held up a hand, as if the gesture would stop the beast. As his mate of several years came toward him, claws dripping with his knight's blood and bits of flesh still clinging to its rakish nails, Byron attempted to reason with the animal.

"Addas, please. We'll fix you. I love you—"

The monster pulled its head back, opened wide, and aimed a well-placed bite.

The maw came down hard on the soft tissue of the neck and shoulder. Clamping down, teeth pierced through flesh and hit bone. The wolf shook its head from side to side with Byron grasped in its maw.

Byron grabbed the wolf's head, trying to pry the beast off, but the wolf's locked jaw proved the action to be less than useless.

The beast's smooth dog tongue slathered over the wound, lapping up the blood as Byron's flesh oozed.

The werewolf released Byron, and as Byron fell, he smacked his head with a heavy *thunk*. The hard concrete split open a new flesh wound. The demon dog took a step away, twisted its head to the side scouring the room, sneered, pulling up a lip and exposed its teeth.

Spotting the stairwell, the wolf shifted its weight, and with a leap and a bounce, the creature raced up and away.

Byron's vision blurred. A hot burning sensation from his rendered flesh and the massive bite wound on his shoulder and neck made his stomach lurch. He vomited.

Byron lay in a growing pool of his own blood and puke.

It wasn't supposed to have gone like this.

Addas and he were supposed to have been together until they were old.

Byron's eyelids fluttered, then closed.


CAM STUDIED EVERYTHING from his forced confinement, but as Eddie got mauled, a funny thing happened. The magic belonging to Eddie that had created his metal confines disintegrated. And not wanting to attract the wolf's attention, he slipped down to the floor, laying quietly so as to not warrant any attention from the beast.

Cam had never been so afraid for his life, ever. He'd also never seen a man shift into a werewolf either. He secretly prayed he'd never have to witness a werewolf shift ever again.

Everton had also fallen from his confinement and lay in a crumpled heap.

Funny the wolf hadn't paid them any attention what-so-ever.

Was that luck? Fae luck? Or had Addas turned on his brethren for other reasons?

Cam, still shaking from the endorphin rush of watching three men mauled and gutted by a creature he'd only ever seen on the movies, realized why the wolf hadn't targeted him. Apparently anger and fear made him invisible.

With relief, Cam let out the breath he'd been holding for what seemed like eternity.

As the creature disappeared, bounding up the stairs, the door at the top banged, slamming shut again.

Cam lay there for a long while. Waiting to be sure the horror had left the building.

As Cam gathered his senses, his fear subsided, and he materialized. Furry, winged, tailed, and horned, a far cry from the demon-beast Addas had morphed into.

But the same type of creature lay beneath Everton's skin. Somewhere within the man that had shared in Cam's captivity, a beast lurked. And he'd seen small snippets of the anger on many occasions. He'd heard the rumble reverberate deep within the barrel chest. The noise signaled the beginning of a snarl or growl. He'd witnessed the glowing red eyes. The bursts of anger the wolf within him created.

Thankfully, Cam had not been around long enough for a full moon. That's when Ev's wolf would have burst forth. The idea of something else, a secondary creature living inside him made Cam shudder.

Cam glanced toward Everton, still lying in a heap. He should crawl over there and see if Everton had survived. After all, Everton had helped him. He'd goaded him into being fae, into discovering his power, and taunted him into learning how to wield it.

Everton had showed him kindness, in a gruff sort of way. And all the ranting he'd done about witches and how horrible they were panned out to be true.

Against his better judgement, Cam, as silently as possible, made his way over to Everton.

The wound in Ev's midsection had bathed him in his own blood. And parts of Ev were on the outside that should have been on the inside. The way Ev had fallen left him in a horrible position slumped to one side, guts hanging out, flesh sizzled from where the silver manacles had burned him. Trying to move Ev proved damn near impossible. His dead weight, almost too much for Cam as Ev outweighed him by at least two times. But after everything the two of them had been through, Cam wasn't about to let the man die alone and abandoned on a cold cement floor. Cam repositioned himself so Ev sat cradled in his lap. Ev let out a groan.

Was he coming to? Would he wolf out and kill Cam? The gaping wound in Ev's belly hadn't healed. But the gash didn't seem as deep or as long as had appeared only moments before.

A bit of intestine hung out the gash in Ev's side.

Cam poked the organ in.

That made Everton jump, and he clasped Cam's wrist.

Cam let out a yip, then covered his mouth.

"Help me?" Everton begged.

His wings flitted and his pointed hairy ears twitched.

"There's no way I can carry you. I'll have to go get help." Cam attempted to shimmy himself out from underneath Ev, his tail flicking back and forth in jerky movements. A wave of anxiety and terror washed over Cam which originated from Ev. The distress made Cam cold and sweaty.

"No, please, don't leave me," Ev pleaded. "You can help me."

Ev's eyes fluttered as he moaned and passed out cold.

Cam wasn't sure what the hell he should do.

Leaving Ev here to die didn't sit well with Cam, despite his need to flee. What if Ev did die? Cam would torment himself, knowing he left him behind. But freedom lay up the stairs, and Cam had no skills to assist Ev. He should go get help.

Cam glanced toward the stairs, his escape from this torture den, then glanced at Ev.

His shoulders slumped as he gave in. He had to stay with Ev.

The beast of a man was so big and heavy, the weight on Cam's lap restricted his blood flow. Within minutes, his toes started to tingle.

Ignoring the stinging sensation which had now traversed into his legs, Cam wrapped his arms around Ev, hugging him tight, and holding him against his chest.

Cam's wings fluttered and sparkled. Cam began to glow, an eerie blue light, and the warmth of the aura enveloped him and Ev.


DEV AND TULLY stared at each other.

"Did you know about this? Did you know Byron sacrificed these creatures and made us drink their... their...what the hell is this shit!" Dev roared.

A huge *bang* slammed.

Both Tully and Dev rushed out into the main study, Dev still grasping the tiny branch in his palm.

Something rushed past the door and up the stairs.

"Byron?" Tully called out, but there was no response. There were some more bangs and loud noises coming from upstairs, glass shattered, and rattling and clanking like pots and pans hitting the tile floor in the kitchen. Another *crash* and *bang*, but after the ruckus, everything went quiet.

"What the hell was that?"

"I don't care. Did you know about this?" Dev held his hand up, the one that still grasped the tiny twig offering.

"About what, the Spriggan? Absolutely not!"

"How long have you been drinking weird green goo? When Byron hoisted it up, everyone in the group went 'Oooh' and 'Ahhhh'. This liquid, you've all drank this before. Haven't you? You all knew this was dead fae fluid." Dev's stomach lurched at the thought of drinking fluid from any corpse. His stomach twisted in knots. If this is what being a witch entailed, if being part of the Shadow Realm meant hurting other things...his mind reeled, thinking about the tiny Spriggan begging to be released from his captivity.

"I've only seen Byron bring it out a couple of times. Dev, I swear, I had *no idea!*" Tully's eyes were huge, and Dev didn't think Tully's skin could get paler.

"I can't. This is sick." Dev glanced around, not sure what to do next.

Tully reached out to try to touch Dev's shoulder, but Dev jerked away.

"No. Don't touch me. Don't come anywhere near me." Dev stepped away, closer to the study's door that would lead him upstairs. He glanced up the stairwell, then back at Tully. "I can't be here."

Dev turned and stared up the stairwell, and noticed the study's door, very apparent now he'd broken the magic seal, as the door hung crooked, hinges bent. He shoved his hand into his pocket and deposited the twig offering there. Hopefully keeping the Spriggan remnant safe, until he figured out what the hell to do with it.

"Dev, please. Don't go. Let's talk. I had no idea. I swear!" Tully begged and moved toward Dev.

"Get away from me." Dev left the study and as he stepped on the stairs to distance himself from Tully, he stopped. Something yanked at him. The sensation reminded Dev of a passing emotion, a memory, a sense of knowing. The emotion signaled comfort and safety.

"Cam?" Dev glanced toward the darkness that enveloped the stairwell as the stairs descended further down.

"Dev, please, can we talk about this?" The desperation in Tully's voice made Dev shoot a warning stare over his shoulder towards Tully.

Tully reached out to Dev again.

"No." Dev jerked his shoulder away from Tully's hand, turned and ascended the stairwell.

He found himself standing on the front stoop of his favorite professor's house.

He had gotten all his wishes.

Whatever he'd summoned from that damn board had all come to pass.

And this wasn't anything he wanted.

# Chapter Twenty-Five

DEV WANDERED THE streets for hours. His fingers were numb from the cold and he wallowed in his misery. The spring days that were bright and cheerful and full of promised life reflected the opposite at night. The damp chilled air permeated down to the bones.

The moon hung clear and bright in the night sky, only a sliver of the orb missing. Its glow illuminated the gnarled bark of the old and well-established trees in the neighborhood. The bare branches appeared skeletal. As much as Dev loved how the darkness normally enshrouded him like a comforting blanket, tonight the shadows made him jittery.

He couldn't go to his new apartment. Tully would find him there. And confronting Tully right now would take energy and the right set of words Dev didn't have.

*Everything had happened too fast.*

It had all been too good. Dev had gotten everything he'd ever wanted. He'd been seen by the Shadow Realm, accepted and made part of the hidden world. Only to find out his greatest desire held nothing more than coldness and evil.

Who could torment and sacrifice such a tiny helpless creature? All for what? Some goo that made him see floating blobs of colour? This was insane. He wanted out.

Even his sister had tied herself to this world, and Dev didn't see her as wicked or evil. But she had warned him the Coven of the Night Grove had a less than stellar reputation.

Maybe Amna and her coven sisters had the ability to remove the Shadow Onyx shard that lay nestled within his arm bones?

He wanted no part of any of this. Sure, he'd wanted this for his entire life, but now? Now he wanted out. He wanted nothing to do with it.

With his mind made up, Dev marched himself over to his parents' house. Amna would know what to do next. Although he didn't look forward to the impending chaos and noise that would greet him there. Especially at this late hour.

As Dev made his way to his family's home, he pictured Tully.

He sure looked as surprised as Dev had been when they'd found the Spriggan.

Dev hoped Tully truly had been kept in the dark. Maybe Byron had duped all the Coven members.

Maybe Tully was innocent in all of this?

Perhaps Tully had been fooled by Byron as much as he had.

And Byron instilled ire; ripples of rage churned in Dev's stomach.

"Fucking asshole." A man Dev had revered and respected for the last four years of his life had turned out to be the most horrible human Dev had ever met. *You should never meet your heroes.* Wasn't that the expression? Okay, so maybe the sentiment didn't fit, but something in the statement about people placed on a pedestal never measuring up to expectations fit. Sure, Radcliffe had started out as an infatuation, a fantasy. The hot professor. Who wouldn't have had signed up for extra classes with *that!*

So many emotions rushed through him. Anger at what he'd seen and been subjected to, betrayal of trust and being deceived. Tricked into giving himself over to the Shadows.

Well, maybe that wasn't fair. After all, Dev had been chasing this intangible world for a long, long time. Far longer than Byron had been around. It twisted Dev's guts, knowing Byron hadn't been the person he looked up to. Byron Radcliff had tainted the Shadow Realm.

One fact remained. Dev had drank dead fae. A lot of it.

The memory of his binding ritual, drinking from the chalice, and tasting the sickly thick and oddly tangy liquid made him want to hurl.

There had been so much dishonesty. Thinking on the last few days, Dev's life had been a whirlwind, and there had been several red flags. Byron admitting at the coffee shop he'd made Tully track him, like some dog. That had sent shivers down his spine. Why spy on someone? Oh sure, witch rules and all, but still. That just seemed so...duplicitous. And the whole *boyfriend* thing with Tully. Dev berated himself for falling so quickly for anyone. Fast and furious relationships never worked out. And the offer of an apartment, one right above Tully, and with a price so low there should have been a waiting list to rent the studio? Again, wishes coming true way too fast. It's like everything Dev had been after and desperate to obtain had been dropped in his lap.

Who has that happen for them?

The memory of seeing Tully for the first time in the coffee shop, smiling, with all those white teeth and glacial-blue eyes, watching the spoon churning and stirring his coffee all by itself resurfaced.

*Dammit. Why couldn't all of this have turned out to be a good thing?*

And to top everything, Dev *still* hadn't written his finals at the university. Four years of hard work, and he wasn't even sure he should show up to write his exams knowing Byron Radcliffe, high priest of the Guardians of the Night Grove murdered and sacrificed harmless fae. How could Dev face him? And with Byron's study blown apart, and the Spriggan dead, Byron surely would know Dev had discovered his cruel and predatory nature.

Dev's hands gesticulated as he walked, talking and mumbling to himself. If there had been anyone around, they would have thought him crazy.

But Dev's internal argument, his talking out loud to himself and the outlandish hand gestures helped him work through his issues. He'd always had conversations with himself. Arguing to unseen people, hashing out theories and problems. And this debate, this crazy magic-soaked, fae-killing, what's-in-it-for-you boyfriend mess was something he wasn't coming to any happy conclusions or satisfying resolutions about. Dev's pace quickened as his internal debate grew more intense, and before long he stood in front of his parents' door.

*Well, this isn't going to be good either.*

Dev closed his eyes and released a heavy sigh. Nowhere in the world right now would provide him a safe harbour.

Reluctantly, Dev reached up to knock, but before his hand even hit the surface, the door burst open and Amna stood there, her hair braided and coiled up. Amna's feet were covered by her favorite fuzzy slippers as she pulled her pink terrycloth housecoat tight around her, protecting her from the chill of the evening air.

"Don't you dare knock; you'll wake Mom and Dad."

"How'd you know I was even here?"

"Really? Don't be so dense. Get in here." Amna grabbed Dev's wrist and pulled him inside. She shut the door behind him, bolted the lock shut, and traced the symbol of a five-pointed star over the door handle. The symbol glowed bright yellow, tails from each of the points rushed over the entire wall. The lines were similar to the ley line globe Dev had seen in Byron's study.

Dev turned up his lip in a sneer. "What the hell is all that for?"

"Something is bloody off tonight, so I warded the entire house. I had just pulled the sheets up to my chin in hopes a good night's sleep would make this weird energy slip off, but I sensed you walking toward the house." Amna quit talking. She pulled away, taking a step back, squinting at Dev. "What the hell is in your pocket," Amna pointed toward Dev's denim. "And why are you all weirded out? Even without being a sensate I can tell by looking at you. I've lived with you too long to know something is wrong with you. What's happened, Dev?"

"Oh my god, Amna, you were right. About everything." Dev's head lowered as he ran a hand through his hair. Dev's foot tapped on the floor.

"Geez, Dev, what the hell did you do this time?" Amna shook her head. "Come on. Let's go in the kitchen, I'll make some tea. But keep your voice down and you'd better tell me everything." Amna turned and made her way toward the kitchen. "And show me what the hell is in your pocket because the funky buzz coming from there I've never sensed before."

Dev followed Amna ready to divulge everything.

"YOU HAVE GOT to be kidding me." Amna's mouth gaped as she cradled her cup of tea.

"Nope. All true."

"That's more than shady, that's disgusting. And Tully's in on this?" Amna shook her head again. She did that a lot throughout the conversation. "I find this hard to believe."

"Well, he's part of the coven, isn't he?"

"But Dev, that doesn't mean he's involved in capturing and sacrificing fae." She grasped Dev's hand and gave his fingers a gentle squeeze. "In fact, I can't see such deviousness in him at all. I like him, Dev. He's misguided with his involvement with that coven, but he's not a bad person. I think you need to go and apologize to him. Make things right."

"Are you crazy?"

"No, and I'm using my witchy senses here. I'm never wrong. I don't see him being mean. And you know he likes you. You deserve to have someone nice in your life."

"This is all crazy."

"I'm telling you, don't let him get away. Maybe he can help you deal with Byron? Maybe the two of you strike out on your own and form your own coven, I don't know, but I'm telling you, he has no part in this. I don't see him being dark."

"You didn't seem so sure the other night when we were here and he'd charmed Mom and Dad to sleep."

"Dev, when have you ever cared about what I say? Besides, I've had a couple of days to think on it some more. You've never brought anyone home. Call my initial reaction sibling protectiveness," Amna waved her hand dismissing the whole incident, "and maybe I was pissed at you. You have no idea how shitty it's been around here without you. Nice Indian boys don't leave the house. So now I have to deal with Mom and Dad. Thanks."

"I know, I'm sorry. I told Tully the same thing. It's not something we do. And yet, here I am. But I can't have a decent relationship with anyone living under my parents' nose. Especially a *boyfriend*."

"True. Listen, I support you, but there won't be anything to support unless you go fix this. Yes?" Amna glared at Dev, who stared down at his knees. "Dev, right? Look at me." Dev rolled his eyes and stared at his sister. "You know I'm right."

"Yeah, I know, it's awkward and stupid, and I feel like a total idiot."

"Well that's nothing new." Amna giggled. "Now, let me see it."

"See what?"

"God, Dev, the twig. The thing the Spriggan gave you."

"Oh, right. Sure." Dev dug in his pocket and pulled out the tiny branch, placing the plant piece on the kitchen table for Amna to inspect.

Amna poked the micro-branch with her finger.

The twig inched away from her touch, grew a tiny olive-coloured vine, which lashed out at Amna's finger.

"Holy shit, did you see?" Her eyes wide with a large grin on her face. "What a silly thing. It's trying to protect itself, but that's hilarious. It's so small."

"I think it's creepy as hell. That used to be the thing's leg." Dev shivered.

"And the Spriggan gave this to you?"

"He snapped off his leg and handed it to me, crawled into my palm and disintegrated."

"I've been a witch for over a year, Dev, and not once has any of this bizarre shit happened. How come you're so lucky?" Amna's eyes glared at Dev belying a possible twinge of jealousy. Dev would have recognized the rather specific glare from years of witnessing the same look whenever their dad allowed Dev to do something his sisters were forbidden to do.

"Seriously?"

"It's exciting! My life's enjoyment right now comes from dealing with Mom and Dad's breakdowns about you not being here and listening to Bahnu and her supposed boy issues. Trust me," Amna sat in her chair and crossed her arms, "this is far more interesting."

"Well it's not interesting to me. And I don't want you messing around with anything like this."

"Oh for gods' sakes Dev. I might be your little sister, but I'm more than capable of looking after myself. Besides, tell me who got bound to the Shadow Realm first?"

"Yeah, yeah," Dev mumbled taking a sip of the tea Amna had made him. "Ugh, how can you drink this stuff?"

"I can't drink coffee an hour before bedtime."

"Why not?"

"I like my sleep. Speaking of which, it's late. You need to go to *your* home and deal with Tully. If Mom and Dad find you here, there's no way they're going to let you slip away without several hours of yelling and screaming and arguing about how you should be living here."

"I suppose. Ugh, Amna," Dev's shoulder's drooped, "I don't want to deal with Tully." Anxiety twisted Dev's stomach thinking about his impending reunion.

"Dev, for gods' sakes, grow up. You've been like this since you were a kid. Something happens that's too much for you to deal with and you escalate the situation into an unbearable scenario, and you walk away. If you'd stop and breathe, examine the problem, you'll see things are not as insurmountable as you might think. Go see Tully. You need to ask him if he knew anything about this. I can almost guarantee you he didn't." Amna relayed her wisdom while pointing to the twig on the table, which inched away at her gesture. "And take his word when he tells you the truth."

"But Amna —"

"Nope. Not hearing any of it. You know I'm right."

"I wish Cam was here...Shit!" Dev's face went white as he fumbled in his back pocket.

"What? And where the hell is your dumbass sidekick? He hasn't been around."

"I almost forgot with everything that's been going on."

"Forgot what?"

"I haven't heard from or seen Cam since all of this started, which is weird. I mean, I know it's only been a couple of days, but—"

"Yeah, but the two of you are attached at the hip, which will be awkward now that you have Tully."

Dev rolled his eyes. "We're not that bad."

"Oh my gods. Yes you are. I swear Bahnu and I had a bet going for years you two would end up together."

"You did not."

Amna glanced to the side as she rolled her eyes. "Yes, we did."

"You two." Dev unfolded the paper he had shoved in his jeans. He spread the paper out on the kitchen table, next to the twig, and pointed at it. "Tully and I went to Cam's Mom's house, which turned out to be the most awkward visit ever," Dev grimaced recalling the odd invitation, but decided not to get into details with Amna, "but she gave me this letter Cam had left saying he'd gone to visit his dad. Which—"

Amna scrunched up her face. "Cam would never do." She finished Dev's sentence.

"Exactly." Dev studied the note.

*Mom, get Dev. Wiccan goats Den* still remained etched across the page. The original note's message had long since disappeared. The new message was still there, and the letters were trembling and shifting.

"Oh my god!" Dev covered his eyes with his palm, rubbing his face.

"What?"

"It just dawned on me. Goats Den. Byron's front door has the image of a goat on it."

"What are you talking about?"

"And the extra pair of boots, Cam's designer boots. The pair with the rainbow-coloured snakeskin."

"Okay, you are making no sense at all."

"And the feeling I got on the stairs..." Dev stared at the dead air between them as a new theory formed in his hurricane of ideas. "If Byron captured a Spriggan and sacrificed the creature he wouldn't stop at that, would he?" Dev remembered the fleeting feeling he'd had while in the basement stairwell after the disastrous discovery in Byron's study. He'd sworn he had sensed Cam. Things were coming together. The pair of boots at the front door that were exactly like Cam's. Tully telling him about last year's coven mishap where they'd lost a couple of members due to some unusual accidents. Tully had chalked up the losses to male witches living short lifespans.

If Byron had been desperate for coven members, and the Coven of the Night Grove had a shitty reputation, what better than to snag a novitiate witch before they had a chance to learn anything different about the Shadow Realm?

Dev remembered the conversation he'd had with Tully the night after being at Cam's place. Tully reminded

Dev he'd been gifted by the god as a tracker. This had to be the god's gift expressing itself. The sensation Dev had of Cam and the note shifting, giving him a hint of what he and Tully had already deduced?

Cam's utter silence on all technology devices surely had to be the largest clue.

Dev was pretty sure Cam hadn't run off to visit his dad. Dev's tracker gift had fired. Dev knew exactly where to find Cam.

If Byron had gone this far into ensuring Dev would become a member of his coven, what's to say he hadn't taken Cam to remove any outside influences? And Cam was definitely an outside influence, most likely one that would steer him away from all this. Cam had never been a big supporter of his occult interest. And after all, Cam and he were besties, like brothers. Dev would have listened to anything Cam might have suggested, and if Cam had any inclination Byron was shady...Dev would never had got this involved on Cam's advice.

Byron must have taken Cam, and that's why Cam came to mind in Byron's stairwell!

Dev stood up from the table and announced, "I've got to go. Cam's in trouble."

Amna scrunched her face up. "Wow. Did you hear what I just told you? Escalate much? Go make up with Tully."

Dev glared at Amna, and then realized that's exactly what he had to do.

DEV HADN'T HAD so many twisted emotions or ever been so anxious in his life as he stood at Tully's apartment door, going to the *only* person who might believe him and help him out. He hoped.

Dev banged on the thick wooden door.

There wasn't any response.

*Maybe Tully isn't home or he's asleep.*

Dev glanced at his watch. The clock read after midnight. Shoot. But waiting for morning wasn't an option.

He banged a second time and waited...this was insanity. If there was a chance Tully had any part in this, he was most likely with Byron trying to—

A light flicked on and illuminated the strip under the door.

With a gust of air whooshing inward and past him, Tully stood in front of Dev, bare-chested in loose sweat pants that hung off his hip bones.

"Hi." Dev glanced at the ground.

"Hi. Are you okay?" Tully yawned and rubbed his eyes.

"I'm sorry for waking you."

"I wasn't sleeping anyway."

"Oh. So, to answer your question, no, I'm not okay. But I need to ask you things, and I think Cam *is* in trouble, and you're the only one I know who might help."

"Wow, that's a lot. How do you get to those conclusions?" Tully raised his eyebrows, but Dev had caught the reaction.

"Look, I'm sorry, I know this is insane, and so am I, but I couldn't deal. And my sister pointed out I do this, a lot. Remember, I became so overwhelmed I walked away from you? I'm so sorry. I always bail when things get too much. I mean, did you see that poor creature? The way the thing shrieked when we found him, and how he begged us for help? Only to die on us? Tully. I mean—geez, this is hard." Dev inhaled and glanced at his feet. "Tully, I really, *really* like you. But I can't be with someone who would do such horrible things to a helpless creature and benefit off its death. Please tell me you knew nothing about Byron's actions."

Tully put on hand on Dev's shoulder, stared at him in the eye, and proclaimed, "Dev, I promise you, I had no idea."

"Really?"

"And I'm sorry I dragged you into all this."

"What? You didn't...Byron did."

"Sure, yes, but you came along on my request, right? I asked you to go see Byron and meet the coven and go get lessons from Byron. I wanted you to join the coven. I wanted us to be together. So it's just as much my fault. I had no idea Byron was killing fae and feeding us their—where ever the liquid goo originated."

Dev let out a huge sigh. "You promise?"

Tully pulled Dev in for a huge hug and whispered into his ear, "I promise. I'm sorry."

Dev snuggled into Tully's embrace.

"There's one other thing."

"What's that?" Tully, still holding on to Dev, pulled back and gazed into Dev's eyes.

"I think Byron captured Cam."

"What?"

"I need to go to the coven house and find out."

"It's after midnight!"

"I know, but I think Cam is in danger."

# Chapter Twenty-Six

DEV'S FOOT TAPPED the car's floorboards, and his fingers were drumming the center console for the entire drive over to Byron and Addas's house. Tully grabbed Dev's hand in an attempt to still him.

He glanced at Dev and smiled. "It'll be okay. Cam's okay. I'm sure of it."

"I can't believe I didn't pick up on any of this earlier. And I'm mad at myself for not chasing down Cam sooner. We've never gone this long without communication. If he's hurt, this is all on me."

"Don't be so hard on yourself. Besides, we still don't know what's going on. You're creating a bunch of horrible scenarios in your head, aren't you?" Tully rubbed the back of Dev's hand.

Dev glanced down at Tully's hand holding his. "You know that doesn't work on me."

"Can't blame a guy for trying. I don't understand why my charms don't work on you. They work on everyone." Tully shook his head. "There are a few things weird about you. You saw the rune marks before you should have, the pentagram on Byron's floor, you siphoned energy at a skill level Byron said shouldn't have been possible, and my charms don't work on you. What's up, witch?" Tully winked and grinned, trying to make light of the situation. They were about to get knee deep in a bad spot and tangle with a high priest.

Dev half smiled. "I wouldn't say your charms don't work on me. All the same, I appreciate the gesture. I don't know why I'm so different."

"Once this mess is done, we'll have to figure out why that might be. Here we are."

Tully stopped the car and put the vehicle in park. They got out and beat a hasty path up to the coven house's front door.

Dev stopped, rotated, and peered off into the night.

"What's going on?"

"I don't know. I get the sense someone's watching. Don't you feel that?"

"You're the tracker, not me. I get to play with metal and charm people. Woohoo, excitement that knows no bounds."

Dev chuckled.

"I can feel Cam." Dev squinted, concentrating.

"What does he feel like?"

"It's weird. I don't how to describe the sensation. You know how you get used to someone, you spend a lot of time with them and there's an energy you get comfortable with? That's what this feels like, and if I look toward the house, the feeling is stronger than if I look out at the road."

"I have no idea what you're talking about."

"Huh."

"Okay, well, let's see if Byron and Addas are up. The lights are on, so that's a good sign. Maybe. I feel weird coming here to confront Byron."

Tully used the goat's nose door knocker and hammered.

"You're going to wake the entire neighborhood."

"If they're asleep, a bashful knock isn't going to wake them."

"I'm not sure I want to wake them. Tully, what if he does have Cam?"

"Then we take Cam and say goodbye to the Coven of the Night Grove."

"You'd leave them for me? I know Byron trained you. Your mother was the one who made sure you got into his hands."

Dev remembered how Tully had been given over to Byron.

"Byron has done some pretty amazing things for me, that's not a lie. And I have a hard time believing he'd stoop to hurting other creatures for the gain of the coven, but I can't deny what you and I discovered in his secret room. I have questions for him too. But until those are answered, right now, I believe in what you're feeling. Can't deny a god-given gift, now can I?"

"How'd I get so lucky to meet you?"

Tully leaned over and kissed Dev. "When we get home, I want you to show me how lucky you think you are."

"Thank you for forgiving me, for putting up with my inability to deal with tough situations, for my insanity." Tully beamed at Dev and hugged him tight. Dev closed his eyes and relaxed into the embrace. Tully jerked and pulled away.

"Dev, look, what is that?" Tully pointed to the sidewalk where he'd been facing.

A dark paw print lay on the stepping stone.

Tully pulled out his phone, hit the flashlight button and held the light over the mark. "It looks like—" Tully bent over and peered at the print closer, as Dev peered over his shoulder. "It looks like blood."

Tully stuck a finger on the edge of the paw print then pulled his hand up inspecting his finger. He held his wet finger up to his nose and sniffed. "I'm pretty sure this is blood. It's tacky though and dark. I think it's been here a while."

"We gotta trace those steps. Look, they're coming from the side gate."

Tully and Dev followed the markings as they led around the side of the house. The paws were huge and even though the trail was inconsistent and irregular, enough blood marked a path to the back door.

"Look at the door!" The panel hung from a single hinge.

They stared at each other for a brief moment until Dev broke the silence. "Something is wrong."

Taking the lead, Dev rushed inside the house, flicked on the first switch he found, which as luck would have it, illuminated the stairwell leading from the door, down to the cellar.

The giant paw marks came up from the basement.

Dev stared at Tully. "You ready for this?"

Tully stiffened. "Not really. Those are huge. What the hell would have made that?"

"I have no idea. The Horned One gave me a gift of tracker, not animal identification. I don't recognize the shape as anything familiar."

"Me neither. I don't know if it's safe, Dev."

"But the marks lead out, not down, so...I think whatever might have been here is gone. Besides, I can feel Cam down there. We gotta go that way."

"Okay." Tully inhaled. Not convinced the house was safe, but knowing Cam lay in the general direction, Tully descended into the darkness, following Dev with one hand on Dev's shoulder.

They inched their way down the stairs

"Look, some of these are smeared."

"So, someone has already been here and stepped over them. Dev, I think maybe we should call the cops."

"Since when do witches call the cops?"

"Since there is blood all over the stairwell!"

"I know Cam's down there. Let's go get him first. We'll call the cops later."

"Ugh, okay. If you say so."

The two made their way down the stairs, careful not to step in the paw prints, past the landing that led to the study where Dev and Tully had been sealed earlier in the day. The prints led farther into the basement.

"Tully, do you remember the loud bang when we were down here?"

"Oh yeah. So much has happened today."

"I think we were here when this went down. That ruckus had to be the door being busted off its hinges. And remember Byron said he had other things he had to get done today?"

"Jesus, I think you're on to something."

"Look, that paw print is partially smeared and there are shoe marks that go up." Dev pulled up one leg at a time to study the bottom of his shoes. Neither of his had any blood on the bottom of them. "Check yours."

As Tully lifted his left leg, the bottom toe of the runner had dried blood on it.

"Definitely happened while we were here. How we didn't notice this..." Dev started.

"You weren't exactly in a happy place. Remember?"

"I suppose." Dev felt the heat rush to his cheeks, embarrassed by his actions. "Come on. You should lead the way. We have to follow those prints down."

"Why me?"

"You've been part of the coven longer and know this house?" Dev suggested.

"Byron never allowed us down here. He said the sublevels under the basement had become unstable. Once upon a time this had been where the coven did spellwork, but he said that happened a hundred years ago. It's a dirt floor and he didn't want us all banging around. Byron told us the chambers were fragile and being down there might compromise the foundation of the house."

As Dev got to the end of the stairwell and put his foot on the concrete floor he turned to Tully. "I think he lied." Dev thumped the floor, and the *tap tap tap* of his shoes against the cement told Tully a different story.

"Who's there?" a voice from the darkness shot out.

Dev grabbed his phone and flicked on the flashlight, looking around for a light switch. The beam of light shone and displayed the giant membranous wings of a creature Tully had never seen before. The wings sputtered a few times, then folded up. A head turned sideways, glancing at them. A single cat-eye reflected light like a demon's eye peering from the shadows.

"I said, who's there?" the voice asked, unsteady but defiant.

"Cam? Is that you?"

Tully found a light switch and flicked the light on.

The amount of blood covering the floor and sprayed up the walls made them both pause for a moment.

"What the ever-loving fuck?" Tully gaped.

Dev scanned the room. His head swiveled taking in the disaster, until he spied the winged creature, cradling a monster of a man.

Its eyes were inhuman. Its tail flipped back and forth as its wings fluttered for a second time. But the voice and the fur and…

"Cam!" Dev gasped. "Cam, what the fuck?" Dev's face scrunched together in confusion and concern.

"Oh my god, finally. Bitch where the hell you been?" Definitely Cam. Dev had warned Tully, on multiple occasions, of Cam's propensity for colourful language.

"What the hell happened?" Dev cried.

"It's a long fucking story. Can you help us? Please? I don't know if I can walk, and Everton is in bad shape."

Dev ignored the mess of blood everywhere and the three bodies lying in unnatural poses on the floor.

Taking stock of the room, the dead naked men were identifiable enough. Gus, even with his face half gone and missing his throat. Eddie, ripped apart with a massive bite mark to his midsection. His guts were strewn around him. The two knights of the coven lay close together in a congealed pool of blood.

Byron lay off to one side up against the wall. His shoulder had been shredded. Dev spied white bone through the torn flesh. Byron's blond hair and beard were matted with crusted blood.

"Jesus Christ." Tully stood in one spot, not moving. He pressed a hand to his mouth. Dev understood. The smell of copper and the sight of the bodies was enough to make anyone need to hold down an urge to vomit.

The metallic scent stuck in the back of Dev's throat. Its odor saturated and heavy in the air.

"Tully, come help me." Dev lent Cam a hand, trying to get his friend up and stable on his own feet. Both his wrists and ankles were raw, and there were huge welts all along his spine.

Cam's legs gave way a couple of times, but Dev kept a hold of him until he found his balance.

"Cam, what the fuck? How?" Dev asked with an arm wrapped around him.

"Short story? Your damn summoning board. Long story, I'll tell you later, please take me and Everton out of here."

"Who's Everton?"

"This is Everton. He's in bad shape. That asshole there sliced him open." Cam had pointed at Byron's body.

"What?"

"Again, I'll tell you later."

It took what seemed like half the night, but between Dev and Tully, they managed to get Cam situated into the car, his wings an issue in the backseat, and Everton out of the basement, which used up every ounce of strength they had. An unconscious wounded werewolf weighed more than Dev had imagined. Cam had warned them about Ev's midsection, sliced through like a holiday ham, but when Dev and Tully went to fetch him, no such wound existed.

As soon as everyone had been tucked into the car and were prepared to leave, Tully glanced at Dev. "I'm going to go into the house and wipe things down, at least get rid of our prints along the door handles and banisters. We need to find a payphone somewhere, which should be fun, there's not many around. We need to call the cops."

"Anonymous call. Yeah, agreed."

"You wait here. I won't take long." Tully kissed Dev. "I'm glad we listened to your feelings. You were right."

"I didn't want to be."

"I know." Tully's lip curled up on one side of his mouth, trying his best to comfort Dev.


THIS HAD BEEN his coven. A group of men he had counted on and called family for the last few years. And yet there were things going on he had no knowledge of, and the men he had trusted had been less than honest with him. Tully wondered if any of the brothers had been in on all of Byron's schemes.

At that moment, Tully understood now what Dev must have been feeling.

Betrayal.

Tully descended the stairwell one last time, removed his T-shirt and wiped everything as he went. He hoped like hell this erased their presence, or at least contaminated the house to the point where they wouldn't be implicated.

*Who am I kidding, this isn't going to work.*

Tully pulled out his phone and punched a few numbers. He waited...and waited. Flicking his phone out to check the screen, he saw the time. It was late. More like it was very early in the morning.

"Hello?" a voice said from the phone,

"Shit. Hi, Sparks, I'm sorry I'm calling at this hour. We need your help."

"What's the matter? What's happened?"

"Lots. I need you to trust me. Can you come to the coven house and...clean up. You'll have to bring anyone you trust one hundred percent though. There's been a situation. I don't know the details. There's so much blood..."

"Oh my god. Are you and Dev okay?"

"Yes, Dev and I are fine. But Eddie, Gus, and Byron are not."

"Geeze! Are they...?" Sparks asked.

"Yeah."

"Shit."

"Exactly. Sparks, I don't know what happened here tonight, but it's shady as fuck. Dev's best friend has been held captive in our coven house. Something seriously dark went down here tonight, but I don't know what. I need to get Dev's friend and a werewolf out of here. I'm going to take them to my place, get them cleaned up, and get details."

"Tully, a werewolf? Is that smart?"

"Probably not, but Dev's friend seems pretty attached to it. Like I said, we need answers, and I don't have any. But we gotta get rid of the bodies and clean up the blood. And there's a lot of it. I need you brother."

"I stepped up for Dev at his binding ritual. I'll be there. I'll bring Wiatt and Kerr. I know I can trust them."

"Thank you. I owe you."

"You owe me nothing. We got you."

Sparks ended the call. Tully slipped his phone into his back pocket and continued down to the basement subfloors. As gross as it all was, he needed a better inventory of the scene. It might help him put together the details when Cam explained later.

There would also need to be some spell work done later to ensure law enforcement would never be involved. He was pretty sure he had at least one book in his library that would give them a reference point on where to start with something that big.

Maybe Uncle Bart would help out too. That man had connections everywhere.

And where the hell was Addas?

When Tully got to the bottom level of the basement, he side-stepped the puddles of blood and bits of flesh as he flicked the light switch off, his hand wrapped up in the shirt.

From over in the corner, Byron groaned.

*God Dammit, he's alive.*

For a brief moment, he wondered if he should go help.

Tully struggled with the notion only for a moment, then decided to leave Byron in fate's hands. A fitting and appropriate punishment. Tully could never follow a coven leader who had been so cruel.

He'd never ignored someone who needed help. But after the things he'd seen, Byron wasn't worth saving.

*What you do comes back to you.*

Witch Law.

Perhaps turning on his high priest would have consequences. Tully shook his head while ascending the stairs, then realized that Sparks would find Byron. He grabbed his phone and called Sparks back.

"Hey, sorry to bug you again."

"No problem. I called the other guys. They'll meet me there."

"Byron's alive. I can't. I'll explain later, but I can't help him. Whatever happens, he deserves it."

"Holy shit, Tully, what the fuck happened?"

"Later, I promise."

"Sure thing. Don't worry. Like I said, we got you."

# Chapter Twenty-Seven

AFTER DRIVING AWAY from the grisly scene, Tully confessed to Dev that he'd called Sparks, and that Byron was still alive.

"Sparks is coming. They'll clean it up. I can't help him, Dev. I couldn't. He took me under his wing, and he did this...whatever this was."

Dev grabbed his hand. "It's okay. I get it."

Everything from that point forward was left in the hands of the gods.

THE NEXT MORNING passed by. Dev and Tully lay in bed together reading, snuggling, talking, and theorizing about what had happened, and all the questions that still remained. Any forthcoming answers lay with the two men who were sleeping off the previous night in Tully's apartment one floor down.

Dev hadn't slept well. Images of unseen beasts and blood splatter haunted his dreams. Tully, too, had a fitful night of sleep. Despite the current midday status, Dev flipped the switch to make a third pot of coffee.

Already well past two in the afternoon, the sunlight in Dev's apartment had shifted and now caressed the far wall. A gentle quiet permeated the small studio, but as relaxing as the day should have been, tensions were tight and Dev's anxiety ran high.

A knock wrapped on Dev's door. Flipping through old books on spell craft, the abrupt noise jostled them out of their current study. Tully's nose, buried deep in an old tome, poked up and stared at Dev.

Dev bounced out of the bed took two steps to the door and opened it.

"Hey. You wouldn't happen to have coffee?" Cam's new cat-like eyes were going to take a while to get used to. Tully had found both him and Everton gym shorts that would cover them for now. But neither Dev nor Tully owned much that would fit the beast called Everton. And most of what Tully had fell off of Cam. Still, some clothing was better than nothing.

"It's already made. Come on in. There are questions."

"No shit."

Tully stood up as Cam flitted into the room. He offered up a chair at the kitchen nook, and let Cam settle while he leaned against the kitchen counter. There wasn't a lot of space for all three of them, but there were so many things to talk about. In the past, Dev and Cam would have gone to a local coffee shop and got comfortable. But given

Cam's current form, being out in public produced a whole new set of issues.

"Where's the other guy?" Dev asked.

"Everton? He's still asleep. Thank god for werewolf healing abilities. I thought for sure I was witnessing him die."

"So, werewolf, huh?"

"Yup."

"And then you would be?"

"Apparently, some kind of forest fae." Cam's eyelids blinked, but there was an extra eyelid that had grown, and they blinked side to side, not up and down.

"He's royal fae." A deep growl came from behind all of them. Everyone jumped. Dev clutched at his chest. "Sorry. I should be thanking you, not scaring you. Everton Lilch." Ev extended his hand as an offering of good will. Tully paused, took the massive paw, and shook. Dev grimaced, unsure. "I promise, I won't bite."

When Dev extended and clasped hands with Everton, he found his hand tiny in comparison pressed up against the werewolf's ginormous paw. Dev bobbed his head in acceptance, focusing on Cam. "Okay. So, where do we start? How about, 'What the fuck, Cam?'"

"You and all your hocus pocus and you're the one asking that?" Cam rolled his eyes.

"Dude, have you seen yourself? What the fucking hell happened?"

"Your goddamn summoning board. That's what. Do you remember our last conversation? I begged you to come over because something was wrong. You thought these," Cam pointed to his horns, "were nothing more than a pimple. You should have stuck around. Shit got wild after you left."

"Wait, a summoning board?" Tully asked, turning to Dev. "Do you still have it?"

Dev walked into the adjacent room over to a book case and pulled the board out from behind some books. "Hells yes. It cost me big bucks. I'll never get rid of this."

"Oh, shit." Tully took the board and studied it. "You bought this at Magix & Mystix, didn't you?"

"Well, yeah. Why?"

"The Coven of the Night Grove made these boards. Byron's idea to make some extra cash, and in the end, each one of these things is designed to lure potential candidates to the coven. Byron desperately needed to fill up the empty spots. What did you wish for?"

"Everything I have." Dev spread his hands wide and rolled his eyes.

"No seriously. I need to know. There's a djinn locked into this board. And you know all the stories about genies and wishes. It's no lie. You get three. And whatever you wished for, is what you'll get, but you'll never be able to guarantee how consequences play out or how the wish will be interpreted." Tully glanced at Dev and then at Cam.

"Well I think Cam wins for outlandish wishes. Just what did you write on those pieces of paper?" Dev raised an eyebrow.

Cam frowned. "I know, I'm an idiot."

"What did you wish for?"

Cam's wings fluttered. "All right fine. This is all my fault. I wrote 'Make me the fairy I truly am'. I got exactly what I wished for. Although in my defense, I had no idea faeries existed. Do you have any idea what I'm expected to do as royalty?"

Tully barely contained his laugh.

Cam and Dev glared at him. Ev, however joined in the frivolity with Tully.

"It's not funny. I'm expected to make baby faeries. With a girl! That's not happening, so how the hell do I get human again?" Cam pleaded.

"I don't know if that's possible, Cam." Tully grimaced. "I mean, I can look into it, and it'll take some time. But I don't think I've ever heard of someone undoing their djinn wish after it came true. I think you're pretty much stuck."

"I don't think this is as horrible as you think. You need to learn how to control all your abilities. You should be able to glamour yourself into a human disguise," Everton offered.

"I don't know how the hell to do anything without screwing shit up."

"Don't be so hard on yourself. You got us out of there," Everton said, repositioning himself so he stood closer to Cam, placing his massive hand on Cam's shoulder.

"What do you mean? I didn't do a thing."

"Not the way I perceived the situation. Just as Byron and his boys began the ritual, a burst of sparkle light cascaded down from where you were strapped to those boards. You cast some kind of spell, whether you were aware at the time or not. And if I had a guess, I'd say some kind of probability incantation. Remember what I told you about fae magic? Luck is one of the bag of tricks fae can employ. You have the ability to change outcomes. Byron's entire ritual went sideways and I think that was all because of you.

"Oh, I don't know. Dev had his own unexpected magical awakening, just before we heard the ruckus. I'm not entirely sure his siphoning energy from the whole area didn't have some effect on what Byron was doing down there," Tully added.

"The two together maybe?" Ev suggested. "Cam has definitely come into his fae abilities. Whether you know it or not. After all the chaos and Addas attacking everyone in the room except you and me, you healed me. So, I'd say you're doing a fine job harnessing your fae magic."

"I didn't heal you! That had to be your wolf."

"Cam, I'm so drained from everything Byron did, it'll be months before the wolf is able to do anything."

"Wait," Tully put his hand up, "what ceremony?"

"Byron attempted to eradicate Addas's werewolf infection. The boy was so close to shifting for his first time, the stench of wet fur lingered around him. But the entire idea of isolating his wolf was a stupid waste of energy. I don't know anyone who's managed to undo the infection. And Byron didn't."

"Wait a minute. Addas was a werewolf?" Dev asked.

"Well, he is now."

"How? When?" Tully asked.

"That would have been my fault, and why Byron held me captive. A year ago I bit Addas in a clan clash. Byron was trying to find a way to *un*werewolf him. He used me for experiments, and I think to exact punishment."

"Oh my gods." Tully went white.

"What's the matter?" Dev's eyes were like saucers at hearing all this information.

"I heard Byron groan when I went to wipe down the crime scene. He was still alive. Chewed up good, but alive."

"You mean Addas infected his lover. That's poetic justice for you," Everton sneered.

"But Byron had gone on and on about Addas not surviving after shifting into a wolf because witch magic and werewolves don't mix, or something like that." Cam said. "And for that matter, Byron kept on extracting my spinal fluid saying that by removing it, I'd be less fae and more human. Clearly *that* was a lie too."

"No, not a lie. I witnessed him do the same procedure with another fae. A young girl. She didn't fare so well after he drained her."

"Wait, he'd done this before? And what do you mean he took fluid from you? Green fluid?" Tully asked.

"Yeah, hurt like a mother-fucker. Came out of my spinal column. The liquid bubbled and glowed bright green."

"I think I'm gonna be sick." Dev covered his mouth, turning pale and hanging his head over the sink.

"What the hell is going on?" Cam threw his hands up in the air.

Everton took a step forward. "The coven captured me during the last clash between my pack and them. I lived in the coven dungeon for almost a year. I *think* I can explain."

For the next hour, Everton shared his history. The constant fight between the werewolves and the witches. How the wolves had discovered the coven had locked down the energy in the area and were using their dominance to their own advantage. Everton's pack were trying to free the ley line from the clutches of a centuries-old coven.

"During the last conflict, my pack had killed a couple of Byron's witches."

"What?" Tully leaned forward. "I didn't know about any of this. But I bet those were the unusual accidents we had been told about."

"Byron would have only brought the most adept witches with him to the fight. Someone like you wouldn't have survived. Trust me, others in your coven were involved. During that battle, I got knocked out and taken prisoner. But I got my revenge. I infected Addas. I was the one who bit him.

"Byron vowed to save his lover. At first, I wondered if Byron's hatred of wolves stemmed from a simple case of racism. He didn't want Addas to become a 'filthy dog', as he like to put it. But after doing some digging, Byron discovered witches couldn't become wolves. I thought everyone knew that. The concept has been around for decades. I've witnessed more than one witch who gets silly ideas into their head that more power is better. They go out and try to combine shapeshifting with sorcery. It's a no go.

"The first shift leaves nothing but a mutated mess of broken bones and clumps of fur. Horribly painful. Addas spent his last year staring down a death sentence."

"So Byron was after a cure," Tully pondered. "Maybe that doesn't make him so bad?"

Everyone glared at him.

"Sure. And there were lots of 'recipes' he'd found which included body parts, or fluid from fae, blood from a werewolf, a host of other things. Not only did Byron keep me to torture, but I remained a constant source of werewolf blood to use in his experiments. Cam turning into a fae was happenstance, but pretty good luck for Byron. Turned out a stroke of luck created the perfect opportunity to capture a fae and use the spinal fluid as a source of healing juice. And Cam had the additional benefit as a bargaining chip to get Dev to join the coven. But Byron also discovered with the last fae he'd abducted that the spinal fluid had other properties akin to a long-lasting energy drink for witches."

"How did I not know any of this?" Tully splayed his hands out to his side

"None of us suspected Byron, Tully. I've been enchanted by him for years at school. He never struck me as someone who would hurt others.

"I think Byron focused every moment of his life on saving Addas regardless of the cost. And he would have gone to the ends of the earth for him." Dev said.

Cam turned to his friend. "Did you fucking drink me?"

"I didn't know."

Cam roared with laughter. "Oh my god, that's rich. I love it. I'm in you." Cam stopped and glared at everyone. "Not like that."

Everton continued, "You know, if you all ingested fae extract...remember what they say?" Ev turned and stared at Tully, being the most advanced witch in the small gathering.

"Once fae-touched you never really are ever human again." Tully said.

"Exactly, I think by drinking the spinal fluid, you've all become partially fae yourselves."

"What do you mean?" Tully cocked an eyebrow.

"Think about it. Addas survived his shift. Why? He wasn't supposed to."

"He wasn't just a witch. He was a witch, a werewolf, *and* a fae." Tully nodded. "So, all the witches from the Coven of the Night Grove are now part fae. Dev that explains why the goddess said you had magic that didn't belong to you."

"Oh, damn. You think?"

"I do. And you got boosted a couple of times. You got the highest dose. At the binding Byron made you drink everything left in the chalice, and when the Spriggan died..."

"The green juice from the Spriggan, when he perished, the remnants in my palm were no bigger than a dime which dissolved into my skin. And even today...all these floating colours." Dev swatted at the colourful orbs. There were a lot of them around with so many people in such a small space.

"So where does that leave me?" Cam asked. "Am I going to be like this for the rest of my life? Byron said extracting the fluid would turn me more human, so what happened? Why am I still like this?"

"I think I might know," Tully offered. "You made a wish, right? Djinn magic is one of the most powerful magics. A granted wish can't be undone. Byron might as well have removed your spinal column and you'd still be fae. It's what you wished for. Welcome to your new life."

"And a long life you will have," Everton added.

"Seriously?" Cam tilted his head as he asked.

"You know fae live for hundreds of years." Ev arched an eyebrow.

"Fuck me."

"Later." Everton grinned and winked at Cam. "Remember, you get us out, I give you one night in heaven." Ev waggled his eyebrows.

"Jesus, Cam. Fae or not, you're still the same. But if Cam's life expectancy is that high, what does that mean for the rest of the coven that is now also part fae?" Dev shook his head.

There were a lot of shrugs.

"So, then maybe me leaching all that energy from you won't make that much of a difference?" Dev bit his lip as he glanced at Tully. "Okay, so wish number one, for the record, was bloody stupid. I'm sure I don't want to know, but your second wish you phrased how?"

Cam turned his head and peered at the wall. "Please don't ask."

"I think we need to hear it." Tully raised an eyebrow. "If the djinn isn't done, we should have some expectation of what's coming."

Cam spun his head at Tully and glared. "You know, for the first time meeting the best friend, you're not winning any points here."

"Cam, I'm sorry, I don't mean to pry, but it's more about safety. I want to know what hurdles Dev might have to face. I'm looking out for him. And you should be too." Tully berated Cam. Dev slid an arm around Tully.

Cam gritted his teeth. "Fine." His greenish-toned skin turned a darker green. He let out a long an exasperated huff. "Are you sure?"

"For Christ's sake Cam, yes," Dev demanded.

"My second wish was 'I want a monster boyfriend.'" Cam dropped his stare to his feet. "And I didn't mean monster as in 'monster' I meant...you know...someone with a big..."

"Oh my god, Cam!" Dev face-palmed himself. And Dev remembered when the two of them had written out their wishes. Right before, Cam had made that exact same reference and had cupped his own crotch.

Tully slapped a hand over his mouth, but even that didn't prevent him from laughing again.

"So we know what you meant, but the djinn in the board took the meaning to be something else." Dev stared at Everton.

Everton caught the look and stared at Dev. "No way, it's not like that."

"Well, maybe not yet, but I think we know where this is going to go." Tully chuckled as he pointed between Cam and Ev.

Dev stood there shaking his head and finger at Cam.

"Oh stop already. Yes, fine. It's all my fault." Cam threw his hands up in surrender, his tail tucking itself between his legs.

"All right, hit me. The third one? What other ridiculous thing did you write down?" Dev prodded.

The first of Cam's wishes had got them all into serious trouble.

The second would land Cam with a monster boyfriend.

Dev didn't think it possible, but Cam went even greener.

"Cam, out with it," Dev commanded.

"This isn't fair. What did you wish for Dev?"

"Mine? Nothing I'm ashamed to say out loud. I wanted a supernatural ability, I wanted to be seen and be part of the Shadow Realm, and I wanted others to respect me for my knowledge and abilities in the occult." Dev listed them off, one on each finger.

"Well, as wishes go, I suppose that's rational. Although I'd dare say your demands ended you up in as much hot water." Everton pursed his lips at Dev, trying to give Cam a little leeway.

"Agreed!" Dev put both his hands up like he was being held at gunpoint. "Lesson learned. No more djinn summoning boards. Okay Cam, out with it. What was your last wish?"

"Please don't make me."

"Cam." Dev glared at his lifelong friend.

"Ugh, fine." Cam shielded his eyes from everyone with one of his hands. "I wrote 'Make sure Dev gets all his wishes'."

Cam peeked out through fingers as he turned his head to look at Dev.

Dev's anger at Cam's flippancy evaporated.

How could he possibly be angry with Cam?

# Epilogue

*A couple of months later...*

"HEY, I'M HOME," Dev announced as he walked in through the front door.

"How's my witchy sociologist?" Tully yelled out. Dev always arrived home close to the dinner hour and tonight, Tully had promised him a home cooked meal.

"Exhausted. It's surprising how many clients I've managed to gain in less than a couple of months." Dev pulled off his shoes and threw them in the closet. It was summer, so his clothes were light. He left his leather satchel in the chair next to the door.

As Dev walked into the kitchen, he saw Tully was making good on his promise. Standing behind the kitchen counter, Tully pulled apart a head of lettuce, making two personalized salads.

"Roast chicken is almost done." Tully winked. "Wine?"

"Oh, yes, please!" Dev responded. "Why did I deserve to get such an awesome boyfriend?"

Tully showed off one of his famous teeth-gleaming smiles.

"It's been a couple of months of insanity. I wanted to take tonight and make the time to indulge ourselves. So tell me, how many times did the goddess show up? Are you being a good emissary?" Tully had on his cooking apron, which had a bear standing upright on it, its paws in the air with a caption reading 'Bear Naked Cook!'

And in fact, that was exactly Tully's state. As he turned away from Dev to open the cupboard, grabbing two wine glasses, Dev was teased with a furry bare butt.

"She comes and goes. Doesn't always show up for each client, and she whispers notions to me. No biggie. Do you need help?" Dev offered.

"I will." Tully grinned.

Dev was still shy and uncomfortable wandering around the house stark naked. Tully, not so much. After taking the main course out of the oven and plating it, and ensuring everything had been set on the kitchen table, he took off the apron and sat at the dinner table, bear and bare bummed. Dev joined him but took the opportunity to run his hand up Tully's thigh.

"This looks delicious." Dev raised his wine glass, and Tully returned the gesture. They touched their glasses together and made the traditional *clink* noise. The gesture had turned into a tradition whenever they enjoyed a glass together.

"Any updates on Byron?" Tully asked.

"Yeah, Sparks called me today at the office. Apparently he's been spying on our old high priest. Byron's still in the hospital and completing physiotherapy. He still doesn't have great use of his left arm. But other than that, he's doing okay. For now." Dev raised an eyebrow and rolled his eyes. The real drama would come in several more months once his werewolf infection had finished its incubation. "Has *anyone* heard or seen anything on Addas? That's the real question."

"Nope. Not a thing. In fact, I chatted with Cam earlier today. He and Ev say 'Hi'."

"Are they coming over this weekend?" Dev asked.

"Probably not. Cam still hasn't got the whole human disguise down, and there's only a few more days until the full moon, so Ev wants to play it safe by staying in the forest. He's almost himself again, but he did offer a place for us if we want to go visit them."

"Really? Did they move in together?" Dev took a bite of his dinner. "Yum, this is good."

"Thanks. Not yet. Cam is still off living with the forest fae, learning forest fae ways. But Ev has a cabin close to the Ancestral Lands. I think he spends more time there than he does with his own pack." Tully chuckled. "That's going to bite him in the ass one of these days. Every pun intended."

"You're terrible."

"And you love it." Tully beamed, his glacial-blue eyes twinkling.

"I do. This is good, what did you do to the chicken?" Dev asked between bites.

"Cook's secret. I'm not telling. If you like this, wait till you try desert."

"Oh, I don't know. I'm getting pretty full," Dev teased Tully. He stretched his arm across the table and pinched Tully's nipple.

"If you continue, you'll end up getting dessert now."

"Oh, well then." Dev dropped his utensils. They made a clattering noise as Dev scooched his chair closer to Tully.

Leaning in, Dev's mouth closed on Tully's. Warm lips, wet and welcoming, made Dev's heart beat faster. Dev placed his hand on Tully's bearded cheek and pulled him in closer, while running his free hand down Tully's furry front.

Dev pulled away. "How'd I get so lucky?"

"You mean, how'd I get this lucky? The smartest, most handsome aurologist in a hundred kilometers and he's all mine. Why do you have so many clothes on?"

Dev continued petting his lover's fur, letting his hand wander down to his lap, finding Tully excited about dessert. Dev stroked Tully's erection a few times, making him shudder.

Tully's cock was weighty in his hands, warm, and velvety. Tully spread his legs so Dev would have full access.

"Do you want whip cream on your dessert?" Tully managed to squeak out in between his moans.

"You can't be ready to come yet." Dev chuckled.

Tully reached under the table and hidden from somewhere underneath, he pulled up a can of spray whip cream. In a slick motion, he flipped the can upside down, held the nozzle over his erect cock, and squirted out a dollop of the cream.

Dev laughed. The cream sitting on top looked like a little cloud top hat.

Making sure Dev had a firm grasp at the base of Tully's cock, he bent over, opened his mouth, and managed to get the whip cream and the throbbing head inside his mouth. With a few licks and swallows the whipped cream disappeared, but that didn't stop Dev from continuing to enjoy his after-dinner special.

"Oh, Dev. Dinner is about to come to a very abrupt end and you'll have eaten too much." Tully wriggled in his seat as Dev's head bobbed up and down.

Tully giggled like a nervous teenager, but pulled Dev up.

Unwillingly, Dev allowed himself to be lifted.

"What? I wasn't done. I want seconds."

"I'll make sure you get thirds and fourths, but first..." Tully stood up from the table and brought Dev up with him so he could unbutton Dev's shirt and pull the garment off him. Dev undid his belt buckle. Tully reached down and unzipped Dev's pants then let go as the weight of the belt pulled the khakis to the floor. Rather dexterously, Tully yanked Dev's underwear down far enough to allow Dev to step out of them.

Tully pulled Dev into an embrace, their hairy chests mashing together. Dev sucked in his tummy a bit as Tully found Dev's meaty member and stroked him several times, then gently squeezed it.

Dev's manhood drooled precum and Tully bent down to lick it up. After spending some quality time orally worshipping Dev, Tully stood up and grabbed Dev's hand.

"Come on. Your choice. Hot bath with aromatherapy oils, a loofa with creamy body wash, hand delivered by yours truly? Or straight to bed for a good old fucking session?"

"I have to choose?" Dev arched an eyebrow while giving Tully a side glance.

"You little minx. No, both it is."

Tully wrapped himself around Dev, hoisted him off the ground, and carried him into the bathroom. Dev laughed.

Despite a tumultuous beginning, he and Tully were enjoying their witchy lives together.


DEEP IN THE forest, hidden away from humans, with werewolves to the southern edge of their lands, Cam stood in a glade, dappled light beaming through the twisted and gnarled branches of ancient maple trees.

Cam held out his hand and unfurled his fingers. Resting in the palm of his hand was the tiny branch the Spriggan had given Dev.

It had taken a great deal of searching with the utmost care in selecting the right spot. A place protected yet still with enough light, open to the sky for rainwater but sheltered enough so winter breezes wouldn't cause permanent frost bite.

Cam placed the tiny twig on a patch of bare soil in the middle of the ancient forest grove.

The twig jerked and bounced, bent in the middle and nearly snapped in two, then straightened out. Minute vines broke free from around the middle and lashed about.

"There, there little one. I've brought you home." Cam smiled. His wings spread out wide, light catching the membranous windows and creating prisms of light, which danced across the long tall grasses.

The Spriggan limb stood upright. One end burrowed into the soil, disturbing the dirt as roots slithered forth and grew, taking anchor and supporting the tiny plant.

The bark stretched and ripped, expanded and flourished. Branches sprouted, and divided out further. Leaves poked out and tiny flowers blossomed.

In the heartbeat of a moment, the stick that had once belonged to an abducted and tortured Spriggan had grown into a beautiful Rowan.

Cam sat at the base of the newly formed tree, let his head lean onto the bark as he sighed in contentment.

Life as a royal prince on the Ancestral Lands of the forest fae wasn't so bad.

In the distance, a monstrous brown and black werewolf ran toward him.

"Nope, not so bad at all."

# Acknowledgements

As always, this is to Lonny. I wouldn't want to be anywhere, but right here, right now, with you. You let me be me.

To Marvin, Brandon, David, and Rachel. You helped steer this project in the right direction and turned out to be more Canadian than I ever thought you could be. Stop apologizing guys, you keep me honest and help me write better stories.

Steve and Kim, thank you for your words of encouragement and enthusiasm that keeps me writing.

And lastly to Raevyn. The human with the biggest boatload of patience and kindness I've ever encountered.

Bear Hugz to you all.

# About

J.P. Jackson is an award-winning author of dark urban fantasy, paranormal, and even paranormal romance stories, but regardless of the genre, they always feature LGBTQ main characters.

J.P. works as an IT analyst in health care during the day, where if cornered he'd confess to casting spells to ensure clinicians actually use the electronic medical charting system he configures and implements.

At night, the writing happens, where demons, witches and shapeshifters congregate around the kitchen table and general chaos ensues. His husband of 22 years has very firmly put his foot down on any further wraith summonings and regularly lines the doorway with iron shavings and salt crystals. Imps are most definitely not house-trainable. Ghosts appear at the most inopportune times, and the Fae are known for regular visits where a glass of wine is exchanged for a good ole story or two. Although the husband doesn't know it, Canela and Jalisco, the two Chihuahuas, are in cahoots with the spell casting.

J.P.'s other hobbies include hybridizing African Violets (thanks to grandma), extensive traveling and believe it or not, knitting.

Facebook
www.facebook.com/jpjacksonwrites

Twitter
@jpjacksonauthor


Other NineStar books by this author

*Daimonion*

*Magic or Die*

# Also from NineStar Press

## Daimonion by J.P. Jackson

Dati Amon wants to be free from his satyr master and he hates his job—hunting human children who display demon balefire. Every hunt has been successful, except one. A thwarted attempt ended up as a promise to spare the child of a white witch, an indiscretion Dati hopes Master never discovers.

But Master has devilish machinations of his own. He needs human-demon hybrids, the Daimonion, to raise the Dark Lord to the earthly realm. If Master succeeds, he will be immortal and far more powerful.

The child who was spared is now a man, and for the first time in three hundred years, Dati has a reason to escape Master's chains. To do that, Dati makes some unlikely alliances with an untrained soulless witch, a self-destructive shape shifter, and a deceitful clairvoyant. However, deals with demons rarely go as planned, and the cost is always higher than the original bargain.

Magic or Die by J.P. Jackson

James Martin is a teacher, a powerful Psychic, and an alcoholic. He used to work for the Center for Magical Research and Development, a facility that houses people who can't control their supernatural abilities, but left after one of his students was killed, turning to vodka to soothe his emotional pain. The problem is he still has one year left on his contract.

When James is forced to return to the CMRD, he finds himself confronting the demons of his past and attempting to protect his new class from a possible death sentence, because if they don't pass their final exams, they'll be euthanized.

James also discovers that his class isn't bringing in enough sponsors, the agencies and world governments who supply grants and ultimately purchase graduates of the CMRD, and that means no profit for the facility. James and his students face impossible odds—measure up to the facility's unreachable standards or escape.

## Connect with NineStar Press

www.ninestarpress.com

www.facebook.com/ninestarpress

www.facebook.com/groups/NineStarNiche

www.twitter.com/ninestarpress

www.instagram.com/ninestarpress